Sexy Summers

Sexy Summers

Sexy Series Book Two

Dani Lovell

Copyright 2013 Dani Lovell

This story contains profanity and sexual content inappropriate for an audience under 18 years of age.

This book is a work of fiction. Names, characters, places and incidents are products of the author's imagination or are used fictitiously. Any resemblance to actual events, locales, or persons, living or dead, is entirely coincidental.

The author acknowledges the copyrighted or trademarked status and trademark owners of the following, mentioned in this work of fiction: Veuve Clicquot Ponsardin, 'Mad Men', 'Don Draper', W Hotels and Residences, iPod, iPad, Nordstrom, Hanky Panky, Ralph Lauren, Chloe, Bentley, Abercrombie & Fitch, Peaches Corner Cafe - Aspen, Silver Queen Gondola, Sundeck - Aspen, Ray Charles and 'Winter Wonderland', Mariah Carey and 'All I want for Christmas', MTV Cribs, Dennis Basso, Escobar Aspen, Belvedere Vodka, Merry-Go-Round Restaurant, Disneyland, Pine Creek Cookhouse, Bounty, The Blind Side, James Blunt and 'Goodbye my lover', Etta James and 'I would rather go blind', Sky Hotel - Aspen.

CHAPTER ONE
WEDNESDAY 19TH DECEMBER

"Linea Nigra," I say out loud, staring intently at the open page on my iPad. *Right, there's a name for it, so it is a real life thing, and it fades afterwards.* Thank god, I can stop feeling like a freak.

"Tilly, are you ready?" Clare calls, walking into my room, and I slam the cover of my iPad as quickly as you can say 'secret pregnancy'.

"Yep, my case is by the front door, is Oliver here?"

"Yes, time to go!" she says excitedly, and I follow her out to the hallway, slipping my iPad into my hand luggage on the way. Today we all travel to Aspen together for Christmas, and everyone seems super-excited. Well, everyone except me. I'm shitting a brick.

I have been advised that although many people do, I should think long and hard before skiing with a little human inside me. I may have swayed more towards hoping for the best and attempting to ski, to hide the truth - had I not grown a tiny bump over the last couple of weeks. Now it's real and I just can't bear the thought of doing anything that might hurt my little baby.

We lock up the maisonette after Oliver loads his car, and we jump in to make our way to the airport. I sit in the back so Clare can sit with Bea's brother, Oliver. Like most of the time, lately, I'd rather be left alone to my thoughts of impending motherhood, and the tiny little wriggler setting up home in my body. *Its ears have developed now, so it can hear my voice...* I think back to the information on the pregnancy app, telling me what Wriggler is up to in there. It's growing soft, little hairs all over its tiny body, and can grasp hold of things now.

I subconsciously stroke my little bump, feeling the tiniest flutter in there. The midwife said it's not unusual to start feeling things now, especially for little people like me. I can't imagine I have a lot of room for it to kick about without bumping into something. I have always had a flat stomach, very flat, in fact - I never even bloated, so it's clear as day to anyone that knows me, that I'm a little bit fucking pregnant.

Only if they saw my belly of course, which no one has, and hopefully no one will. This isn't exactly a beach holiday.

I'm used to the idea now; I found out a couple of weeks before my beautiful best friend Bea and her equally beautiful boyfriend, Daniel, went on their first trip back to the States since he moved here to be with her. When they met on the way to LA in September, neither of them dreamed that Daniel would move over five thousand miles to live here with Bea, but I have never seen two people more disgustingly in love than those two, so one way or another, they were going to be together.

I found it quite hard initially. Daniel met Bea in LA, I met his best friend Luke, and we had the most amazing, sex crazed holiday imaginable, but as my feelings towards the 'playboy of the year' started to get a little stronger, I knew I had no choice than to break away from him and never see him again. It hurt. Quite a fucking lot, really, so when Daniel charged to London on his white horse (or jumbo jet, or whatever), to sweep Bea off her feet, I felt a little bit broken, to say the least. I didn't realise at the time, but my hormones were going freaky-crazy because of little wriggly pants in here.

Luke obviously has no idea about our baby, I haven't spoken to him since we returned from LA, and I have a feeling that when I finally do tell him, he's going to run, screaming for the hills - or mountains of Aspen, and never look back. He's not exactly 'daddy material'. I wonder if this has ever happened to him before... he told me that our 'incident' without a condom was the only time that had ever happened, but can I believe everything a man-whore says? *Oh, alright,* he may like his ladies, but he's not a total lying douche bag.

"Shall we stop for a drive-through breakfast? I'm starving," Oliver says with a yawn, snapping me out of it.

My hand jumps from my small, swollen belly to my thigh. "Could do," I respond, trying not to sound like I could eat a horse.

"Okay, it's right here, what do you want to order?" he asks. And here I experience difficult situation number one. What I would absolutely *love* to order right now, is a bowl of hot sweet porridge with a knob of butter stirred in, a pinch of white pepper, a light sprinkling of salt, and a small tub of ketchup on the side. But as that would probably give the game away, I settle for a plain old bacon roll.

~~~~~~

We pull up at the drop off zone, and Oliver unloads our cases before handing his keys over to the meet and greet parking attendant. My stomach churns and I can't tell if it's Wriggler trying to grab a vital organ, the revolting bacon roll I reluctantly consumed to ensure he's happy in there, or the fact that I'm about to get on a plane, to spend two whole weeks with the unknowing father of my child, pretending I have hurt myself so much that I can't ski, and hiding my weirdo eating habits and growing belly from all of my friends. *Ah. It'll probably be the latter.*

"Til! Clare! Over here!" Bea calls from a short way down the ramp as she slides out of their fabulous new Bentley. Bea loves Daniel's LA car so much, that she persuaded him to get another one for the UK. Money grows on trees for those two. I have to admit, though, it's the motherfucking sex god of cars.

"I'm so excited! I can't tell you how thrilled I am that I get to spend our amazing holiday with my family and best girlies," Bea says, looking like she's about to burst into tears.

"I know, thanks for inviting us all along, it's going to be so much fun. I feel like I haven't been skiing in forever!" Clare replies, "How about you, Til? You looking forward to hitting the slopes?"

Oh fuck, I haven't thought up my mystery ailment yet... "Yes, it'll be great, Christmas in the snowy mountains!" I say, hoping to sound super-enthusiastic and avoiding the subject of skiing altogether.

"Come on then, enough chatting, let's get checked in," Oliver says with a roll of his eyes as he helps load Bea and Daniel's luggage onto a nearby trolley.

After check-in and passport control, we meet up with Bea's parents; Emily and Edward, and sit down for coffee, waiting for the gate to open. Daniel strolls over and sits next to me, leaning in to kiss my cheek. "Hey Til, how you doing? Everything okay?"

We have formed a fantastic friendship, Daniel and I. He's so caring and really looks out for me, just like Oliver does. I think that at 5'3" and of a small build, these men want to look after me. I'm more than capable of looking after myself, and I'm sure they know that, but I love our close friendship, and I wouldn't have it any other way.

"I'm fine thanks, Daniel. How are you? How's London treating you?"

"Amazingly, thank you for asking. So, I spoke to Luke last night, he says he's looking forward to catching up with you." My heart thumps in my chest. I know he's only looking forward to it because he thinks we're going to have crazy sex again, and I can't help but get a rush of excitement at that thought, too, but after I tell him - which I plan to do as soon as I see him - I doubt there'll be any sex, ever again. I have contemplated the idea that we might remain fuck-buddies; fuck-buddies with a baby... doesn't really have the same ring to it, does it? And as my feelings started to deepen towards him in LA, I don't think it'll be wise to start having amazing sex with him again. I need to be the best single mum I can be, and pining after my bad-boy baby-daddy is not going to be conducive to that. As if he'd want to be fuck buddies after all of this explodes anyway.

"Oh, that's nice, it'll be good to see him again, too," I manage, my heartbeat almost audible.

"Tilly, he's a good guy, you know," he says quietly, his voice soft.

"I know he is, but Daniel, we had a bit of fun in LA, that's it, what do you want me to say?"

"Hey," he says, holding his hands up in defence, "I just want to make sure you know that, don't read him wrong. He likes you, Til."

"So you say. Daniel, we were fuck buddies, that's all."

Our conversation is interrupted by the tannoy announcement, calling for passengers on our flight to head to the gate. Daniel stands and puts a gentle hand on my shoulder, "I just want to make sure you know."

"Thanks, Daniel. There really isn't an issue, I was sad to have left him and LA, back in October, but everything is back to normal now. It was just a bit of holiday fun. Now, go and be with your sickeningly amazing girlfriend, I know it's killing you to have left her side for five minutes," I say with humour and he grins one of his beautiful smiles that made Bea fall so head over heels in love with him.

I watch as he walks over and casually slips both arms around her waist from behind. She rests her head back onto his chest and he kisses the top of it, smiling contently. So in love... *What the fuck is wrong with me? Snap out of it Til, this sort of romantic P.D.A. would have made you puke a few months back.*

~~~~~~~

Take-off was uneventful, poor old Bea looked petrified, but Daniel held her the whole time, and even preoccupied her with a mini-pash or two. *Mmm, I'd quite like a pash right now...*

Daniel and Bea decided that as everyone was travelling in economy, so would they. I certainly can't afford to fly in any other cabin, and Clare didn't want to, so I think they thought it'd be nicer for everyone if they travelled in this cabin, too. I, personally, think that if you *can* fly first, you *should* fly first, but I'm clearly not quite as thoughtful as they are.

I have a window seat in an emergency exit next to a stranger, while Bea's parents, Oliver and Clare (who - by the way - aren't a couple, shockingly), and Bea and Daniel all sit in pairs in nearby rows. I curl up in my seat, cover myself with an airline blanket and close my eyes. I'm knackered, and could really do with a sleep, but I'm too shit-scared about what's ahead to do anything but think.

I feel a tiny flutter in my belly and the image of that dinky baby on my iPad screen this morning comes back to me. Tiny weeny little legs with disproportionately big feet, all curled up in a little ball with a giant head and minuscule, cute little features. I cup my barely-there-bump under my blanket again. *It's just me and you for now, Wriggler. You're my lovely little secret.*

At first, I totally shat myself, wondering how the hell I could be a mum. Don't get me wrong, I adore kids; my nephew, Jack is the most amazing little boy on the planet. I always wanted kids one day, I just never really thought about when... or how. And I never told anyone about my desire to be a mother. My own one was a poor example.

It took a little while to get used to the idea, I'm fifteen weeks along now, so I'm into my second trimester and am feeling about a gazillion times better than I was in the first, the morning sickness having diminished. Granted, I still feel like I haven't slept a wink for about a week solid, but apparently - that's normal.

I know I should have told someone about it, but the further along I get, the harder it seems. It's not like I know my mum, and my beautiful, amazing dad passed away years ago, so the only people I would confide in about this, are my sister, Gemma, or my best friends Clare and Bea. Gem would be the obvious choice, she's had a baby before, she's my sister and would support me through anything, but she lives in LA and if she knew that I hadn't told anyone else, she'd worry herself silly about me.

Clare and Bea have been so busy sorting out the new changes at their cake shop, and what with Bea's new life with her man and all their travels, I just haven't seemed to find the time to sit down and make a big deal out of it. It's also news for Luke first, in my opinion.

I suppose it has been quite a long time really, to have kept it to myself. I've known for about eight or nine weeks now, and Wriggler was made a few weeks before that. I remember it well, it was the only time we didn't use a condom... *good god, it was so hot...* Bea had just cooked the four of us a delicious pasta dish for dinner in my sister's pool-house, where I always stay when I visit. Bea and Daniel decided to chill out on the sofa, so Luke and I made the most of the beautiful warm swimming pool. Gemma and her husband, Jay, were at a dinner party, so we knew we had the garden all to ourselves.

It started with an outstanding snog in the water before things got predictably raunchy, and Luke untied the bows at either side of my bikini bottoms. He reached his hand between my legs as we kissed. Thinking about it now sends a tingle right to my bits and pieces. God, it was so hot. I slid my hands up and around his broad, muscular shoulders and clenched his unruly hair in my fists. He pushed his shorts down his muscular thighs, his erection springing free underneath the water, and he pressed him self against me, his thick hardness desperately routing for a way in.

Not long after, I was clinging on to him for dear life, my legs wrapped around his incredible body, taking everything he was so enthusiastically offering. He paused briefly to carry me from the pool, still buried deep inside me... *mmm...* and he pressed me up against the side of Gem's house to fuck me against the wall. Bea and Daniel could have walked out at any moment, but neither of us could have cared less, when I'm... *correction...* when I *was* fucking Luke, it was like nothing else existed, just our wild, crazy, animalistic sex. I can guarantee that getting caught was the last thing on either of our minds while he was thrusting into me over and over again. I still have a friction burn mark on my back. *Well worth it.*

Shit. This is not helping. I squirm into my seat, wishing I'd stop thinking about sex. I'm so horny. I think it must be something to do with pregnancy; I've needed sex before, but now I can literally feel a clenching inside whenever I think about it.

Luke was convinced that he hadn't come inside me - in fact, so was I (I won't go into detail... but it was kind of obvious), so I never once thought that I'd get pregnant. I had no clue at all, until I missed my period when we got back. Even then I just put it down to my emotional breakdown, I didn't think that the breakdown might have been to do with missing my period. But anyway, turns out you *can* get pregnant that way, and I did. The perfect situation when you live five thousand miles from the womanising father of your child. God, I could really use a cup of tea right now.

~~~~~~~

The rest of the flight was spent quite the same; subconsciously stroking my belly, reminiscing about the animalistic sex with Luke. *Sex... spending the day in bed that time... well, in bed, in kitchen, on floor, in den, on stairs... oh yes, that was a good day.*

"Are you coming Tilly?" Bea asks, "They're calling the flight now," she adds, pointing to the screen at Chicago

O'Hare Airport, where we're catching the onward flight to Aspen. Thank god this is only a short flight, as soon as we get there, I'm going to bed. Oh... maybe I should talk to Luke first. *Oh shit...* The nerves make a comeback and my stomach tangles as I follow the rest of the party towards the plane.

~~~~~~~

Approximately three hours later, cars are awaiting our arrival outside in the snow. It's absolutely beautiful, it's dark, but the snow sparkles, the mountains surrounding the airport glowing electric blue in the moonlight. Clare, Oliver and I say our goodbyes to Bea, Daniel, Emily and Edward, and climb into one of the limos.

Trust Daniel to arrange special transport like this; he's so lovely. Bea and Daniel are staying at their house with her parents, and the three of us are heading off to Daniel's sister's house. I don't think she is staying there with us; Daniel said the housekeeper will let us in, but it's nice of her to let us use her house, considering she doesn't know us.

I'm falling asleep in the limo, it must be about four in the morning at home. Why, oh why didn't I sleep on the plane? At least I'm on my way to a bed, Daniel's plan to head straight to the houses and meet up in the morning was perfect, I don't think I'd have been able to keep my eyes open if I had to meet up with everyone tonight. Telling Luke will have to wait until tomorrow. And I'm totally okay with that.

The journey only takes about fifteen minutes, so we're soon pulling up to the most amazing wood and stone built house, surrounded by snow covered pine trees. Steps lead the way up to the glass front door and first floor verandah. The three of us stare at it, it's incredibly beautiful.

"Fuck me," I say, "it's bloody massive!"

"Wow, I wonder what it's like inside," Clare says, somewhat awed.

"Let's go and find out! Bagsie the biggest bedroom!" Oliver says as he opens his door and legs it up the steps. Clare and I make a dash for it to catch up with him, trying to grab the best bedroom first. On my way up the snowy steps, I slip slightly; my hand instinctively holding my tummy, while the other grabs the handrail, reminding me just how precious and fragile this little Wriggler is. It's so unlike me not to have a laugh with the others, but I'm not risking anything.

I slow to a walk and wait by the front door for the driver to drop off the cases, introducing myself to the housekeeper. It's a good excuse as to why I'm not running around the house like a lunatic, so I show him indoors and ask him to leave the bags nearby. Clare returns a while after, laughing, and out of breath, telling me what room I'm left with. I honestly couldn't care less, as long as there's a bed that I can pass out in - I'm happy.

I say goodnight and make my way to the room that Clare directed me to and fall down on the bed. The room is fantastic, the huge window looks out to gorgeous snowy trees, night-lights accentuating the stunning surroundings. I pull the huge Abercrombie and Fitch t-shirt I once stole from Oliver from my suitcase, and change into it, pulling on a pair of fluffy ski socks before tucking myself into the cosy bed.

If Bea could see me now, she'd slap me to kingdom come, girls just shouldn't wear 'frumpy' to bed according to her; silk and lace, all the way. I have countless pretty nighties and silk pyjamas at home that she bought me as gifts before trying to throw away my baggy t-shirts and shorts. She never did find this one.

The bed is so deliciously comfortable, I nod off almost immediately. Thank god.

CHAPTER TWO
THURSDAY 20TH DECEMBER

Oh my god, I'm never going to be able to afford to bring up a child on my own. Where am I going to live? Clare's not going to want a baby around the place... *Oh here we go again.* These questions always seem to keep me awake after I stir in the middle of the night needing a wee.

I had hoped, as I stayed up until like, five in the morning UK time, that this wouldn't happen. I check the time again, three fourteen am local time; ten fourteen at home. So I have had a good five hours or so, but I could really do with more.

I roll over and close my eyes, hoping to drift off again, but I feel like I've had about twenty espressos; wide a-fuckin-wake. *Sod this.* I clamber out of bed and contemplate rifling through my case to find a jumper but I can't be bothered, and it's really quite warm anyway, they definitely know how to insulate houses here. It only needs to blow a cool breeze at home for the house to feel like a flipping freezer.

I plod down the stairs having a good look around me as I go. It's absolutely gorgeous; thick, rustic, wooden banister rails and balustrades, cream walls and giant, undressed windows everywhere. As I get around the corner on the large staircase, I see the huge open plan lounge ahead of me, so beautifully decorated, the burning fire adding to the cosy ambiance. *Is it safe to leave a fire on overnight?*

I make my way across the room towards the kitchen at the back, around the corner. The huge windows showcase the beautiful dark sky contrasting the brilliant snow. It's a winter haven, and I love that I'm up, appreciating this, all on my own. Well, with Wriggler of course.

I find the kettle on the far counter and flick the switch while I search cupboards for mugs and tea bags. When I find what I need, I lean against the counter, facing the increasingly noisy kettle and close my eyes, wondering how on earth I'm going to tell him. Do I just pull him aside and say, 'by the way...'? Do I ask him to dinner and do it in a public place so he can't go too crazy? Do I shag him one last time and tell him afterwards? *Oh Tilly, shut the fuck up. You are not shagging him again. Well, not unless you've told him and he still wants to shag you... which he won't, so forget it.*

I lift my head and let out a long, loud sigh of resignation, when a deep, familiar voice purrs in my ear, making me jump from here to next Thursday. "I'm going to fuck you right here, baby, right now, and you're gonna love it." *What the fuck?* Before I can make my body react and turn, his warm hand skims under my nightshirt, gliding up my thigh to caress me. Goosebumps spread rapidly on my skin as he slowly moves to stroke my clit. Hot lips caress the side of my neck and I let out a loud, desperate moan.

I know who it is, of course I do, I know his touch, I know his smell, his words repeated from the first time we ever did it. He presses up against me and continues to touch me, licking and kissing my neck, slowly making his way up to my ear. My eyes close, my breathing erratic, I so need this.

His breath heavy in my ear, I can feel his heartbeat pulsating through his chest onto my back as he moves his fingers from my swollen clitoris to my thigh. Grabbing it, he raises my knee onto the counter top, almost lifting me off the floor, and immediately, forcefully sinks inside me. "Fuck!" I cry, it's so unexpected, but so good - so incredibly, amazingly, fucking good.

"Oh, fuck, yeah..." I moan loudly as he pounds into me against the kitchen counter. I push away from the surface a little with my hands, enabling him to move deeper, but also protecting my belly from the harsh corner of the work top.

He licks my neck from my collar bone to just below my ear and whispers, "You're so fucking tight, you need this, don't you? You need me..." and it turns me on so much. He remembered, I love it when he talks like that.

"Oh, yes," I cry again, reaching behind me to cling onto his neck, I don't want him to move away, I want his face pressed against me, breathing, grunting, licking...

He moves fast, pounding into me, pushing deeper with each thrust and I'm going to come any second now. "You missed my cock, baby?"

"Oh god, Luke, I'm going to come..."

"Come on, baby, come hard," he growls and puts his fingers back down there, lightly flicking from side to side. I immediate explode, crying out, pulling his neck down to my face and sinking my teeth into his flesh. The fierce spasms shooting through me don't stop, and my wailing continues as I hear and feel him join me, with a short, sharp thrust. The intensity is so much more than I have ever felt before, it's so much stronger, completely taking over. *Wow, wow, fucking wow! Oh my god, if pregnancy is the reason for this, I'm going to have another one.*

Luke wraps an arm around my waist and pulls me back off the counter and onto my feet in front of him. I remain facing the other way and look down, panting, remembering that I really wasn't supposed to do that. He runs both hands down my sides and forwards, towards my belly and I spin around before he feels it. I look up at his smiling face. *Oh jesus, he is so much hotter than I remember, and I remember him being the hottest fucking man on the planet.*

"Hey," he says, his voice raw and sexy, "good to see you. You want me to make you tea?" *Oh, how sweet is that? No, Tilly! Stop that.*

"No. No, thank you. I can make my own. Are you having one?" I straighten up, moving away from him. That was *so* not supposed to happen. *Shit. Maybe I should tell him now...*

"Yes, please, sweet-cheeks." And there's that gorgeous dimpled smile again, he needs to stop with that sexy, cheeky thing he does. He sits at the island in the centre of the kitchen and watches me.

"No problem," I say, busying myself with the mugs and kettle, *he's so god damn good looking.*

I put the used tea bags in the convenient countertop bin and turn to hand Luke his cup. I'm not hanging around, I can't like him, we're not having a holiday fling again. Besides, I won't be able to tell him if we start getting all fun-and-frolics-and-sex-in-wild-places, again.

"Aren't you going to sit down?" he asks.

"Uh uh," I say, shaking my head. "I aught to get back to bed, try to sleep."

"Oh. Sure," he says, looking a little disappointed, I think. "Won't you at least tell me that that was fun, like always?"

I smile, I did always say that after we had sex, but at the time, nothing was happening - no deep feelings, no seriousness, no... babies. "Yes, that was fun, Luke. Really fun. How did you even know I was down here? Why are you here, anyway? I had no idea." *Or I'd have had a lot more trouble getting to sleep.*

"Well, the plan was for Dan, Bea and her folks to stay together, Dan's mom and dad and Alexia together, and your two friends, you and I together, in this house. I think they put all of us together because they thought we might be more raucous or something. I heard someone coming downstairs and thought I'd check it out, I followed you down here - watched you for a bit. I wanted to help you find everything but I couldn't take my eyes off of you, you look freakin' hot in those socks, damn..."

Oh don't start or I'm going to rip your trousers off. Great, so I'm living with him for two weeks. I am going to have to work damn hard to stay away. "Oh right, okay. Out of interest, Luke," *because it really doesn't matter,* "did you just use a condom?"

"Sure I did, always have, always will, baby. Well, except that one time in the pool, and that was a one off. So don't panic, you're safe, no kids or diseases to worry about," he says with a chuckle. Hmm, that's what you think, Summers. *Tell him, tell him, fucking tell him now, it's an open opportunity, Tilly, do it!*

"So, can I come with you?" he interrupts my thoughts.

"Huh?"

"You said you're going back to bed, can I come?" *Oh, why are you making this so hard, you sexy motherfucker?*

"Er... Luke, I don't know... look..."

"Hey, it's cool, hot-lips. You wanna sleep? Go get some sleep. I can save fucking you even harder until the morning."

I laugh out loud, this is what I remember from LA, this naughty, frisky, cheeky fun that seemed to go everywhere with us. I let myself forget about Wriggler for a minute, and say exactly what I want. "Come on then, bad-boy, let's do this." I know I shouldn't, but *Christ*, he's just so hot, and I'm just *so* horny.

"Hell, yeah!" he says with a wink as he steps down from his stool and follows me towards the stairs, holding his tea.

"So were you here when we arrived?" I ask, stepping up the gorgeous stair case.

"No, I was at Danny's, I thought you'd all be going there, and I wanted to say hi to him, I haven't seen him for a while."

"Oh, okay," I reply as I get to my room and open the door, *shit, what am I doing? Sex should not be on the agenda. Again.*

I put my tea down on the bedside table and plonk myself on the messy bed, crossing my legs underneath me, leaning back against the soft, tall headboard. Luke stands against the wall and crosses his ankles, watching me.

"So, do you miss him? Daniel?" I ask.

"Sure I do, he's my best bud, but I know he's happier in London with Bea, and I still get to catch up with him when they come to LA every few weeks. I'd like to come to London soon, they've invited me countless times. Would that... uh..." he pauses.

"Would that what?" I ask.

"Would that bother you? I kinda wanted to join Daniel back when he first flew over, but I didn't want you to feel... you know, uncomfortable. We left things a little weird. You said you weren't interested in seeing me again."

Oh god. I don't want to get into this. Can't we just have sex? "Luke, you can do what you like, if you want to come to London, come to London. I'm sure you'd love it."

"And the not seeing me again thing?"

"We were holiday fuck buddies, you're a fun-loving playboy, I was the female equivalent - why would we make plans to see each other again?"

"Was? So, what, you're not anymore?"

Oh, this is not going how I thought it would. "Never mind. Look, don't let me stop you from coming to London to see Daniel, I shouldn't even be a consideration in that decision. Do whatever you like. Would you make a big deal about not seeing one of your other women?"

"No. But we did more than I do with other women."

I don't even know what that means, and I'm not going to try to understand. *Get out of this one, Til, don't get into emotional bullshit. You're not going to fall for this player again. Sex, that's the way to do it.* "I liked what we did," I rise onto my knees, my legs apart, "want to do it again?"

"There's that naughty girl I remember," he says, putting his cup down on a chest of drawers and striding towards me like an animal that's found its prey. *Thank god, a distraction.* "You look fucking hot like that."

"Yeah? Looking pretty hot yourself, Lukey" I say, taking a long slow look up and down his thoroughly toned, huge, muscular body. His white t-shirt clings - but not too tightly - to his torso, highlighting the dips and curves of his muscles. His arms, those enormous, strong arms that can pick me up and throw me about like I weigh no more than a feather. The muscles flex as his hands clench in anticipation. His huge erection is prominent through his low-slung baggy pyjama bottoms... or lounge pants... or whatever it was he called them in LA. He's more than ready, and so am I.

He stands at the side of the bed and I crawl to meet him there. I grin, salaciously, before running my fingers under his t-shirt and up his chest. "So, you think socks are sexy?" I ask, grinning.

"On you they are, on your hot little legs, when you've got nothing but a t-shirt on. By the way, you really shouldn't walk around a strange house with no underwear on..."

"No? You didn't like it?" I ask, lifting his t-shirt up his abs. He helps, pulling it up and over his head and as he's pre-occupied with that, I sit on my bum, my legs either side of his body and yank his trousers down, grabbing his cock in my hands and immediately bending to take the tip into my mouth.

"Oh, Jesus, fuck..." he says, making me giggle around him.

"Mmm..." I moan as I move my tongue around him and pull back to say exactly what comes to mind, "I love the way you taste." I do love it, I missed it, he has the best tasting cock in the universe.

"Taste me, baby, suck me dry." And that is the sort of talk that brings me to orgasm without even a touch.

Thoroughly turned on, I open my mouth and take as much of him as I possibly can, he's so hard, I can't help but groan and moan as I plunge him deeper into my mouth, sucking relentlessly. My tongue ripples slowly over the tip every time I pull back, and then I sink him further and suck hard, over and over again, my hand pumping in rhythm.

"Your fucking mouth is amazing, Jesus Christ you know what you're doing. Baby, I'm going to come so freaking hard..."

I yelp, desperately needing him to come, I need his pleasure, I want to hear it, feel it, remember it. I shouldn't be doing this, I shouldn't be confusing my fucked up emotions... but it's just. So. Good.

"Ah, yes! Fuck!" he cries as his release shoots into the back of my throat.

"Mmm," I moan, desperately drinking it in, loving it. *God I love blow-jobs.*

I take one last gentle suck, before releasing him and looking up at his face with a grin.

"Jesus, Tilly. That was fucking awesome," he says, lifting me up off the bed. My legs wrap around his waist and I hold on to the back of his neck as he looks into my eyes for a moment, before running his tongue along the parting of my lips. *Oh yes, kissing... let's do that.* He softly rests his lips against mine and looks up to my eyes again. I don't want to gaze into his amazing blue eyes, I know all of those feelings will come rushing back to me and make me want him again. *You want him now, Til. Stop kidding yourself.*

"Say it," he says with a smile.

I grin and move my mouth against his, gently kissing his soft, full lips. "That was fun," I say, and of course, again, I mean it. "Doing that to you was always fun. I love making you come like that."

"I love coming like that. I'll have to repay that favour later. But right now, you're going to kiss me."

"Are you going to say 'please'?"

"No. Kiss me."

"No! You kiss me!"

"Kiss me motherfucker!" he says and we both burst out laughing, before he presses his gorgeous mouth against mine. It's divine, his tongue working in precise rhythm with mine, our lips gliding against each other softly. *Oh wow, I forgot how amazing this is.*

He walks with me to the huge window and presses me against it, it's freezing, even through my t-shirt, but being caught between the cold hardness of the glass, and the hot strength of his body is the most amazing sensation. He reaches between us and pulls my t-shirt up, breaking away to pull it over my head. I make a mental note to keep close so he doesn't notice Wriggler.

He presses me back against the window and I gasp loudly and tense as my warm skin touches the freezing glass. "Cold, Princess?" he asks with a cheeky smirk.

"It's freezing..."

"I'd better warm you up then," he says as he looks down at my now fully-erect nipples. "Mmm, would you look at that." He cups one of my boobs and lowers his mouth to my nipple, sucking it in. I groan loudly as he very lightly takes it between his teeth and flicks it with his tongue.

"Mmm, that's so good..." I moan, my boobs have been so sensitive ever since I missed that first period, and this is like the best massage in the whole world, with a great chunk of sexual arousal thrown in.

He groans and holds the other in his free hand, my legs tightening around his waist. He follows suit with his mouth and teases my other nipple. I arch back against the window, pushing against him and close my eyes in ecstasy. I feel my belly pressing up against him and revel in the fact that Wriggler is wedged between Mummy *and* Daddy. Even if Daddy has no idea. *Oh god, don't do this, Til, don't think of them together, don't picture him as a doting father...*

He lifts his head and kisses my jaw. "These are bigger..." he says, firmly fondling my breasts in his giant hands, "how'd that happen?"

"Uh huh, I don't know..." I lie, grabbing fistfuls of his gorgeous, messy blonde hair and yanking his head towards me, devouring his mouth. *One way of changing the subject.*

He takes me back to the bed and kneels onto it, with me still hooked to his front. He lowers us down and again - feeling his belly pressed firmly against mine, makes me think how safe our little baby is right now. Tucked away inside me, cosy and warm, covered by Luke's big protective frame. I so wish I'd made this baby with a different Luke, a committed Luke, a family man Luke. But then, I suppose, that just wouldn't be the Luke I like so much. *Damn it, why do I always have to like the fucking bad-boys?*

I know he's ready for me again by the hard rod, digging into my thigh. I need to prepare for how we're going to do this without him seeing my midriff region. I reach down and grab hold of him. "So, you want to prod me with this thing?" I ask with a huge grin on my face and Luke laughs.

"I want to prod you, poke you, do all sorts of probing with that thing."

I laugh with him, "Good, because I want to be prodded, and poked and probed, more than you could possibly know..."

"Oh really? You want *me* to prod and poke you, or you just want to be prodded and poked?"

"Do you want your ego stroking or what?"

"I want something stroking..." he says and those dimples pop, he is seriously the best looking man I have ever met. All that smiling he does doesn't do him any harm either. I grab his neck with my free hand and pull his face to mine for a deep, passionate, impatient snog. We both moan and my hand tightens around his cock, sliding my hand up and down his length.

I break away and push his chest so he lifts to give me room to turn underneath him, I crawl up to the head of the bed and rise to my knees on the pillows, holding the top of the head board with one hand. "Fuck me this way," I demand, turning to look back at him.

He has a big, dirty grin on his face, "Hell, yeah, I'll fuck you this way!" he says excitedly and kneels behind me, lifting one of my thighs to position himself. "Holy fuck! What am I doing? Why does this only happen with you?"

"What?" I ask, wondering why he's not currently pummelling me to infinity and beyond with his man-stick.

"I forgot the condom, Princess, and I don't have any more on me. You got any... right here, right now, so we don't have to move?"

I giggle at his impatience. "No, Luke. I wasn't planning on having sex this holiday."

"What? Why not? You knew I'd be here..."

"Yeah, but I didn't want to get into it again... listen can you just do me and we'll talk about this after?"

"We can't, not without a condom."

I want to scream, I'm bent over a motherfucking headboard, with my favourite cock mere centimetres away, I want it! "You been tested recently?" I ask.

"As always... but we can't Til, I can't, it's not what I do."

"Do you trust me not to have anything dirty?"

"Yeah... but Tilly..."

"Just do it, god damn it - it's fine, nothing will come of it, I swear." *Because you already gave me a baby.*

"I don't know, I want to so badly, I mean he's rock solid over here..."

"Luke, I'm practically dripping on the pillow, just fuck me hard and fuck me good, and do it right now. Do it!"

I can see his mind working over time, but I know his dick will win eventually. It better had. He leans towards me and I feel him there, teasing my entrance, *oh yeah... just a bit more, go on...*

"You can't get pregnant, no?" he asks. I'm pretty certain you can't get pregnant when you already are, so I'm not technically lying if I say no... am I?

"No. Fuck me, big boy, come on."

And without a second thought, he sinks deep inside.

"Holy shit-balls, it feels so good," he croaks as he slides out and thrusts back in again. "I want to fuck you like this, every time."

"This is your last time, sweetheart, so make the most of it," I say, between moans as he pounds into me, deeper, further.

"I'm fucking you all vacation, baby, and you're going to love it so much, you'll want to take me home afterwards," he groans, his voice monotone with concentration.

"Unlikely. So do me like it's your last, Summers."

He growls loudly and works faster, taking one hand from my hip and putting his fingers in my mouth. I suck, swirling my tongue, coating them with saliva for his next trick. When he's satisfied, he takes them from my mouth and straight to my clit, where he circles lightly.

"Oh god, yes... Luke, it's... oh wow, amazing."

"Like I said," he says, between breaths, "you're going to love it."

"Oh yes, I do, I do, keep going, you want it too, you love it too, tell me..."

"I fuckin' love it," he says, his thrusts sharper, faster, "you feel amazing, Princess," he cries, grabbing a breast with his free hand. I cry out in ecstasy, "Luke! Yes! Oh god, yes, I'm going to come Luke, I'm going to come so hard."

"You turn me on so much, Tilly, I swear to god, we're not leaving this here," he says as he licks my neck again and kisses my jaw.

"Oh... oh, yes, Luke!" I cry, the industrial strength orgasm ripping through me, my eyes clenched and my hands squeezing the headboard so hard it hurts.

"Oh Jesus Christ, baby, can I... can I... holy shit... can I..."

"Yes, come inside me, come deep inside me, Luke..." I cry, answering the question he was so desperately trying to ask, and he cries out my name, slamming into me, clenching my breast almost painfully in his hand.

"Ah!" I cry, his last thrust so deep - so good.

His head slumps to my shoulder, his arms wrapping around my chest, his soft lips dropping tiny kisses onto my skin. "Uh..." he mumbles, echoing my thoughts exactly. "Remind me why I shop around again? I want to keep the model I've got right now."

I giggle, "No you don't darling, you have a condition I like to call 'post orgasm love disorder'."

He laughs, lazily, still collapsed against me, "You're the funniest chick I know."

"You're the funniest *'dude'* I know. Now are you going to get off me or what?"

"No. You stay where you are little lady."

I giggle and shove him away, "Get off, you pillock."

He releases me and leans back onto his haunches, "Pillock? I have no idea what that means but I'm guessing it's no way to talk to a guy suffering from 'post orgasm love disorder'".

I grab the duvet to cover myself, before turning to settle into the bed. "I'm sure the patient will snap out of it pretty soon. You'll survive. Now go on, piddle off and let me catch a few more winks."

"Piddle off? You speak a whole other language, Princess." he lifts his side of the duvet and slips into the bed next to me.

"In case you didn't understand, it means piss off, now go on, on your bike."

"You don't really mean that, I get it, you've got 'post orgasm bitch disorder', you'll get over it soon. Now get over here and let me use you as a pillow."

I laugh out loud, "Luke, come on now, we're not doing this."

"But I'm cold and lonely," he says in a cute voice.

"You've just had roasting hot sex, you're not cold. And since when are you lonely? You have more 'company' in your life than anyone else I know."

"Yeah, well right now, I only want yours, so get over here my little love bunny and show me some affection."

I roll my eyes and smile in defeat, it's just impossible to think seriously around him. I slide over and tuck myself into his side. He's so cosy and warm and comfortable, and although I know I really shouldn't be doing this, I decide that as long as I know the score, just tonight - it'll be fine. God knows I need a big hug right now and he gives the most perfect bear hugs ever.

"Oh, and Luke? That was super-fun."

My tummy flutters and I wake in desperate need of a wee. My arms are cradling my belly and I'm tucked, comfortably in the big strong arms of Luke. *Oh shit.* I'm not supposed to be enjoying this. I try to slide out of his arms but he only tightens them around me. "No, Princess," he mumbles sleepily, "stay, keep me warm, don't make me sad..." and with his eyes still closed, he sticks his bottom lip out like a little kid. *Christ! How does anyone say no to this man?*

"I need a wee, Luke," I say quietly, matter of fact.

"So go ahead, we can wash the sheets later," he says with a sleepy grin, "okay, but come straight back and stroke my big dick, okay?" I can't help but burst out laughing, how can he be so funny when he's still half asleep?

I slip out of his embrace and grab my t-shirt from the floor, holding it against my stomach as I dash into the en-suite. I take care of business and start the taps to run myself a bath, no doubt everyone will be up soon and we'll need to head out to get the ski gear. *Shit, do I really want to spend all that money when I'm not even going to be using any of it, just to keep my secret?*

I step out again, with my t-shirt on, nicely hiding child, and look over to the bed. Luke is fast asleep again, looking too gorgeous for words. He's lying on his front, the duvet covering him from the hips down. His back is one of the most amazing sights I've ever seen, I'm tempted to straddle his bum and just lay on top of him, touching his hot skin. At least Wriggler's got good genes, if he's a boy and looks like daddy, he's going to be set for life.

I stroll over to the huge, crescent shaped window and look out at the beautiful morning view of pine trees and perfect white snow. A balcony would make this room just about perfect. My mind wanders as with always lately, I'll definitely take Wriggler on holidays in the snow, kids love snow.

Maybe I'll go somewhere with Gemma and Jay so Jack and Wriggler can have snowball fights together. I picture my little toddler in a hat with a giant bobble, waddling through the snow outside, falling down onto its bottom and giggling in excitement.

"Pretty out there, huh?" Luke's sleepy voice brings me back to the now.

"Huh? Oh, yeah, it's gorgeous."

"Like you," he says, patting the bed beside him. I smile and stroll over to sit down on the edge of the bed. "What time is it? We're meeting at nine to go to the ski store for you guys."

"I don't know," I say, standing again to walk around the bed to get my phone. "Oh shit! Luke! It's eleven o'clock!"

"Oh..." he says, rubbing his eyes, "whoops."

"Why didn't anyone come and get me? Or call me?"

"Hey, don't sweat it, let's get ready and go get some breakfast downstairs, then I'll take you to the ski store later."

"Really? Is that okay?"

"Sure it is, hot-lips. So, you wanna shower with me?" he asks, wiggling his eyebrows. *No chance! You'll definitely notice in the shower!* No, I'll get dressed, have breakfast and then sit down and tell him. Yes, that's the new plan.

"No, I'm running myself a bath, I'd like to just get dressed quickly on my own if you don't mind. I'll meet you downstairs." I say, grabbing one of the fluffy towels from the top of the chest of drawers and backing towards the en-suite."

"Sure. See you down there in about half hour."

"Okay. See ya," I say as I enter, close the door and immediately lock it, so I know there's no chance of him seeing my wet, naked, newly pregnant body in broad daylight.

~~~~~~~

Dressed in black snowboarding trousers and a long-sleeved, loosely fitted, grey t-shirt, I make my way down the stairs. Although I'm a skier, rather than a snowboarder, I really liked the look of these trousers, and they cling nicely to my bum. I thought I'd better find something to accentuate a different part of my body, so I could try to conceal my stomach a little easier. And who cares if I don't snowboard? I'm not doing either on this trip so I'm literally wearing them for the sake of it, anyway.

Luke is sitting at the kitchen island when I walk in, looking devilish in his über cool snowboarding gear. Now Luke *is* a snowboarder, he told me all about it in LA, and he looks the part. *Mmm, he looks hot.* The housekeeper I met last night is standing at the hob and she turns to smile at me as I walk in.

"Good morning, ma'am, what can I get you for breakfast?" Before I can answer, Luke looks at me and interrupts.

"Hey Princess, looking *hot!* I'm having eggs Benedict, you want some?"

I turn to the housekeeper, "If you're making eggs Benedict, I'd love some, thank you."

"You want to sit in the dining room? It's all laid out." he asks and I scrunch my nose, shaking my head.

"Naa, too formal, I'll just sit here with you," *and tell you a big fat secret.*

"Cool. You look hot in this, you want me to teach you to snowboard?" *That would have been so much fun. Here you go Til, now's you're opportunity. Go.*

"Actually, Luke, I want to talk to you about something."

"Sure, hot-stuff, shoot."

Fuck, fuck, fuck, here we go. "Well, the thing is... I, um," The housekeeper interrupts, putting our breakfast down in front of us.

"Can I get you a hot drink?" she asks.

"No thank you, this is fine." I want to slap the bitch for making me delay this. Okay, okay, she did just lovingly prepare my favourite breakfast, and I'm being particularly harsh, but I really need to say this, and now I don't want to!

"I'll leave you to eat then, please leave your plates, I'll clear up when you leave."

"Thanks, beautiful," Luke responds with a cheeky grin, and she exits the kitchen, leaving us to finish this awkward conversation. *Yikes.*

"You were saying? You, um?"

"Yes, I, um, I don't really plan on hitting the slopes, while I'm here..."

"Really? Why not? You're in Aspen, baby!"

"Yeah, I know. Look, the others don't know about this. Luke, I need to tell you something."

"Sure, what is it?" He looks at me, concerned; so cute. I know as soon as the words come out of my mouth, this will all change, he won't be caring, jovial, funny-guy-Luke anymore; he'll be cross, he'll be afraid, he'll be out that door in a flash. I can't do it. I can't. Maybe I can sleep with him again, have a bit more of this gorgeous Luke, and then tell him after. But that's *such* a bad idea. *Just do it, you pussy.*

"I um, I had an accident last time I went skiing and I really, *really* don't want to do it again." *You fucking wimp, Tilly! But quick thinking; well done for that.*

He looks at me, confused, and I want to slap myself. *Idiot!* "Is that all? Shit, Til, must have been bad, you look scared-crazy. You know, if you want, I can take you out, we can take it real slow, get you back in the swing of things?" He puts his hand on my thigh and I hate myself. He's so fucking sweet, and I'm lying to his face, withholding from him the most important information of his life.

"Luke, I don't know how you'll understand without me getting deeper into it, and I don't want to do that. But I *really* can't put a pair of skis on."

"Okay, how about a little fun snowboarding? With me? I'll be gentle, I promise."

I shake my head and he simply nods. "Okay, say no more. Well! This will be fun, we can plan a load of other fun shit to do instead."

God, he has a heart of gold. Yes, he shags a different woman daily, but he openly admits that, and whoever he's with knows the score.

"Luke, that is really so sweet of you, but don't change your plans, I'm happy to chill out around here and go out for walks and stuff. You go and have fun doing what you're supposed to do on a snowboarding holiday."

"No way! Tilly, you can't spend every day on your own, we'll do stuff together, it'll be fun. Just like LA, but with snow..." he pauses for a moment, "you're okay with that though, right? I mean, after all the weird shit that happened before?"

"Luke, I'm going to be totally honest with you, because I know it won't change anything, okay?"

"Okay."

"Okay. At the end of the LA trip, it all got a bit weird and I said we weren't seeing each other again because... well, how do I put this? Um... you like fun, yes?"

"Yeah?"

"And me, too, yes?"

"Okay, yeah..."

"Well, I kind of started liking you. Like, more than 'fun'. And it freaked me out because I don't 'do' relationships, and neither do you, and I really didn't want to end up like Bea and Daniel were at the time, pining for you, with no hope of ever being together. So the easiest thing was to just break away from you and not have to deal with it."

He surprises me, smiling a giant, mischievous, childlike grin. "Tilly..." he sings teasingly, "you totally fell in love with me. You think I'm awesome, you want to be Mrs Summers."

I giggle, he's so cute, and funny, and yes, awesome... "You are massively gorgeous and I'm sure girls do fall in love with you, frequently, but no; I wasn't in love with you. I just wanted you. I got jealous at the thought of you with other women, which freaked me out even more because I don't get emotionally attached like that. I'm not telling you this because I want anything to come of it, I just thought maybe you should know why it got weird."

"Totally, I felt like that too, Princess," he says, casually, chewing on some breakfast.

"No, you didn't. You don't need to say that just because I did. I know you're not into it, and honestly neither was I, so it was completely alien for me to feel like that."

"Think what you want, but I don't make shit up. So what does that mean for this vacation? Can we still do stuff and have fun together or what?"

"Yeah, we do have fun, I think I'm ready for another taste of Luke..." I say with a cheeky wink.

"So, are you still jealous at the thought of me and other women?"

"Um... I don't know. I think I've just accepted it, it's who you are and what you do. I know that I left LA and you had a new girl on your arm within a few hours, I'm not daft. I just had so much fun, I wanted to carry on having fun instead of some other girl taking my place. It would fuck me off if you shagged someone while you're having a holiday fling with me though."

"I wouldn't do that, my god, what kind of person do you think I am?" I simply shrug and he smiles slightly before continuing. "I like this, I like that we can just talk like this, totally open, nothing hidden." *Yeah, about that...* "I like you, Til, I like all the stuff we do together, which is weird because most girls bore the hell out of me in five minutes flat. Like I said, we did more than I've done with anyone in a long time. I don't want you fucking other guys either, but hey, I've gotta accept that that happens..." he pauses, "don't I?"

"What?"

"You with other guys."

"Well, I wasn't a virgin when I met you, so... duh."

"That's not really what I meant." he says, putting his knife and fork down on his cleared plate. "Oh, by the way, there was a letter for you on the hearth, did you see it?"

"No?" I put my cutlery down, hop off my stool and head to the fireplace. I don't know how I missed the A4 page, folded in half with 'TILLY' written in massive letters on the front. I open it up.

'Morning sleepyhead,

As you were both still asleep at ten, we had to go without you. Hope you had a fantastic 'sleep'. Text me if you want to meet up later, we can make another trip to the ski hire place for you. You naughty little minx, didn't take long for you two to find each other ;-) Maybe lock the door next time so I don't have to walk in and see you cuddled up like husband and wife. Very cosy.

Only teasing, can't wait to meet him later,
Love you, Clare.
(Oliver is making me sign his name, too.) And Oliver.
Xxx'

Those two need to do it and get it over with.

Luke surprises me suddenly by scooping me into his arms and collapsing on top of me on the giant sofa. I laugh hysterically as he tickles my waist, kissing my neck simultaneously. *No, no! Away from my Wriggler bump!* I squirm underneath him and manage to distract him by hooking my legs around his waist, tightly. He looks at my face, those dimples...

"You know, your ass looks pert as apples in these pants," he says with a grin, "you have a great ass, let me see it."

I laugh, "No! Listen, Luke, can you do me a big favour?" I ask, folding the letter and tossing it on the coffee table that sits between us and the amazing log fire.

"Anything, if you'll show me your sweet ass."

"Okay, I'll show you my *'sweet ass'*, if you can help me persuade the others to drop the subject, when I tell them I'm not skiing. I really don't want to make a big deal out of it."

"No sweat, sugar-lips, I can do that. Can we act, like, together and all?"

"What do you mean?"

"You know, in LA we were all, like, couples; Danny and Bea, you and me, your sister and Jay. Can we do that here? Then we can say we're doing our own thing, instead of skiing with everyone else."

"Oh okay, good idea," I just know this is going to make everything difficult. I am going to have an amazing time, I'm not going to want to tell him about Wriggler and when I do, I'll end up in love with him, begging him to be the active daddy in our little family. Which is *not* going to happen. I am letting myself have fun with Luke, but I *have* to tell him soon and I *have* to keep my wits about me. Remember the type of man he is, a lovely one, but a ladies' one. *He's not ours, Wriggler, we must remind ourselves regularly. He's not ours.*

"You love it." he says, his face closing in on mine.

"Love what?"

"You love acting *together* and all. Admit it, you love me, you want my babies." He kisses my lips softly.

I laugh with him, but also at the irony of it all. *I've already got one of those, darling.* "Yep. I love you, I think we're a match made in heaven, I think we should go and pick out china patterns."

"Sure, baby, and I'll get right on building that picket fence."

"I think it's *you* that loves it, *you* that loves me. *You* want to see me cradling your cute little bubba." I say. And immediately I know that I've gone too far. My heart thumps painfully in my chest, wishing it were true. *Why the fuck did I say that?*

Wriggler does some sort of acrobatic manoeuvre, I can feel it, *really* feel it, much more than I have felt before. I desperately want to put my hand to my belly and tell him what's just happened. *Right, that's it. You're telling him. Maybe not right now, but you're telling him. Soon.*

"We'd have seriously good looking kids, you and I. Come on, let's go make one," he jokes, "come on..." he says, standing up and holding out a hand to me as I curl my body a little so I'm not lying flat out in front of him. I take his hand and he pulls me up off the sofa.

He walks to the kitchen and flicks the kettle on and I look at him, confused. "So... you want to do it while we boil the kettle again?"

He laughs out loud and walks towards me, "No, I want to show you something else first. After that, you can show me your ass and then make us some good looking babies." *Oh god, please stop going on about babies.*

"Okay, I'm intrigued."

He makes us both a steamy cup of tea and asks me to follow him as he carries the cups up the stairs to the door right next to mine. I open it for him, and he leads me inside. It's quite similar in layout to mine, only with different furnishings and... *oh... a balcony.*

I walk straight over to it as he opens a drawer and pulls out a t-shirt.

"Here," he says, "take your clothes off and put that on."

"What? Why?" I ask, confused.

"Just do it. You'll see." He turns to place the tea down on a unit and I whip my top off, throwing his t-shirt over my head in record time, before he can see me. I pull my trousers off and throw them on the nearby chair, so I'm left standing in the middle of the room, in his huge t-shirt and my ski socks.

Luke gazes at me and slowly strolls towards me, a sexy smile and those delicious dimples adorning his gorgeous face. As he reaches me, he tugs on either side of the t-shirt and pulls me into his body. He's so huge next to me. I'm short with a really small frame, and he is built like a brick shit house and nearly a foot taller than me. I wonder if his body would be quite as amazing if he wasn't a personal trainer.

"You have no idea how freakin' hot you are right now, baby. I want to fuck your god damn brains out."

I laugh, I don't know why I don't expect these comments to come out of his mouth, but they always take me by surprise.

"So, the thing you want to show me, is it your man-pole? Because if it is, I hate to break it to you, but I've kind of seen it already."

He grins, "You are definitely the funniest chick I know. And I know a lot of chicks."

"I'm sure you do. But I think we've established that we find each other super-funny, so what did you bring me here for?"

He leans down and lays a lingering, soft, open-mouthed kiss on my lips. My eyes close, I'm almost hypnotised by these kisses of his, I've missed him so much.

"Wake up," he says against my mouth, "I'm not finished with you." I grin and open my eyes as he releases me and quickly changes into some tracksuit bottoms and a sweatshirt, before sweeping the duvet off the bed. He tells me to sit and wait. He then opens the balcony door and disappears outside. A few moments later, he re-enters and collects the tea. *What the hell is he doing?*

"Okay, Tilly, you can come out now." he calls and I make my way out to the covered balcony, shivering as I approach the door wearing nothing but the t-shirt. He's sitting in a huge, round, cushioned chair on the bedcovers. "Sit, baby," he says, patting his lap.

I sit on his lap and bend my legs up to my chest, squashing Wriggler, and he wraps the duvet around us both before handing me my tea.

"Relax and look around you."

He wraps his arms around me and I sink into his chest, enjoying this warm nest he's created. I sip my hot tea which is steaming out here in the snowy air, and look at the beautiful view, the same view I enjoyed earlier from my bedroom window. It's so peaceful and quiet."

"Wow, it's amazing out here."

"A Christmas winter wonderland, I thought you might like this."

"Oh I do, I love this. Thanks Lukey, you're a really thoughtful motherfucker, you know?"

He laughs a gorgeous, hearty laugh and kisses my head. "You are something else, girl. Drink your tea before it gets cold, it won't take long out here." he says, taking a long sip of his own. "Are your ears cold, Princess? I've got a couple of hats here..."

"No, my ears are okay for now, thank you." I rest against him and close my eyes, the urge to hug this huge, cute, adorable man becomes too much to resist. I put my cup down and turn to straddle him, under the covers, wrapping my arms around his muscular torso, pressing my cheek against his shoulder. My legs bent either side of his thighs, I squeeze him tightly, revelling in the comfort and warmth of Wriggler's daddy's body.

He puts his tea down and again, wraps his arms around me, sinking back into the chair. "I love how you can just curl up against me like that, and fit under my chin, you're so tiny."

"See, you do love me."

He chuckles and squeezes me tightly, "It wouldn't be too hard." *It would for you, you womanising philanderer. You gorgeous, beautiful, caring, sexy, womanising philanderer.*

I close my eyes and imagine what it would be like to keep him; to be wrapped up in these giant, protective arms every day, to feel the warmth radiating off his luscious body, have him hold me whenever I need it, have him want me, need me, love me... *Tilly! Watch yourself!*

"Wanna sit on my dick, baby-girl? You got me hard as rock under here."

I burst out laughing, I can never feel sombre with Luke around, he turns that happy dial to 'max' as soon as my mood takes a nosedive, and without even knowing it, it seems.

"Do people ever come out here?" I ask, referring to the outside area below us, wondering how visible we are.

"Sure they do." He grins.

I grind against him and become immediately excited when I feel his erection throb even harder through his tracksuit bottoms. "You *are* hard as rock, Lukey, I think he needs a bit of attention down there."

"I think so too, *poor little bugger,*" he says in a terrible cockney accent. I giggle and reach underneath me to try to free him from his trousers. He lifts his bottom and slips them past his buttocks. I grind against his hard length, through the gusset of my lace knickers. It's so arousing, he's so arousing; watching his slightly amused but totally turned on face, hearing the grunt noise he's making under his breath. I slide my knickers to the side and grab hold of him, guiding him there.

"Hey, wait up..." he says.
"What? No! We're about to fuck here!" I cry out.
"Shh," he says through a laugh, "we need a condom."
"Oh what? Where are they?"
"Inside."
"Oh come on, Luke, you can't bring me to this point, and *not* let me put you inside me."
"Wow, so romantic," he says and I laugh again.
"Seriously though, Luke, we've already done it without, why can't we just carry on? It's fine, nothing can result from this... please? Let me sit on your big hard cock..." I say with a deep, comical, trying-too-hard-to-be-sexy voice.
"I want it so badly, baby, it feels so good..."
"So do it, just because you don't use a condom with me, doesn't mean you'll forget all the time. Let's have a couple of weeks without condoms... it's so nice to feel you properly, I never have sex without one, neither do you, so let's enjoy it, let's be naughty."

"You're such a bad influence," he says as he thrusts his pelvis up, forcing himself inside me.

"Oh fuck!" I cry, god, it feels so good. I ease down onto him fully, taking his whole length inside me and it's a feeling of complete and utter perfection.

I slowly move up and down, grinding with every down movement, riding him with expertise, still completely wrapped in the duvet.

"Feels so good, baby, you're so ready for me. You like this? You like riding me outside where anyone could see?" he growls quietly.

"Oh, fuck, yeah," I moan, "it's so good, it's so cold, but so hot... oh god yes, it's hot." I moan, increasing my rhythm, his strong hands on my hips, lifting me and slamming me back down against him. He moves one hand up to my chest and caresses one of my breasts making me moan louder.

"Shh, someone could be down there, or do you like that? You like someone hearing us and not knowing where we are?"

"Oh... oh yes, I like that..."

"You sound so freaking hot, right now, they're going to wish they were fucking you, they'll wish they were me sitting under you, watching you..."

"Uh huh, uh huh, yeah..." I say, my orgasm fast approaching, his talk doing so much for me, I love everything that's coming out of his mouth, his voice, deep and gravelly, it turns me on so much, every move we make together, every thrust he indulges me with. My muscles tense, my hands grip his shoulders, I lean forwards to bite his lip and the climax hits hard, crashing through me, taking everything I have, "I'm coming... oh god, yes, yes... uh!" I cry and he clasps his hand over my mouth to silence me as he grunts loudly, thrusting deep and hard inside me.

I wrap my arms around his neck and press my cheek against his, panting and moving slowly against him, coming down. He holds me tight, flush against his body, his heart beating wildly through his chest.

"Wow, that *was* fun..." I whisper with a grin, and he chuckles, breathlessly.

"Amazing fun," he says, "we'll do *that* again before the holidays are out."

"Mmm, yeah. I am so tired."

"So sleep Princess, we've got nowhere to be," he says, softly, lifting me and cradling me sideways in his lap. He rearranges the covers so we're totally wrapped up. "You good?"

"Mmm, yes thanks." I smile and enjoy the closeness. "Luke, are your family sad not to be with you for Christmas?"

I ask, purely because I wonder as I lay here on him, how there isn't a family somewhere, wanting this lovely man home.

"They're cool, we don't always see each other at Christmas because my parents divorced, so I've always spent alternate Christmas's with each of them. Now I'm grown-up, it just depends what we're all up to, as to where I spend it."

"How old were you when they split up? Don't answer that if it's too personal."

"No, not at all, I was about nine, I think, it wasn't a big deal, they were never really together anyway."

"So who did you live with?"

"My mom, but I saw my dad most weekends and for vacations and stuff like that. I was a happy kid, I didn't know any different. How about you? You missing your folks?" he asks.

"Um, no. My dad died when I was nineteen and I don't know my mum."

"I'm sorry, Til. You don't talk about it much, huh?"

"No. It makes me sad, talking about my dad. I miss him a lot, he was an amazing man. There's not a lot that upsets me, but thinking about him is one of the few things that does."

"Okay, let's stop talking about it."

"It's okay. Sometimes I like to talk about him, even if it makes me sad, just so everyone knows what a good man he was."

"Well, if he brought you and Gemma up, it's pretty obvious what a good man he was."

I smile up at his face, "You may be a bad-boy when it comes to the ladies, Luke, but you have a heart of gold, really. You're a good man, too."

"Alright, alright, you're totally in love with me, I get it."

I giggle and swat his peck. "You're totally in love with yourself."

"Til, can I ask you something?"

"Yeah..."

"I know you said you had a fun time with me over the summer, but did you really have a great time? I mean, I have never had so much fun with a girl before. I know you had fun, but, was it like, *amazing* fun or just... fun?"

I smile and look up at his face, "You're getting all insecure on me, that's a side of you I'd put money on never seeing."

"Insecure? Me? Pah! No, but seriously, I have wondered ever since, if you were feeling how I was, if you enjoyed yourself as much as I did."

"Yeah, I did. I had an incredible time, I was quite looking forward to having an LA fuck buddy to call up every time I went to my sister's... but I changed my mind about that when I started liking you for more than just sex."

"You say it like there's something wrong with liking me, am I that bad a catch?"

"Oh come on, Luke," I say with a grin, "you forget I was the female equivalent of you, we don't *do* more than sex. You're an amazing catch in some ways, but no one wants a man who can't keep his dick in his pants; no one wants a catch that doesn't want to be caught. Stop making out like you're the relationship type, I'm not even the relationship type, you don't need to play that game with me."

"I can keep my dick in my pants," he says with a frown and a pout, like a child.

"Have you ever *had* to keep your dick in your pants?"

"Once, yeah. A long, long time ago. And I didn't *have* to; I wanted to."

That does surprise me, I'm intrigued. "Really? Who was that? Didn't work out, obviously, did it fall out of your pants accidentally?" I ask playfully.

He smiles a very small, very shy sort of a smile, one I've never seen before. "Actually, no, it didn't. Hey, let's talk about something else, this is all a bit too deep for your first day in Aspen. What shall we do?"

Oh! I really want to know what happened! Damn it, he obviously doesn't want to discuss it. "Okay, um, I don't know, what shall we do? I'm quite enjoying your hot bod right now."

"Let's chill out here then, I'll take you for lunch later and then we can come back and get ready for dinner tonight, I think it's here."

"How do you know this stuff?"

"Daniel texted me earlier, they all know we're together, obviously, so he sent me today's plan of action. They won't be back from skiing until about four, four-thirty."

"Okay then," I say as I snuggle back into his chest and enjoy feeling so warm and cosy out here in the chilly, winter wonderland.

CHAPTER 3
THURSDAY 20TH DECEMBER (CONT.)

"Hey, Princess..." Luke's voice stirs me from a deep sleep, from my happy dream about Wriggler; I had her in my arms, she was the tiniest little thing, wrapped in a pink blanket, wearing a white hat that Luke's mum had knitted. *Oh, so sweet. Are you a girl, Wriggler?*

"Wake up, hey..."

"Mmm?" I say, as I stretch and gaze at the impressive chest I'm pressed up against.

"What were you dreaming about? You were smiling and telling me to look at her; look at who? You secretly fantasising about a threesome?"

I giggle but holy fuck, that could have been bad! Since when do I talk in my sleep? "No idea, but before you go out looking for potential third candidates, I'm not into it."

"Ah, shit," he says with a cheeky grin, "so you wanna go grab some lunch now?

"Yeah, okay." I say, starting to move, when he holds me still, pulling me closer into his body.

"I've never really looked at a chick asleep before, it's not usually part of the deal, but you're cute when you sleep, your cheeks flush pink, you look so... peaceful." *Oh my god. Luke!*

"Luke, why are you acting weirdly? We're fuck buddies. Stop being lovey dovey, I know you're in love with me and everything, but..." and before I can get any further, he grabs my face and devours my mouth, his tongue caressing mine, his lips soft, but in full control. I completely succumb to his touch, relaxing fully against him, giving in. He stands effortlessly and carries me inside.

He sits on the bed with me, and slowly pulls away, resting his forehead on mine. "I don't get bored of you, it's so odd."

"Wow, what a compliment," I say with a chuckle, "but as fascinated as you are by me, we're not having sex, we're going out to eat. So you'll have to let me go."

"Well that's no fun."

"Nope, see? You'll be bored soon enough."

He laughs and releases me, and we both get changed quickly before heading out to Luke's hire car. It's like his car in LA, a big SUV type car; so 'him'. We both climb in and he drives us about three minutes down the road, before parking up and walking me to a place called *'Peaches Corner Cafe'*.

"Have you been here before? You seem to know where you're headed," I ask as he opens the door for me.

"Yeah, I've eaten here quite a few times, they do some great food, healthy too, a lot of organic stuff."

Ooh, organic, this will be good for you, then, Wriggler.

A short while later, our food arrives; a roasted vegetable sandwich for me, and a Caesar salad with seared tuna for Luke. It looks amaze-balls and the next fifteen minutes or so are spent in total silence as we devour our delicious food. I'm so flipping hungry.

When I finish, I look up at Luke who is sitting back in his chair, smiling at me. "See something you like, lover-boy?' I ask.

"As a matter of fact, yeah," he says with a smirk, "I love zucchini, and that chunk on your cheek looks really appetising."

I grab my napkin and wipe my cheek, rolling my eyes. "Hilarious. And it's called courgette."

"It's *called* zucchini."

I raise my eyebrow in amusement, "Courgette."

"I'll show you my courgette in a minute, now get over here and sit on my dick."

Yet again, I burst into a fit of laughter, I'm sure he's a hell of a personal trainer, but he'd keep me in shape just from laughing. Well, that - and all the sex. "In the middle of the cafe? You're *that* bad?" I ask through the giggles.

"I don't know, sweetheart, I think, based on the noise you make, that I'm actually pretty good."

I shrug, casually, "Meh... I could take it or leave it."

"You love it. You want it right now," he leans forward across the table and looks around to check for nearby, prying ears. He speaks with a low, quiet, ridiculously sexy tone, "you're thinking about it - right now, about the huge boner in my pants, you want to lick it and suck it, wet it... slide down onto it." *Oh. Yes. I. Do.*

Inside - I am basking in the naughty. I want him to continue, I want him to yank me onto the table and shove his hand into my trousers. "Am I? How on earth would you know that?" I ask, leaning forward onto the table to meet him.

"I can see the filth in your eyes. They're looking at me saying, 'take me, take me now, big boy'," he says in his very amusing, very awful girly voice, before reverting back to the deliciously sexy tone that makes me tremble with need, "and I want to feel you, I want to sink my fingers into your..."

Suddenly, we're not alone, someone stands at our table, waiting to take the plates. I'm flushed - hot, and unable to hide the sexual need written all over my face. You just can't say things like that to a horny, pregnant woman! I want to scream *'fuck me. FUCK ME!',* but I doubt that would be appreciated by the staff and patrons of this lovely corner cafe.

"Let's go," Luke says, standing to leave. I'm quite disappointed, I was enjoying that. I stand and move next to him, and he slings his heavy arm around my shoulders, walking with me to the door. Just before we reach it, he bends down and mumbles against my loose hair, "you're so ready for me right now, aren't you?"

I look up at his face, he's grinning at me, his blue eyes sparkling and his dimples screaming for me to brush my lips over them. He's got such a cheeky face, I guarantee he was a seriously mischievous looking child... I bet Wriggler inherits that, it'll be so cute.

"Maybe..."

"Maybe? Are you telling me there's a chance you're not soaking wet and wanting me more than life itself? Wow, well it seems I need to continue."

We arrive at the car and he opens my door, pushing me up to help me into the tall vehicle; his giant, strong hands on my bum... oh, I love his hands, so masculine and powerful... and talented. He holds the top of the door with one hand and puts the other on the roof as he leans right in until his face is practically touching mine. His biceps bulge through his many layers, he's *massive*.

He whispers against my lips, "I'm so hard just thinking about what I'm going to get to do to you, I don't believe you don't feel the same, you want me to sink deep inside you just as much as I do. Go ahead, feel..." I glance out of the corner of my eye to check that there's no one in the immediate vicinity, and as I extend my arm to his fly, I move my face infinitesimally closer, and brush my lips against his, my heartbeat wild, my blood burning though my veins. I rest my hand on him as I open my mouth to move the kiss to the next stage. He wasn't telling a lie, he absolutely *is* so hard, and I would like nothing more than to sink to my knees and swallow him deep into my throat.

He kisses me back slowly, erotically. With my one hand stroking his hardness as best I can through his thick trousers, I curl the other around his neck, pulling his face into mine, taking the kiss to another level. I moan slightly at his masculine grunt, as he releases the car frame and pushes me back against the headrest with his kiss. He holds my face in both hands as he clearly loses himself in this super-passionate, rather public moment.

I take my hand from his cock and plunge it into his messy, dark blonde hair, greedily, pulling him into me, pressing him against me. If I could yank him into the car and in between my legs right now, I so would. I writhe in my seat and Luke takes one hand from my face and rests it between my legs. A high pitched grunt escapes me as he rubs the fabric of my trousers over the sensitive area. Everything other than Luke and I escapes me. I've no thoughts on my surroundings, who might be watching, what sort of a whore I look like for getting my vag rubbed in public; I couldn't care less. All I know, is that I want this man, right now. I want him to crawl in on top of me, pull down his trousers, and fuck me like his life depends on it.

A car toots its horn nearby and we both snap out of our oblivion, slowing the kiss and opening our eyes. I look directly into the electric blue outlining his oversized pupils, and in this moment, I understand completely how you can get totally lost in another's eyes; to delve into their inner secrets. As an unromantic cynic (apart from where Bea and Daniel are concerned), I feel quite uncomfortable about this discovery. I'd really rather not know what it feels like to have a glimpse into someone's soul. If I didn't know him better, or was a naive searcher of the idyllic happy-ever-after, I could fall in love with him in this instant. *Could?*

He's gazing right back at me, searching for something, searching for answers that he won't find. I know he likes me a lot and he's confused by his feelings towards me, but that doesn't mean he can, or will, ever fall in love. It's just not what people like us do; we play about and move on to the next bit of fun. I am going to be giving all of that up now, to focus on being a responsible mum, but that doesn't mean I'll succumb to the belief that everyone finds their soulmate, I think a very minute number of people are ever truly happy in love, and I am under no illusion that I will be an exception to that.

"Let's go Princess, I want more of you than I can have right here," he whispers, still gazing into my eyes. I giggle; he's a horny bugger.

"I love that," he adds.

"Love what?"

"When you laugh, your nose wrinkles up, it's cute. I noticed that the first time we met at the noodle place in LA, when you fell head over heels in love with me."

"What?" I giggle, "you mean when you fell in love with me; you're the one remembering my wrinkly nose!"

"Whatever, sweet-lips, let's go get some," he says as he kisses me quickly and pulls out of the car, shutting the door behind him. *No, come back and kiss me some more!*

He jumps in his side and starts the engine, before pulling into the road. He turns to look at me, smiling, and I wonder what he's thinking.

Again, it takes only a few minutes to get back to the house and Luke parks up. He walks around to open my door and lifts me out of the car, under my arms, like I weigh nothing. Instead of putting me on the ground, he rests me against him, my legs and feet dangling, and kisses me on the lips. I put my hands on his shoulders and pull back, to kiss each of his dimples.

"I love these," I say with a smile, "they're so cheeky, I don't think you'd be as much of a bad-boy without these dimples."

"You can thank my mom, I get them from her. Why do you like bad-boys so much?"

"I just do. Long story. But it means I like you, so don't complain."

"I'm not complaining, I'd hate it if I liked you and you didn't like me back... I've never actually had that problem, apart from when you said you didn't want to see me again. I didn't like that."

"Of course you've never had that problem, look at you, you're a fitty!"

"Oh, I'm a *fitty,* huh? I have no idea what that means, but I'll assume it's a good thing, and I'm glad you think so. I might just let you suck me off for that."

I burst out laughing and he lowers me to my feet, bending to kiss me once more as I laugh. He takes my hand and leads me to the steps which have been covered in a new layer of snow since we left. I remember my near fall last night and slow down, holding on to the rail to keep steady.

"Hey, don't worry about slipping, baby, I got you," Luke says, putting an arm around me and pulling me into his side. He has no idea that I'm not worried about myself, or that he's actually protecting our baby right now, not me.

As we open the door, the most delicious smell captures me immediately. "Mmm, what's that? It smells amazing!"

"Must be dinner... who cares? Let's go to bed."

I smile, "I'd like to get a drink first. And won't the others be back from skiing soon?"

"Yeah, but we can be quick. Come on, Princess, let's get that drink and go." He heads to the kitchen, tugging me along behind him, smiling as I go. I haven't smiled or laughed as much as I have in the last day or so, since I came back from LA in September.

Come to think about it, I've completely forgotten how miserable I was up until yesterday, he's got such a way about him that takes you away from all the crappy shit that accompanies real life. It's as if he's constantly introducing me to *his* world, where everything is bright, and vibrant and positive; every day is sunny, the grass is always the greenest and happiness is available on tap. *Oh, how I'd like Wriggler and I to live in that world.*

As we turn the corner to the kitchen, the housekeeper, Pam - I think Luke called her - is again, standing at the cooker, stirring the contents of a few pots. She turns and welcomes us warmly.

"It smells amazing in here, what are you cooking?" I ask, I don't see how I can be hungry when I just polished off a delicious roasted veg sarnie, but still, I think I could eat whatever this is as well.

"It's dinner," she says, "I am making you guys a Yankee pot roast."

"Ooh, what is pot roast? I've heard it mentioned on tv and stuff, but I don't really know what it is. I want some already though."

"It's beef roast with vegetables and broth. It's traditionally made with potatoes, but I like to pour the broth over mashed potatoes, so that's what I'm making for you."

"That sounds incredible..." I say, practically dribbling.

Luke is standing still, staring at me with his arms crossed. "So you've never had pot roast before?"

"No, but I can't wait to try it."

"And you're hungry after lunch already?"

"Don't look at me like I'm a pig, can't you smell?" I ask with exasperation, why isn't he appreciating this?

"Sure, I can smell, but I also only just ate a half hour ago... with you."

Okay. Maybe this is completely abnormal, but how do I explain? *Oh, didn't I say? I'm starving again because I have your child growing inside me.* Hmm. No.

"Okay, I'm just appreciating the smell, that's all," I say as my stomach rumbles.

"What can I get you?" Pam asks.

"It's okay, I'll get it," I respond, not wanting her to take her eyes off that cooking for a second, what if it burns?! I open the huge fridge and take out a bottle of water and start to drink it. Luke strolls over and presses his front against my back, resting his hand on my hip. He runs his other hand down my spine, over my bottom and in between my legs. I almost spit my water out as I glance over to Pam to check if she can see. Luckily, she's facing the pots and pans, away from us.

Luke bows his head to mine and whispers in my ear, "Feel good, Princess? Want more?"

I lean back against him, his fingers pressing and circling into the crotch of my trousers from behind. I want to stop immediately, but at the same time, I really don't. This is naughty, and dangerous and such a complete turn on.

I nod. "Uh huh," I whisper.

He uses more pressure, circling slowly, and I subconsciously grind my hips into him, encouraging him.

"Water good?" he asks, his voice louder, sounding completely normal.

It's a struggle for me to answer, but I manage, "Yep..."

Pam is still facing the cooker as Luke moves his hand away, he spins me around and kisses me, slowly unfastening the popper of my trousers and sliding his hand inside. *Shit! Wriggler!* I close my eyes and pray that he hasn't felt a difference in my belly size, I'm not ready to tell him, not just yet. He moves his hands until he is inside my knickers, and I'm so desperate to moan, his fingers rhythmically making magic in my Hanky Pankys.

He breaks away from the kiss for a moment to whisper in my ear, "Do you like this? She could turn around at any minute, and she'll see me standing here with my hand in your panties, making you want to come..."

A tingle spreads all over my skin, his deep whisper, his fingers moving, his words... oh yes, we need to go and have sex right now.

The clatter of pans and spoons in the background doesn't stop us, I wrap my hands around his neck and rise onto tip toes to whisper in his ear, "Fuck me somewhere, anywhere, now..."

He continues with his fingers and smiles, "You'd like that, wouldn't you? I was thinking of making you come here, now." He works his fingers faster and I close my eyes, trying to remember I'm in the kitchen with the housekeeper, and can't have a screaming orgasm.

"Let's go... please? I want to come," I whisper and he simply smiles, but makes no move to leave. My back is to Pam, so I have no idea if she turns around, only Luke can see that.

"I've always thought a pot roast is a great first meal for a winter vacation. Something nice and hearty after a long, active day out in the cold," Pam says, and I look straight up at Luke's face for reassurance, she clearly hasn't turned around, because he hasn't stopped.

"Absolutely, 'Perfect Pam'," Luke responds, "I bet everyone will love it, you're a great cook. What time are they arriving?" he asks.

I'm standing here, on the verge of an explosive orgasm, while he continues to have a normal conversation with the fucking housekeeper! I can't do this, but oh... I think I'm going to come...

"They're arriving at seven, dinner will be served shortly after that."

Luke wraps his free arm around me, as if he's cuddling me, and I push my face against his chest, burying myself in his thick jumper. I need to moan. It's coming, my thighs clench, my pelvis rotating slightly against his hand, and just as he pushes his fingers inside me, and I prepare for the mighty detonation, Oliver calls out from the lounge area.

Luke whips his hand out of my trousers, and wraps both arms around me quickly, as if we've been doing nothing but hugging. *Fuck no! Oliver, I could fucking kill you!*

"Here you are! You missed a great day, Til... hi, you must be Luke, I'm Oliver, Bea's brother," he says as he enters the kitchen and walks over to us.

"Hey, Oliver, I've heard a lot about you from Daniel, good to meet you."

Oliver opens the fridge and pulls out two bottles of water and as Clare enters, he hands her one.

"Hi Til, we missed you today, have fun?"

"Hiya, yes thanks, it was great, this is Luke, by the way, Clare."

"I gathered. Hi Luke. I've heard lots about you from Bea and Daniel," she says, "... oh, er, and Tilly..." she adds as an obvious after-thought. She kisses his cheek and Luke looks at me with a raised brow. I feel bad, It's obvious that I haven't talked to Clare about him as much as Bea.

Clare kisses him on the cheek and smiles sweetly at me. "I'm desperate for a cuppa, shall I make us all one?"

"I'll make it, you two go and change into something comfy, and then you can tell me all about skiing," I say, needing a reason to cool off, alone for a moment.

"Great, back in a bit," Clare says and she and Oliver head to their rooms to change.

Pam walks over and makes a shooing motion with her hand, "I'll make tea, sweetie, you two go relax, I'll bring it through," she says with a warm smile.

Luke and I sit together on one of the three large sofas surrounding the coffee table. The fire crackles in front of us, it's such a cosy haven in here. Luke moves to sit right up against me, putting an arm around my shoulders. I look up at his face and smile, resting my head into the side of his chest. "I was milliseconds away from coming then, you know."

He grins, showing off those irresistible dimples, "If they'd have come home just a few seconds later... but I still want to take you to bed, I want to taste you."

"Oh, Christ, Luke, shut the fuck up. Or I'll seriously come in my pants right here, you've got me so horny."

Luke laughs, "Will they be long? Maybe you can sit on me real quick?"

I laugh with him, "No, they won't be long, and as much as I love dangerous sex, bouncing on your lap in the middle of the lounge, in the middle of the day, with friends about to walk in - is just too much."

"It is? But letting me make you come in the kitchen with the housekeeper at the stove isn't too much?"

I giggle again, "Okay, okay, so maybe I would do you in the lounge, but not now. I need it, trust me, I do, but we'll have to wait. It was hard enough trying to make conversation when I'd just been on the verge, it'll be even harder if I've just had a raging orgasm."

He pauses for a moment, looking into my eyes. His are so warm, so happy, but they're doing that searching thing again. "You know, Til, I can't thank Bea enough for hooking up with Daniel on that airplane, or I'd never have met you. You've totally changed the way I feel about women. Sure, I've always loved women... a lot," he emphasises those last two words, "but I've never really seen further than... the outside."

Whoa! Careful there Luke, you might actually start sounding like a good-boy! "That's because all you do is shag them. You - and I, actually - don't get to know anyone."

"I've never really wanted to, but you intrigue me. Not that I wanted a relationship when we met, or anything, the same as you, but I wanted to keep seeing you, and your fine-ass body."

I look at his face, his gorgeous, happy face, and I smile, slowly, "You know why that is?"

He raises an eyebrow, suspiciously, "Why?"

"Because you *lurve* me."

A broad, delighted smile crosses his face and he turns to close in on me, wrapping a hand around my side, against my ribs. He tickles me, burying his face in my neck, growling and brushing his teeth against my skin, biting me gently. I screech and howl with laughter, pushing my hands against his hard chest.

"Get off me you animal!" I cry, between fits of giggles, pushing against him as I writhe underneath.

He continues, forcing me down on the sofa so he's half on top of me. My laughter gets louder as the tickling gets worse. "Stop!" I cry, I can't take any more.

He slows and chuckles, locking eyes with me. He lowers his face to gently kiss my lips, and I wrap my arms around him, to fully accept his invitation.

"Huh hmm..." I hear Oliver clear his throat, obviously, and we both giggle, sitting upright and straightening ourselves out.

Clare and Oliver sit on another sofa, watching us with amused smirks on their faces. Luke throws his arm around my shoulders again and relaxes back, resting an ankle up on the opposite knee, causing his thigh to press firmly against mine. *Grr, I just want to straddle him and snog his fucking face off.*

Pam enters with a tray of tea and little pastries, and puts it down on the table in front of us.

"Thank you, Pam, I hope that hasn't kept you from looking after my yummy dinner," I say, smiling jovially - but I damn well mean it.

"Your dinner is cooking slowly and perfectly, Miss Burton."

"Gah!" I cry, "Don't call me that, I'm Tilly, please call me Tilly."

"Okay - Tilly. Enjoy your tea, everyone."

"So, how was your first day?" Luke asks, looking genuinely interested. I lean forward and pour our tea from the pot, turning to hand Luke his. "Thank you, Princess," he says, and heat flushes my cheeks at his term of endearment in front of my friends. I see Clare grinning as she pours hers and she catches my eye and winks. They haven't seen me acting like this with anyone for... well, not since my ex, Scott, so about six years or so. Bea has; she saw how we interacted in LA, but these two certainly haven't.

"It was fantastic, we had a great first day, didn't we Clare?" Oliver says, turning to look at her, grinning.

"Brilliant, the snow was perfect. You'll love it Til," she says, and I stumble, not knowing quite what to say.

"Well, I, er..."

"I actually wanted to take Tilly out over the next few days, we're not too fussed about skiing yet, and I know some really cool places I'd like to show her," Luke interrupts, and I gaze up at his face, surprised. I doubt he knows how grateful I am that he's taking the heat off me a little.

"What?" Oliver asks, "You've come to Aspen for a skiing holiday, and you're not going to ski yet? Are you crazy? I thought you loved skiing?"

"Well, I did, but I had a fall last time and it has given me the heeby jeebies, plus, Luke has told me about some amazing sights, so I really want to do that."

"I can visit whenever I like, so I quite like taking time out to do other stuff, too," Luke adds, as his hand searches mine and gives a gentle squeeze. I could just kiss him all over for this. And he has no idea of the real reason he's doing this for me. *Ouch.*

"Oh, okay then. But we'll miss you on the slopes, make sure you join us out there after Christmas," Clare says and rests back into the sofa with her tea. I don't respond, I'll cross that bridge when I come to it.

The next hour, or so, is spent chatting comfortably, Clare and Oliver tell us every detail about their day, and Luke shares information about the best slopes and places to visit in Aspen. The men seem to get on well, as expected, they're both friendly guys and have common interests in Daniel and Bea and their cars, which is the next topic of conversation.

After a while, Luke heads upstairs to change for dinner, and the rest of us lounge by the fire, chatting.

"He's gorge!" Clare whispers enthusiastically, "And he seems like a great bloke, Til. You've been at it like rabbits all day, haven't you?"

I laugh and raise an eyebrow, "Not all day, we had to eat."

"Okay, okay," Oliver butts in, "enough of that, I'm not Bea you know, stop talking about sex."

"Aw, jealous Olly? Not getting any?" I tease.

"I get plenty, ta very much, but I'm not keen on hearing about your pursuits. You two are too close to the family, it's like hearing about my sister doing it... bleugh..." he says, quivering in disgust. Clare turns slowly to look at him with a raised brow, he simply blinks at her, and looks down at his hands, awkwardly. *What's that all about? Oh... my... god...*

"Eur! You two are shagging aren't you? Oh my god, I knew it!" I cry and they straighten up immediately, attempting to look innocent.

"What? No! Oh my god, Til, where did you get that from?" Clare asks, she looks mortified, maybe I should have kept that revelation to myself... but they *so* are.

"Til, I don't know what you think you know, but me and Clare, we're not... we're just friends, sweetheart. Close friends, yes, I'll give you that, but we're not... you know... doing anything together." He looks at Clare and she at him, they both feign innocence, curling their lips up at one another in mild disgust. "Like I said, you two are like my sisters."

"Okay, if that's what you say." I hold my hands up, not believing them for a second. I do think of Oliver as a big brother, and I imagine he sees me as a sister, but there's something different about him and Clare. She used to fancy him back when we were in college, when we first met Bea, but he had a long term girlfriend back then and showed no interest in Clare. So she got over it and it has never been discussed since, but in the last few months, they've been spending so much time together, alone, and I've been more than a little suspicious.

"Seriously Til, sort out that vivid imagination," Olly says, rolling his eyes and relaxing a little. *Hmm.*

My phone makes a noise in my handbag, so I stand to head to the table by the front door where I left it to check my messages.

~
LA Luke 20 Dec 17:54
Get your sweet ass upstairs and show my meat some love.
~

I laugh, loudly and reply straight away.

~
20 Dec 17:55
Show your meat some love yourself. I'm busy.
~

His reply is almost instant.

~
LA Luke 20 Dec 17:55
Get busy with me, Princess. I wanna lick you... come up. My room.
~

I quiver, I want that so much.

~
20 Dec 17:57
Lick me later, when we have more time, and then... ;-)
~

I'm selfishly glad that I didn't tell him about the baby straight away. If I had, I wouldn't have enjoyed this time with him, I wouldn't have been reminded what it's like to enjoy myself, to mess about with someone... to get fucked. Christ, I would have gone a long time without any. Better get some more, while he's still willing. I know I need to tell him though, and I will... I will.

    I make my excuses to Clare and Olly, telling them I'm going to change for dinner, and I make my way up the stairs towards Luke's room. As I approach the door, my mobile phone buzzes again.

~

LA Luke 20 Dec 18:01
I want you now. :-(

~

    I smile, slipping my phone into my pocket and I slowly turn the door handle, pushing it open just a little. I slip in silently and as I turn to close it, Luke appears out of nowhere, grabs me by the waist and spins me around, forcefully pushing me against the door, his lips pressing against mine, his tongue immediately searching.

    I clutch his unruly, damp hair in my fists and kiss him back, moaning loudly. He lifts me, effortlessly, keeping me pressed against the door, our faces level. I subconsciously acknowledge his lack of attire, only a small white towel around his waist, his body warm and damp from the shower. I wrap my legs around him and my stomach flips in excitement, I clench in anticipation.

    He caresses the side of my face with his hand; it feels good, so intimate, he's offering a different side of him than the one everyone else sees. I wonder if he handles his other women with such caring tactility, when he's not throwing them around the bedroom.

    "I like you, Tilly," he says as his lips travel down my neck.

    "Just as well, really," I say with a smile as he continues. I close my eyes and enjoy every touch of his soft lips.

    "I mean it, I really like you. I missed you when you left."

    My heart beats wildly and I writhe against him as he takes my earlobe in his teeth lightly, his excited, yet, gentle breathing, all I can hear. "Did you miss me?" he whispers, vulnerability laced through his masculine voice. I pause for a short while, enjoying the affection he's showering upon me, afraid to speak for fear of something too true escaping. "Til?" he asks, gently probing.

"Yes," I whisper, almost too quietly, "I did. I missed you."

"Luke... hey, Luke?" A loud knock on the door behind me and Daniel's voice interrupts our 'moment'.

Luke sighs, "Kinda busy in here, dude," he calls back, still kissing my neck.

"Oh, okay, hey Tilly," Daniel calls, making me laugh. "Hi, Daniel."

"We're all downstairs about to have an aperitif, can you resume that later?"

Luke chuckles silently and drops his head to my shoulder. "Be down in a minute."

"Cool." Daniel responds, and I hear his footsteps retreat to the stairs.

I smile and pull his head up by his hair, he's smiling too. "Come on, bad-boy, let's go for dinner. We can pick up where we left off, later."

He pouts like a kid, "But I'm hard, I need you..." he lowers his head to trail kisses along my collar bone. I close my eyes, leaning my head back against the door, needing him, too.

"Don't say that, I'm so horny."

He growls and lifts his head to kiss my mouth, resting there, he looks into my eyes, "That's not something I can hear, right now. Come, the sooner we eat, the sooner we fuck. Let's go show our faces."

He releases me and I go to change in my room.

I slip on a pair of jeans and a cosy woollen jumper, and as I'm pulling on my big socks, a fully-dressed, gorgeous-looking Luke walks in. He's wearing jeans that skim his legs to perfection, showing off his incredible thighs. His v-neck, charcoal sweatshirt is soft and expensive looking, and fits impeccably... he looks like a bloody fitness model. "What is it about you?" he asks with a smile, "You're changing me; I never used to find socks a turn on *at all,* but now I think they're really freaking hot! It's all I want you to wear for the next two weeks."

I laugh as I stand, pulling my hair into a pony tail, "Okay, if that's what you want," I say as I pretend to unbutton my jeans.

He walks over and holds my wrists still, "Okay, okay, it's all I want you to wear for *me*." He brings my hand to his mouth and kisses it, "I don't want them seeing what's mine."

I raise my eyebrows,"Oh, what's *yours* eh? You think I'm yours?"

He smiles and frowns, "Weirdly, yes. Let's go."

I follow him out of the door, wondering what exactly that means. Is there a chance we might be able to work something out? Do I want that? Yes. I do. I knew when I left LA that I'd want more with him, but he's not that kind of bloke. *Is he?*

~~~~~~~

The meal with everyone was lovely. The food was exactly as I had expected, bloody amazing! It was a little awkward, trying to avoid having a glass of wine without making a big deal of it, I was handed one, so I kept it - occasionally bringing it to my lips to simulate drinking. The taste of the pungent liquid on my lips actually makes me heave a little, I've heard that some women find the thought of alcohol repulsive when pregnant; I think I must be one of them.

It was lovely to catch up with Bea's parents, Emily and Edward, they've been like parents to me since Dad died and I try to see them as much as I can, I'm always invited over to theirs for Sunday lunch with the family, and I go whenever I can, although I've been MIA in recent weeks.

Daniel's parents are also lovely, just as Bea said, so welcoming and happy. His sister, Alexia, is hard to make out; she is very quiet, seems quite nice, maybe a little prudish. I'm also not sure if she 'gets' my British humour, she doesn't seem to laugh much. Well, she does for Luke, she couldn't help but laugh at their private jokes, giggling that squeaky noise, flicking her hair about like she's in a shampoo advert. I know I sound jealous, I'm not, I just found it really fucking irritating.

Luke managed to peel himself away from Alexia long enough to join Bea, Daniel and I out on the verandah for 'one for the road' at the end of the evening. Everyone else decided to stay in the warmth, around the fire, but I really wanted a moment with the LA crew.

I had a hot chocolate with Bea, while the boys had a beer together. They held us close; Daniel had Bea tucked into his side, her arms wrapped around his waist, and Luke's arms were wrapped around my chest from behind, pressing me into his front. It felt just like LA... well, except LA was hot... *Mmm, smoking hot, what a hot, sexy summer that was...*

Anyway, it was great to get a moment like that, just the four of us. We told Bea and Daniel about the skiing situation, and they reacted pretty much the same as Clare and Olly did; disappointed, but accepting. I'm so grateful that Luke made the whole thing that much easier for me. I owe him one.

I managed to get a little time alone with Bea during the course of the evening; she said I seem so much happier now that I have seen Luke, and I reluctantly agreed with her. I don't want him to be able to shape my mood, I haven't let a man do that since Scott, but it's totally out of my control here, and I'm not really comfortable with it.

Bea is glowing, she adores Daniel's Aspen home and is so excited for their first Christmas together, I can't help but smile with her. They are perfect together, and so lucky to have found each other. One day, they'll have a baby, just like me. The difference being; they'll have the security of a loving relationship - she'll have the father of her child with her, supporting her... in the know.

When the front door closes, and the guests have gone, I slump on the sofa and curl into a ball, closing my eyes and enjoying the relaxing heat of the fire warming my chilly body. Clare and Oliver both said their goodnights a short while back and went up to bed separately. Luke had a message on his phone about a work emergency and had to make a business call in the study. What could possibly be so critical about personal fitness, I've no idea.

I subconsciously cradle my slightly rounded tummy and relax fully, wondering what little one is getting up to in there. I'm not feeling much in the way of flutters today, some days he's livelier than others, and he's still so tiny, he might have moved so I can't feel him... her. I can feel the difference inside, if I poke my belly, I can feel a hard ridge, or if I run or hop or something, I feel a heavy, full sensation, almost as if there's a grapefruit sitting in my pelvis.

It's strange, but I like it; it reminds me that I'm never going to be alone, even if... *when* Luke decides to do a runner, it'll always be me and Wriggler. *Oh... Wriggler, I don't want to tell him. He'll leave and I'll go back to being a miserable bitch again. I promise I'll be happy when you join me out here, though, I will, I'm so excited to see you.*

I drift off, comfortable and warm, thinking about those ten little fingers and ten little toes. Mmm, so cosy.

CHAPTER 4
FRIDAY 21ST DECEMBER

I need a wee, badly. I moan and turn in bed, preparing to sit up when Luke's voice startles me. "No..."

I can't recall coming to bed last night - to Luke's bed. I blink a couple of times, attempting to clear my head, it's not like I've been drinking. I'm naked, except for my knickers, but all I remember is falling asleep on the sofa. I slip out of bed, to grumbles galore from Luke, and dash to the en-suite.

When I finish, I head back to find him sprawled out in all his naked glory, looking ridiculously gorgeous. I pick up the jumper I was wearing last night, and pull it on to cover my torso. I notice I'm still wearing my socks and smile.

Sitting cross-legged on the bed next to him, I gently run my fingertips along his washboard abs, he is the sexiest man alive, without a doubt. I lean down to lay a gentle kiss on his chest, and watch as his mouth curls into a slight smile as he sleeps. I try to picture him as a dad - but I can't, he's probably great with kids but nowhere near responsible enough to have and take care of one of his own.

I check the time on my phone, which is on the bedside table; again, no recollection of this. It's only six thirty, so I should probably get some more sleep, but I feel wide awake - I must have slept like a log. I climb off the bed and take a thick blanket from the chair, heading towards the balcony. Opening the curtains just enough to crack the door, I slip out into the ice cold morning with the blanket around me. It's peaceful, I feel so cosy, wrapped up like this, my thick socks keeping my toes toasty.

I stare into the snowy pine trees ahead and listen as the weightless snow floats to the ground. It's silent, not a bird rustling in the trees, not a gust of wind rushing past; nothing. I rest against the railing and close my eyes, taking a deep, cool, fresh breath in.

Wriggler tugs at something gently, making me smile, I can't wait until she's bigger and I can feel big kicks. I feel happy in a strange way, I have my little secret with me, I'm getting more and more excited about his or her arrival, and I'm with Luke having such a wonderful time. I would probably be a lot more happy if I could share my news with everyone - have Luke be the excited, expectant father, but thinking that way is unrealistic and I daren't get carried away in case I persuade myself that it could happen.

I hear the door creak behind me, and Luke's huge, warm arms wrap around me, his head sinking to kiss my neck, making my knees go a little weak.

"Morning hot-lips, want me to make you come?"

I grin, resting my head back onto his chest, and giggle, "Good morning, bad-boy, I always want you to make me come. I'm just enjoying the quiet out here so early in the morning, it's amazing."

"Cool, huh?" he says, lifting his head and looking towards the trees with me, "I want to take you somewhere today, I think you'll like it."

"Ooh, sounds intriguing."

"But it's real early, we can go back to bed for a while if you like."

"If you want to, I just woke to use the loo and felt awake, so came out to see dawn in the snow."

"I'll tell you what, buttercup, let's go out, you and I. Right now."

"Now?" I ask, "Where?"

"Just get your warm stuff on, we'll shower when we get back," he says, kissing my cheek and releasing me to head indoors.

About ten minutes later, I'm sitting on the floor of the hall, pulling on my snow boots and Luke emerges from the kitchen with two lidded, disposable cups of tea, wearing a gorgeous smile. As I stand, he hands me a cup. "Ready?"

"Yep, let's go," I reply, following him to the door. He wraps an arm around me as we descend the snowy steps. When we reach the bottom and I head towards the car, he tugs me in the opposite direction, towards the mass of pine trees.

"I would've made you coffee, but I noticed you've been taking tea a lot, so thought I should stick with that. That okay?"

I have been drinking tea, I thought it would be less of a caffeine overload for the baby, but what I'm surprised at, more than the fact that he has been thoughtful enough to make it in the first place, is that he noticed.

"Tea is great, thank you. I've gone off coffee a bit. So where are we going?"

"I thought - as you like to look at it - that we'd go for a walk around here." He points up at the balcony to his room as he talks, and I realise that we are headed to the area I look out to from his balcony, and from my bedroom window. He holds my free hand and leads me into the trees. It's still so peaceful, even from below the trees.

"This is really cool Luke, I love it out here," I say as I look up at his face, smiling.

"Good."

I take a sip of my steamy tea, and stroll along with him, wading through the deep, powdery snow. "So, what happened last night? Did you take me to bed?"

"Sure did, I got back to the living room and you were out cold in front of the fire. I tried to wake you but you were out for the count, so I carried you up to bed. You were cute, you smiled at me and put your arms around my neck. That's 'cause you love me, you know," he says as he raises a brow and takes a sip of his tea, smiling.

I laugh, "Yeah, yeah. So how did I not wake up when you undressed me?"

"You stirred a little, you really don't remember?"

"No, it's weird."

"You must have been real tired! I started undressing you, but you got fidgety when I got to your pants and you pulled them down yourself."

Blimey, even when I'm unconscious, I know what I'm doing. "Oh right. Weird. You uh... you left my socks on..."

He smiles and blushes a little, "I couldn't help myself, Princess, your legs look so freaking hot with those things on."

"I'm surprised you didn't jump me," I say with a snigger.

"Oh, come on, Tilly, I might be a bad-boy, but I'm not going to try to have sex when you're practically comatose."

"I'm sure I'd have come around." I grin, looking up at him through my lashes.

"I bet. So, forget that, how's work? We haven't really talked a whole lot, yet."

Wow, Luke getting off the subject of sex! "Work is okay, thanks, boring as always, but it pays well and I get to take my holidays, so it'll do," *and I can deal with it because I'll be taking maternity leave in a few months.* "How's your work?"

"It's cool. Why don't you look for something else if your job's boring? I bet there'd be a bunch of travel firms ready to snap you up."

"Thank you, Luke - but it's okay, I doubt anywhere else would give me as much annual leave as I get now, I've worked there forever so I get quite a lot."

"Sure, if you're not unhappy, it's all cool."

We continue walking through the trees together, chatting, and it's probably one of the most refreshing mornings I've had. The snow creaks under our boots, the early morning air fresh and invigorating. Our voices are gentle, respecting the sheer perfection of our peaceful environment.

"So what are we going to do today, Lukey?"

He grins, "Lukey..." he repeats, testing the word, "not very 'bad-boy' is it?" he chuckles with me, "I want to take you somewhere for lunch. It'll be good, you'll like it."

"Luke, you really don't have to take time out from snowboarding, you know. Entertaining me isn't your role here."

He comes to a halt, looking at my face. He takes my empty cup and drops it, with his, into the snow beside him. Reaching for my pockets, he pulls me towards him. "I know I don't have to Til, but I want to... I like hanging out with you, and there's shit I want to show you, starting with the main man trying to burst out of my pants right now." He wiggles his eyebrows.

I smile broadly and immediately place my gloved hand against the hard bulge in his snow trousers, "Show me then..."

He chuckles and bends to kiss me, curling one bare hand around my neck, and clutching my buttock with the other, pulling me against him. He lightly brushes his lips against mine, before licking the centre of my top lip, parting them a little; our combined breath casting warm clouds between us in the cold air. He presses a little harder, his lips moving rhythmically, invitingly.

I groan, and wrap my arms around his neck, encouraging him to move faster, harsher... dirtier." *I so friggin' need this.*

He squeezes my buttock hard, it hurts but it's so good and I cry out in need. A dark thrill spreads from deep within, prickles covering my skin, I want him so much, right here in the silence... no one around - but still that exciting possibility of getting caught.

He slips his hand down, in between my legs from behind, and hoists me up until I wrap my legs around him. His incredible strength is such a huge turn on. His fingers press against me and I grind into them, silently begging him to move... or rub... or stroke... grope... fondle, fucking anything! Just get me off!

"Hold on," he says as he lets go and proceeds to unzip his coat between us, he pulls it off his arms, kissing me meanwhile, and with both hands, flicks the coat out and lets it float to the snow behind us. I suppose he's hot... or something? He wraps his arms around me, squeezing me tightly, and ups the tempo with the serious pash we've got going on. I'm so ready to rip the rest of his clothes off when he pulls away and says, "Wanna wrestle, Princess?"

Before I even have time to figure out what he's talking about - let alone respond, he has pulled off some seriously acrobatic manoeuvre, flipping me, throwing me, dropping me; I've no idea, but I'm completely stunned to find myself on all fours, on top of his flattened coat, Luke pressed up against my back, kissing my neck. *What the...?* "Whoa..." I whisper, amazed, totally impressed, but not in the least surprised, the way he threw me about the bedroom in LA, it was only a matter of time before he did so here.

His hands make quick work of pulling my trousers and knickers down my thighs, and his cock is immediately against me, forcing its way in. I cry out, everything about this is what I love, everything about what he's doing, where we are, how dangerously sexy this is.

He grunts as he eases all the way inside me, he seems so big, so much deeper. I lift my head back, eyes firmly shut, my mouth forming the perfect 'O', and his cold hands grab my hips, hard.

"Fuck, you're so freaking hot," he cries as he pulls back and immediately sinks back in. "Jesus, baby, I'm gonna come too fast."

I moan out loud, he's not the only one. "Me too, Luke, this is so fucking good... and dangerous... talk to me..." I ask, knowing it'll make us both come faster than a speeding bullet.

"You want that, baby girl, huh? You want me to tell you how hard I am, how good it feels to pound your ass like this out in the open," he growls as he thrusts into me harder, faster, "anyone could be out here, someone could have seen us back in the yard, and decided to come join us... oh, fuck, yeah..." he growls again.

"Yeah," I cry desperately, so close already, "yeah, uh huh, I'm gonna come, keep going... Luke..."

"Baby, I'm gonna come so hard. You want it, don't you? Out here, under the trees, your bad boy so fucking deep inside you." And that's all it takes, just two little words... 'bad'...oh yeah... 'boy'...

"Oh shit, oh god! Luke!" I cry, not too loudly, but loud enough for anyone in this woodland to hear, and the sharp spasm shoots through my body, it's so intense, so unbearably good, and so fucking long! "Oh god, yeah... yes!" I cry again, riding through it, willing it to stay with me for a few seconds more, my hands grasping at the coat beneath me.

Luke thrusts deep and hard one last time before calling my name and grunting, collapsing against my back.

I pulsate around him, still buried inside me, as he pants against my back. "God, Luke, that was fucking amazing - quick, but fucking amazing."

He laughs. "Short 'n' sweet, just like my naughty girl. You're just as bad as I am."

"I never said I wasn't, darling..."

"I think two wrongs make a right, here; you and me."

I grin, wondering what to make of that comment, but agreeing with it, anyway. We do create something special together. Well, we already have; Wriggler. *Oh yeah, Wriggler, forgot about you for a minute.*

Luke slowly lifts away from me and does his trousers up. I pull mine up as he lays down next to me and pats his coat, gesturing for me to follow suit. He holds out his arm and I snuggle into him, half on the snow and half on his coat, gazing up between the trees to the clear morning sky.

"Well, that was fun," I say with a smile and he turns his head to look at me, his dimples beautifully on display.

"It was, I've never had sex in the snow before, most girls wouldn't do what you just did."

"Oh really? And what is that supposed to mean?" I ask, accusatively, but lightheartedly.

Luke grins, "Just that you like the same things as I do, I get to do stuff that really turns me on, with you, and it's a lot of fun. You're different to other girls is probably what I'm getting at."

"Okay then, I'll allow that. Because I am, and I like a bit of naughty."

"I figured that the day we met, remember Nordstrom?"

I smile, remembering our first kiss, just an hour or so after we met. We all went shopping together, after Bea and Daniel unexpectedly reconnected while we ate at a noodle bar, following their first meeting on the aeroplane. Bea wanted to get some underwear from Nordstrom so we all joined her, much to her embarrassment. She ran off, determined to lose us, so I took the opportunity to flirt with the hot slice I'd just met. I already knew at this point that we'd be getting naughty later; he was just such a bad boy, so much fun and totally my type.

Anyway, after a while of picking up the tiniest scraps of lingerie to tease him with, he dragged me behind a full clothes rail and introduced me to his talented mouth. I don't think, before that experience, I had ever had a snog like it, just thinking about it makes me swoon.

I had no idea how long we were pashing behind that clothes rail for, but after a while, my naughty streak reared its very attractive head, and I subtly brushed my hand against his very erect cock, through his shorts. I remember clearly, opening my eyes as I did, and watching his reaction. His eyes shot wide open, and he smiled into the kiss briefly, before pulling away and telling me how hard he was going to fuck me later. I nearly passed out, this was a man after my very own heart.

"Of course, how could I forget that?"

"You couldn't, baby, I'm awesome."

I laugh and wrap my arm around his hard torso, I feel a sudden pang of guilt; I shouldn't be acting so casually around him, like everything is fine. He's laying here in the snow, cuddling me, laughing with me, and has absolutely no idea that I'm carrying his baby. *You'll go to hell for this.*

"Tilly, I hate to get all serious on your ass, but can I ask a question?"

"That *was* a question, but yes, you may ask another..." I say, jovially.

"I know you said it's okay, but I'm not used to boning without a raincoat, so it's kinda weird for me. Do you take birth control pills or what?"

Oh, shit. Inside, I'm tied in knots, I can't lie to him but I can't tell him the truth either, I'm not ready to give him up yet. He clearly doesn't want a baby, or he wouldn't have asked the question in the first place. *Shit, shit, shit.* I look anywhere but at his face and nod, I can't say the words, I don't lie with ease.

It seems to do the trick, he squeezes me and kisses my forehead. "Cool, sorry, I didn't want to question you but I've got to know the answer, you know? Now, it's all good."

I feel guilty as hell.

"It's so peaceful out here, huh?" he says staring up at the now overcast sky. I gaze at the side of his handsome face and something deepens inside me, emotionally. I want to squeeze him and tell him I'm sorry for lying, I'm sorry for keeping this from him and that I'm sorry I haven't told him how much I want him. I really want him, for Wriggler, yes, but for me, too. Could he ever give up his women and be a boyfriend and a dad? I really don't think so.

"Hmm? Oh, yes, it is. I love early mornings, before anyone else is up. Aren't you cold, Luke?" I ask, we're lying on his jacket and he doesn't even have gloves on.

He chuckles a little, "No, I'm good. Are you cold? You need warming up again?" he winks.

"Already?! How can you possibly be ready to go again?"

"When it comes to your tight little body, I'm always ready... so?"

I laugh again, "So, no. You can wait until later, lover-boy." I hear a rustle in the distance and rest up on one elbow, leaning against his chest. "Ooh, we're not going to get mauled by grizzlies are we?" I ask, half-joking, half-serious.

He smiles in amusement and brushes the hair escaping my bobble hat with his fingers, "I like your bangs, they suit your pretty face..."

"'Bangs'," I repeat with a grin, "sounds funny, we call it a fringe, but thank you, I like it, too. Now - can you answer my very pressing question?"

"No, Tilly, we're not going to get mauled by grizzlies. For starters, the bears here are black bears, but they hibernate for winter, so we can come out and fuck in the forest as often as you like." He holds one of my boobs in his hand and leans in to kiss my neck, mumbling against my skin, "Wanna head back to the house? I want to see these babies..."

~~~~~~~

At around midday, I clamber down the snowy steps again and wait for Luke to join me at the bottom to take us wherever we are going. It has been such a fun morning; after our 'session' in the snow, we walked back to the house and went at it again, in Luke's room. You couldn't get bored of 'Luke sex', no one could, he can keep you wanting all day.

I managed to have a shower on my own - somehow, he really wanted to join me but I made up some excuse about wanting to shave my legs in private, so he left me alone for a short while. It's getting more and more difficult to avoid him seeing me naked, I am going to have to tell him, before he figures it out himself.

We dress separately and meet in the hallway before heading downstairs for breakfast with Clare and Oliver. Olly is so excited about their day at Snowmass Mountain today, he's like a big kid! It's great to have a catch up with them before they go out, I wish I could spend more time with them while I'm here.

"Ready?" he asks as he skips carelessly down the steps, jumping the last few. He has no fear... kind of reminds me of who I was a few months back. Wow, how carrying a child can change so much, so quickly.

"Yep, where are we going?"

"For lunch, I told you," he says with a great big smile, winking. Those dimples seems to get deeper every time he smiles at me. "I thought we could walk there, it's not far at all, about three minutes in the car, twenty minutes walking, you good with that?"

"Yeah, that sounds like a great idea," I reply, and he throws an arm around my shoulder, guiding me out towards the road.

As we turn the corner onto the main road, Luke takes his arm from my shoulder, and reaches down to hold my hand. I look up at his face and he's already looking at me. "You're okay with holding hands, right?" he asks.

"Yes, it's fine, why do you ask? We held hands earlier on in the woods..."

"Yeah, but we're out in public now, thought I should check."

"It doesn't bother me in the slightest, Luke, aren't you afraid it's cock-blocking you though?" I ask with a grin as I squeeze his hand.

"I'm blocking my own cock, Princess, he's all yours right now."

"I feel so privileged," I say, sarcastically, pressing my free hand to my chest. But in reality, I do feel privileged. I doubt he's blocked his own cock for anyone. Well, except that one girl that he mentioned yesterday. I wonder what happened with her...

We walk along the pavement at a steady pace, chatting and joking around as always for about fifteen minutes before he takes a left turn and shortly after, a right. After a few paces, he stops and points at a large building at the base of the mountain. "This is Ajax Mountain, or Aspen Mountain as they call it now." He gently tugs my arm and walks towards the large, brick built flight of steps. "Wait here for me, I won't be long." He kisses my hand and jogs towards some nearby offices. I look around for a restaurant, wondering where lunch is.

Only a few minutes later, Luke returns, wrapping his hand around the back of my neck and pulling me in for a kiss, without saying a word. He lingers for a moment before pulling away and smiling a beautiful smile. "Let's go."

"Where to?" I ask, wanting to continue with the kissing.

"Up here," he points to the large glass building at the top of the steps.

As we approach, I notice the small cable cars travelling up the mountain and the sign reading; 'Silver Queen Gondola'. "Are we going up the mountain?" I ask.

"Uh huh," he responds, "that's where lunch is; up there." I immediately smile broadly, excited.

He leads me inside where the modern red and black gondolas churn through the building, passengers exiting on one side, and climbing aboard on the other.

"Hey, Luke!" A voice calls out as we wait, and Luke turns towards it.

"Matt! Hey, how's things? I haven't seen you in a long time, bro." They exchange slaps on the back and a small man-hug.

"Sweet, I didn't know you were in town, dude, you didn't call?"

"We only just got here, I haven't been out yet. I'm just taking this beautiful lady to lunch; Matt, this is Tilly," he says as he wraps his arm around me, pulling me into his side. I can't help but smile shyly at his introduction.

"Sweet... jampiece," he says, nodding at Luke with a downward smile, in approval. *What the hell is jampiece?* "Hey Tilly, great to meet you."

"You too," I say with a smile, shaking his hand.

"Anyway, enjoy Sundeck, good day for it. Text me or whatever, there's sick fresh powder out, we'll shred the gnar."

"Not today, bro, but yeah, we'll do it."

"Cool, here, hop in..." Matt says, guiding us to the front of the queue and gesturing towards a bright red gondola, "this one's done," he says to the other guy controlling the queue, kindly letting us ride up alone. He smacks the side of the gondola with his hand and gives Luke a thumbs up as the gondola moves towards the exit.

"Sweet," Luke says and returns the thumbs up as our doors close, and we start our ascent.

"I have no idea what you two were just talking about," I say as I sit back in the seat while Luke takes an iPod from his pocket and places it in the allocated slot in the gondola. "Wow, a docking station?"

"Yep, as this is your first time up here, I thought you could use a little light background music," he says as he finishes fiddling and sits back, putting an arm around my shoulders. He rests his feet up on the bench opposite and crosses his ankles, smiling confidently.

Just as I begin to frown in question, a very familiar song starts to play; Winter Wonderland by Ray Charles.

"Oh! I love Christmas music!" I cry enthusiastically. How perfect, listening to a real Christmas classic whilst journeying up a beautiful snowy mountain with the most fun and thoughtful man I think I've ever been with.

"Well, good; so do I."

I look out at the incredible view; pure white slopes, pine trees topped with powdery snow, skiers gliding elegantly down to the base, and to make everything even more perfect, the sky is the most perfect blue, the sun beaming.

"Luke, I love this, I didn't think I'd see any of this as I'm not skiing. Thank you."

"Don't thank me, Princess, I want to be here, too," he says as he sits up to join me, looking out through the glass. He tugs my scarf down and kisses my neck, wrapping his arms around me from behind, before resting his chin on my shoulder, gazing out at the spectacular view.

A snowboarder on the slope below takes an impressive tumble - almost burying himself in the snow, making Luke chuckle, "Whoa, that kid blasted a dookie!" he says in amusement.

I turn to look at his face, laughing, "What the hell does that mean? I am definitely new to this slope lingo."

He shows off his dimples as he replies, "That just means he fell real hard."

"Okay, and what about jampiece?"

He laughs out loud and kisses my cheek, "A jampiece, my hot, sweet, baby girl - is what you are. You are a total jampiece."

"And by definition?"

"By definition; something that is excessively cool, beautiful and/or fun. You are all of those things, but Matt was referring to your beauty."

"Ah..." I say with a smirk, raising my eyebrow and nodding, "so I'm a jampiece... I like this."

"I like this, too," he responds, "a whole lot." He kisses my neck again, but this time, he doesn't stop. His lips softly caressing my skin, his tongue gently stroking with each small touch. My eyes close and I smile, listening to the jolly Christmas music, feeling totally relaxed in the company of the man that I'm falling for, more and more with each hour that passes.

Even when we were apart, I felt more for him every day. That feeling of wanting something so much, knowing it won't happen, just like Bea went through. And it's not just him I've been wanting, I've been wanting the father for my child, I've been wanting the domesticity of a normal family. *Jesus, if I could go back six months and hear myself now, I'd think I was having some sort of hallucinogenic episode. Who the fuck am I, and where has fun-loving Tilly gone?*

"I think you should suck my big dick," Luke says with a smile against my neck, making me remember that a little bit of 'fun-loving' Tilly is still in there. I laugh loudly and bring my hand up to the back of his neck as he continues to kiss me. I press his head into me, loving his closeness.

"I would love to suck on your big dick, bad-boy, but as our little pod is almost entirely made of glass, and we pass another every few moments - just a few metres away, I think we'd get caught."

"Would that be so bad? I really want you."

I giggle again, "Really? So if I sank to my knees right now and took you out of your trousers, you wouldn't bat an eyelid?"

He pauses, breathing against my neck for a moment as he weighs it up. "Okay, okay. Not here. But later, I want to do something naughty." He proceeds to run the tip of his tongue from the base of my neck up to my jaw, and I shiver with excitement.

"Mmm, yes please. Naughty is definitely on my 'to-do list', today."

The song ends and another fun song starts to play; Mariah Carey, 'All I want for Christmas'. Such a classic and I can't help but wriggle, dancing along.

"I like this," Luke says, nodding at me, "but I'd rather you did it..." he pauses as he pulls me up onto his lap sideways, "on my lap. Don't stop - wiggle."

I grab his face in my hands and smile as I lean in to kiss his beautiful lips. I close my eyes and linger, totally absorbed by the moment, by his fun naughtiness, by his supreme masculinity, by his attraction to little old me.

"All I want for Christmas is *you*," he whispers, as he breaks away, looking directly into my eyes. He's not laughing or joking about; he means it."

"Well, you've got it. We're in stunning Aspen for two weeks of festivities, it's going to be such a fun holiday." I say, not even thinking about what'll happen once I break the news.

"Can I ask you a question, baby?" he says, his head tipped to the side, holding my gloved hand in his.

"Of course you can, lover-boy."

"You never really told me why you like bad boys..."

I sigh, silently, and look down at our hands. Snuggling into his chest, I get comfy before I let the truth about the past flow. I know I needn't be honest about it, but I feel there's no reason to withhold the truth, no reason why Luke shouldn't know a bit more about me. Okay, we're still only temporary fuck-buddies, but he's also Wriggler's dad, and if he wants to have anything to do with the baby, I think he should know as much about me, as he wants to. "Well, it starts with Scott. My last real boyfriend."

"He was a bad-boy?"

"No, anything but. He was as good as they get; loving, attentive, completely besotted by me. Or so I thought at the time."

"Go on," he prompts, removing his gloves and then mine. He wraps one arm around me, and threads the fingers of his other hand through mine, comfortingly.

"Well, our relationship was lovely; he always put me first, we never argued, we were like a very happily married couple, I suppose. A little old before our time, but blissfully content. Then, one day, when he was at work, some girl came to the door and told me that he'd been fucking her for two years."

"Holy shit..."

"Naturally, I didn't believe her; my wonderful, attentive boyfriend would never do that to me, she must have got the wrong house, or whatever - but then she started talking about Scott. That's when I knew it was true, the things he said to me, he was saying to her. She was very sweet and compassionate, so I asked her to come inside so we could talk more. She stayed for a good couple of hours. Apparently they weren't too serious, but she found out he was sleeping with someone else, followed him home one night and found out about me, too."

"Wow, Til, I'm sorry you had to go through that bullshit."

"It's okay, it was crap at the time, but it lead to a really fun stage of my life. Had he not done that, I might never have known who I really am."

"But that still doesn't explain the bad-boy thing..."

"No, well, after what happened with my *good-boy*, I found myself going for bad-boys, wanting nothing more than a quick fling because that way, I knew where I stood. I was in control and nobody could hurt me because I expected bad behaviour. Nothing shocked me and no one ever managed to get inside my head to take over my feelings and emotions. I also had so much fun with these types of guys, they liked that I wasn't pressuring them for more and we had a great laugh together. I learnt a lot..." I wink at him, cheekily, "and really enjoyed my life that way."

"Enjoyed? So you're not enjoying it anymore?" *Oh, crap, here we go.*

"Like I said before, Lukey..." I smile coyly at him and fiddle with his fingers, "you got to me a bit, you were the first person to tweak at my emotional frigidity, I started feeling things for you that I hadn't known since way back in the early 'Scott' days. That's when *we* got weird. I'm used to naughty sex in limos with fuck buddies, not romantic trips up snowy mountains with Christmas music and hand holding."

He looks at me with a smile and a cheeky twinkle in his eye. "But you love it, don't you? Admit it, you want this until you're old and decrepit, you want the sexy motherfucker from LA as your husband. Come on... you know you want to come clean."

I laugh out loud, I love how he turns anything remotely serious or uncomfortable into a laugh fest. "Luke, my darling man, I want all that shit, just about as much as you do. Alright?"

He nods slowly, smiling, "Aight, I can deal with that answer. Seriously though, Til, it's great to know a bit more about your past, why you're who you are. And personally, as much as I don't want to think of you hurt, I think Scott did the best thing for you. I think this Tilly is awesome."

"Thanks, lover-boy, I know that's your way of telling me you're totally head over heels in love with me." I giggle and accept the smiling, soft kiss he plants on my lips.

"What happened to the other girl?" he asks as he slowly pulls away.

"Laura's a great friend of ours now. She is blissfully happy with our other friend, Jamie. They make a gorgeous couple; she actually thanks Scott for bringing us together, if he hadn't shagged us both, she'd never have met me, the girls or Jamie."

"Wow, it's cool you could be friends after all that."

"Yeah, it wasn't her fault. She had no idea either. So, now that I've told you that, one of these days you're going to tell me about the girl who you kept it in your trousers... pants for."

He looks down with a shy smile and shrugs. Wow, he really doesn't want to talk about her, I wonder what makes her so special? Makes me a bit jealous actually. "Don't worry, not now. But one day you'll tell me." He smiles, the relief evident, but something in his eyes tells me he wants to talk about it. I hope he wasn't terribly hurt, I couldn't bear to think of this gorgeous, gentle giant in a place of darkness and grey. *Shit, Til, you need to stop falling in love with him; you're a fucking idiot. Maybe I just think I love him because I have his beautiful little baby inside me... Oh shut up.*

"Okay then, how about you answer me this: when 'working' with your lady clients, have you ever had a husband catch you... at it?"

He laughs heartily and squeezes me tightly. I feel so comfortable tucked in his arms in this private space, the beautiful view passing us by, his fucking sexy face smiling at me like that; it makes me want to snog the hell out of him, take him back to England and make him my bitch. "Sure, I've been caught a few times."

"Oh my god, really? What happened?"

"Well, it hasn't happened a whole lot, but a couple times, the guys turned a blind eye - they married hot young chicks and knew they were having fun on the side, just grateful to have them on their arm for events. That's why they hired me to do the... um... 'training' - keep 'em happy. They'd hire the guys they thought their wives wanted to play with."

"And of course they all want to play with sexy Luke Summers, who wouldn't?"

"Well, naturally..." he says with a jovial smirk.

"And any others who weren't so happy about it?"

"Yeah, one guy tried to beat the shit out of me while I was literally in his wife; broke his hand, I took him to the emergency room and we agreed to end the contract and never tell a soul that he broke his hand punching some guy in the bicep."

I laugh out loud as he continues. "And then one guy - who's into some serious shit that I don't even want to know about - got some of his 'colleagues' to pay me a visit. That was the worst time, I got fucked up real bad, I was in the hospital for a while."

My heart hurts suddenly, a chill spreads across my skin and I immediately want to wrap my arms around his neck and hold him to me. The thought of him getting pulverised by a bunch of Neanderthals is enough to make my stomach churn. I feel immediately sick. *Holy fuck, I have never felt this protective over anyone before. Well, apart from Jack and*

Wriggler, but this is a man; a grown man for shit's sake! "Oh my god, Luke, were you okay? How long ago was this?"

"About a year and a half, yeah, I was fine. Just a few broken ribs and shit like that. They tried to fuck up my face, but if nature wants something perfect, you just can't mess with it."

His attempt at playing this down isn't working. "What happened to your face?

"Not a lot; broke my nose, fractured a cheek bone and eye socket... not enough to flaw perfection," he says with a wink, but I'm mortified.

"I can't believe I didn't know about this, you never mention it..." I gently run the tip of my finger down the bridge of his perfect nose, it's hard to believe it has been broken. I look at both sides of his face wondering which was the damaged side, and he silently, nonchalantly, points to his left side.

I cup his cheek bone in the palm of my small hand and lean forward to lay a soft kiss just underneath his eye. His eyes close and I have to fight back the tears that are desperately trying to force through. I'm not a crier - yeah, okay, since I got pregnant I have cried all the time - but in general, especially around men - I do not cry.

My mouth twitches downwards at the sides and I blink repeatedly, wishing I could control this. I continue to lay gentle kisses all around his eye socket, I can't stop thinking about the bones underneath his beautiful skin, broken and cracked, he must have been in such terrible pain. A tear rolls down my cheek and I close my eyes, pressing my forehead against his. He wraps a hand around the back of my neck and whispers to me, "Tilly, I was fucking someone's wife. I deserved it. I knew she was married, I just assumed their arrangement was like the others. Don't be sad."

I snap my head back and wipe my cheeks with my hand. "I know, you're totally, right, I don't know what's frigging wrong with me, I don't do crying. Ignore me."

"No, no, don't do that. Come back and kiss my face again, don't be embarrassed. You care about me, that's all. If you told me something had happened to you, I'd probably want to go shoot the fucker." I smile, grateful for his understanding and for trying to ease my discomfort. "Please? I was enjoying your lips on me, I don't 'do' intimacy, so this feels... good."

Oh so honest. And so incredibly open with me, so vulnerable for such a big, strong, confident man. "Me neither, I haven't been like that with anyone since... well, anyway, I forgot that it's actually quite nice."

I kiss his face again, closing my eyes and really absorbing the affection we're sharing. I hadn't even noticed that the Christmas music has changed to a slower, quieter number... how convenient of it. It seems like we've been in the gondola forever, but it must have only been about fifteen minutes. I wish we could stay in here - in our bubble, all day long.

A few more minutes pass, Luke's hands cradling my face as I lay more and more kisses over his precious, damaged bones. It feels, almost, like kissing him like this will heal him - my affection, my love for him will fuse his broken face. He looks so perfect, how can he possibly have been beaten so badly and have no marks on the outside? Someone up there wants this man to stay beautiful. *For me?* No, you imbecile, not for you, for every 'twenty something' female with a pulse that takes his fancy.

"We're nearly at the station," he whispers, holding my face, guiding my lips from his cheek to his mouth. My eyes remain closed, and I softly caress his lips, moving slowly, caring for him so much. He introduces his tongue ever so lightly, brushing my lip, deepening the connection and I welcome it, readily.

A barely-audible, masculine groan sends a warm tingle to my groin, his hands gently gripping my face; he's enjoying this as much as I am. He wants me too. We pick up the pace, our hands caressing each other's faces, our lips entwined. *Good god, I can't get enough, I wish I could hold him close, twenty-four-seven.*

We pass through the last mechanism and the gondola jolts, interrupting our increasingly-heated moment. "We're getting out here, Princess," he says against my lips, and I open my eyes to find his burning into me, needy and raw. *Maybe he could fall for me, too, after all?* "We'll pick up where we left off later, on the way down." He winks at me with a cheeky grin, flashing his sexy dimples, and I'm reminded that this isn't all lovey dovey romantic mush, we're having so much fun, too, just like LA.

I was so worried about this trip, in fact I was very close to cancelling, but thank god I didn't. Although I haven't done the 'deed' yet, I am so grateful for the time that I have had, and to experience the usual fun with this added, unexpected intimate romance, has totally made my Christmas.

Our pod slides into the station and the doors open as it slows. Luke takes his iPod and stands, taking my hand to help me out. "Enjoyable journey, ma'am?"

I giggle, "Quite satisfactory, thank you."

"Satisfactory? That won't do, I'll have to work harder on the way down. Maybe you'd prefer some cock."

Again, I burst out laughing, not expecting it. "Only if it's yours," I say with a grin, "but on a serious note, that was lovely, Luke, I really enjoyed the journey up here. I'll always remember that about this trip."

"I hope you remember more than just that. I can recall a pretty memorable kitchen encounter that shouldn't go amiss. Oh, and a balcony encounter... a backyard encounter..."

"Yes, yes, I get the message. I will remember all of the steamy moments, too."

'Great, and we still have a whole lot of time to create more of them. If you'd let me, I'd rip your clothes off and fuck you right here," he says with a cocky smile, and I can't help but get excited.

A moment later, we are standing outside a restaurant called Sundeck, at the top of the mountain. I am absolutely awed by the beauty surrounding me. I'm not normally one for waxing lyrical about natures's 'amazingness', but right now, I am left so thoroughly speechless by the incredible three-sixty view of the surrounding valleys and peaks; it's something you don't miss when you haven't seen it, but when you do, you want nothing more than to experience it every day of your life. *Especially if I get to do that ride up with hot stuff every time...*

Luke takes my hand and squeezes it, "Earth to Tilly..."

I tear myself away from the pretty to acknowledge the sexy beast, "Hmm?"

"I was asking what you thought and you were ignoring me. Totally understandable, considering you've never been up here before."

"Oh, I'm sorry, it's just so stunning, bizarrely emotional. I mean, I've been skiing - many a time - but I can't say I've seen a view quite as special as this before."

"It's something, huh?"

"Thank you so much."

"Don't mention it. So, do you want to head inside to eat now?"

"Hmm?" I ask again, turning to have another look at the view behind me.

"Let's head in for food, I'll bring you back out here after, so we can toast the view together."

I smile up at his happy face, "That sounds more perfect than anything else I can think of right now."

He guides me towards the door, past tables of skiers taking a breather and racks upon racks of skis and boards in the deep snow outside.

CHAPTER 5
FRIDAY 21ST DECEMBER (CONT.)

We eat a delicious lunch together in the bistro-style restaurant, the beautiful fireplace and rich wooden finishes make this place a welcoming haven that I will be very disappointed not to visit again. In decor, it is really quite similar to Alexia's house; rustic and warm. We see a whole host of people that Luke knows, and he introduces me to each and everyone.

He orders us both a glass of bubbly to take outside, and leads the way to an empty table on the deck. "This okay for you, Princess?"

"Perfect, thank you," I say, gazing around at the view again. I will have to think of an excuse about the damned champagne, though.

"Want the wedding to be up here?"

Uh...what the fuck? "I beg your pardon... what?"

He chuckles and grabs my hand, "Relax. I'm only messing with you. It'd be cool though, to do something like that here, ya think?"

"Oh god, I really wondered what the hell had gotten in to you! Do you think about stuff like that?"

"Sometimes, but I don't usually see myself in the scenario. I saw a snowy wedding once - in a movie or something, and the first thing that came to mind was this place. If I get married, I'll ask the lucky lady if she'd do it here."

"Oh yeah, completely different, it'd be incredible. But if you ever get married, I'll eat my hat."

"What, you don't think a bad-boy like me could get married?"

"I'm sure you could, I just can't see you ever wanting to."

"Well, I didn't think I ever would, but I never say never, and as I get older, I think I might just see myself with a ball and chain."

"And there's my point, lover-boy. Ball and chain."

"So you think you'll ever get married?"

"Doubt it." *Not unless I fall out of love with you and find a man who flicks my switches like you do...*

"Why not? You don't want to get tied down?"

"I never really thought I'd get married, after Scott. I used to imagine my wedding as a kid and while I was with him, but when we broke up, I swore off all thoughts of 'happy ever after'."

He nods and shrugs nonchalantly, saying nothing.

We sit beside one another at the picnic style table, sharing the view, and Luke holds his glass up in front of us, "To the beauty all around, and I'm not only referring to the landscape."

I hold my glass next to his and smile, looking at his face, I roll my eyes, shyly, before touching the flutes together, "To the beauty all around."

He wraps his arm around me and slides me into him until I'm pressing hard against his body. I smile and rest my head against the crook of his arm as he looks into my face with a matching smile. Leaning down towards me, he purses his lips and I respond, immediately, by kissing them. Instead of a quick peck, he lingers, squeezing me, holding me tightly against him. I relax completely, this feels so perfect, so comfortable... so right. This is what I want - him. All of him. I love him. *Fuckers.*

He pulls away, and his eyes remain closed for a moment before he stirs and smiles. "Drink up, Til, and we can take the lift back down. I want a real kiss - like, a real, *real* one..." he winks, keeping his eyes locked into mine.

I return his sexy smile and run my hand down his thigh to his knee, and back up again, pausing just before I get to his willy. God, I'd love to put my hand on it, right now. And as if he can hear my thoughts, he whispers, "Don't stop there, naughty-girl, I can see you want it."

I contemplate for a matter of seconds, it doesn't take much to persuade me, and I check around us to see what the people are doing. His jacket slightly covers that part of him anyway, so I glide my hand further up until I'm resting on his very hard cock, and by god, I want to rip his trousers open and sink to my knees to suck on him.

His eyes still burning into mine, I see mischief, I see excitement... oh... I see the man I want to fuck for the rest of my life... "I can see what you're thinking, Princess. And it's exactly what I'm thinking."

Hmm, somehow I doubt that. "Really? You can see how much I want you in my mouth? How much I want to slide under the table and suck you?"

"Jesus, Tilly! Fuck, I need to be in your mouth right now. Tell me how much you want me."

I could go to town telling him my exact thoughts about him, but I won't. He wants dirt, not romancing. I squeeze him gently through his trousers, desperately wishing I could feel his powdery soft skin in my hand, running my fist up and down his hard length.

"I want you more than you realise. I want to pash you right here for at least half an hour with this view in front of us, I want to take off my gloves and run my hands underneath your clothes, up your bare chest, feeling your toned body. I want to straddle you and press my body against yours, feel this pushing into my trousers between my legs," I say, clutching hold of him harder, "I want to grind into you until I come so hard, right here..."

He closes his eyes and growls before taking me by complete surprise and grabbing me by the waist, swinging me around and sitting me on his lap, my legs either side of him. Most of the champagne spills out of my glass into the snow in the process, helping me out somewhat. He puts a hand around the back of my neck and looks purposefully into my eyes, "Tilly, I want you so bad."

I giggle, gazing right back at him, "You mean you want me so *badly*. And you know how tempted I am to dry hump you right now, but we're already getting some strange looks from half of the people up here. I don't see many other girls straddling their... um, straddling men."

"Straddling their..." he repeats in question, "what were you going to say?"

"I don't know... 'boyfriends' I suppose."

He smirks and raises a brow before continuing, "What with the grammar lesson and negativity about public displays of... *affection*, I don't think I like that response."

"Public displays of affection? I think public sex is slightly different to a P.D.A."

"You love it," he says with a cheeky grin and stands effortlessly, holding me under my buttocks with one hand, my arms around his big shoulders. He takes my glass and puts it on the table with his, before strolling with me hooked to his torso, towards the gondola station again.

A few moments and some strange looks later, Luke steps into a gondola pod and sits, refusing to release me. He tells the 'dude' manning the station that he wants us to be alone so again, no strangers join us, although there are a lot less people descending in the pods, as there were ascending.

I remain straddled on his lap and immediately lean forward to kiss his delicious neck, nuzzling his clothes out of the way and inhaling his lovely scent. He smells so fresh and clean, the chill in the air somehow accentuating that. He slides his hands under my jacket at the back, and inside the waist band of my trousers until his hands are cupping my bare buttocks, as the doors close and the gondola slides out of the building.

He squeezes hard, making me moan loudly against the soft skin of his neck. "I could seriously fuck you so hard right now," I mumble, holding his face with one hand, the back of his head with the other.

He makes a growling noise deep in his throat, "Let me rip a hole in your pants?"

I giggle and pull away to look at his face, now cupping it in both hands. "No, I refuse to walk home with a big hole in my crotch. I also refuse to pull them down in view of everyone in passing gondolas, so the sexual frustration will have to remain until we get back. As much as I want it."

"Fuck, I want you," he whispers as he pulls my face towards him forcefully, devouring my lips with his own. His tongue immediately joins mine, desperately caressing me, taking charge.

I let out a loud, high pitched moan as I writhe against him, feeling the hard bulge through our layers. I can't control my body's urge to rock against him, grinding, rubbing, easing the pressure of frustration. He moves his hands to my hips and pushes me harder, rocking me back and forth. My god, it's so frigging good.

"God damn, I gotta have you, baby..." he says against my mouth. He runs his hands up my sides and reaches my boobs, fondling them firmly so I moan loudly, their sensitivity excruciating, but so good. I rock my pelvis faster before coming to a halt and reaching between my legs to touch him, I can't take any more. Using both hands, I quickly unfasten his trousers and lose one inside his underwear. I find him hard and waiting, and so fucking tempting.

He groans loudly, "Uh, Tilly..."

"No one can see..." No one *would* be able to see *it*, but should anyone in a passing pod look into ours, they'd definitely get the right idea.

"You make me crazy."

"You make me hot," I respond, jovially with a cheeky smile, as I hold on to his shoulder with my spare hand, running the other up and down his rock hard cock. He grabs my hips with his hands and grimaces, rocking his head back and squeezing his eyes closed.

I lean forward and run my tongue up his throat, from the dip, over his Adam's apple, to the bottom of his chin, "I wish I was doing this to your cock... I want to taste you, my favourite dick on my tongue..."

Luke chuckles; a deep, sexy chortle that only makes my hunger for him intensify. "Your favourite, huh? Well, in that case..." he says as he moves one hand from my hip to the fastening of my trousers. I give up stressing about the Wriggler bump, I'm covered by clothes and am in a sitting position on top of him, I very much doubt that he can feel the increase in size of my belly. I'm far too in the moment to stop him, and even if he does notice... is he going to question how much weight I've gained while my hand is clamped around his dick? Unlikely.

"In that case," he repeats, sliding his hand down the front of my trousers and into my Hanky Pankys, "I want to taste my favourite pussy." I grin, thoroughly enjoying our exchange, before my eyes close of their own accord and I whimper loudly as his fingers graze my clitoris.

I pump harder on him and he pushes his fingers inside me, causing me to cry out loud. "Fuck, Luke, I want you inside me..." He takes his fingers from my knickers, leaving me at a loss, and puts them in his mouth, smiling a little.

He sucks indulgently, before taking them out, "I tasted my favourite pussy, Princess, and it was so good." A grin slowly grows on my face.

I stand up, letting go of him, my trousers still undone, and I gesture for him to sit sideways on the bench-type chair. He complies, leaning backwards against the side of the gondola that faces the ascending pods, straddling the bench, looking at me, questioningly. I quickly kneel on the bench between his legs and unzip his jacket, "Hold it open," I order, and as he does, I bend down to his cock and take him as far in my mouth as he will go, without hesitation.

"Holy fuck!" he cries, and I smile around him as I lick and suck and devour him. He tastes so good, I love the feel of his warm, soft skin against my lips and tongue, his clean, masculine smell... *Uh, I could suck on this stick all day long.* I have no worries of being caught, I'm pretty sure Luke's coat is screening me from those other pods, but I couldn't care less, I am enjoying this way too much. Luke would never let anyone see me doing this, anyway.

As I hold him in one hand, my other grabbing his thigh, keeping my balance, I increase speed and suction, moaning loudly, letting him know exactly how much I love this.

"Oh god, Til..."

I moan in high pitched response, not wanting to break away until he comes down my throat.

He growls loudly, letting go of his jacket and sitting up, forcing my head away from him. I sit up, already starting to complain as he leans forward, grabbing my face and pushing me against the other side, before taking my lips zealously. His tongue forces its way into my mouth and he groans loudly as he moves against me, kissing, biting, brushing my lips.

I pull off his sexy hat and grab fistfuls of his messy hair, holding his head to mine as we pash it out. Again, he reaches down to my knickers and slides his hand inside to lightly flick my clit, making me wail loudly into his mouth. "Come, Til, come for me, I want to hear it, I want the people on the slopes below to hear it, I want everyone to know I'm making this jampiece come hard, right now..." He pants heavily against my lips, staring into my eyes, moving his fingers with unbearable precision.

It would be too easy, far too easy to just come. I want to, but at the same time, I want him in my mouth and I want to make him come, so much. I push his chest away and bend, forcing his hand from my underwear, and take him in my mouth again, stubbornly. I hear his chuckle in surprise, and see the jacket open up as a shield again. Oh, having him fill my mouth is by far one of the best sexual experiences... in the world... ever. I am so turned on, I will probably just come along with him.

"Someone is going to see us, Princess. You like that, don't you? he says, his voice raspy and sexy.

"Mmm..." I moan, not really answering either way, but not stopping, so my thoughts on the subject - pretty obvious. He chuckles again and follows with a loud, exhaling sigh.

"I love this about you..." he whispers and I wonder what exactly he means; does he love that I go public? Or that I give a good BJ? That I don't care about being caught if I get what I want? That I love to please him? That I am completely obsessed with his knob? I just don't know, but he's about to come and I am enjoying it far too much to bother asking. I'll figure it out another time.

"Oh shit, Tilly it's too good..." he says and totally surprises me by scooting back, taking himself from my mouth and grip. I sit up again, ready to grumble. "We can play this game all the way down, if you like, but I'm not coming until you do," he says with a cheeky wink.

I smile, "I want to make you come first, I love you in my mouth."

"I think we should fuck and come together."

I laugh again, "We can't fuck in here, Lukey."

"I know," he takes my hand and kisses it, followed by a cheeky lick, "we'll wait until we get back. Just bear in mind how fucking horny I am, because you're gonna get it."

"Can't wait. In the mean time, snog me until we get to the bottom."

He smiles a shy sort of a smile and slowly moves his head towards mine, staring into my eyes the whole time, "It would be my pleasure, hot stuff.

~~~~~~~~

The remaining few minutes in the gondola were lust filled and amazing. We kissed non stop, held each other, ran our hands all over each other through and under our layers... I couldn't wait to get him back to the house, I was hot, wet and had far too many clothes on. As did he.

By the time we got to the base station, our hats and gloves were back on, our jackets zipped and flies done up. No one would know what we'd been up to. We were giggling and excited, acting like a couple of teenagers. His arm wrapped tightly around me, we walked towards the exit, smiling and happy.

Luke's friend Matt catches us as we take the steps down to the main paved area below the building, and makes Luke promise to give him a call to 'go shred the fresh pow' with him and 'Queenie' - whoever that is. I'm learning a whole new side to Luke and I really like it, I find it so... sexy. Maybe he can talk to me in his 'snowboarder dude' lingo sometime.

I love that he can be the casual fitness trainer LA guy, the smart, sophisticated hunk out for dinner, the cool snowboarder in Aspen, the bad-boy, the good-boy - he's just so many amazing different people rolled into one and it makes him so unique - I am, reluctantly, very much in love with each and every one of his 'people'. The question is, can he add father and boyfriend to that list?

As we get to the pavement and begin the walk back to Alexia's house, Luke stops suddenly, crouches down on his haunches and points to his back, "Hop on, your carriage awaits."

"A piggy back ride?" I ask, loving his childish predilection.

"Totally!"

Amused, I climb on his back, wrapping my arms around his shoulders and he stands effortlessly and starts to walk towards the house. I move my head forwards and press the side of my face against his, hugging him tightly.

"Luke, I really want you to go out on the slopes with Matt, I know you must really want to, and he does, too. Please would you go? Forget about looking after me..."

"I want to spend the time with you though, you know that. I'd love to take you out on the slopes, but there's a good reason why I can't, so between slopes and fun with you, I know which I pick..."

I could melt at his unbelievable sweetness, and managing to resist the urge to tell him as much, I simply squeeze him a bit tighter and think of a compromise. "Okay, how about this, I would love to see you in action, just hearing you talk the talk makes me want to shag your brains out, so, how about you go out with Matt and... Queenie, is it?" I ask and he nods, "And take me with you. You can leave me at the mountain restaurant and I can watch you snowboarding down to me. That way you get to have fun on the slopes with your friends, I get to watch and we can have some lunch together or something. That's if you don't mind me hanging around with you and your 'mountain crew'."

"That won't be boring for you?" he asks and I shake my head vigorously.

"Definitely not! I'd love to watch you doing your thing!"

He pauses for a moment, considering my suggestion, "Okay, cool, if you want to do that, let's do it, but only if you're sure you'll like it."

"I'm certain. Yay! I can't wait for you to excite me on those slopes."

Luke snickers and squeezes my thighs a little tighter, "You know I can turn you on wherever we are..."

I return the snicker and agree, "I won't argue with that, bad-boy."

As we walk into the driveway, a few minutes later, I loosen my hold on him, preparing for him to release me.

"Uh-uh, not yet," he says walking towards his hire car and unlocking it with the key in his pocket. He walks towards the boot and opens it wide.

'What are we doing?" I ask.

"I want to get you something... in the trunk," he says with amusement, and I look inside and see nothing but a big, duck down coat.

He moves it to cover the hard rim of the outer edge of the boot floor and just as I go to question what he's doing, he pulls off another impressive wrestling move, flipping me from his back to his front, and quickly lowering me so I'm laying on my back in the boot, my legs still hooked around his waist.

"Whoa!" I cry in surprise as he leans down on top of me and kisses me through a huge smile. He reaches behind himself to my feet and pulls off my boots, dropping them to the ground below him. He then kisses me again, slowly biting my lip whilst moving his hands to my fly to unfasten it.

"I thought you were getting me something in the *trunk*?" I ask in a whisper and he looks into my eyes, his twinkling with mischief.

"I am; I'm getting you *fucked* in the trunk," and with that, he steps back and yanks my trousers and knickers down, pulling them off one leg completely. Grateful for my jacket covering my belly, I revel in the naughty moment. As he sees to his own fly, I have a quick look around us; the boot of the car is facing the house, pulled right up to the wooden garage door. As the main house is up another level, there aren't any windows near us. To the left of us is the side of the stone flight of steps, and to the right, thick trees separating this property from the next. We're totally safe to fuck like rabbits until the others get back from their day on the slopes. Not that it'll take that long.

He leans back down on top of me, guiding himself to me. He nudges forward, pushing against me but not quite inside and I moan desperately, closing my eyes in anticipation. He starts to unzip my coat and I quickly grab his hand in mine, squeezing it, and I guide it up to my head. I rip my hat off and put his hand around my ponytail. "Hold my hair," I demand, never having tried this before but needing something else to preoccupy his hand.

"Won't it hurt?" he asks, breathing heavily, hankering for the inevitable first thrust.

"I think I'll like it, just do it..."

And immediately, he groans and eases himself inside me, slowly. I cry out in ecstasy, I've been so desperate for this feeling since the gondola. His hand tugs on my ponytail at the same time, yanking my head back and that, combined with the overriding pleasure of his cock burrowing deeper and deeper inside me, is out-of-this-world-amazing.

I grunt, loudly, unable to keep quiet, and I couldn't give a shit. I have the hottest, most delicious man pumping his hard meat inside me and the world can just fucking know about it.

"You want me so bad, baby..."

"Oh Luke!" I cry, "I so fucking do, so, so, so *badly,*" I respond, emphasising the correct use of the last word.

He chuckles and pounds into me again, "We're in the middle of a serious... grr...." he pauses and growls as he thrusts again, "a serious fucking in the trunk of my car, and you're giving me a grammar... oh fuck... uh... a grammar lesson..."

It's my turn to giggle, briefly, before I switch straight back to moaning in ecstasy. "Badly, oh yes, Luke! ...Badly..." I cry out loud, grabbing hold of his buttocks and squeezing, trying to pull him deeper, make him go faster, anything to make me come. I squeeze so hard it must pinch because he makes another loud growl and shouts out before pulling on my ponytail, jolting my head back.

"Oh fuck!" I cry out, in pure pleasure.

"Shit, sorry, Til," he whispers, as he continues to thrust harder and faster.

"No, I like it... yank my hair, pull it, it's so good..."

I move my hands from his bum to his head, pulling off his hat and threading my fingers into his hair, grabbing fistfuls and pulling, forcefully.

"Oh, yeah, god..." he moans, tightening his hold on my ponytail again and returning his lips to mine.

He thrusts, I grind my pelvis repeatedly, and we kiss like we'll never get enough; it's hot, needy and so frigging good. He feels so big, so hard, so bloody incredible; pounding into me. The waves build higher and higher, I'm totally on the brink and I'm going to crash so fucking hard...

He breaks from the kiss, keeping up the exquisite rhythm, and runs his tongue up the side of my neck to my ear, taking the lobe in his mouth and biting down gently as he pulls on my hair making me explode violently around him, yelling loudly and gripping tufts of his hair tightly.

"Ah, fuck!" he yells and he slams into me, forcing me further into the boot, my head pressed against the seat backs. His eyes squeezed closed, breath held, his face the most amorous picture that you'd only ever see in a moment of sheer, sexual pleasure. "Oh, god!" he whispers, collapsing on top of me, burying his face in my neck, "so hot, so... so hot."

I hook my feet together around him, squeezing him between my thighs, clamping him tightly against me. I still have my trousers and knickers hanging off one leg, his bum is hanging right out of his trousers and we're half lying in his car, half standing on the driveway. If anyone saw us now, they'd probably laugh themselves stupid. I giggle, quietly, just thinking about what we must look like from outside.

"Another, less enthusiastic lover, might be self conscious about this laughter..." he mumbles against my neck, lazily, not moving an inch.

I laugh louder, turning the slight giggle into a deep, belly bouncing guffaw. He slowly lifts his head and gazes down at my face, his eyes glazed, his dimples - beautiful. "Seriously, if it were anyone else..."

I jovially swat his huge bicep, hardly touching him through his thick jacket, and snort as I try to talk through the fit of giggles. "No, no..." I manage, "it was amazing, and super fun as always..." I take a short break to calm the giggles and say with a smile, "I was just chuckling at what we must look like, and then you made me laugh more..."

He takes a look behind him, at his bum and my legs, and laughs with me, "Well naturally I knew my sex was great, and yeah, I see your point. But I don't give a fuck, it's a big trunk, I'm getting in there with you..." he says as he proceeds to clamber in with me, bum in the air like a crazed nutter.
God, you've got to love this man.

CHAPTER 6
SATURDAY 22ND DECEMBER

A cool breeze blows my hair from my face and I roll over in bed, opening my eyes - to find I am all alone. He can't have been gone long; I stirred not so long ago to his lips on my neck, his arms tightly wrapped around me, whispering in my ear about being sexy and beautiful and all that smooth-talking gibber jabber that I love.

I rub my eyes as I sit up and look around, noticing the curtains moving from the open balcony door. We definitely didn't go to sleep with it open...

Last night was fantastic fun, but so relaxing, too. It was great to feel like 'me' again, around my friends. After the sesh in the boot of the car, we came in and chilled out in front of the fire for a while, laughing and chatting about his Aspen slope friends and how he and Daniel have enjoyed trips here a couple of times a year, since they met.

When Clare and Oliver got back from skiing, they told us that Bea and Daniel would be having dinner with us, and when they arrived, Pam laid on the most delicious buffet style dinner I have ever eaten. I seriously stuffed mine and Wriggler's faces to maximum capacity.

Afterwards, we all sat around the fire again and talked well into the night. Bea and Daniel curled up together on one sofa, occasionally taking themselves from the conversation to smile lovingly at each other and share a kiss or two. I was transfixed, bizarrely - watching their every move, feeling how powerful their love for one another is. I never thought these revolting words would ever come out of my mouth, but their love is simply beautiful.

I can't imagine ever having someone feel for me, how Daniel feels for Bea. She is so lucky to have someone as wonderful as he is - love her so much, but I hope he counts himself just as lucky because Bea is one of the most amazing girls on the planet. The best friend anyone could hope for, and, as is plain for all to see, a besotted, doting girlfriend. What a couple; disgustingly beautiful to look at and so incredibly happy.

Clare and Olly sat on another sofa together, but as you'd expect from 'just friends' - they weren't all over each other. Clare wants to think again, though, if she thinks I didn't notice the awkward glances they gave each other every time Bea and Daniel, or Luke and I shared a kiss or a cuddle. I really want to know the deal with these two; they have had sex, for sure, but is there anything else going on? I hope he's not fucking her about, I'll cut his flipping balls off with a spoon if I find out he's playing games with her.

She's so sweet and innocent, not a loud mouth like me or strong minded like Bea, she's a gorgeous girl inside and out, who'd never hurt a fly and who is constantly shocked by the shitty ways of the world.

As for Luke and I - well, like I said, we too had a kiss here and there, I sat curled on his lap, his big, strong arms wrapped around me the whole time. We shared the odd, whispered, private joke about car 'trunks' and 'outdoor pursuits' making us both laugh together, and it made me think that to Bea and Daniel, this must be like watching us in LA, because this is exactly how we were then. Only I had no idea how much easier it was then, to have no secret, to have no fear that - although I was leaving, I didn't have to worry that I may never see him again. Oh god, I hope that he will want *something* to do with Wriggler, I couldn't bear it if he disappeared completely. I wouldn't expect him to settle down as a family, but I would do anything for my baby to have a dad that wanted to know. A dad like mine.

~~~~~~~

I kick back the covers and drag myself out of the cosy bed, wrapping the blanket around me as I stroll towards the balcony. Approaching, I see him leaning against the railing facing my favourite view of the garden, wearing his tracksuit bottoms and a white t-shirt. His huge, broad back hunched as he leans forward, each and every muscle on display through his top, I can't help but fall a little deeper. Here he stands, all alone, having no idea that I am gazing at his delicious, sexy body, wanting nothing more than for him to love me and our baby, to complete our family unit. *Wow, these revelations... how Tilly has changed.*

I approach him silently and rest my body against his back, wrapping my arms and the blanket around his tummy. He turns his head in surprise and then looks back out to the trees, letting go of the railing and crossing his arms over mine.

"Morning Princess," he whispers, and I notice his usual, jovial, morning personality has gone awry, leaving a calm, thoughtful one in its place. I'm not complaining, he doesn't seem sad or unhappy, just a little... preoccupied.

"Good morning, bad-boy, why are you out here?"

"I was awake and you were still sleeping, I wanted to catch some of the dawn that we enjoyed so much yesterday. I think this early morning Aspen smell will always remind me of Tilly Burton."

I smile, snuggling my cheek into his warm back. I hope that's true, I hope he does remember things about me forever. Well, once he knows about Wriggler, I'm sure he'll never forget me completely. "I really enjoyed that. I'm enjoying this, too, aren't you cold?"

He stands straight and tugs at one of my arms, guiding me around to his front. He wraps his arms around me and rests his head on top of mine. The warmth of his body through his t-shirt welcomes me into his embrace. "No, I'm not cold, but you can keep me warm anyway."

"Okay." I respond, more than willing, enjoying the closeness. He must be feeling some of what I'm feeling... he just must be. I know the type of bloke he is, and I know he doesn't hold his usual type of women like this - he doesn't stick around long enough to feel anything for those women. He does feel something for me, it might not be as much as I feel for him, and he might not want the things that I want... but he definitely feels more than he does for anyone else. Apart from that girl he won't talk about.

"So, what shall we do today? I still have a lot of places to show you, or, I thought that maybe we could just hang out here all day?"

"Oh yeah?" I ask with a grin, looking up at his face, "You mean in bed?"

He returns the smile and winks, "Well... in bed... maybe take a stroll in the yard again... maybe kick Pam out and use the kitchen again, see what other rooms we can *relax* in."

I giggle, "I like it, let's do that. We have plenty more days to go out and explore." *And I'm so frigging horny, I'll take everything he offers me.* A day of Luke sex... I don't think anyone could say no to that, especially a horny pregnant person.

He looks into my face and unexpectedly shouts, "Woohoo!" in a high pitched, excited, girly fashion, making me howl, before he picks me up and runs inside with me, throwing me on the bed from quite a distance, and leaping on top of me.

~~~~~~~

We wake up together, in the media room of this stunning house, in the early evening after a day full of fun, amazing sex. We've worked our way around the house, and found some rooms I never even knew were here. This being one of them. It's a gorgeous room, not the type of 'cinema' you see on 'MTV Cribs', but a much more cosy, homely one. There is a huge screen, of course, but instead of big leather recliners on several levels, this is just a dark, luxurious room, with comfy, fabric sofas surrounding the screen.

We decided to come in here and watch a film, but managed to pash for the entire duration. We've had so much sex today, I don't think either of us had the energy to go at it again, and it was just so great to lay on this sofa together, cuddling and kissing... I never want to give this up. We eventually fell asleep together, I lay on top of his huge, hard body, and he held me, tightly.

As we stir, my head is on his chest, facing away from the screen, and one of my hands rests on his peck, the other holding on to his bicep.

"Hey, sweet-cheeks," he says, his voice gravelly and tired, "that was a good sleep."

I stretch slightly, not wanting to move from his embrace. "It was great, you're a comfy mattress."

"Sure I am, but that's because you're so itty-bitty, you barely cover a half of me."

I grin against his chest, loving it. "I don't want to move from here, do we have to?"

"We gotta get up, Til, we've probably missed the food..." he takes his hand off my back to check his watch, "yeah, it's six, and don't forget we're out tonight."

"Oh, I completely forgot about that. Yeah, we should get up, I'm bloody starving, too. Damn it."

"I'll fix you something, babycakes," he says, stretching his arms above his head as I start to move away from his warm body.

I totally forgot that we all arranged to go out tonight. Bea said last night that her parents, Emily and Eddy-boy are out for dinner with Rose and Henry; Daniel's parents, so they thought we should go for a night out. I have to get my wits about me before we go, I need an excuse as to why I won't be drinking, I don't think I can fake it again, I must have killed numerous plants with vodka since finding out about Wriggler; someone is going to notice one of these days.

It helps that when everyone else is drunk, they don't notice the sober person, pretending to be drunk. I haven't been out that much since Wriggler, but our crowd has always gone to the pub at least twice a week, and I was always there before. I didn't want to go after I found out, and I avoided it as best I could, but when everyone started texting me, asking what was up, I had to start making an effort in order to hide my secret. I could have just told them the truth, but call me old fashioned - I think the dad has a right to know before my friends.

I look down as I stand and drag my eyes from his toes towards his delicious face, pausing as I get to his middle. His t-shirt has ridden up on one side, flashing a few abs, and his low slung trousers expose his hip... I can see that sexy trail of hair traveling from his belly button down... down... disappearing into his waistband. And as I focus on that region, I notice his seriously impressive erection, dancing up and down under his trousers.

Shit. I shiver from the sudden spasm between my legs - I want to run my nose down that happy trail, I want to pull back that waistband and see my prize, then slowly lick the bead of liquid off the top... I know it'll be there. Then I'll gently take his swollen, rounded tip in my mouth and close my lips around him...

"Hey... up here, Princess." He snaps me back to reality, staring at me with the biggest, most amused smile on his beautiful face. *Those dimples!* "See something you like?"

'Yep. Your big fat erection."

He laughs loudly, throwing his head back and closing his eyes. He's even sexy when he laughs... of course he is, that's one of the first things I loved about him; funny *and* sexy.

He wiggles his eyebrows and hooks his thumb in his waistband, slowly etching it lower, showing me more and more of that sexy (neatly trimmed) hair. I glance up at his face and he winks, blowing me a kiss before saying, "Later, beautiful. Later."

I frown and pout like a child, stomping my foot and turning my head away from him, and in two shakes of a lamb's tail, I'm in the air, cradled in his arms. '"Poor Tilly's not a happy baby..." he says, kissing my cheek, "just a few hours and you can suck it like vacuum cleaner."

I turn to his face and smile, my tantrum gone, "Good. 'Cause I'm gonna. Might even catch you unawares in a quiet corner of the bar, later."

I see the excitement in his face and the twinkle in his eye, "Now *that* sounds more like it."

He walks with me upstairs to the kitchen, where we find Pam clearing away dishes.

"Hello, gorgeous young lady," Luke says, walking over to her, still holding me in his arms - and he kisses her cheek.

She blushes a little and swats his arm, gently. "Oh, you're a naughty boy, Luke. Put your girlfriend down, poor thing is probably starving. I have left two bowls of chunky soup on top of the stove for you, it's chicken and vegetable. Clare and Oliver have already eaten and gone up, so go sit and I'll bring some fresh bread. Can I get you anything else?" I immediately cling to the 'girlfriend' comment, and wonder if Luke is going to put her straight.

"Pam, if I didn't already have a beautiful lady in my arms, I'd be scooping you up and running back to California with you. Your delicious soup and bread will be good for me, thanks."

"Oh and fine for me, too, thank you so much for putting some aside. It smells wonderful."

"No problem, Tilly. And Luke - if I were twenty years younger, I'd consider taking you up on that offer, but I know that all you want from me is my cooking."

"It's a lie!" Luke cries, playfully and winks at her.

She smiles and collects the bowls of soup from the stove, handing them to us. He puts me down on my feet and we make our way to the island to eat. Pam leaves a slate board full of warm slices of fresh bread in front of us, before turning back to busy herself once again. I am so excited to eat, the soup looks absolutely delicious.

"So you've known Pam a while then?" I ask, their familiarity doesn't come after a few days.

"Uh huh," he says, taking a spoonful of soup, "she looks after Daniel and I when we come out here together, she's the best Aspen 'mom' ever."

I smile, enjoying the affection he has for her. "So why isn't she at Daniel's now?"

"Oh, he has Marsha at his place for the holidays, I asked Danny if we could have my Pam over here for the holidays. There are three of them, the Berkeley's employ them to work in the three houses. Pam's in love with me, too."

I laugh, "How could she not be? She seems really lovely, I can see why you asked for her. It's very indulgent - all this, I've never been on holiday and had staff to make all of my food and clean up after me like this."

"Good fun, huh?"

"Yeah, feels a bit naughty, like I should be helping."

"Pam loves it, she'd hate you to think you need to help."

"I know, but still. Anyway, she called me your girlfriend..." I ask, wondering what his answer will be.

He simply shrugs. *Hmm, what does that mean?*

We continue to eat together, chatting away and thoroughly enjoying the soup. It's thick and loaded with chicken and chunky veggies; absolutely amazing, I need the recipe for this because I will crave it until I get to meet Pam again. Hopefully I will, if we ever have another of these trips...

that's if everyone wants Wriggler tagging along. Maybe when Bea and Daniel have a baby together, it'll be easier.

We go upstairs to get ready and as we get to my door, Luke pulls me close to him and looks down at my face. "I'm looking forward to being with you tonight."

"You've been with me all day," I reply with a smile, slipping my arms around his waist.

"Oh, I have, my little love-muffin, but I'm not talking about boning."

I giggle as I reply, "No? You talking about the blow-job I offered? Because I think we covered that a few times today, too."

He groans and smiles, "*So* good... but no, I'm talking about being with you. You and me, out together with friends. Like a couple would."

Oh wow, like a couple! "Well, I'm looking forward to that, too. It should be a fun night. Can't wait to catch up with everyone and to dance with you again, I loved dancing with you in LA."

He grins and presses me up against the door, circling his pelvis and grinding against me, "Let's dance then..."

"Later, Lukey, I need to get ready," I say, reaching my face up to meet his, and gently brushing my lips over his. His eyes close and he bends further to press his mouth against mine more forcefully, opening to allow his tongue to run along my lips, before I welcome it inside. I grab the back of his neck and moan as our tongues tangle together, our lips caressing. He puts one hand on my hip and the other cradles the side of my face, holding me to him.

Butterflies flit in my belly, the excitement of having this huge, masculine, adorable man pressing me between him and the door, his gorgeous soft lips moving with mine, our heartbeats throbbing through our chests, pounding against each other...

"Good evening lovers," Clare's happy, sweet voice interrupts us as she whisks past in the hallway, heading for her bedroom.

Luke pulls away and grins as we hear her bedroom door close behind her. "Suppose we better get changed."

"Yeah, I've got to go or I won't be ready in time. But I'll meet you downstairs in about an hour."

"I'll be waiting, Princess."

We manage to tear ourselves away from each other, and go our separate ways to dress. It feels bizarre being all alone, having been with Luke for such a long time, and I am disgusted with myself for actually starting to miss him after as little as about five minutes. *Jesus, Tilly - fuck. Get a frigging grip.*

After a quick shower, I hear a knock at the door as Clare's head pokes around, "You decent?" she asks.

I scramble to get the towel adequately covering my belly, which seems to be swelling by the minute. I notice Clare's slight frown, questioning what I'm hiding, but I'm relieved that she doesn't ask.

"I just wondered what you were wearing, I thought maybe we could get ready together, I've hardly seen you at all since we got here, and I feel like we've been missing each other a lot at home, too. Is everything okay, doll?"

I smile, convincingly, loving having my friend here. We have been 'missing' each other a lot at home, but it's mainly because I don't want her to find out the truth, and keeping this from my best friends has been horrendous; very hard, but in my eyes, very necessary.

"Yes, everything is fine, we're just busy bods at the moment. Getting ready together sounds perfect, I miss you." I say with a playful pout, but totally meaning it.

"Me too. So? How's everything with Luke? From what I've seen so far, he's great! I really like him, *so* your cup of tea!"

I giggle, shyly. "I know, he really is. And things are great thanks, he's been so amazing. This is what LA was like, Clare. We were always having such a laugh together."

"Well, all I know is, my Til is back. She's been somewhere, and I don't know where exactly, but I know we all have to go into our own little world sometimes. But Luke and this trip has brought you back, I needed to see that Tilly spark again - and I have. If he is the reason for that, then I'd re-think your 'fun-loving' lifestyle and keep hold of this one."

"Thanks lover, but you know, it's not quite that simple."

"You're not going to do a 'Bea and Daniel' are you? *'We love each other so much but won't dare try long distance so we'll just be miserable'*?"

"No, I don't feel like that, besides, I *can* up and move to LA if I really want to. It's just not as simple, he's not up for it, and I've never been up for that sort of thing... he's a lady-loving playboy and I know it."

"Well it's clear as day that he's totally besotted by you, I can't see a trace of playboy, just a hilarious, fun loving, sweet guy... the male version of you."

"Thank you, darling."

I grab my make-up bag from the bathroom and plonk myself on the floor, cross-legged, in front of the full length mirror, while Clare sits at the vanity, to apply hers. This is how we do it at home and I love the familiarity of it. We chat easily together, talking about how much fun Clare's having on the slopes.

Apparently, Bea and Daniel are so cute together when they ski; if Daniel is ahead of Bea, he slows to wait for her to join him, then they stop just to share a kiss. Bea fell today and apparently Daniel was so caring, helping her stand up and checking her over, Bea just stroked his cheek and kissed him, telling him to stop worrying. I'm a bit sad to be missing it all but so grateful for the amazing time Luke's showing me.

"So how about you and Oliver? You getting on alright?" I ask, fishing.

"Yeah, we're having good fun. We always do, you know that."

"Uh huh, I know. So... I'm getting vibes..."

"Vibes? What sort of vibes? Not what you were on about the other night?"

"Well, yes, Clare. You two are being weird, I know you've been at it, don't even bother with that ridiculous show of denial you both put on the other day, so what's happening? Are you serial shaggers now or what?"

Clare puts her blusher brush down on the vanity table with some force, rolling her eyes and sighing, "For fucks sake,

Til, we're not shagging, can you stop going on? We've always been mates, so I fancied him way back when... so what! It doesn't mean I'll be in love with him 'til the day I die."

"Who said anything about love? I'm asking if you're shagging the guy... geez Louise, calm down!"

"Sorry, Til, but it's getting a bit annoying, having to worry how I'm acting in case you think something's going on. Nothing is, okay?"

"Doesn't mean it hasn't gone on..."

"Tilly!" She shouts, warning me to stop. This reaction - which is highly unlike Clare, she rarely gets angry - only confirms my thoughts. They may not be in a relationship, but Clare can't hide a lot from me, something has happened. I'll let it go though, I don't want to upset her, it's not like I don't have secrets of my own.

"Okay, sorry, sorry. There'd be nothing wrong with it, though, if you did do something together." I add, quietly, pushing my luck and she simply glares at me. "Just saying." I add with a cheeky smile and Clare joins me with a roll of her eyes.

"Anyway, so what are you wearing?" she asks, changing the subject, tactically.

"Dunno, what do people wear out in Aspen? Full on party gear? Jeans and boots? I thought maybe a mixture of the two... skinny jeans and heels with a nice top?"

"That's what I thought, finished off with an ugly winter jacket," she giggles.

I finish off my make-up with a last layer of mascara and break our chatter by drying my hair. I wonder - in this 'me time' with my head upside down and the loud hum of the dryer blaring - what Luke is doing... maybe he's still in the shower - naked, smoothing foamy suds all over his muscles. His wet, tanned skin - flawless and toned... Maybe he's putting his clothes on, pulling his trousers up those muscular thighs, buttoning his fly, fastening his belt with those perfect fingers of his... Maybe he's thinking about me - about kissing me and having naughty sex... Maybe he's got a hard on... I squeeze my thighs together as my inner muscles clench in anticipation, my mouth watering at the thought of his cock. *You're obsessed, woman.*

When I return to reality, turning the dryer off and standing straight, smoothing my fringe with my fingers, Clare is strolling across the room in her underwear towards her clothes on the bed. I watch her, absently gazing at her tight flat belly. I wonder if mine will ever go back... it certainly doesn't look like that anymore, although I do have a new love of my neat, tiny, wriggler bump, with or without the weird brown line up the middle. I also look forward to the day that I can walk around, in front of my besties and Luke, and not have to cover up. Mind you, that day may never come with Luke, depending on how he takes the news.

"I know you love me and everything, Til, but I didn't think you were *that* into me..." Clare says, and my eyes shoot straight up to her face as she stares at me, wondering what the hell I'm doing.

"Oh!" I cry and laugh out loud, giving me a moment to figure out what to say. "No, I was just admiring your perfect belly, maybe I shouldn't have had my belly button pierced, do you think I should take it out?" It's all I could think of, but I immediately regret it, knowing what she'll follow with.

"I like it, it's 'you', but take it out, let's have a look..." *Shit. What now?*

"Um... oh, never mind, I'll think about it another day. I don't have much time left to finish getting ready and I need to sort my fringe out."

"No, you're getting ready anyway, let me see, won't take a sec. I want to see what pierced belly buttons look like without anything in..." *Oh for gods sake, leave it Clare, would you?*

"I'll do it tomorrow, the ball is on pretty tight, I don't want to risk not being able to get it back on." *Totally lame, Til, you sound like an idiot.*

She looks at me with a frown, "Alright... everything okay?"

"Yes, why wouldn't it be? Anyway, what do you think about this top?" I ask, holding up a loose fitting, floaty, charcoal, silk vest, praying she goes with the new subject and drops the old.

"That's lovely, with which jeans?" *Thank god.*

"My black skinnies and black, super-high stilettos... sound good?"

"Hot, darl, boiling hot. Luke isn't going to want to leave the house once he sees you in that."

I smile and continue to get ready, hoping Clare isn't over-thinking the belly button thing.

A short while later, I'm leaving my room. My hair is perfect, my usually slightly-too-big-at-the-waist jeans fitting snugly, my blouse floating perfectly over me, covering Wriggler, clutch bag in hand and heels clicking gorgeously on the wooden stairs. Clare has headed back to her room for her bag. As I get to the bottom of the stairs, I see Oliver sitting back on one of the couches ahead of me, talking out loud to no one in particular, he looks gorgeous as always, dressed for an evening out. He is always impeccably dressed for nights out and functions, but by day, in his work gear, he looks rugged and scruffy in a sexy kind of a way.

A moment later, I realise he's talking to Luke as he emerges from the kitchen looking absolutely bloody gorgeous in his pale blue fitted shirt, jeans, and scruffy, square-toed, suede cowboy boots. *Oh, fuck me, I could actually eat the man alive.* His collar is open, with his top button undone, I can see that dip in his throat at the base of his neck... what I'd do to be able to kiss that soft spot right now, I bet his neck... and the rest of him in fact, smells incredible. His naturally highlighted hair - clean, but gorgeously messy, in true Luke style.

He stops, mid-walk, mid-conversation, when he sees me. We both stand, rooted to the spot, eyeing each other up and down appreciatively, saying nothing. My belly churns with excitement, I want him. I love him. We continue to stare, time seeming to escape us, neither of us thinking about Oliver, who's probably feeling super awkward right now. We don't care about the rest of the world... at least, I don't, anyway.

I take a tentative step towards him, and he does the same, only he doesn't stop, and continues with great strides - slamming his drink down on the dresser before reaching me, forcefully grabbing me and thrusting his hard body against me, cupping the back of my head and pressing his mouth to mine. His eyes close firmly, and mine follow, the warm rush spreading from my toes to the tips of my fingers, my lips excitedly indulging in his affection.

I moan quietly, immersed, thoroughly lost in the moment. His tongue so forceful, the slight, barely audible grunt that escapes his throat sends evidence of my arousal straight to my knickers. My hand weaves through his soft hair, clasping at tufts and yanking gently.

He walks me backwards towards the wall by the stairs and presses me against it, not breaking the connection once. He slides his free hand down my back, over my bottom and between my legs, lifting me effortlessly so my legs wrap around his waist, our faces level. The feel of his strong fingers pressing against me only spurs my need more, I tingle and clench, our kiss escalating into a wild, salacious pash.

"Oh for fucks sake, seriously? I'm right here... she's like my sister, mate..." Oliver's disturbed groan interrupts our moment, and we pull away from each other guiltily. Luke slowly lowers me to the ground, staring intently into my eyes... I shyly break the eye contact, looking down before sheepishly over to Oliver.

"Sorry, Olly... I got a bit carried away. Won't happen again."

"Sorry, dude." Luke adds.

"Too damn right it won't, I need to scrub my eyeballs with a scourer after that, gross." Olly says with a shiver, making me giggle.

"Alright, alright, it's not *that* bad, I'm not *actually* your sister, you know. I'm sure you wouldn't cringe at the thought of Clare getting down and dirty..." I know it's wicked of me, but I couldn't help it, I want to see his reaction, and bingo... it's exactly as I thought. Oliver shakes his head and looks down, stuttering.

"Well, er, that's, you know - totally different, we have a different relationship, and it would probably still be a bit, you know, uh... weird... and that..."

If I wanted a clear as day answer - that was it. And if that wasn't enough for me to know that these two have definitely shagged, as Clare makes her way down the stairs, looking incredibly hot in her tight jeans, sheer, partially sequinned pink blouse and nude, suede stilettos - Oliver's eyeballs practically fall out of his head. It's classic, he clearly can't hide his attraction to her - even if he desperately wanted to, which I'm sure he does. *Where have I been? How long has this been going on?* His eyes drag from her feet up to her beautifully wavy, thick blonde hair, his mouth slightly ajar.

It's getting awkward, so, as I have already made him feel unnecessarily uncomfortable, I decide to throw him a bone and break the ice. "Ready Clare?" I ask.

"Looking sexy, girl!" Luke adds, stepping over to her and kissing her cheek.

"Thank you Luke, and yes, I'm ready. Just need to get my ugly ski coat on..."

"Yeah, me too," I say, laughing, moving to pull away from Luke, to go and get my jacket, when he grabs my hand, stopping me.

"No, wait, I've got something for you..." He lets go, leaving me at the bottom of the stairs with Clare, and walks purposefully to the back of the far sofa. He retrieves a large box, and walks straight back over, handing it to me. It's so much heavier than Luke makes it look.

I frown - smiling, wondering what on earth this is... it's like a bloody wedding dress box. I take it over to the sofa, Luke following me, and start to remove the lid. I brush aside some tissue only to find my hands deeply buried in the softest, most luxurious fur I've ever felt.

"I bought you a coat, thought you might find it useful here," he says, casually, as if it's nothing. He reaches down into the box from beside me, and pulls out the coat. My mouth drops open as I see it in full length; the most incredibly gorgeous, Dennis Basso, designer fur; the large, lengthy collar, a rich, deep shade of charcoal grey, so perfectly soft. The main fur of the shin length coat, a beautiful mocha brown, in luscious, fat, horizontal ridges.

I slowly look up at his face, he is casually holding out the coat, waiting for me to turn and slip my hands into the liquid silk lining. I am stunned, fuck buddies don't buy each other fur coats worth - most likely - many thousands of dollars... do they? "Luke..." I whisper, looking dazed into his unusually innocent, sparkly blue eyes, "I... it's..."

"Beautiful, huh? Come on, Princess, arms in." I turn and hold my arms behind me, as he effortlessly slides the elegant coat up to my shoulders. The huge collar brushes my jaw and cheeks, I feel a million dollars. I slip my hands into the silky pockets and draw the coat to a close at my front, I feel cocooned, safe and warm inside.

"Wow, Til! It's stunning!" Clare cries enthusiastically from the stairs, reminding me that there are still other people in the room.

I nod with her and turn to Luke again, he's grabbing his keys from a side table casually, as if he gives ladies furs all the time... maybe he does...

"That sounds like the car pulling up outside, shall we go?" he says.

"Luke, I... thank you so much, I don't know what to say."

He waves his hand and grabs a random cowboy hat that I hadn't noticed, sitting on the back of one sofa. He places it down on the top of his head, flicking the front of the rim with his finger. *Fuck me, that is one sexy cowboy...* The boots, I've seen plenty, but I have never seen the man in that hat before... *phwoar*... he is bringing that to bed tonight!

"Nothing, Til, it's just a coat. You look damn hot in it though, I picked well."

"When did you get it?"

"Just after I left you to get ready, I'd already made a call so it was easy - I've got contacts." *Hmm, probably not the first fur purchase he has made, then. Just how much money do personal trainers earn?* He pauses, looking me up and down, before wrapping his arm around my waist and pulling me towards him. Burying his face in my neck, almost knocking his hat off, he kisses me and mumbles against my skin, "You're gonna let me fuck your god damn brains out wearing that, and not a lot else, sweet-cheeks."

I giggle and press my palms against his torso, my tiny hands barely emerging from the ends of the fluffy sleeves, "fine by me, as long as you wear that hat... and not a lot else."

He growls against my neck and squeezes me tightly, before releasing me slowly to turn and adjust himself, away from view.

I look over at Oliver who is curling his lip in disgust, and Clare, who's grinning, cheekily, like she's seen something she shouldn't have. "Suppose I'm going to be the one to look like a tramp in my ski coat then!" she says with a roll of her eyes.

"You could never look like a tramp, Clare, you look hot." Olly says, clearly meaning every word, but looking slightly awkward.

"Couldn't have said it better myself, shall we head out to the car?" I ask, needing to get out of this house so I don't cancel the night out and jump Luke right here and now on a side table, fur coat and cowboy hat 'n' all.

We all leave the house and make our way down the stairs to the limo, where we greet Bea, Daniel and Alexia before heading off to town. Bea apparently knew about my furry gift, and also had a beautiful new purchase herself, so she thoughtfully brought another short, hip length coat with a fur collar along for Clare, so she wouldn't be left out, and she looks hot in it; we all look so glam in these new extravagant items.

We get out of the car as we pull up in town, and organise ourselves. As Alexia steps out, Luke rushes forward to take her hand and help her out.

"Thanks, Lukey," she says with a big smile, and I feel a sudden rush of anger, *that's what I call him, not you - bitch.*

I continue to watch as he puts an arm around her and kisses her cheek. "You look smokin' tonight, Lex."

"So do you, you better make sure I get a dance later."

"As always, babycakes, as always."

Wow. The jealousy boils violently inside, I want to punch her in the fucking face, stupid bitch, that's *my* Luke, that's *my* dancing partner, *my* baby-daddy. I am shocked by the way I feel, I've never been jealous like this before, even when I was in love with Scott, I never felt the need to get violent with anyone, even after I found out he'd been shagging everything in a skirt. But she's doing my nut in. Ever since we got in the car they've been all chatty and giggly, and the fact that she doesn't talk to me at all just makes me think she's a jealous witch. I don't know why Bea thinks she's so great.

As I shoot daggers at the pair of them, I feel an arm link through mine. "They're just friends, Til," Bea whispers, and kisses me on the cheek.

"Huh? Oh, yeah, I know. It's cool," I say, nonchalantly, like I wasn't just plotting to shove her under an oncoming steamroller.

"Good, as long as you do. She likes you, she's just a bit shy in social situations."

Like fuck she is. "Yeah, fine, Bea. I don't have any issues," I lie. Bea nods in acceptance and releases my arm to join hips with Daniel again.

Luke tears himself away from *'babycakes'* and comes to stand with me, wrapping his arm around me and bending to kiss my lips, briefly. "I've been thinking about your naked body all the way here... I'm getting hard visualising inside your panties," he whispers in my ear. His low, breathy tone, raw and sexy, I fight the desire to grab his hand, bury it inside my coat and press it between my legs. His 'to-the-point' statement makes me laugh, completely forgetting about my thuggish jealousy of a moment ago.

"I'm glad you feel that way, I'm really horny for you, I want to make you come," I whisper back, smiling cheekily, knowing he'll be having to rearrange himself again soon. I bet Alexia wouldn't know where to start - getting him hard.

CHAPTER 7
SATURDAY 22ND DECEMBER (CONT.)

We arrive at a nightclub after a short walk along the pretty, brick promenade. There is snow all around, but the walkway is (thankfully) clean for pedestrians. Two streams and rows of trees covered in Christmas fairy lights run down the centre of the promenade, with shops, restaurants and bars on either side. I am so grateful for this beautiful warm coat and the big man holding me close to him. I'm cosy and toasty in the freezing night air.

An impressive bar made of ice sits outside in the centre of the walkway, with patrons standing close-by, drinking tall flutes of champagne. We walk past and towards the main entrance to 'Escobar'. There is a large queue of people waiting behind thick, red ropes, but Daniel and Luke lead us straight past it, towards a large, bald man in a black suit and turtle neck, manning the door. When he notices the boys, he flashes a big, friendly grin and his intense, blue eyes sparkle.

"Jeff!" Daniel shouts, in greeting, obviously fond of the doorman.

"Danny, Luke, great to see you. Alexia, looking stunning this evening," he says as he reaches out to hug her. "Back for the holidays, and with some beautiful ladies, I see..."

"Jeff, this is the love of my life; Bea..." Daniel says, and I hear Clare swoon behind me, she's a sucker for romance.

"Well, what a pleasure to meet you, Bea," Jeff says, pulling her in for a hug, too.

"And her brother and friends are with us also," he says, quickly introducing Clare and Oliver.

"Jeff, it has been a while," Luke says, "I couldn't stand the distance any longer, I just had to see you." They laugh together before he introduces me. "And *my* amazing woman is Tilly." *His* amazing woman? *Ooh...*

"Amazing? Probably. Beautiful? Definitely. Wonderful to meet you, Tilly." He opens his arms, beckoning me with his fingers and I step forward into his bear hug.

"You, too, Jeff." I say as I step back and out of his embrace. He unclips the rope from the post to let us all through, shaking the mens' hands and giving Clare a hug too. How very familiar of him.

We walk through the doors and down two flights of stairs that look strangely like a jetway to an aeroplane, and as we near the bottom, I immediately feel the stifling heat of an obviously bustling nightspot. A friendly, uber-cool looking blonde guy who clearly knows Luke and Daniel, meets us at the bottom and directs us through the packed venue to our VIP table at the back, complete with a stripper pole and private bathroom. *I hope we don't have to sit here all night and watch some bikini-clad contortionist opening and closing her legs around this pole. If I wanted to see someone's vag pop out the side of their thong, I'd go to a strip club.*

The cool blonde guy - Ian - has a quick chat with Luke and disappears into the crowd. I stand and take a good look around me, taking in the atmosphere. On closer inspection, I notice that the club is set out like an aeroplane, with curved metal walls and screens where the windows would be. That would explain the entrance. I wonder if Daniel brought us here because of his and Bea's affection for aircraft, since they met on a plane.

It's jam packed in the club, super-loud and hyper but looks like a whole lot of fun. The music is fantastic, and should the situation have been different, I would have loved a full-on, alcohol fuelled dance sesh, followed by a full-on, alcohol fuelled sex sesh with Luke, back at the house.

The eclectic mix of people could keep my eyes preoccupied all night. There are the groups, pretty much like us, 20-30 somethings from out of town; there's the 'jampiece' snowboard crowd; the moustaches; the fat, rich men with white hair, perma-tans and pinky rings; the over-cooked cougars; the 'undressed to impress' groups of young single girls looking for their sugar-daddies; the cowboy hats; the fur coats... it's fantastic!

"It's so cool in here!" Clare shouts to me, with a huge smile on her face. "Bloody hell, look at her over there!" And I follow her line of vision to another VIP table where one of the guests is stuck upside down on their stripper pole with her stiletto heel wedged into her bouffant hair-do.

"Ouch! That's not what you want!" I say, laughing as we watch two of her male friends struggling to get her down.

"You going to show me how to do it?" Luke's voice surprises me as his arms wrap around me from behind. I casually hold them, slipping them a little higher so they sit just under my boobs; above Wriggler.

"Is there going to be a stripper?" I ask.

"No, this is for us to have fun on. Wanna give me a show?"

I turn in his arms and put mine casually around his neck. "I'd rather give you a private one."

"And there he goes..." he says, rolling his eyes and pulling me tightly against his body, so I can feel his erection though our clothes. I lean up and pull on his neck slightly so I can kiss him, his lips are so inviting, I can almost taste him already. Just as our lips touch, our eyes locked, our hearts beating wildly - *someone* disturbs us.

"Here's your champagne guys." *Oh my god, I'm going to slap her, I bet she chose that exact moment on purpose.* We both turn to Alexia who is holding two champagne flutes for us.

"Thanks, Lex," Luke says, taking an arm from around me to hold his glass.

"Yeah, thanks," I say, reluctantly, wishing I could throw it in her face. *Oh my god, Til, what the hell is wrong with you?*

Luke sits on one of the couches and pulls me down onto his lap. We all toast together and everyone starts to drink. I put the glass to my lips and then place it back down on the table with the ice bucket, bottles of Veuve Clicquot, Belvedere Vodka and glass jugs of soft drink and water. I look around and directly into the eyes of Clare who's frowning at me in question. It's not really a surprise to me, I would normally have had a half-glass swig of my first, given how much I adore it. I just mouth 'headache' at her and point to my head, looking away immediately, hoping to have answered satisfactorily enough to end the subject.

Bea and Daniel stand to talk to some people Daniel knows, and Oliver refills his and Clare's glasses as they chat together. Alexia talks to the blonde guy - Ian, again, leaving us alone. Thank god.

"So you like it here?" Luke asks loudly over the music as he kisses my neck.

"Yes, it's really cool. I like the layout."

"Have I told you how hot you look tonight, Princess?"

I giggle and wriggle in his lap, turning to face him. "Yes, you have. And you're looking damn hot yourself, cowboy, I love this look on you." I say, taking his hat off and putting it on my head.

He grins and brushes my fringe from my eyes, "A little big for you, maybe we'll get you one; suits you."

"So what are you? Snowboarding 'dude' or cool cowboy? Bad-boy or good-boy? Fun-loving wild boy or sophisticated gentleman? There are so many Lukes and I don't know which is the real one."

"Never judge a book by its cover, Til, you never know what treasures may lay inside. I'm all of those Lukes, and more."

I nod. "I'm happy with that, I like all of you," I say, resting one hand on his cheek and leaning forward to place a chaste kiss on his perfect, pert mouth.

"All of me, huh? Which bit is your favourite?"

I smile, "Oh, I don't know, could be your big strong arms that keep me warm when I'm cold, maybe your rock hard abs that tense when you're standing between my legs; or your thighs - those delicious, muscular thighs that I secretly stare at through your jeans. Maybe it's none of that, maybe it's your handsome face, your irresistible dimples, your soft mouth. Or... could just be your massive cock."

He laughs loudly and takes his hat back before holding the back of my neck and pulling me in for a long, slow kiss.

"I want to watch you come, right now." *Oh the good Lord Jesus Christ, I want him to watch me come right now, too...* I clench my inner muscles and wriggle in his lap again, feeling in need of a good-old rogering.

"Are you trying to frustrate me?"

"Not at all. I'm trying to get you to let me fuck you. Now."

"Now?" I ask, astounded, "Here? No chance!"

"Not right here, no." He looks at me, his head tilted to one side, assessing my reactions. "Do you want to come?"

I pout, a smile forcing its way through, "I always want to come, these days."

He stares into my eyes, his face seriously contemplating something, deliberating whether or not to go ahead with it.

"Come with me," he says as he grabs my hand and stands, sliding me off his lap in the process. He peers around us and strolls casually, holding my hand, to the private toilet, nearby. Punching in a code, he slips in, pulling me behind him, and slams the door, pressing me up against it, forcefully.

"You want me," he says, one of those phrases that turns us on, ridiculously so.

"*You* want *me*." I respond, mixing it up a bit.

"You want my cock, baby."

"Oh yeah? You want my..."

"Your..?"

"My aching... hot... wet..."

"Uh huh..." he grunts, breathing deeply, running his nose up the side of my neck and kissing my jaw.

"Pussy."

I watch as his eyes clench shut and his forehead wrinkles with his frown, both of his hands pressed against the door, either side of my head. "Jesus, Tilly..." His face moves like lightning, pressing against mine, his tongue entwined with mine before I even get a chance to react. I moan loudly, knowing that no one will hear us, and I hold his neck with both of my hands. Just the feel of his soft, warm skin on my hands makes my chest lurch, painfully. *Shit, I love him so much. Why do I have to love him? I love every inch of his gorgeous body.*

His hands move from the door to my fly as the kiss increases in frustrated need, I need to come, I need him to make me come... and I need to feel him come, just as badly. He breaks away from the kiss and bends to kiss and lick my neck, my chest... he slides down my body until he reaches my fly. I pull off his hat so I can see his face, and drop it on the nearby sink.

He unfastens my trousers and pulls them down, along with my knickers, to my knees. He takes off my left shoe and then removes the jeans from that leg only. "Put your leg up on the sink, Til." he orders, and I do what he says.

I'm standing against the door, holding the handle in one hand, the wall with the other, with my legs wide open and a foot in the sink with his hat. He gazes between my legs and groans loudly. He closes the space between us, kneeling, hovering in front of my bits. His warm breath teasing me, his hands grabbing hold of each thigh, tightly, my flesh bulging through his splayed fingers.

"You're so fucking beautiful, Til..." and immediately I feel his hot, wet tongue run up my centre, making me cry out in ecstasy. He doesn't waste a minute, he's licking and lapping and kissing me over and over, it's so agonisingly good, I moan and cry out, continuously begging for more. I take my hand from the door knob and fist it in his hair, pulling hard.

He growls so loudly and presses his face against me, hard, moving down slightly and pushing his tongue inside me. It's so good. He moves back to my clitoris, where he sucks and flicks lightly with his tongue and I can feel it brewing deep inside, it's rolling through my body, thick and fast.

"Oh god, Luke, oh fuck yes..." I cry, preparing for it, getting ready for the imminent explosion to burst through my body, and as it hits, I cry a long, high pitched moan, my eyes locked on his head, moving between my legs. My foot kicks against the far side of the sink, every muscle in my body tensing, his hands squeezing my thighs so hard, it hurts... pleasurably so.

"Oh fuck!" I shout, my standing leg weak, pulling his hair hard, unable to let go. *Holy fucking shit-balls, pregnant orgasms are the best!*

I moan as he slowly runs his tongue up my centre again, before kissing all the way across my groin to my raised thigh. He releases my legs, leaving creamy-white hand prints, and holds my hips to keep me steady. He looks up at my face and licks his lips, sensually. "I love how you taste... how you come... there's something so special about Tilly."

I rest my head back against the door with a thud, panting, and I smile. He stands up against me, and kisses me hard.

"That was... totally amazing... oh wow," I murmur, still catching my breath from my crazy-incredible orgasm.

"Too right." He slips his hands around my waist, catching my blouse, pulling it tight against my belly. *Oh, please don't look down...* "I couldn't have waited to get home for that, Til."

"Well... I can't wait either." I say as I drag my hands down his hard chest to unbuckle his belt.

He steps back, shaking his head. "Not yet." *What the...?*

"Why? I want to taste you, too..."

"I am so freakin' horny, baby, but I'm going to wait - I want to fuck you so hard, you'll still be feeling it next week."

"Fuck me then..."

"No, Princess. Make me wait for you... I want you to tease me until I'm ready to explode in my pants."

Oh. I'm really quite annoyed about this, I was so ready to suck him silly, taste him, feel him come in my mouth. So ready to go outside to the bustling club, knowing I've just made my man come with just a door separating us from all of these people.

Well, fine. If he wants to be like that, I'll fucking tease him until his knob turns blue, and then he can sodding well sort himself out. Pig.

I gently shove his chest away, pushing him backwards so I can get my leg out of the sink and pull my jeans and knickers back on. "Fine, you want teasing? You've got it," I say, unable to hide my childish huff. And why the fuck should I hide it? I want to give a frigging blow job!

"Hey, hey, hey... what's this?" he says, holding my arms and searching for eye contact. "Are you mad?" he asks, as his mouth curls into a smile.

I smack his arm in frustration. "Don't laugh at me Luke," I respond, trying to shake myself free, bending to reach for my shoe.

"No," he says, tightening his grip on my arms and pushing me back against the door, "I'm not laughing at you, look at me," he demands, and for some bizarre reason, the stubborn side to my character bows down, and I stop what I'm doing to look him in the eye. "Are you mad? Because you're not sucking me off?"

I pause for a moment, thinking about how stupid this must look. It is stupid, why the hell am I so mad? I just want him so much. "Yes." I admit, reluctantly. "I just want it. You got to do what you wanted... why can't I?" I ask in a small, whiny voice, like a child.

"Til, I wanted to give *you* everything. This, in here, is about *your* pleasure. I'll wait until later, I want to fuck you after you suck me, and I don't want to do all that in here. I don't want to see my girl on her knees in a nightclub bathroom, right by a toilet."

Oh my god, his girl again... I can't imagine him having an issue with any other girls getting their knees dirty. "Okay, fair enough. I'm sorry, I just... you know."

"Yeah, sugar-lips, I know. You just love me too much, to not give me a BJ every place we go."

I giggle and press my hand against his pecks, "Yep, totally."

We share one more long, sensual pash before I put my shoe on, straighten myself out, and slip out of the bathroom, hopefully unnoticed, with Luke.

We must have been out all of about thirty seconds, when Alexia calls over to Luke, "Hey! Luke! Come and say hi to Sebastian and Cole!" He kisses me on the cheek before heading over to them. *Hmm, fine.*

I take the time to see what's happening around me; Bea is dancing with Daniel nearby, locked in a tight embrace, noses touching, their movement slow and sensual, totally contradicting the loud dance music. They kiss slowly, lightly brushing their lips together, and I see Daniel saying something to her, making her smile - prompting her to stroke the hair at the back of his neck. They are so in love, watching them fascinates me.

My attention is grabbed suddenly by the loud squeal of Clare, spinning around the stripper pole with one bent leg and one hand. Oliver stands by, laughing exuberantly, holding their empty glasses. How can she possibly be drunk already? *Crikey, I'm getting old.*

I step over to the drinks table and pour myself a glass of orange juice, before sitting on one of the sofas to observe the fun. Now it's Oliver's turn on the pole and wow! He's good! Clare watches, her face a stunning picture, lit-up and happy, laughing contagiously at him. He's putting on a great show, seemingly - solely for Clare.

Bea and Daniel join them, laughing - Bea trying to pull Oliver away so she can have a go herself. Watching my friends from the sidelines like this, having so much fun together, makes me feel so lucky. I don't know what I'd do without them all, even Daniel has become so important to me, in a short space of time since LA. I hope nothing changes when I have my baby, I hope we stay just as close, I know they will have a huge part to play in the life of my child. They are my best friends - but I pray that we manage to keep our tight knit friendship just as firm as it is now. Having my sister in the States, and with Dad gone, they're all I have here.

I smile and turn to look in Luke's direction, only to see him standing with Alexia, his arm around her waist, laughing happily. The other two - Sebastian and whats-his-name - are nowhere to be seen. I'd love to know what's so fucking funny, Alexia is practically falling over herself. Her hand rests on his stomach, the other on his shoulder as she leans into him and says something in his ear. He glances over in my direction and smiles, before looking straight back at *her* to answer her question with amusement.

My fury boils to a whole new heat as he bends down and sweeps her off her feet, giggling and smiling as he throws her over his shoulder. She smacks his bum and in turn, he swats hers. *That's fucking it!* I have had enough of this bullshit, he doesn't mean anything he fucking says, I'm stupid to believe he's not shagging anyone else, it's in his god damned nature! We have to stop. Now.

First thing tomorrow I'm going to tell him about the baby and get the fuck away from here. I should never have let myself fall for him, the way I have. I know who he is and what he's about and he's showing me first hand, right now. But...

first things first - I'm going to give him a taste of his own frigging medicine, see how *he* likes it.

I stand - furious, hot and determined, searching for someone. I see a small group of fairly handsome looking men, drinking and laughing, and I decide that they'll do. I walk directly to them, picking - in my opinion - the most good-looking. I grab his hand, interrupting them and not giving a shit, and tell him, "Dance with me."

He raises his eyebrows and smirks, silently agreeing, and follows me a few steps away into Luke's line of vision. I turn to face him, wrap my arms around his neck and press my body against his. It feels totally wrong, and very uncomfortable, but I don't care. I'm doing this.

He places his hands on my lower back and smiles, trying to figure me out. "So, I'm Jason, what's your name?"

I shake my head, "Don't speak, just dance." I don't want to get in conversation with the guy, I don't want anything but to make Luke feel just a smidgen of what I feel when he shoves his nose up *her* backside.

We grind together, and I close my eyes, trying for a moment to forget it's not Luke. I notice that subconsciously, I'm trying to distance Wriggler from him. I'm so horribly uncomfortable doing this, which is yet another 'new' for me, I have danced with countless men in my time, and never felt weird like this.

The guy holds my hips and turns me around, pressing my back into his front. *Bleugh.* I move with him, circling my hips, grinding in time to the music, hoping I can end this soon. I glance up and notice Luke talking to *her*, looking at me. She's looking up at his face, clearly deep in conversation about something, he's nodding, but his attention is on me. *Good.*

He frowns and cocks his head, and as I start to feel a little better, hoping he feels as jealous as I do, the man slips his hands around my waist, and rests them low on my belly. I am so out of my comfort zone; having another man touching my precious cargo is unbearable, it's not his to touch. My protective instincts are clearly setting in, and I look up at Luke again to find him smiling through that frown, amused.

The anger is uncontrollable, I am fuming! I tear the hands from my belly and stride, angrily to the seating area to grab my clutch bag. Luke manages to pull himself away from the oh-so-*amazing* Alexia to come over and join me.

"Hey, enjoy your dance with Jason?" he asks.

"What?" I ask, angrily, "You know him?"

"Sure I do, he's a friend of a friend."

Oh for gods sake. "Yes, thanks. He's a nice guy." I say, straight faced, without emotion, looking anywhere other than his face.

"Too bad you're not his type then, huh?"

I turn quickly, ready to pounce angrily, "How do you know? We were having a great time."

"I'm sure you were sweet-cheeks, but gay guys don't usually go for the ladies."

Oh my god, ground, open up, please? I close my eyes and sigh, defeated. "Fine."

"Were you trying to make me jealous? What's going on, Tilly?"

I look at his face and realise that he just doesn't see our relationship the way I do. We're still just fuck buddies, nothing more. Just because I'm in love with him, doesn't mean we'll ever go any further, and trying to tell myself that he just might be father material, is living in a dream. He'll want nothing to do with me, and nothing to do with Wriggler.

"No, Luke. I was just dancing. Go back to Alexia, I'm sure you're dying to continue with your hilarious conversation."

He holds my shoulders and slouches a little to near eye level. "You're jealous of me and Alexia? You're kidding?" He smirks, making the blood boil inside again, rage surging through my body.

"Just fuck off, don't take the piss out of me, don't laugh at me, and don't fucking touch me!" I shout, shrugging out of his hold.

"What the fuck is wrong with you?" he shouts, frowning, now looking quite furious himself.

"Fuck off Luke!" I scream, trying to get my voice heard over the music, frustrating me massively. I'm so hot, I must be bright red. Luke raises his hands, showing his palms, pouts and shakes his head. He turns and walks away through the crowd, leaving me standing there embarrassed, angry and totally alone.

I look around, no one is looking, no one saw what has just gone down over here, which is great, but makes me realise exactly how alone I am in this situation. No one knows how much I love Luke, no one knows that I now want a 'forever', no one knows that I have his beautiful baby growing inside me. In this moment, it's just me, and it's so hard.

Tears sting my eyes and my mouth twitches. These damn hormones! The only thing I can think of to make me feel comfortable right now, is to get the hell away from here, away from the noise, away from my clueless, happy friends, away from the chaos and Christmas cheer, away from Luke. I grab my coat and clutch bag, and slip away through the heaving club. This is where being short comes in really handy, no one can ever see me in a crowd.

I run up the stairs and dash outside at the top, totally avoiding any kind of niceties with 'Jolly Jeff'. I continue to scuttle in my heels until I get a good distance away from the club, taking care not to slip. I haven't even noticed the freezing temperatures in my silk vest, but I slip on the fur coat, needing some sort of comfort. I find a bench in the middle of the promenade and sit, my hands either side of me, my head bowed, eyes - teary. What the hell do I do now? I don't know my way home or the driver's number.

I sit back, lifting my legs and crossing them on the bench, wondering where the hell to go from here. I rest my head in my hands and close my eyes, horribly sad, confused and desperately scared. It's back to how it was before, and it should never have changed.

I have to tell him, and then we need to figure out how to move on from here. If he wants to know the baby and be a big part of its life, I'll contemplate finding a place to live in LA, for the sake of Wriggler. It'll be hard leaving my girls at home, but other than them, there's nothing important enough to keep me there. Enabling my child to have a relationship with his or her father, is far more important than missing home.

Then, of course, there's the likely option that he won't want to be that much of an active dad, happy enough to see the child here and there, whenever I visit Gemma. Which would mean, not a lot of change for me, apart from my own place to live and a way to find enough money to raise the baby without help.

Or... the option that he won't want to see the baby at all. That would kill me, and as much as I know the type of guy Luke is, I just can't see him being *that* much of an arse-hole.

My mind moves to the last option; the nonsensical idea that I don't like to even contemplate because of how devastatingly unrealistic it is - but my head has other ideas. *Torturous bitch.* The option where Luke tells me he's excited and that he wants to be in the baby's life, that he wants to see his baby every day, he wants to see *me* every day. That he loves me, he wants to be with me, he wants to live together and raise Wriggler in the perfect family setting. *Oh Wriggler, I can't guarantee that I'll have a happy ever after, but I will make damned sure that you are the happiest child there is, whatever happens. I'll do everything I can for my precious baby.*

I take a long, deep breath in and exhale slowly. Just one night of amazing, swimming pool sex, and my life and emotions are all over the shop. Why am I in love with a bad-boy? An amazingly hot, caring, sweet bad-boy. *No, Tilly! Think of Alexia, think of his ten billion other women in LA, think of what he does for a living! He trains women and fucks them as part of the deal. He's a no-go zone and you know it... you just thought... you hoped, that you were wrong.*

I feel suddenly exhausted; physically, mentally... exhausted. I can't do this anymore, all the hiding, the lying, the avoiding... it's too much, and with all of the other emotions that come with pregnancy, I just can't continue. I bring my knees up to my chest, wrap my coat around them and lean against the back of the bench on my side. I rest my cheek on my knees, close my eyes, and let the tears fall, ignoring all of the people around me, not caring what they think. It's okay to forget and lose myself in my own world for a short while, like Clare said earlier.

I snuggle my coat around my face and feel the warm, salty tears spill over the bridge of my nose onto my knee. I'm so alone and I can't do anything about it until I tell Luke about the baby. I just wish I could pick up the phone and call my sister, tell her everything, tell her how much I need her and love her. I wish I could sit in Bea's living room with the girls, a Chinese take-away and Don Draper on TV, relaxing like we used to before I started avoiding it.

I wish I hadn't gone crazy at Luke back in the club, it's not his fault that I was getting carried away with wishful thinking, he's always been open and honest about his lifestyle and I knew it well, I should have just remembered that, before getting so comfortable in his company. *Sod this for a game of soldiers, pregnant emotional shit sucks, incredible orgasms or not.*

I listen to the footsteps and commotion all around me, clicky stilettos, the clonking of boots amongst the buzz of voices, it's quite calming - I can imagine this to be how a baby hears the world, from inside the womb. There's one noise that stands out though, and it's definitely boots, the rhythm is familiar, the depth of the noise, specific. It stops, right by me. I know who it is without even looking up. He has come to find me, and I need to apologise. I should hide my tears and pretend to be emotionally stable but I just don't care, the fatigue is too much and I can't do it, I can't act anymore.

I don't even bother to look up when he sits next to me and effortlessly lifts my curled body onto his lap. He puts one arm around me, the other hand resting on my head, and I sink into his warm, welcome body.

"You don't have to tell me what the problem is. You don't have to make me jealous - I can feel that way on my own. You don't have to *be* jealous - no one else does anything for me but you, and lastly, you don't have to be sad. Whatever it is, if you want to tell me, go ahead, if not? That's fine too, but know that I'm here; you're not alone, you're loved and cared for, more than you know, Tilly." His tone is warm and caring, but his words tip me over the edge of this emotional roller coaster, and I begin to sob against his chest.

"I... I'm... I..." I attempt to speak, a brief stutter of the word 'I' clearly all a twenty seven year old pregnant lunatic with psychotic tendencies can manage.

"Shh, I know there's more to it than what happened in there - when you're ready, you can tell me."

I wrap my arms tightly around his middle, thoroughly appreciative of his understanding. This man's parents must be pretty incredible people, to raise such an impeccably perfect human being, I do hope that they will feature in our child's life.

"Ah, the fur-ball has arms!" he says, cheerfully - making me smile.

"I'm sorry," I manage.

"Til, don't. You had reasons for what you said, I don't know what they are, but I know they are there and are valid. There's nothing going on with me and Lex, you know, we're as close as brother and sister; I tease her for being prudish and dorky, she tries to give back in return. We just don't see each other that way, Til, she's too straight-laced for me, and I'm too much for her. She likes quiet, submissive, typewriter types. Does that help clear it up?"

I nod - sniffing, my chest convulsing. It makes sense; Daniel and Luke are so close, he probably would be close with his sister, too. She doesn't look like a dork, she's gorgeous - in fact, and stylish, elegant, sophisticated... *Oh god, I'm remembering why I don't like her.* But I can see how she might have a few nerdy tendencies. I'm not even sure all of this was about her anyway - it was more the realisation that I've let myself get too far with a playboy, panic about his reaction to the news, and having no idea what the future holds for Wriggler and I.

"Do you want to go home, Princess?" he asks, brushing his chin against my hair. I simply nod against his chest, thinking how nice it would be, to be tucked up in bed right now, naked and warm in Luke's arms. I know everything he just said points to the reasoning that he isn't shagging other girls, but that doesn't mean we'll ever have anything more than another holiday fling.

"I'll call the car," he says as he stretches back to try and manoeuvre his mobile from his pocket.

"Actually, Luke, could we walk for a bit? I know it's freezing but I'd like to get some fresh air and then collapse in bed when I get home. It's not far is it?"

"No, about fifteen minutes or so. Will you be okay in your heels, baby?" he asks, surprising me, he's actually thinking of my inappropriate footwear.

"Uh huh," I nod, sniffing, still tightly pressed against his chest, "I'll be fine. If it gets too snowy, you can carry me until it's clear again."

"Sounds like a plan, shall we go now or aren't you done loving me yet?" he asks, and I giggle, although he's hit the nail on the head; *no, Luke, I'm not, but I have to be.*

"We can go," I say, straightening my legs out and turning to slide off his lap. As we both stand, he holds me in his arms and looks down at my face.

"Look at me," he says, his voice gentle, yet firm.

I do as he asks, trying to forget that I probably look scary as hell from all the crying. *Holy crap, you need to get a grip, all this crying... it's weird.*

He gently places both of his cold hands on my face and droops his head to lay a soft, simple kiss on my lips. He pulls back again and smiles at me, brushing my cheek with his thumb, staring deep into my eyes. "Okay?" he whispers.

I return his sweet smile and nod, wondering how on earth I will ever stop loving this beautiful man.

"Let's go." He reaches down to take my hand and slips the other in his pocket as we start the walk back to the house. It's a gentle, easy, calming stroll. The evening crisp and chilly, but so peaceful, even with the cars passing and people having fun around us. We don't talk, we just hold each other's hand and amble towards home, Luke occasionally lifting me effortlessly into a cradle-like embrace to avoid snowy patches, giving me a wonderful opportunity to study the face I seem to know better than my own.

When we enter the house, I kick my shoes off by the door and Luke follows, before lifting me again, and carrying me up the stairs to his room. He deposits me gently on the end of the bed, and immediately switches on his en-suite light, pulling the bathroom door to a little, and turning the main bedroom light off. He opens his curtains and the balcony door, before returning to me - not saying a single word - and lifts me to my feet.

The room is very dimly lit and romantic. He slips my coat off my shoulders, throwing it on the chair, and he grabs the bottom of my blouse, lifting it up - prompting me to raise my arms so that he can slip it off with ease. I should be covering up, I should be hiding the bump, but I see little point. He'll know tomorrow, anyway. It feels good to let go a little, hiding is so tiring. From the front, in this dim light - it's probably not even visible.

He steps back and removes his own jacket and shirt, slowly unbuttoning, one at a time. The sprinkling of light from the bathroom catching his tanned, ripped torso. *Amazing.* I undo my own fly, slipping my jeans down my legs, leaving me standing at the end of the bed in my black lacy underwear; the cold breeze from the balcony causing goose-pimples to spread rapidly over my bare skin.

Luke walks over to his drawers and opens two of them. When he returns, he turns me and unclasps my bra, gently pulling it from my body, before slipping one of his huge t-shirts over my head. I put my arms through and turn back to him, standing before me in jeans, his hat and nothing else.

"Sit down for a minute," he whispers, and as I do, he sinks to his knees on the floor, and lifts one of my legs. I smile as I see the big, warm ski socks in his hands as he gently holds my calves, one at a time, sliding the socks on. I don't think a man has ever put my socks on before, certainly not a hot, semi-naked cowboy. And just for a moment I can imagine him taking care of me when I'm big and fat and round - waddling about, ready to pop. I can see him as the doting husband, worrying about his wife, the devoted dad, tending to his baby... the perfect Luke, the one I could spend forever with, the one who want's to spend forever with me.

He stands again, once my feet are socked, and walks around the bed to turn it down. "Climb in, Princess," he says, his voice a gentle murmur. I tilt my head ever so slightly and look up at his face, wondering why he's being so gentle and calm, instead of ripping my clothes off and fucking me against some piece of furniture somewhere, as is the norm for us. I stand and walk over to him, pausing to look up into his eyes and I smile a little, before curling myself in a ball in his bed. It smells like us.

He walks back around to his side of the bed and I hear his belt unbuckle. I turn to face him and watch as he takes his trousers down, unveiling those mouthwateringly muscular thighs. He slips into the bed next to me and prompts me to raise my head so he can slide his arm beneath me. I snuggle into his warm flesh, my hands and cheek pressed up against his chest, his other arm wrapped tightly around me.

"What's happening?" I ask, quietly.

"We're going to bed..." he whispers.

"You're not going to flip me into a crazy position and fuck me senseless until we both collapse?"

He chuckles and squeezes me a bit tighter. "Not tonight, baby. You're tired, I'm tired, and after what happened at the club, I want to show you that there's so much more to how I feel for you, than sex. We don't need to fuck like rabbits for me to want to be with you, and I think you need me to demonstrate that."

Oh my good holy man above, he's getting deep - Luke, Mr Light-hearted Funny Man - is actually showing me his 'husband material' side. Well I never. And where exactly is he going with this? Appeasing my emotional instability so I don't go off on one again? Telling me he could be falling for me, too?

"Oh, okay. You could just tell me that and then shag me silly... I still owe you a blowy." I say, making light of it.

"I could, but I won't. I wouldn't feel like you'd truly believe me if I did that. Anyway - not everyone has amazing sex all day long you know, maybe we should start trying to be a bit more normal."

"No way!" I cry, swatting his chest with my fingertips, "I love our crazy sex schedule! While we're here and can, I'd like to stick to it, thanks..."

He laughs again before responding, "Okay, we'll continue to be abnormal, woodland creature types. But not tonight, I just want to sleep with you and hold you; take care of my Princess."

His Princess? Here we are again with the '*his*' thing. Have I missed an important conversation here? Does he see me as his girlfriend or what? Am I *his* because I'm currently his fuck buddy? No, that makes no sense. God, ending this and telling him about being prego is going to be the hardest thing I've ever done. I so desperately want to keep him, but this is all just so temporary, as all fuck-buddy relationships are.

"Okay, Lukey, whatever you say." I try to forget about everything, I'll just enjoy this calm before the storm. "Anyway - why did you leave the balcony door open?" I ask, curiously.

"I love the cold night air here, especially when we're warm inside; it's cosy. And I want you to seek my body for warmth when you sleep, I want you to get cold, and reach for me. That way, I can keep a tight hold of you all night."

Oh my god, I think I need to cry again. *Hold it in, wuss, don't you dare.*

CHAPTER 8
SUNDAY 23RD DECEMBER

Wriggler's moving... really moving, I can feel it so undoubtedly, and it has woken me up! I have read enough pregnancy books to know that this isn't that common, but I remember Gemma telling me that she felt Jack partying around in there really early on, too.

I stir more thoroughly to find myself spooning with Luke, his shallow, short breaths on my neck, his body pressed tightly against mine and our legs tangled together. His hands... his hands are... *oh my god,* they're there. He's touching it, he's holding her...oh my god, his large hands are totally covering my belly, the t-shirt scrunched up around my ribs.

I lie totally still, wondering what to do... if I wake him, he'll consciously feel it, if I don't and go back to sleep, he might wake first and then notice. She moves again, it's like I have a little lizard in there or something, exploring the wonders of my insides. Maybe she knows... maybe she can feel him... *Daddy*.

I picture his handsome face laying behind me on the pillow; his happy smile, his gorgeous dimples... dazzling blue eyes. *He's* the father of my baby. This beautiful man and I, *together*, made a tiny little life; the miniature person growing inside of me is a part of *him.* I still find the thought of it totally incredible, and somehow, the fact that his body has been able to give this precious bundle to me, makes me love him all the more, with all of my heart. Yet he still has no idea about any of it.

I continue to lie here, letting Wriggler indulge in the unknown attention of her dad, letting myself fantasise about how it could be. It feels so good, I wish I could stay like this all day, without even having to tell him anything. The cool breeze from the open balcony sweeps over our entwined bodies and I appreciate his want to hold me and keep me warm.

"Be with me..." His sleepy slur startles me, he's awake. I spin, quickly, turning to face him and cuddle into his front. His hands quickly settle on my bum and he pulls me closer, his eyes still closed and a slight smile on his face. Then I realise what he said. '*Be with him...*' Is he actually awake? Does he know he said that?

I snuggle against him and close my eyes, assuming he's asleep and talking gobbledegook. He's so warm and safe, his skin is so soft, I could never get tired of this.

"Hmm?" he asks, nudging me, squeezing a buttock.

I snap my head up to look at his face, his eyes are half open, a smile plays on his lips. "What?" I ask, wondering what's happening.

"Be with me... will you?" he says it again.

"I am with you..."

"You know what I mean. Will you be with me? Be mine? You know, the big 'g' word?" he says as the smile on his face grows.

I frown, "You mean your girlfriend?" I ask, stunned. He's actually asking me to be *with* him?

"Like, duh... yes, my girlfriend, I want to try being together, we make such a hot couple," he says, winking.

I push back from his chest and rest up on my elbow, looking at his face in disbelief. "You're serious? You want to be my boyfriend?"

"Wouldn't be more serious if I broke a fibula."

"But... you're... we're..."

"I'm a bad-boy, you live in England... all that shit?"

"Well... yeah?" I answer, in shock.

"Well, to start, being a bad-boy doesn't have to change - I know you love it," he grins, "but I can and have changed aspects of it. The women to start with. I have no interest in other women, Til, who could want more when they have you?" I can think of someone, but Scott and Luke are so different, it's not even a factor. "And, so you live in England? So what? We're not Danny and Bea, we can do long distance, can't we? You come to LA to see your sister - you can come to see see us both. I can come to London as often as I can to see you and hang out with Danny... we can talk every day and video call... *that* could be *good,*" he says, emphasising that last word with a wiggle of his eyebrows. "So, I don't see why we can't try, and if it works out, maybe you'll come and live in LA one day. You said you'd like to, back in September."

Oh my good god. I can't quite believe this. He wants to be with me. And it seems he has it all worked out. "How long have you been thinking about this?"

"Since you left LA, but I thought I wouldn't see you again, back then. So, when I found out we'd be here together for the holidays, I thought maybe there's a chance that we could try."

"Luke, I... I don't know what to say... You really want to give up your women?"

"I already have. I'll be honest with you, though, Til, after you left, when we left it as 'over' - I tried getting back to my old life."

"Okay... so tell me, what happened?" I want to know, it might hurt - but his honesty is really important to me, if we're ever going to try to be something...

"Okay. Well, I went after a girl... a lady. I did the usual - flirted, got her back to her place... and, well," he closes his eyes and grimaces, "I tried to fuck her."

I purse my lips and inhale, sharply. It hurts like a motherfucker. I can't be cross with him though, and surprisingly, I don't feel any hostility towards him at all, we weren't an item and had planned never to see each other again. Still hurts though. "Okay..."

He pushes up on his elbows and leans forward to kiss my neck, apologetically. "It was bad. I really needed to clear my head and that's how I've always done it. But it wouldn't work Til, I couldn't get it up." He looks at me with a horrified expression on his face. "It's the first time that's ever happened to me before. I didn't want her, I wanted you. I tried to think about you, because that was sure to make him stand to attention, but my mind wouldn't let me, every time I tried to picture your naked body in front of me, I kept seeing her, and it did nothing for me. It got awkward."

"Oh, shit... what did she say?"

"Well, I told her the truth. She only wanted fun and wasn't interested in anything more, so she was okay about it. In fact, she was very sweet, told me to come get you and never let you go."

Wow. This is bizarre, I'm actually feeling affectionately towards this woman who got naked with the love of my life.

"Okay. Well, that was honesty. Thank you. And I have to say, it pleases me that you can't get it up for anyone else... your meat is mine!" I say, giggling, trying to ease his worry about telling me.

"You're okay about that?"

"Well I can't say it makes me happy to think of you kissing and getting intimate with someone else..." I have to pause and shake the image from my head, "but I understand that it happened when we weren't doing anything together. We weren't even in contact then. And you didn't dip it in."

He laughs and pulls me down on his chest. 'No. I didn't. And I'm glad the 'problem' occurred, because I'd hate to have slept with someone else. I probably wouldn't have been able to go through with it, even if I had managed to get a woody. But I can tell you, every time I thought of you after that - I had no problem picturing your sweet-ass body and getting hard as nails. So..." he pauses briefly and continues softly, "how about you? Wanna tell me anything?"

He makes me smile; he's jealous. "No. I don't want to tell you anything."

"Oh. Well that's okay."

"Because there is nothing, Luke. I haven't done anything with anyone else, since you."

"Oh thank god. I couldn't bear that. So, what do you think? Wanna be my girl?"

I smile and stroke his face. "More than anything." That's not strictly true, more than anything - I want him to want to be a dad to our baby, but in light of these most recent events, I think I'll give it a little longer, let us get used to our new status, maybe he'll want me too much to leave. At least I know, if he does want the baby, that he's not with me just for that reason. My god, I hope he takes the news well, I can't lose him after this.

"But as much as I love having you as my boyfriend, I'm afraid I have to leave you. I am desperate for the loo."

He chuckles and swats my bum, releasing me, "Go pee, but you better come back here and show me what a good girlfriend you are."

"Totally," I say with an excited giggle, and kick back the covers to make my way to the en-suite.

Afterwards, we lay in bed together, wrapped in each other for a while before making long, sweet, incredible love. It feels so good to be able to call him my man for real, whilst having him worship my body the way he does. Of course I avoid any positions that show off my naked belly, but it's still amazing none-the-less.

We get out of bed at about eight, I hadn't realised it was so early but I'm glad we had time for all of this mornings activities; I had completely forgotten that today is the day that Luke is taking me out with his friends, Matt and Queenie. I seem to have some memory problems at the moment - must be another pregnant thing. I can't wait to see him in action on the slopes, it's going to be so hot. Luke throws on his tracksuit bottoms and we head downstairs for breakfast. I'm still wearing his t-shirt and socks, but I'm decent.

As we approach the bottom of the stairs, holding hands, we slow as we see the carnage before us. *Crikey!*

"Wow, guess we missed a great night!" Luke says amused. We stroll slowly over the the centre of the living room where we find bottles and bottles of champagne all over the place, glasses knocked over, packets of crisps everywhere. Bea and Daniel are fast asleep together on one sofa, wrapped in each other, Bea with one hand pressed on the centre of Daniel's face, squashing his nose. It's a hilarious picture.

We find Clare and Oliver passed out on the floor in front of the fireplace, they're not hugging or anything, they're laying in opposite directions, but their heads are together, up close to each other and Oliver has his arm stretched in front of him, alongside Clare's body. Alexia is hanging off another sofa on her front, and a man I vaguely recognise from last night is fast asleep, sitting on the floor, his head resting on Alexia's thigh.

"How long do you think they've been asleep? And who's he?" I ask, amused by this comical scene. This would have been me, back in the pre-Wriggler days, and now look,

Miss Sophisticated herself; Alexia, hanging head first off the sofa, her hair a crazy mess, crisps stuck to her clothes and a strange man dribbling on her thigh.

Clare and Bea are just as bad, I think I can even hear Bea snoring. They're going to feel like shit when they wake up.

"Not long by the looks of it, and this is Seb - a friend of mine. Let's take some pictures and leave them to it. Great blackmail material." He gets his phone from his pocket and starts to snap a few shots of the hilarious scene. I bet Alexia will hate this!

We laugh again and make our way to the kitchen where the loyal Pam is slaving away, whisking up a pancake batter.

"Morning beautiful," Luke says, smoothly.

"Good morning, you two. Wow, considering the scene in there, you look surprisingly fresh."

"Yeah, we came home early, last night. We're responsible like that."

"You just can't keep your hands off each other..." she sighs, "young love... breakfast?"

"Yes please." I say, excited about whatever Pam has in store for us today, ignoring the 'love' comment.

"I have been pre-briefed by Daniel that Miss Hart likes pancakes and strawberries, so I'm making chocolate chip pancakes with Maple syrup and fruit salad, and bacon and eggs. You can help yourselves once I finish the pancakes.

"Sounds amazing, thank you." I respond.

"My girlfriend here got that right, it sounds damn good. Thanks Pammy." He looks at me and winks, his excited smile the cutest thing I've ever seen.

We eat the delicious breakfast together and as I finish up, Luke waiting patiently beside me, his hands on my thigh, Clare stumbles into the kitchen looking horrendous. "Oh dear god..." she says, putting her hand to her forehead, steadying herself as she loses her balance. Luke's rushes over to her and holds her arms to guide her over to the stool next to me at the breakfast bar.

"Here, sit there." he says, picking her up and putting her down on it.

She grabs hold of his shoulders in surprise, "wha-oa!"

I giggle, it's so funny to see her like this, Clare *never* gets a hangover. "Not well, chicken?" I ask sympathetically, and she whimpers in response, leaning forward to drop her forehead on my shoulder. I stroke her hair and giggle again. "Oh, poor Clare."

"What is this? Horrible... just horrible... do I have a bug?" she mumbles, amusingly.

Luke steps over and rests his hands on her shoulders, gently massaging, looking at me and smiling in amusement.

"Oh... ohhh..." Clare moans, "Never... ever, ever stop. I think I love you more than she does right now..."

Oh my god... we haven't quite got to that bit yet! Luke simply looks at me with a huge grin and a raise of his eyebrows.

"No, doll, you don't have a bug. This is what we call a minging hangover, Clare, and you're suffering for once. But you have probably only had about two hours sleep; if you drink a bucket load of water and tuck yourself into bed, you'll feel much better later," I say, feeling for her.

"Really? Oh god, I hope so, I feel like I've ingested something poisonous," she murmurs, her eyes still closed.

"That'll be the alcohol, darling."

She grimaces and raises one hand to cover her ear, "Oh dear god, shh... don't... too much Champ... oh god, I can't say the word..."

I laugh again, this is so unlike her. "Go to bed, sleep it off, you'll be okay later."

"Yes..." she says, sliding off her stool and dropping straight to her hands and knees, crawling out of the kitchen, "night night..."

~~~~~~~

When I finish, we make our way up the stairs to change. Half way up, we're greeted by Clare, fast asleep, sprawled up the second flight. We both stop and look down at her, amused, before Luke picks her up effortlessly and carries her. We part ways as I enter my room and he takes Clare to hers, agreeing to meet downstairs in half an hour to head out.

After my amazingly hot shower, I dry myself off and as I walk over to the wardrobe to get my ski clothes, I catch a glimpse of my naked body in the full length mirror on the way. *Holy fuckaroony.* How the hell has that happened? My bump has suddenly sprouted - it's a proper-proper bump-bump.

Blimey, there's no way I can hide *that*! I read that this can happen, that you can suddenly pop out in front like you've swallowed a melon. I'm not *massive*, but I am very clearly impregnated, and I am going to have to tell Luke about this very, very soon, because he will notice this, for sure.

I stand still, gazing at my body's fresh little development. I hold the bump, turn to see it from all angles, wondering how much it has changed since the fifteen week stage just a few days ago. In a couple of days, I'll be able to check to see what happens at sixteen weeks. Wow, and just four weeks until I'm half way there. I feel another pang of guilt. How can I keep this from him? I love him, he wants to give up everything his life is about, to be *my* boyfriend, how can I be so dishonest? *Because you're a selfish bitch, Tilly.*

I realise I've been standing, staring at myself for far too long and need to be downstairs, sharpish. I throw on my underwear and ski stuff, noting how tight my ski trousers seem since I last wore them, the day before yesterday! My tight black polo neck jumper really clings. Oh this is going to be hard work. I put on some light make-up, my jacket, and tie my hair in a ponytail, covering my ears stylishly with a chunky, knitted headband, my fringe neatly escaping from the front.

Downstairs, Luke greets me with the usual compliments and one of his dramatic embraces, throwing me backwards across his knee and kissing me passionately, making us both laugh, as always. The others - minus Clare - are all still in the lounge, pretty much the same as they were before, only Bea's hand is no longer pressed up against Daniel's nose, instead they are tangled together, faces touching, affectionately.

Once we're ski-suited and snow-booted, we leave the house, Luke collecting his board from the verandah en-route to the car. God, he looks so damned sexy like this, I'm pretty sure that once I see him attached to the board - goggles down, I'm going to want him to do it to me, just like that, somewhere deserted. *Ooh... kinky... leg restraints...*

"It'll probably take about ten minutes to get there, you set?" he asks as he climbs into the car next to me, having put his board in the boot.

"Yep, so tell me where we're going."

"We're headed to Aspen Highlands, where Matt, Queenie and I will do Highland Bowl. Are you sure you're okay with staying at the restaurant on your own?"

"Yes, please don't worry about me. I can't wait to see you snowboarding! So, what happens at Highland Bowl?"

The huge smile on his face speaks volumes, he is so excited about this. "Well, it's an off-piste adventure and it demands serious physical fitness, because you've got to hike to the top before you can come down. There's an epic energy up there, when you reach the top it can get quite emotional, I've done it many times, but it still knocks my socks off when I get up there, the three-sixty views are unbelievable. It's for extreme skiers and snowboarders, not for the faint hearted; it can be quite hairy. I wish I could take you to experience it."

I love how passionate he is about these things, he goes so much deeper than you could ever expect when you first meet him. He is a great big onion, with hundreds of amazing layers... I especially like the cowboy layer, too. "That sounds amazing! How long does the hike take?"

"Don't worry, I won't leave you too long, I think we'll cheat and use the snowcat today, to save time, it takes us about a third of the way up, to the first access gate, and then we'll hike the rest. The hike should take about a half hour. The ride down is the best fun, I can't come to Aspen and not come here a couple times - it's super-steep and as the traffic is low up there, the freshies last.'

"Freshies?"

"Yeah, like soft, new powder, it's freakin' fantastic."

"Sounds it, I'm excited for you."

He glances at me briefly with a beautiful smile, before turning his eyes back to the road. "Thank you, baby. It is fantastic fun, but I'm going to look forward to getting back down to the restaurant to see my girl. You better have a hot kiss waiting for me."

"Of course I will, I'd have more hot stuff waiting for you - if I could."

He turns to smile again, and winks at me before continuing with details of the day. "So we'll park up and head up on the Deep Temerity lift to meet Matt and Queenie, drop you at Merry-Go-Round, which is midway between the base area and the Bowl. You should like it, it has fantastic food and a bar."

"Great, I might sit outside, so I can see you coming."

"You don't have to be sitting outside for that, hot-lips..." he says cheekily, making me giggle, and we continue the short journey comfortably.

We park up at the base of the mountain and head over to the ski lift. The mountain in front of me looks absolutely beautiful, like most of the mountains here. Aspen is simply a stunning place to visit. Luke clips one of his feet onto his board and pushes himself to the lift with one leg. He looks like such a pro, and it's hot. We sit on the three-seater lift, and pull the bar down to secure ourselves.

Luke holds my hand in his as I take a long, appreciative look around me; it's so picturesque, and so quiet - only the smooth slush of skiers below us, gliding elegantly down the slope. I wish I was skiing with them.

"You love it out on the slopes, don't you?" he asks.

I nod, still captivated by the perfect, white brilliance of it all.

"I don't understand, if you like it so much - why don't you come out with me and take it slowly? I don't want to push you, Princess - and I wouldn't, but I can see how much you love this environment, I can see how much you want to join everyone. I'll take care of you, make sure you're okay."

I could just die. I love him so much, he's so unbelievably kind and thoughtful. I get the sudden urge to tell him right now; he needs to know! "Luke, I really... I'm... the thing is..." I pull my hand out of my thick ski glove and rest it on his handsome face as I stare into his perfect, bright blue eyes... and he interrupts.

"It's okay, Til, I know, you don't have to explain. But, one day - I hope you'll let me bring you out here again and get you back in the swing of things. I want to share this place with you so much."

Damn it. Although, in hindsight - that was probably a good thing - nobody wants to freak out on a chair lift. And how bloody sweet of him, I hope he'll *want* to bring me back again, one day. "I'd like that." I respond, gazing at his face.

He leans towards me and kisses me slowly, "You're the most beautiful girl I've ever known - I love every little bit of you," he whispers, and kisses me again. My heart pounds in my chest as his lips touch mine, my eyes remain wide open, staring at his face... he didn't mean that in *that* way, did he? Just hearing the words 'I love' come out of his mouth turns me into a giddy mess, even if that's not how he meant it. So I make light of it, as we do.

"See - I told you you're totally in love with me," I say against his mouth with a cheeky grin, and he pauses, staring at me, into my eyes - my soul.

"I am, Princess," he says, quietly, looking my face up and down, taking in my every feature, "I totally am in love with you."

Oh my god! Oh my god! Holy crap-nuggets, oh my...
"Uh... you... uh..." I stutter, totally thrown and utterly overwhelmed.

He chuckles and holds my face in his big gloved hands, "Yes, I, uh, I, uh..." he says laughing, "I love you, like, really, *really* love you."

My mouth drops open and a smile forces its way through, "I... wow, I wasn't expecting... wow."

He simply shrugs his shoulders, almost apologetically and tilts his head to the side, "That okay?"

I laugh, still shocked, "Of course that's okay. I... well, I... I love you, too," I say timidly, a bit apprehensive about admitting it finally, I've been holding it in long enough.

"I had hoped you might. Well, would ya look at this, the fuck buddies have only been an item a couple hours and they love each other already. We better get your finger sized up..." he says with a grin and I smile at his joke. I wonder how this changes things - maybe he really won't want to leave, when I tell him. *Oh, but what if he does?* Now that I know he loves me... I'd be even more broken.

"You really love me?" he asks, vulnerability pouring through his expression by the bucket load.

I smile and stroke his precious face again, skimming over his dimples. "Yes, I love you. I have done for a while, but was trying to ignore it and get over you."

"Well you don't have to anymore. I fell in love with you way back, I think I really knew about it when you were leaving LA - when we went for brunch with Bea and Danny. I saw you feeling their heartbreak, looking at them with such sadness and compassion, I wanted you to feel that way about us."

"I was. I just hid it well. I didn't want to admit my feelings to anyone, not even to myself, and especially not to you."

"Hold up - you told me you hadn't fallen in love with me, the other day, when you were explaining why it all got 'weird'."

"I know. I wasn't about to tell you then either. Luke, you have to understand, I know you, I know your life, it's hard to believe that you could give up what you know to be a boyfriend..." *...and a Dad, but we'll get to that later.*

"I understand that, but I want nothing more than to give all of that up, for you. I need you to be confident about us, and not worry that I'm going to be bad when you're not around. I'll be bad *with* you, but that's where it stops."

"Okay. I'll probably have a few worries when you're working with your women though - knowing what you used to do with them, I suppose I'll have to try and get used to it."

"I don't have to do that anymore, baby. I did it because I enjoyed that life. I've got you now, I don't want it. I'll stop with the trainer thing."

He'll do something else? Just like that? "You can't just change careers because you got a girlfriend *today*, what will you do for money?"

He smiles, knowingly as we reach the top of the lift and raise the bar, stepping off the seat before it swings around to descend again. "We'll talk about it later, sugar-lips, that's not something you should be worrying about." He unclips his foot from the board and picks it up, taking my hand, walking towards the restaurant. It's a large, one story building in the shape of a wide, isosceles triangle, with a glass frontage.

"Where would you like to sit?" he asks as he wedges his board in the snow, leaning it against the rack, "Inside or out?"

"I'll sit inside for now, I'm a bit cold. Maybe I can get a place by the window..."

He strides inside, confidently, finding me a table by the window immediately. "This okay?"

I smile, "Perfect, thank you. Go and enjoy your adventure, I'll see you later."

"I'm not done yet, sit and I'll be back," he says before walking away from the table.

I frown, but settle myself, taking my jacket off and staring out into the pure white morning. *He's in love with me.* He has just told me that he loves me, on a ski lift, totally out of the blue. I'm struggling to believe it to be honest - we're just fuck buddies... Well, I suppose we're not anymore, he's my boyfriend and I'm his girlfriend and we actually love each other. Oh my god, this is fucking crazy! Neither of us were looking for *this*!

"Hey, Princess, here you go," Luke says, surprising me, as he places a steamy cup of hot chocolate in front of me.

I look down at the drink and back up at his face, his expression totally casual.

"Thank you, darling, I could have got this myself."

"Pah," he says, waving his hand, "what are boyfriends for, huh? You want a snack, too?" He bends down, resting one hand on the table and the other on the back of my chair.

"No, thank you. This is great."

He slowly moves his face to mine and rubs our noses together as he whispers, "I'll be thinking of you sitting here, waiting for me so you can tell me that you love me again - the whole time I'm up there."

I smile broadly and look into his twinkling blue eyes, "Is that right?" I ask, brushing my lips against his, "I think you'll be picturing me totally naked, except for a pair of big socks, bending over for you in front of the fireplace."

"Holy fuck, I like your visual better - but while you're bending over, naked, I still want you to tell me that you love me again."

Oh my god, he's so cute! I giggle, "No problem, big-boy. I bet you're hard already, aren't you?"

"Too fucking hard - wanna feel?" he asks, flashing his dimples and winking.

"Dude! So good to see you!" Matt disturbs our intimate moment, calling out from behind him. Luke immediately stands to turn and greet him and they share another slap and man-hug.

"Hey, Tilly, is it?" Matt asks, leaning forward to take my hand, and I nod. "Great to see you again, Tilly, this is Queenie, my hotdog of a wife," he says as he turns back and waits for her to finish greeting Luke. *Hotdog? Is that a compliment?*

"Babe, this is Tilly, she's... uh, she's with Luke,"

"She's my girlfriend, Queen," Luke says, rolling his eyes.

"Hey," she says stepping towards me and stretching out her arm for me to shake her hand. She's so pretty with gorgeous, long, strawberry blonde hair, a welcoming smile and... wow, gigantic boobs! Blimey, she's hot. This is the reason men hit the slopes in Aspen, clearly. And they're *married?* I'd have never guessed, they seem so... cool, I suppose I imagine all snowboarders to be stereotypically wild at heart and carefree. I don't really think about their regular lives off the slopes.

"Hi, Queenie, great to meet you, I've heard lots about you."

"Good to meet you, too, and feel free to call me Kat, most people do. It's great to see Luke with a proper girlfriend at last."

Yep, and that's me! He chose me! "Luke's really looking forward to heading out with you today, I'm sorry I can't join you."

"It's cool, I'll get to know you a bit better when we get back down," she says with a smile and warm, understanding tone. I wonder what Luke has told them.

"Shall we head out?" Luke asks as he slips his gloves back on and grabs his hat.

"Sure, catch you later, Tilly." Queenie/Kat says, smiling before she slips her hand into Matt's and walks outside.

Luke strolls over to me and bends to kiss my lips, "I'll try to go fast, don't go anywhere."

"Oh, I won't, and take your time, enjoy it, I really want you to."

"Thanks, Til. See you soon. Enjoy your hot chocolate," he says, picking up the cup and taking a cheeky slurp.

"Cheeky! Off you go..." I say as he gives me one more frothy, chocolatey kiss and disappears around the corner and out of the door.

I watch through the window as they get themselves sorted and head out towards the snowcat. I sigh, trying to take in the many events of today... and it's not even lunch time! I cannot believe I have a boyfriend, but the biggest, most amazing revelation today is, of course, his declaration of love.

This has to make things different, I mean, I'm not saying this will make him *want* to have kids with me right now - but if he loves me, surely he won't want to leave me because of this. No, we can do this together... he'll want that, he'll love me enough to get over the initial shock and learn to adapt his life to become part of our baby's life. Even if we're not living together straight away, as long as he wants to be an active dad, we can work it all out... can't we?

It doesn't feel like I've been sitting here for long at all when I see the three of them returning, looking like they're having fantastic fun together, gliding down that long slope ahead of the building. Oh, I'm so envious, I'd love to be out there with them right now; but I have this melon to think about, and as much fun as it looks, I'd rather feel comfortable knowing that I'm not putting Wriggler in any unnecessary danger.

I step outside, leaving my scarf, gloves, and drink on the table, and stand to wait for them to get back to the restaurant, watching, utterly transfixed on my hot bad-boy. He's just so fucking edible right now, I never knew how much snowboarding turns me on.

They all approach, laughing and joking, and as Matt and Kat slow to detach their boards, Luke glides all the way over to me and stops directly in front of me, his arms hanging down by his sides, his knees bent, facing me, panting. His face is covered by his goggles and hat but when he smiles, I melt. He beckons me with his finger and I step forward to meet him.

"Hey, beautiful. Miss me?" he asks as he holds my arms and pulls me towards him for a gorgeous, long, lust filled kiss.

"Uh huh," I mumble into his mouth, in answer, as he takes it to the next level, holding the back of my head and pashing me right here in front of the restaurant, in full view of everyone. *So good...*

He continues for quite a while, not giving a crap about who's watching. Me neither. It's just so slow and deep and incredible. He pulls away slowly and my eyes open a fraction, the brightness surrounding us, dazzling my vision. I focus on his perfect face, remembering for just a split second that underneath this pure skin - are damaged, imperfect bones. *That'll never happen to him again, he'll never go through that again - not while he's with me.*

"I missed you, too. It felt like I was up there forever."

"You enjoyed it though?" I ask.

"Sure did, broadway!"

"Broadway? That means good? God, I'm going to have to learn this one day, do you have a snowboarder's dictionary, by any chance?"

He chuckles and squeezes me, "No, but I'm sure I can get one."

"What are you going to be like when I'm back in the UK? If you missed me for that short period of time?" I ask, smiling.

"Hmm, yeah, we should probably talk about our options later."

Matt and Kat stroll over to join us. "Dude, you were tearin' it up!" Matt says, high fiving Luke.

"That was the front, except for that damn fruit-booter cutting me off, did you see that? Ass-wipe." Luke replies, making me giggle, I have absolutely no clue, what-so-ever.

"Let's go in," Kat says, "I could eat a damn horse."

"Cool, I gotta take a freak-a-leak so I'll see you back at the table." Matt responds before grabbing his wife by the buttock and pressing her up against him, giving her a laughing kiss, before disappearing inside.

What a totally cool couple.

We have a great lunch together, Matt, Luke and Kat talking about their fun hike and how incredible the 'fresh pow' is, up in the bowl today; Matt telling me how he and Kat met - working together, teaching kids to ski - and explained that she's his 'Queen of the Mountain', hence the nickname, which seemed to stick with most of their snowboarding crew.

I don't delve too much into their personal lives, we don't have much time for that while we eat, but sitting there, next to Luke, watching this great couple interact and finish each other's sentences... it's insightful. That's what we could have; Luke and I could be like this in a few years time. If we last, I hope we manage to keep the spark going like these two seem to have.

The boys decide to board the rest of the way down, after Luke very sweetly double checks if I'd mind, which of course, I don't. Kat, or Queenie - which seems to come so much more naturally after listening to the boys calling her that all day - says she'll take the lift back down with me; keep me company.

As we sit down, and lower the bar, I thank her. "You really didn't have to come down on the lift, I'd have been okay on my own, but thank you for keeping me company."

"Hey, it's cool, I wanted to. I'd like to get to know you a little better, Matt and I think the world of Luke, he's a good guy."

I nod and smile, unable to hide my affection for him, "I think so. He isn't what he seems on the outside."

"True story! We went to LA on vacation one year and stayed with him - boy, he has so many different lifestyles. I'm a mountain chick, all the way, and that'll never change, but Luke can be whatever he wants - he is a natural here and most would probably think he's born and bred, but in LA, he was the total California fitness guy."

"It's true, but I think that's one of the things I like most about him, he's just so... vibrant, and energetic -

enthusiastic to experience everything to the max, wherever he is, whatever he's doing - he has to live it, breathe it." I say, smiling like an excited, loved-up teenager. "So, did you enjoy your trip to LA?"

"We sure did, we took our little boy to Disneyland, he'd wanted to go for so long, so we surprised him for his birthday. He loved it, and he adores Luke, so staying with him was almost as exciting as Disneyland."

They have a child? Wow, you'd never know, I am really surprised, they're so... so, cool! *And Luke is great with their son... interesting.* "Oh, wow, I didn't know you had children."

"Just the one, Logan, our pride and joy."

"You two seem so... free-spirited, I hadn't pictured you with a child. That's lovely, how old is he?"

"He's seven. We didn't plan to have a baby - he was a beautiful surprise. We'd been together for a year at that point."

"Oh right, but you were both happy about it?"

"Definitely, I was worried about how Matt would take the news, we were still young and hadn't been together all that long, but he was so excited, I can still picture his face now. He took the worry away instantly and made it perfect."

"That's sweet, so did you get married after he was born?"

"Yeah, we got married 2 years after he was born, the little dude walked me down the aisle with a little bobble hat and ski goggles on his head."

"So cute! Don't take this the wrong way, but you two still act so 'new' together, you seem so in love, you've still got the spark. That doesn't seem to last long for a lot of couples with kids."

"It's true, I think the stress can get to people, but Matt and I have always taken time for ourselves too, to keep it strong; we have sex, like, *all* the time."

Oh my god, I wasn't expecting that... "Oh! I'm so happy for you," I say with a laugh, hoping she'll 'get' my sense of humour, and luckily, she laughs.

"You gotta work at it from both sides. As long as he always makes you feel wanted and special, and you always tell him how much you appreciate and love him - you'll keep something alive. It's not the same for everyone, but I like to take care of myself - make sure he has good reason to still think I'm hot, even after all these years. He thinks I look hot in a potato sack, but I want to feel at my best for me, and for him. If you think you're beautiful and sexy, then he will too."

She really has no idea how much advice she's giving me here, I'm looking at her pretty, happy face, listening to her talk so lovingly about her man and little boy, and it's giving me so much hope. I can still be me, I don't have to become someone else to be a good mum - Luke can be the Luke I love, and still be a great dad, and the fact that Matt took the news well, gives me just that little bit of a boost. I can do this, I can tell him. It's not going to be as bad as I think. We could be just like Matt and Queenie, we just need to put into it what they do.

"I have a great best friend who helps me out sometimes, she takes Logan now and again so that Matt and I can have some time to be a couple. She's got him now, he skis so she takes him out on the slopes and he loves it."

"That's great, you sound like you've really worked out how to love life."

"We do. We have a great life and I couldn't be more thankful for that. I love my boys more than anything."

My crazy emotions are playing up again - I just stare at her like a bloody idiot, welling up. I swear, the advantages to being pregnant in the bedroom are fantastic - but this emotional crap is fucking ridiculous.

"Hey, you're going to be fine. Luke loves you so much, he couldn't stop talking about you up there, it's so great to see him like this. Honestly, you're the best thing to happen to him in a long time. I can tell you're worrying about stuff..." she says, pausing and nodding a little. *What? Does she know? How could she? No... she can't... can she?* "but you need to relax and go with it, it's not going to be as hard as you think. He'll be perfect."

Okay, now I'm completely baffled. She sounds like she's talking to me about the baby - but she can't possibly know that I'm pregnant... can she? Am I that fat?! Oh my god. *No, no, no.* I can't be - or my friends and Luke would definitely know about it too, I mean come on, I've been having sex with the man, if Queenie can know just by spending a couple of hours with me, there's no way he wouldn't know. *Ooh, what if he does know and is just waiting for me to tell him?* No. That's ridiculous. Just take what she's saying as relationship advice and stop over analysing.

"Thank you for the advice, I will really take that with me. I'd love to be as happy as you two, ten years down the line."

"It's cool, I'm only telling it how it is for us. You two are going to be great together, for a long time to come, I'm certain of it."

And just like that, the seven minute ride down the mountain is over and we're approaching the boys at the bottom of the lift.

"It was great talking to you, I hope we'll get a chance to meet up again."

"Me too, today was fun," she says as she lifts the bar and we both lurch off the chair as it moves around to collect some other people going up. Once we're out of the way, she hugs me. "You'll be great together, I know it," she says, reassuringly, and I unexpectedly hug her back tightly, holding on to her, so grateful for her support. I needed to hear that so much.

CHAPTER 9
SUNDAY 23RD DECEMBER (CONT.)

After joining the boys, we set off separately, Matt and Queenie - to go and collect the 'dude' as Matt calls him, and Luke and I to the car to head home. I have a really hard time trying to keep my hands off him in the car, I can't stop looking at him, knowing that he feels the same way. Not to mention the fact that he looks so fucking hot - his hair a mess, his face windblown and gorgeous. *Mmm.*

I sit back in my seat, just gazing at him as he drives, we're both clearly tired, although for very different reasons, so we're happily silent, enjoying the journey. "You were so extra-specially sexy today, Lukey," I say quietly, resting my head against the seat back and bringing my knees to my chest, curling up. "I want you to kiss me."

His gorgeous smile absolutely blows me away, it makes my belly flutter wildly and goose bumps run all over my skin. I am so overcome with love for this man, I think I would do anything for him. Move to LA? In a heartbeat.

He slows and it takes a moment for me to realise that he's parking up at the side of the road.

"Where are we going?" I ask, still totally mesmerised by his splendour.

"Home. But you want me to kiss you..." he unclips his seatbelt and leans over to me, cupping my jaw with his warm hand, his lips brushing mine as he gazes, fixedly, into my eyes, "and what my girl wants, my girl gets, especially when I want it more." I begin to smile as he presses his delicious, soft lips to mine. His eyes close and I see his brow furrow slightly, before I follow suit, getting lost in this exquisite moment of tenderness - love.

He brings his other hand to my face and holds it gently, but firm enough for me to know he won't let go without a fight. I wrap my hands tightly around the back of his neck, his tongue gently caressing mine, our kiss thoroughly passionate... but not about sex.

He slows and gently moves away, still clutching my face. "Tilly, I'm not going to lose you again. It has taken me thirty one years to feel this and I will die before I give it up."

I smile, wanting to burst into tears but managing to control it somewhat. "I so love you. It feels weird to come out and say it, but I really, really do. I never thought I'd have this, I've never felt like this before."

"I know, me neither. I think I haven't settled down for a reason, because I was waiting for you. There's not one single woman that I have ever met - and you know I've met a few - that comes anywhere even close to you. No one that I would even consider spending my life with - except you."

I giggle, quietly, shyly. "You'd consider spending your life with me?"

He smiles one of his huge, dimply smiles again, "I'm *gonna* spend my life with you. Starting right about..." he looks at his watch, "now!" I laugh, looking into his warm, kind eyes. "So kiss me and make it official," he says, pursing his lips, and I do just that.

"I'm sorry about last night, Luke," I say, pulling away, "I went crazy and it wasn't fair on you. These feelings are just so new to me and I didn't think that you felt the same. I didn't know how to deal with it and then... the ugliness occurred."

"It's okay, I get it. But don't ever feel insecure like that with me, sweet-cheeks, okay? You're my little love-bunny and you're going to have to get used to it," he says, kissing my neck, making me laugh... yet again.

We must have stayed in that spot for at least half an hour, talking and kissing, in our own world. It was a rare moment where neither of us was thinking about sex... okay, okay, so I was definitely looking forward to getting home and ripping off his skiwear, but it wasn't *about* sex, it was just us, talking about us... being 'us'.

When we arrive back at the house, walking through the door arm in arm, we are greeted by the entire gang looking a whole lot more civilised than they were this morning. They're sitting in the living room, surrounding the fireplace on the sofas, having afternoon tea and cake, put on - no doubt - by impeccable Pam.

"Hey, you're all looking a whole lot healthier than you were this morning... Dan, how's your nose?"

I giggle and Daniel looks at Luke quizzically, "My nose? What happened to my nose?"

"Ah, nothing, just your little wifey trying to rearrange it for you."

"What?" Bea asks, totally confused and I laugh out loud as they frown at each other, questioningly.

"Hey, Seb, so you managed to peel your face from Lex's thighs, huh?"

Alexia's face is a picture, she sits up straight and tucks her hair behind her ears, "Oh my god Luke, stop this, we get it, we were drunk." She looks really pale, she must have a serious hangover. They all must. Euw, the thought of it makes me want to be sick. I've no idea how I'll ever drink again, morning sickness was like the worst hangover ever, non stop for two weeks. Luckily mine was short-lived, I've no idea how women who have nine months of it do it; you'd never have more than one child! *I wonder how many we'll have? No Tilly! One step at a time - my god, who am I?*

Luke laughs out loud, "You sure were, and I got evidence, too," he says teasingly, to moans and grumbles galore. He takes off his outer layers and jumper, his arms delightfully on display out of the sleeves of his fitted white t-shirt that stretches across his pecks perfectly. *Sweet Jesus, I'd like to lick those nipples right now...*

As I subconsciously gawk at his impressive torso, he steps over to me and starts to remove my scarf and hat. I smile, enjoying his attention. He drops them on the side table nearby, and starts to unzip my coat. I immediately stop him. "No, it's fine, I'm not hot." I say, worried about exposing the melon in the tight polo-neck I'm wearing.

"No, but you will be in here," he says, continuing.

"No, no, I'm fine, thank you," I say, grabbing hold of his hands and clutching them together, in front of me.

"Til, you'll be baking in here, the fire's so hot," Clare says, and a rush of anger floods through me, making me want to scream at her.

"Clare, I'm not a fucking child. Thank you."

Bea's head swings around and they both stare at me like I've grown two heads. "Tilly!" she says, shocked.

"S-sorry... I, I just..." Clare stutters as her cheeks flush pink, clearly embarrassed, and I hate myself.

"Sorry Clare. I didn't mean to bite your head off, sorry. I'm fine." I say, hoping the room will ease back into conversation and stop staring at me for losing my temper.

Luke frowns at me and leads me to Bea and Daniel's sofa to sit down. Pam brings in an extra couple of tea-cups for us and as the room starts to make noise again, discussing something to do with the Aspen property market, Luke looks down into my face and whispers, "What was that about, Princess?" He looks concerned.

"Nothing, I just know when I need to take my own coat off. I'm fine."

"Okay, okay," he says, raising his eyebrows, and nodding, dropping the subject. Geez, this is getting tough.

I already feel a wave of heat engulf my torso as Luke leans forward to pour the tea, I'm fucking boiling. I'll have to go and change before I start sweating by the bucket load. Just as I sit forward to stand, Luke sits back again and puts his arm around my shoulders... *oh god man, don't make me any hotter than I already am...*

"Hey, can I get your attention for a minute..." he says, and I just know what he's about to do. I'm totally for it, but couldn't he wait until I change into something a bit cooler?

"I am the most excited dude in Aspen right now, because this hot piece of ass sitting next to me has agreed to be my girl. Yep, that's right, Luke Summers is off the market, tell the papers, I am totally in love with one Tillifer Burton."

Another heatwave tortures me as my excitement at his words bubbles over. I giggle. "Tillifer?" I ask, laughing.

"I think it has got a nice ring to it, Tillifer..." he says, testing his new name for me.

I shake my head and smile.

"Oh my god, that's amazing!" Bea cries, "Although totally expected; you two are *so* made for each other. So you love each other?" she asks, grinning like a cheshire cat, "I knew it!"

"Yep," Luke replies, "I love the ass off this girl and I can finally say it."

I grin, ignoring the beads of sweat growing on my forehead; getting up to change right now would be incredibly bad form. "It's true, I love him like mad, but I'm sure you all knew that already."

Clare winks at me with a smile and scrunches up her nose, she's probably got goose pimples, she loves a bit of romance.

Alexia surprises me by standing and stepping over to us, bending to kiss my cheek and then hugging Luke. "It's about time you told her, I'm so happy for you guys," she says, beaming. *Okay, so my explosion last night was totally unfounded.*

Clare follows suit and kisses Luke on the cheek before bending to hug me. *Oh dear lord, please don't add other people's body heat to my discomfort.*

She wraps her arms around my shoulders and presses her cheek against mine. *So. Frigging. Hot!* She pulls away slightly and looks directly into my eyes, frowning. Her eyes look up to my forehead, and back down again to my eyes. Oh shit, I'm sweating. "Til," she whispers, "go and get changed now, this isn't good for you; passing out won't do either of you any good."

She stands to go back to her seat and I'm left wondering who, exactly, she's referring to by 'either of us'. Am I just making everything about Wriggler today, or do these people actually know my secret? Because this just seems too weird.

Luke looks at me with a big smile and leans in to kiss me on the lips. "I'm going to go and put something more comfortable on, I'll be back in a minute." I say, and stand to make a move upstairs. Bea holds her hand out to me and I take it, looking down at her, everyone else chatting amongst themselves. "Love you, I knew you'd work through it. I want to know all the details, okay?"

I smile, I love her so much, too. "Totally, we need a little girly time."

"Oh yeah, do you need to do any shopping? Me and Clare are going to hit the shops tomorrow for some last minute, Christmas Eve purchases, wanna come?"

Sounds wonderful. "Oh yay! I'm there, it'll give Lukey-boy a chance to buy something fabulous for his incredible new girlfriend..." I say loudly, winking over at the hunk.

When I get upstairs, I grab some clothes from my room and go straight to Luke's, closing the door behind me and heading for the balcony. I open both doors wide and start to strip off, I am so fucking hot, you could fry an egg on any part of my body right now. When I get down to my underwear and socks, I stand outside and let the freezing air engulf me. I close my eyes and drop my head back, resting my hands on the melon, as she has a little dance in there.

A couple of minutes pass as I stand, enjoying being absolutely fucking freezing, before a warm vibration soothes my neck and large hot hands slide around to cup my aching boobs. "What are you doing, my little love-bunny? You'll catch your death out here..."

I moan and rest my head against his chest, sliding it to the side so he has better access to my neck. He squeezes my breasts firmly and lightly pinches my nipples through the lace of my bra, making me cry out; they're so sensitive, so sore... and this is heavenly.

"You want me, huh?" he asks, pinching the skin on my neck with his lips, "you want your guy to make you scream right now?"

"Oh!" I cry as he lifts my bra cups up above my boobs and immediately rolls my nipples between the tips of his fingers and thumbs. He kisses my neck and jawline over and over, licking slightly so the cold air catches the damp patches and makes me shiver. My skin feels cold but my boobs are on fire; hot, heavy and begging for more of his touch. He squeezes again, before taking one hand and sliding it down my side, and inside my lace knickers.

"Holy fuck," I cry out as he gently circles, slowly, matching his caressing rhythm at my breast.

"You're so hot, your boobs are hot... shit I need you, baby..." he says, taking his hand out of my knickers, and pushing them midway down my thighs. I bend forward slightly, making myself totally available to him, open, ready and needy.

He kicks a low table in front of me and tells me to stand on it, giving me some extra height for him, and as I do, I feel him there, pushing, nudging. His large, rounded tip easing its way inside me. It's... indescribable. The pleasure of feeling him slowly moving further and further inside me, my god - nothing on God's earth feels as good as this.

"Oh god, Luke, you feel so good..."

"Fuck, you are so damn tight, baby... fuck!" He groans loudly as he pushes as deep as he can go, before pulling back and repeating. I can almost feel every single ridge, every vein... everything that makes Luke - Luke. With one hand on my hip, keeping me steady, and the other on my breast, still caressing, firmly, he starts to pump faster. I grab the railing in front of me and hold myself rigid, creating a resistance against his thrusts, forcing him deeper inside me.

"Argh..." I cry through gritted teeth, needing it harder, I'm so hot and ready for it and it's going to knock my fucking socks off.

"Jesus, I've got the hottest girlfriend... in the fucking... world..." he says as he thrusts faster, "God, I love you, Tilly, so... fucking... much!" he cries, clearly about to lose control.

"Yaha... I say, nodding continuously, needing him to keep going because I'm about to... yeah... I'm, I'm going to... "Holy fuck!" I cry out as the climax crashes through me, forceful waves erupting again and again, his rhythmic thrusts prolonging the ecstasy.

"Til!" he shouts, releasing my breast and grabbing hold of my other hip, slamming me against him as he comes hard, growling, digging his fingers into my flesh. "My god!" he cries, panting behind me, and rests his forehead against my spine. "What the fuck - that was probably the hardest and fastest I've ever come in my life... uh..." his exhaustion from the quick, hard fuck evident.

I imagine what we look like, standing on the balcony, me on a coffee table, my knickers half way down my thighs... and actually, it turns me on a bit. "Do we look fucking hot right now, or what?" I ask, amused, enjoying the sound of his deep, hearty chuckle.

"You look fucking hot right now baby, and that's fo sho! We were loud, Til. We probably just woke the bears from hibernation."

I laugh, loudly, resting my hands on top of his, on my hips. I step down from the table, breaking our intimate contact, and turn to press my body against him, trying to avoid standing naked in full view. I slip my knickers back up my legs and look up into his gorgeous face.

"I want you to make me feel like that everyday that I'm with you. Think you're up to the challenge?" I ask, grinning.

"Too fucking right I am, if I get to do that to you every day, I'm in heaven already. So, what's going to happen? Are you going to come and live with me or what?"

I laugh out loud, 'Wow, such a tempting invitation!"

He chuckles with me and wraps his arms around me, I'm really, really cold all of a sudden, and standing out in the snowy air, naked, is not helping. His huge strong arms, however, cover a large portion of my top half, making me feel cocooned and protected.

"I would love for you to move to LA and come live with me, you freakin' awesome señorita."

"Ah, now that's more like it. Yeah, I'll have a lot of stuff to sort out, but I think that could work, señor..."

"Awesome!" he cries, squeezing me tighter and kissing my head.

"Now, I've got a pretty cool surprise planned for you tonight, my little pumpkin-pie, so we've gotta go get showered and ready to head back out by about six."

"A surprise? Ooh! How exciting! You spoil me, Lukey."

"I sure do, Tillifer, and that's not ever gonna stop." He leans down and kisses my nose, swatting my behind and bends to pick up my coat, to wrap it around me. "Now, go back to your room and get ready, wrap up real warm. I'll catch you downstairs in an hour. Okay?"

"Okay!" I say, excitedly, looking forward to whatever he has planned for us.

An hour later, I'm downstairs as agreed dressed in skinny jeans, flat, black boots, a vest top, a loose fitting, knitted, black jumper and my beautiful fur coat. He did say to wrap up warm - I hope this is the sort of attire he meant. I put my clutch, hat and leather gloves on the side table and sit down next to Bea on the sofa. I link arms with her and rest my head on her shoulder, snuggling. "I miss you, BB," I say quietly.

Daniel is in the kitchen, Alexia and Sebastian have gone and Clare and Oliver are playing 'snap' on the carpet in front of the roaring fire. I'm starting to feel the heat again in my beautiful coat.

"I miss you, too, doll. I can't tell you how relieved I am to have the Tilly we know and love back."

I smile, "I know, Clare said the same thing yesterday. I'm sorry, I've just..."

"Til, I was there too. You don't have to explain anything to me. I know you're not the type to admit stuff like that, even to yourself."

I look down at my hands, not really knowing what to say, because I feel like I'm lying. That's not the reason I've been distant.

"We'll have a lovely day tomorrow, the three of us hitting the shops together, then a nice family get together at ours in the evening."

"I'm really looking forward to it, too. I can't wait to see your house! You have a house in Aspen, it's so cool!" I say with a huge grin. This time last year, not one of us had a boyfriend, and look at us now, Bea has her incredible Daniel and their amazing lifestyle; houses all over the bloody place - and I have Luke. He's all mine and I couldn't be more happy about it. Oh yes, and I'm having a baby... mustn't forget that whopping great detail.

Luke trots down the stairs happily, whistling to himself. Is it normal to want to squeeze your boyfriend to death, twenty four hours a day? It's not, is it? *Oh god, I'm such a freak.*

"Where's that divine bedroom beast of mine?" he asks, and I stand, giggling, and stroll over to the table to get my things. "You ready, Princess?"

"Yep, is this okay?" I ask, gesturing to my clothes.

"Delicious," he says with a wink, approaching me and bending to plant a soft kiss on my lips.

~~~~~~

The journey takes around half an hour in the car, and when we get there, Luke speaks with a few people before leading me over to an incredibly romantic horse drawn sled, and my mouth drops open in excited surprise. "We're going on that?"

"Yep, your carriage awaits, you really are a Princess tonight," he says, holding his arm out to welcome me on first.

"Oh, wow," I say as I step up and sit down, "this is amazing, I've never been on one before."

"I know it seems corny, but this and the snowcat are the only vehicles up here and I thought this was a little more romantic than the cat."

"It's totally corny, but amazing, thank you so much," I say, turning towards him and holding his face as I kiss his mouth. "This will be so much fun. Who'd have thought it? You and I being all romantic, we're so not those people."

"We are now, sweet-cheeks, so you wanna get used to it, okay?"

"Yes sir!" I say, saluting before having a good look around me. It's dark but oh-so-pretty.

We start moving, causing the cab to jolt slightly and I throw my hand over to Luke's lap and grab his thigh. "Like that, is it?" he asks with a smirk. He wraps his arm around my shoulders and pulls me close, tucking me into his side. I pull my stunning fur tightly around me as I rest my head against his shoulder and snuggle into his big body. "Thank you, this is so wonderful."

"You're welcome, Til. I hope you're hungry..."

I am famished. "Yes, I am."

"Good, because the food at this place is fantastic. I've been here a couple times with Danny and a few of the others, but we skied cross country to get there, which is another option, but I didn't think you'd like it."

"No, thank you." I smile and nuzzle his shoulder with my face. Could there be a more thoughtful bad-boy out there?

I think the answer is absolutely, categorically - no way. He's one in a million, and he's mine now. *He's ours, Wriggler!*

It's so cold out here, much colder than it was earlier when I was getting banged on the balcony...*ooh, that was fantastic...* but I'm enjoying it, my hat is keeping my ears toasty, my gloves are doing their job, and my ball of fur coat and smoking hot boyfriend are all I could need to make this journey the most romantic, cosy experience, ever. I think I like romance, as it happens... what a revelation. Another one.

The night is so clear, so silent; the stars bright as anything, no street lights, no engines - just the huge, perfect moon spotlighting this idyllic setting, the soft slushing trot of the horses' hooves in the snow. Luke tilts his head to rest on top of mine and cups my face with his free hand. I close my eyes as tingles spread underneath my skin, absorbing all of this addictive affection. I just never knew I needed this so badly. How could I have lived for so long without it? Without him?

"Are you warm enough, beautiful?"

I grin and nod against him, "Mmm." I stretch my arm around his belly and hold on tightly. He smells delicious. "Yes, thank you. I'd like to stay out here like this, all night."

"I think you'd get cold pretty fast."

"Not if I'm with you I wouldn't. Did I tell you how much I adore my coat?"

"I believe you did. I'm glad you like it," he says, like we're talking about a DVD or something."

"Luke, it's a big deal you know, this coat."

"No it's not, I thought you'd find it useful."

"Exactly. You thought. About me. And it must have cost a fortune. Do you buy coats for lots of people?"

He lifts his head and looks down at my face, "Tilly, I have never bought a fur coat for another girl, ever. I bought one for my mom when she came here one year, but that's it. So don't go thinking like that. And so it cost a few bucks, so what? You're my girl and I've got money. If I want to get you something, I will. And lastly, yes; I thought. I'm always thinking about you, I think you've been on my mind, permanently, since September."

My grin spreads from ear to ear. "That's 'cause you *lurve* me..." I tease, and his responding chuckle sends vibrations to my lady bits.

"Uh huh, yeah, but not as much as you *lurve* me..." he replies, lowering his face to kiss me and I immediately wrap both arms around his neck and hold him to me, prolonging the pleasure. Our romantic sled ride fully consummated by our offering of love for one another; a sublime, sentimental kiss. *Who the hell are you and what have you done with Tilly?*

We climb out of the sled as we arrive outside *'Pine Creek Cookhouse'.* The snow begins to fall and as I look at the quaint, little, wooden building, thick snow lining the roof, warm lights glowing through the windows - I feel a surge of excitement at the thought of spending the evening in this romantic cabin with my luscious Luke.

We enter the warm haven, hand in hand, and I take in the incredibly welcoming ambience. The decor is exactly how I'd imagined as we were nearing; antler chandeliers, mellow, soothing lighting, people gathering around an impressive wood burning stove with Irish coffee. It's wonderful.

Once we have taken our top layers off, we are greeted with a delicious plate of charcuterie and red wine. As much as I adore my red wine in real life, I still can't stomach the idea of even taking a sip whilst pregnant. It honestly makes me heave just thinking about it. Nope, Wriggler will just have to wait another eighteen years to have his first taste of booze... or maybe twenty one years, depending on where we live...

"Don't you want your wine, baby?" Luke asks, snapping me back to the present.

"Hmm? Oh, no, not really. I'm not really in the mood for drinking this holiday, I think I'm having enough fun without it. Call it a detox."

"Okay, that's a different Tilly to the one I remember, but it's fine by me... I'll join you."

So sweet! "Oh no, please don't do that, you enjoy it. Please?"

"I can take it or leave it, Princess," he says with a shrug. Gorgeous man.

Three courses of incredible, American Alpine cuisine later, I am stuffed to the rim. We shared our dishes to experience the best of everything we could order, and it was fantastic. Now, I'm sitting facing a rather large chocolate brownie with a huge dollop of vanilla ice-cream on top, a squirt of cream, and lashings of chocolate sauce. How on earth I can even contemplate eating this after the ridiculous amount of meat I have just consumed, I've no idea. But it looks heavenly. Luke is staring at his walnut-pecan pie as if he might be able to shrink it a little before he has to eat it.

"We should probably make a start on this..." I say, holding my spoon, wondering where to begin.

"You're right. We really should. Ladies first," he says with a grin, rubbing his full belly.

"Okay..." I break a little off with my spoon and bring it to my mouth, and I'm almost brought to orgasm. "Oh. My. God. Incredible."

"It looks good. I wouldn't mind smearing some of that on your little body later and having a midnight feast," he whispers.

"Naa, Bea and Daniel beat us to it on that one, they're obsessed with chocolate sauce and all that stuff."

"Really?" he asks, laughing, "he never mentioned that one, surprisingly. So what else can we try then?"

"Maybe we could put black treacle on my nipples, you'll be there all day trying to suck it off," I say dryly with an amused smirk and to my horror, the older couple at the next table turn to look at me, stunned. Did I say that loudly? *Whoops...* I can't help but giggle even louder, though, as the gentleman looks back to his wife and wiggles his eyebrows, suggestively, before winking back at me.

"I think she's on to something..." Luke says to the man, and the couple laugh quietly with us. How often can you talk about nipple treacle with the old couple next to you in a restaurant? This evening is just so memorable, the romance is fantastic, but being us, having a laugh and enjoying the banter we so love, makes it complete.

We stay a little longer to have a hot, after-dinner drink with the older couple, and then head back outside in the heavy snowfall, to the sled. The ride back is quiet, calm and very, very sleepy. We cuddle up together and close our eyes, fully relaxing to the hypnotising rhythm of the horses.

Back at the house, everyone is in bed, as expected after last night's shenanigans. We get ourselves a drink and, of course, make the most of the empty downstairs area by having seriously crazy, half dressed, hardcore sex all over the living area, finished off with slow, intimate love making on the rug in front of the fire. I know it's so cliche, but it's fucking fantastic, and I'd recommend fire-front sex to anyone. The lighting, the warmth, the intensity... mmm, it definitely gets a 'yes' from me.

CHAPTER 10
MONDAY 24TH DECEMBER/CHRISTMAS EVE

The morning goes super-fast today, after we wake and go for it one more time against the bedroom door (yes, we got distracted on the way down for breakfast), we enjoy breakfast with Clare and Oliver. The boys get ready and leave as soon as Bea and Daniel arrive, ready to hit the shops for their last minute shopping and to get a little bit of Christmas skiing in.

We're a lot more casual about it, we chill out in our pj's for a while with a cuppa, Bea joining us when the boys leave, and we chat about everything and anything.

"This is definitely one of the best holidays I have ever been on," Clare says, enthusiastically, "I mean, I love a beach holiday - obviously, but this is just so cosy, and the excitement of Christmas is so much more intense here with the snow and serious festivities. It's nice for us both to be able to enjoy a break away together, knowing that the Cakery is in good hands. I'm having such fun."

"Well, you can come back whenever you like, girlies." Bea responds.

"Thanks, sweetness, now you've got a house and all..." Clare says, excitedly.

"I can't wait to see it tonight, Bea, Luke says it's amazing," I add.

"Oh, it is. I adore it, I don't want to leave! I just can't quite believe how lucky I am."

"You've got it all, Bea... treasure it," Clare says, softly, with her hand on her heart and her head tilted slightly.

"Alright, alright, let's not get all romantic and crap," I interrupt, the old Tilly returning briefly, and I stand, making my way to the stairs, "I'm going to get ready - you girls need to help me find something to buy Luke, I haven't had to buy a boy anything for god knows how long. Well, except Olly, but I mean... a *boy-boy*."

Clare responds a little too quickly, "Oliver *is* a boy-boy."

"Alright, Clare, I was simply saying that I haven't had to buy a *boyfriend* a gift for ages. Blimey, what's gotten into you?" *Like I don't already know...*

"I could ask the same thing of you, Til," she says, quietly, but sharply. Quite unlike her. I choose to ignore it, I don't want to piss her off about Oliver and I don't want her to elaborate further.

I go and get ready and we all meet downstairs shortly after. The limo takes us into the shopping precinct nearby, and we start by browsing in a gorgeous clothes boutique where we try on lush winter coats and accessories. Bea buys some gloves for her mum, and we move on to some more man-friendly shops, to buy some things for the boys.

Ralph Lauren is a must for Bea, Daniel seems to wear so much from there. We all separate and stroll around the shop, looking for different bits and pieces. I see a few nice things, but it is impossible to buy clothes for a man, I mean, he needs to try it on for a start, and will it suit him? Will he like it? It is fashionable at the moment? I am just going to have to give up on the clothes idea, I know about girls fashion, and I know that Luke looks hot in everything he wears - but boys clothes on a hanger? I have no idea.

I stroll over to look at some accessories and I see Clare brushing her fingers over a tan leather wallet. Knowing that Oliver lost his wallet the day before we left for Aspen and is using an old one until he gets a chance to buy another, I know exactly what she's thinking, but this is way more than we usually spend on each other.

"He'll love that," I say, wondering how she'll respond. I wish they'd feel comfortable enough to come out in the open and be a couple.

Clare nods, deep in thought as she opens it up. She suddenly puts it back down and frowns. "Hmm? Who? I was just looking for... um... for my dad."

"Clare, darling, no you weren't. Your reaction tells me exactly who you had in mind, and I think he'll love it," I say with a supportive smile.

"Oh for fucks sake, Til, get over it. I was thinking of my dad." *Whoa!*

"And it's just a coincidence that Oliver lost his wallet before we came here?"

"Yes!" she snaps, her face red with fury, "would you just get over it, there is nothing going on and I'm fed up of you bringing it up all the time."

"What's the problem? Why can't you both just be honest with everyone?"

"Don't fucking go there Til, I mean it..." I don't think I've ever seen her this angry, but I need to get through to her that it's okay. She's never hidden stuff from us before and it's unnerving.

"I will fucking go there, just be honest!"

"Oh, like you are? Like you're honest? Don't start all of this bullshit with me Til, you're being the biggest fucking hypocrite that I've ever met. Why haven't *you* told anyone? Huh?"

Oh Shit. My stupid badgering has come back to bite me in the arse. And she... knows? "Told anyone what?" I ask, in the hope that she's talking about something minor like... like... having sex in the kitchen.

She looks around and lowers here voice, "You know exactly what I'm talking about. Why haven't you told anyone that you're pregnant?" Her face softens and she frowns, putting a hand on my arm. I stare at her, not really knowing what to say... how long has she known? "Tilly, please, just say it. To me."

I'm suddenly overcome with emotion, she's gone from being furious with me - quite rightly so, I am a huge hypocrite - to being so gentle and caring. Knowing that I'm not completely alone anymore is an unexpected relief. A tear falls from my lashes and I wipe my cheek immediately, before anyone around us notices. I simply nod, and with that confirmation, I turn into an emotional wreck, nostrils flaring, eyes flooding.

"Oh darling..." Clare says, clutching my wrist. She looks around us and leads me to the dressing rooms, grabbing a blouse from a clothes rail en route. Bea is obviously deep in the mens department and totally unaware of the drama unfolding over here.

Clare locks the door behind us and turns to give me the biggest, most needed hug ever. "Oh Til, why didn't you just tell me? Why hasn't either of you told anyone?"

I sniff and wipe my wet cheeks with my fingertips. I look down at my feet and clear my throat. "Well, it's not that simple."

"Oh god, oh no... why?" she asks, obviously worried about the pregnancy.

"Oh, nothing like that, Wriggler and I are both fine..."

She smiles, "Wriggler?"

"Oh, yes, that's what I named it. It wriggles around a lot, I can feel it really early on."

"Oh my god, that's so amazing... I need to hear so much more - but first, why isn't it simple?"

"Well... Luke doesn't know." I wince, waiting for it.

"What?" she cries, loudly, "Why not? It's his baby, isn't it?"

"Oh yes, I wouldn't have been that stupid with anyone else."

"You forgot a condom?" she asks.

"Yeah."

"Til, you have to tell him. I hate to say it but you're being really selfish right now."

I nod because she's right. And I'm ashamed of myself. "I know. And I hate myself for it, but I wanted to tell him in the flesh, and then we got here and he surprised me in the middle of the night with a sesh in the kitchen, and it just went on and on, and now the girlfriend thing; I'm afraid to ruin it all and lose him. I'm worried to find out that he doesn't want to be in our lives." I whimper most uncharacteristically, and drop my head on her shoulder.

She strokes my hair. "Darling, whatever happens, he deserves to know, and it's not fair that you're keeping it from him. So your.. what? Three months?"

I shake my head, "More, it works out at sixteen weeks tomorrow, pregnancy date calculations are weird. Anyway, that's the date I got from the midwife."

"And it's most definitely Luke's baby?"

"Oh yes, no doubt at all. It's Luke's."

"Bloody hell, Til, you're four months pregnant and you haven't even told the dad... your boyfriend!"

"Please don't, I already know how bad it is. After the whole boyfriend/girlfriend thing happened, I thought maybe he'd take the news a bit better - be more likely to hang around, so I planned to tell him in the next day or so."

"Good, you should. Til, he's not going to be like your mum. I can understand your fears, I know what sort of a guy Luke was, and I know you want your child to be wanted by both parents because of your mum and everything, but you have to accept that whatever happens is going to happen, and nothing you do will change that. Especially prolonging this."

"I know. I will tell him."

"Good, because seriously, I will be on your back until you do. The guy needs to know his life is about to change, and he deserves as much notice as you got, even though he won't now."

"I know, I know."

"How long have you known?"

I pause, nervous to tell her, "Um... since the end of October."

"What?" she cries, her eyebrows raised in disbelief, "And you didn't tell us? Does Gemma know?"

I shake my head, guiltily. "No."

"Why not? How can you possibly have been doing this all on your own? Okay, so I've had suspicions for a couple of days now, but I was waiting for you to tell me something yourself."

"I'm sorry. But I don't think it's right for me to tell my friends and sister before Luke even knows. It's his baby and I think he should have been the first person to find out."

"Well, I agree with you there, and he would have been if you'd have just told him straight away."

"I'll tell him. I promise I will."

"Today Til, you have to."

I nod, agreeing with her. God, I hope he doesn't run. "Does Bea know?" I ask, there's no way she could keep this from Daniel.

"I don't think so, I haven't spoken to her about it, but she's not daft, if she doesn't have suspicions already, she will know soon enough. Til, hasn't he noticed? I mean... in bed - you've got a little bump."

I gasp, "Oh my god, can you notice really badly? I've been trying to hide it."

"Yes, I can notice, but only because I know you, and I've been really looking for it. But how hasn't he when you're naked?"

"I've just been a bit creative with positions and stuff. And a lot of the time, we've been... I've needed clothes on..."

"Oh my word, you are so daring, you've been doing it outside haven't you?" she says with a grin.

"A lot. I can't get enough, he's just *so* good, Clare."

"Well, I'm glad for you, Til. I really am, I love him, he's great and so perfect for you."

I grin, sniffing. "He is, isn't he?"

Clare nods. "Just tell him, doll. I'm here for you, whatever happens, okay? You're not alone now. My god, I have *so* many questions for you, I want to know everything. That's some holiday souvenir you brought home!"

"Girls? You in here?" Bea's voice calls from the entrance to the fitting rooms. I sniff again and wipe under my eyes.

"Do I look okay?" I whisper and Clare licks her thumb and wipes some mascara from under my eye. "Good thing I love you," I say with a smirk.

"Love you," she whispers and kisses my cheek, "let's go."

"Yes, we're here," I call out as I open the door.

"Oh, I wondered where you were."

"Sorry, I just wanted to try this on and we couldn't see you," Clare says, in explanation.

Bea looks at the blouse with a frown... "Clare... that's like, a size fourteen... I assume it was too big?"

Clare looks down at the very conservative blouse and nods, I can see her wondering how to get out of this. "Hmm. Yes, it is, isn't it. I, um... I wanted a baggy look, it didn't work. Anyway, have you got what you needed?"

~~~~~~~

We continue to shop, finding a few gifts for the boys and some wrapping paper and gift boxes. We decided a while back to leave our gifts for each other at home under our tree, to exchange when we return. It seemed silly to add to the luggage allowance. I find a few little things that I think will be perfect for Luke, considering he is so hard to buy for, so I really hope he'll like them.

Just as we step out of the gift-wrap shop and make our way down the street for coffee, I feel strong arms wrap around me from behind and warm breath caressing my neck. To the side of me, I see Daniel embracing Bea, too.

"I've missed you this morning, Princess, wanna go somewhere and fuck?" Luke whispers in my ear, making me burst out laughing. I lean back against him, smiling.

"Definitely. Let's do it."

He turns me to face him and kisses me softly, looking directly into my eyes. I'm dazzled, still, by his incredibly handsome face. "Excellent. I could really slip my hand into your panties right now."

"Oh, I'm so pleased to hear that..." Oliver says in disgust, rolling his eyes and turning to Clare, shaking his head.

We both giggle and share one more kiss. He looks at my face again and cocks his head to one side, "Are you okay, baby?"

I nod, "Uh huh, I'm fine, thank you."

"Sure? Your eyes are different, like you've been crying or something?" How does he notice this stuff? Bea didn't even notice, but then again, she wasn't up close and personal like my man is right now.

"No, it's just the cool breeze, it makes my eyes water."

"Okay, as long as my girl is good."

"Are you coming for a coffee with us?" I ask, hoping they will, we've only been apart for a few hours and already I need him near me, holding me. It's as if I run on Luke powered batteries that can only go so long without being charged. I can't remember ever being so dependant on anyone, especially not emotionally. I feel like I've stepped into someone else's life, and I love it too much to ever leave.

"Sure... Danny?" he calls, disturbing his and Bea's clearly private conversation, she's smiling and flushed and he's got naughty thoughts written all over his face. "You wanna join the girls for coffee?"

"Sure," he replies, and they look to Oliver for his approval.

Sitting around the table in the warm coffee shop, all I can do is gaze at him, thinking about Wriggler. I'm psyching myself up to tell him. I will tell him today, absolutely, definitely. I will find the appropriate time and he will know. He will be shocked, maybe a little cross that I have kept it from him, but he'll be okay. He'll be fine, maybe even a little excited. He won't leave us. *Oh fucking fuckers, I hope he doesn't leave us. I think my heart would just stop beating.*

"Did you buy me stuff?" he asks, cheekily, making me grin. Again.

"Maybe. Did you buy me stuff?"

"Yep. But it's all in the car so you can't go exploring my bags."

"I like surprises, anyway."

"Good," he says, "me too." *Oh god, I hope that's true!*

"So when are you off to the slopes?" I ask, enjoying the fact that he will be able to do what he so loves again, instead of having to stay in with me. Though I will look forward to his return; I am definitely ready for him to throw me about again... maybe somewhere naughty. Oh, and also because I will be discussing Wriggler with him. *Yes, Tilly. Get with the programme, stop thinking about sex; hot, hard, scream-worthy, bad-boy sex...*

"I don't know if I'm going to go, I want to come home with you." he says, reaching for my hand as he sips his coffee.

I play with his fingers and smile. "Do you?"

"Yeah. I really do. And not just to poke you with my baton either."

I giggle quietly. "What do you want then?" I ask, softly.

"I want to fall asleep with you on the balcony again. Just you and me, wrapped up warm inside the comforter, listening to the snow fall." I gaze up at him and realise that I'm witnessing yet another Luke now. In-love Luke. Gentle, sweet,

I-love-you-with-all-of-my-heart Luke. And I feel so special to be the one that this Luke comes out for.

I clutch his hand in both of mine and hold it to my heart. "That would be lovely, I would really, really, *really* like that. But you've agreed to go with the boys; they haven't spent any time on the slopes with you, I'd like you to go and have some fun with them."

He pouts playfully. "Oh. You don't want me?"

I giggle at his joviality, "Of course I want you. But I have to wait until you've had some fun. I can't keep hogging you. When you come back, we'll have some time together before we go to Bea and Daniels. And then, after..."

"Mmm, after? I like the sound of that. What about during? Maybe we can get up to some mischief during dinner..."

"Sounds... creative. I will look forward to it."

We continue with our group coffee date, talking about the plans for Christmas Day, tomorrow, which I'm really looking forward to. Just one little huge thing to get through first. I'm shitting myself.

We leave after we have all warmed up and rested a little; the boys head off to ski, and we visit a couple more shops before hopping back in the limo and going home. Bea stays in the car and continues back to her house to get ready for dinner, and Clare and I climb the stairs to Alexia's luxurious pad.

We go straight upstairs to Clare's room, to wrap everything. It occurs to me that I haven't even been in here yet, I've been so preoccupied with me and Luke, that I've spent no time exploring the rooms in which my friends are sleeping.

Clare's room is gorgeous, and clearly the master suite of the house. She has a beautiful stone fireplace facing the end of her bed and double french doors on either side to the large, covered balcony. Her en-suite is bigger than our entire maisonette at home, with a beautiful oval, stone bath centring the room.

"Bloody Nora, Clare, this room is flipping gorgeous!"

"I know, if you were quicker on your feet..."

"Naa, my room is fine, I'm in Luke's most of the time anyway. This must be Alexia's bedroom," I say, strolling slowly around, scoping out the features and fittings. I open the balcony door and step out to a different view than mine and Luke's rooms, but a beautiful one none-the-less.

"Come in, Til, it's freezing and I have a gazillion questions to ask you, you're forgetting that we have a little baby to talk about."

I smile and re-enter the room, closing the doors behind me. "Yes, we do. So go ahead. Ask away," I say as I sit, cross legged on the floor next to her, taking the cellophane from the rolls of wrapping paper.

"So, you're sixteen weeks."

"Tomorrow."

"Sixteen weeks tomorrow," she nods, "so that means you're due when?"

"Eleventh of June."

"Ooh, just before my birthday! How exciting. So, how has it been? What's it like? Does it feel funny? Did you have morning sickness? Oh my god, how did I not notice? You've been so ill! I hadn't even connected the two until now."

I nod and shrug, "Yeah, I felt really shitty for a while, I wasn't sick all the time, but I felt like I had a really bad hangover, or like... car sickness - for weeks. I had two weeks where I thought I was going to be sick every time I moved, but that passed, thank god. I'm feeling a lot better now, just tired."

"So the bad two weeks, is that when you took that time off work?"

"Yeah."

"You've been avoiding going to the pub and stuff... I thought that was all to do with you missing Luke!"

"It was at first, before I knew, but I also felt really emotional and couldn't work out why - turns out, I had pregnancy hormones to blame."

"It all makes sense now; you not drinking... hang on, what about all those vodkas I bought you when you *did* actually come to the pub."

"Mmm, about that..."

"You vodka'd the plants, didn't you?"

"Uh huh. Sorry, doll." She tuts and rolls her eyes. "But what could I do? If I'd have asked for sparkling water, you'd have all bombarded me with questions about what's wrong with me!"

"Yes, you're right. We would have..." she gasps suddenly, "Oh. My. God! *That's* why you never have any tampons anymore!"

I laugh out loud, "How the hell do you know about my tampon supply?"

"Oh darling, I've been nicking your tampons for as long as I can remember. I always run out," she says, waving her arm like I should already know this.

"Ah, I see, that explains a lot." I say, remembering all those times when I could have sworn I had a full box left, but only had a couple loose in the bottom of the drawer.

"Can I see? Please?" she asks, smiling excitedly.

I rise onto my knees and lift my jumper and vest top to reveal baby Wriggler's bump. Clare gasps again and immediately reaches out to touch it. "Oh..." she says, taking one hand and putting it to her mouth, her eyes well up and she smiles sweetly, "hello little baby... oh Tilly..." she sobs as she throws her arms around my neck, "I'm so sorry you've been doing this on your own. I wish I could have been there for you. I wish I'd have concentrated more on what was going on at home." She cries on my shoulder, holding me tightly.

"You couldn't have known, Clare, I would have done everything to stop anyone finding out before Luke. I just shouldn't have left it so long."

"I'm so happy for you, Tils, you're going to be the most amazing mum in the world."

"I hope so," I say, determined to do my best.

"Let me see again," she says, releasing me and sniffing. She bends and kisses my belly, "You're too cute, Wriggler, I know I can't see you and everything, but you're still the cutest little thing, ever. This is Auntie Clare speaking, I'll be your favourite. Okay, maybe Auntie Gemma will be your favourite, but your Auntie Bea and I will come very close. Then of course you'll have Uncle Jay and Uncle Daniel... you'll like them a lot. But no one will be as perfect for you, as Mummy and Daddy. Oh, and if you're a boy and you take after Daddy, you're going to have all the girls chasing after you because your dad is seriously hot..."

"Er... I am still in the room you know..." I say, chuckling, "I'm glad to know you think my boyfriend's good looking and everything, but let's not forget that he's mine."

"Nope. Of course, all yours and obviously always will be. He loves you so much Til, you know that don't you?"

"Actually Clare, I think I do."

The rest of the afternoon is really lovely. Clare still swears she'll beat me with a pole if Luke doesn't know by tomorrow, and that's fine. I probably needed a big kick up the arse anyway, so it's a good thing that someone knows and can keep me in check.

The boys are really late coming back from skiing - a fault with a lift or something, so Clare and I are sitting in the lounge, ready and waiting as Luke and Oliver burst through the door. Luke smiles gorgeously when he sees me and bends to kiss me as he passes, before disappearing up the stairs after Oliver, to get ready.

"You'll have to do it later, or tomorrow, there'll be no time before we go," Clare whispers and I nod in agreement. "Hell of a Christmas present!" she adds, grabbing hold of my hand and squeezing it, supportively.

Luke says he'll drive us to Daniel's, rather than waiting for the limo to get back, we were supposed to be using the car that has only just taken Daniel home and if we wait for it, we'll be even later for the meal.

"You can always leave the car there," Oliver says, as we reach the bottom of the steps, "if you want to have a drink."

"I'm cool, I don't think I'll drink anything tonight," he replies, squeezing my hand and winking at me, and I know he's privately referring to our conversation at the restaurant last night about abstaining from drinking, with me.

The journey takes about fifteen minutes or so and as we pull up to the beautiful house, I am awed, again. "Wow, it's amazing! What beautiful houses the Berkeleys own."

"You'd like Danny's folks house here, that's something spectacular."

"More spectacular than this and Alexia's house?"

"Oh yeah." Good god, they *do* have money growing on trees, I read somewhere that Aspen boasts the highest real estate prices in the entire United States, and these houses are fucking massive. And they're only holiday homes! I am starting to realise just how wealthy the Berkeley family is. Bentleys and what-not aside.

Bea opens the door and welcomes us into her new, stylish - yet totally welcoming home.

"This is absolutely stunning, Bea. Look at you; Lady of the manor!" I say jokingly, no malice intended.

"I know, it's so absolutely gorgeous, I'm a lucky girl. Do you see why I don't want to leave?"

She greets Clare, Oliver and Luke, and leads us into her fabulous living area to join the parents. Bea's parents, Emily and Edward immediately stand to hug Clare and I.

"Darling, how are you?" Emily says, holding me tightly. She's sort of adopted me since my dad died, and I love her for it. My mum ran away when Gemma and I were very young and we haven't seen or heard from her since. I don't remember much about her and my dad was more than perfect, so I don't think Gemma and I were too badly affected, but it's never nice to know you weren't wanted, hence why I want Luke to want our baby so much.

"I'm great, thank you."

"I'm glad to hear it, I thought we'd see you out on the mountains, it's not like you to miss out on some skiing."

Here we go again. I shrug and pull back, kissing her cheek, "I'm just not into it this year... and..."

"I know, darling, you're spending some quality time with your lovely new boyfriend. I understand. I'd have done exactly the same when I met Edward. It is wonderful to see you with such a strapping young man, we've been waiting for you to meet your special someone," she says, extending her arm to beckon for Luke. When he joins us, she raises onto tiptoes and he bends for her to kiss his cheek. "Hello, dear, I was just telling Tilly that the two of you make a stunning couple. Enjoy each other."

He smiles at me and slips his arm around my waist, "Thank you, Emily. I certainly will, I'm a lucky guy."

Emily scoots away to hug Clare and Oliver, while Luke smiles at me. He just gazes, saying nothing, holding me into his side. After a moment, he bends to kiss my forehead and whispers in my ear, "I love you. Now let's go some place and fuck like rabbits."

I giggle as he turns me to slip my coat off my shoulders. "Wow, you look hot in this," he says as he sees my loose fitting black top with open back. I've teamed it with my normal skinny jeans and boots. He bends and lays a soft kiss on my bare flesh, in full view if everyone. He's so affectionate, I love it.

As we all gather with drinks, I decide to stroll around the huge, beautiful room, taking in the exquisite, luxurious furnishings and incredible architecture. The room has an extremely high, wooden ceiling and a glass wall running all the way to the top at the back; traditional with a fabulous modern twist. The enormous, designer-looking Christmas tree fits perfectly, and the elegant decorations sprinkled throughout the room create such a warm, festive ambiance. It's so stylish, if Daniel hadn't arranged for a designer to come in and set these decorations up, I would most certainly put Bea's name on it. It's her to a 'T'.

I gaze out of the glass onto the patio outside, lit in the deep night by the warm, amber glow streaming from the lights of the pathway leading to the lawn. Luke joins me, his warm hand slips into the back of my open top and rests on my rib cage. He turns me slightly to press against him and I wrap my arms around his waist, resting my head on his chest. We stare out, into the night, together.

"It's a great house, huh?"

"I love it. I love being here."

"Want me to show you around?"

"Oh, definitely, I want to see the rest of the house." I turn and call to Bea, "Bea? Do you mind if Luke shows me around?"

"No!" she calls back, waving her hand, "Go! See the rest of the amazingness! Oliver and Clare are already having their tour."

We start downstairs, he shows me the fabulous kitchen, where Pam and Daniel's housekeeper are preparing our food, and then we move on to the rest of the rooms downstairs. It's absolutely huge. The beautiful swimming pool and gym on the lower ground floor are hugely impressive, I can't wait to use them. He leads me up the stairs to see the four incredible bedrooms. They could all be classed as master suites, with huge dressing rooms and bathrooms. We pass Oliver and Clare in the hallway, looking just as excited about Bea's new holiday home as I am.

Luke guides me to another door, behind which is a long, straight, carpeted staircase. We make our way up to the top to a small, lobby style library, with a couple of plush love seats and walls lined with wooden book cases, filled to maximum capacity. It has an addictive smell of leather and books, combined. There is a huge, round window to one side facing the stunning view of the white peaks of Aspen. What an incredibly idyllic place to spend a cold, snowy afternoon with a cup of tea. I want this!

Luke tears me away from this book-lovers haven to pass through yet another door to an absolutely gorgeous roof terrace, complete with covered pergola and outdoor lounge furniture. The area without cover is thick with snow, but under the shelter is clear and sheltered from the cold. The view is breathtaking. This is, by far, my favourite floor of this stunning house.

"This is just... I have no words. I adore this."

"I thought you would." He stands behind me and wraps his arms around my chest. "Sometimes, I take a day out and spend it up here, on my own."

"Out here? All day?" I ask.

"No, I spend a while in there, reading, and then I move out here for an hour or so with my book. It's the only really peaceful thing I like to do."

Another Luke. "You read?"

"Sure, I don't get a lot of time to, so I like my day up here while we're on a ski break."

"You will always surprise me."

"You like surprises," he says, and I smile, loving that he remembers every tiny thing I tell him.

"I do. Not as much as I like you though." I turn in his arms and lift my head to reach his. He meets me and we kiss; a long, lingering, loving kiss. He slides his hands down my side as our lips are locked, our tongues entwined, and he cups my buttocks, squeezing them hard. A loud moan escapes me and I immediately thread my fingers through his hair and pick up the pace of the kiss. I rise and fall on my toes, rubbing my body against his, needing this constant contact. One of his hands moves up my back to hold the back of my neck and he groans deep in his throat. He pulls away, briefly, breathing heavily as he whispers, "I need you, baby, I need to feel you, hold you. I need your skin."

His lips lock with mine again and my hands automatically search for the bottom of his jumper and slip inside, running up his hard, warm abs. "Your hands are so cold..." he says against my mouth, before walking with me, still kissing, through the door and back into the library.

He closes the door behind us and walks me to a far wall, pressing me against the shelving. I unfasten my own jeans before he gets a chance, and push them, along with my knickers, down my thighs. By the time I'm done, he has done the same, and he flips me around to face the books. There is a wooden ladder to my left, resting against the shelving, and he takes it and slides it in front of me. "Step up."

I do as he suggests, making me the perfect height. There are convenient handles on the shelving, I assume to keep ones balance when climbing the ladder, so I clutch hold of one, and raise one leg to rest on a higher shelf of the book case, putting me in perfect position for Luke.

"Oh god, you look fucking amazing, he says, as he brushes my hair away from my neck and kisses me, gently. "I am going to fuck you right here, baby, right now, and you're going to love it." *Those words again!* I grin in anticipation, I love it, I love it already.

He slips his hands into my top and around to my bare breasts, holding them, caressing them divinely. He presses his torso against me and I feel him digging into my skin. I want him to keep his hands on me, it feels so good, so I reach down between my legs and hold him tightly, guiding him to me. I glide my hand up and down, enjoying the heat of his oh-so-ready cock. He nudges forward, forcing himself inside me and I cry out loud as he pushes further and further until he fills me completely. My now destitute hand moves to hold his balls, his skin tightly clenched. I handle them gently, slowly moving to caress and manipulate until the skin softens. *God, this turns me on.*

"Shit, Princess that's so good," he says as he glides back out slowly and pushes deep inside me again, making me moan out again. His movement makes it impossible for me to hold him any longer, so I release him and grab one of his hands on my boob, forcing him to squeeze harder. It hurts, but it's just so fucking good!

He continues to move, his rhythm slow but punishing, making me want to beg him to pound me hard and fast. Gradually, in his sweet time, he picks up the pace, I push against him again to create some resistance, and the effect is overwhelming, I suddenly cry out as my orgasm comes from nowhere, bursting inside and rolling on and on. My legs tingle and my knees weaken as it rips through me, taking every ounce of energy that I possess. He thrusts deep and hard and groans loudly behind me, stilling as he lets go.

"Tilly, my god!" he cries in a whisper, collapsing against my back.

I pant and rest my head against the ladder. "Luke, promise me we can do this every day?"

He chuckles and kisses my back. "You don't have to ask me that every time we have sex, baby girl, we can definitely do this every day. Maybe not on a ladder, but we can do some other crazy shit."

I laugh and immediately want to turn and hug him. I love how he makes me laugh. "We better get back, bad-boy, we don't want to be late for dinner. I don't know about you, but I've worked up an appetite."

CHAPTER 11
MONDAY 24TH DECEMBER/CHRISTMAS EVE (CONT.)

We get ourselves sorted and head back downstairs after a bathroom trip for me. It's not always convenient to have sex without a condom, when you're out and about.

Everyone is making their way into the large dining room as we return and we follow, grinning at each other like naughty school kids. Clare catches my eye and sends me a questioning look, and I shake my head, no. That's not what we were doing upstairs. She raises one eyebrow and taps her watch, reminding me that I have to tell him, tonight. I nod, subtly and continue to my place at the large table.

There are elegant decorations adorning this room, too, with mistletoe dripping from the huge chandelier above the table. There is a roaring fire to one side of the room, and a large window, facing the front aspect of the house, on the other. The snow falls outside, creating a fabulously festive, cosy ambiance.

We all take our seats, and Henry, Daniel's dad, strolls around the table, filling up the wine glasses. I don't draw attention to myself by saying no, I just let him pour the glass, knowing I can now ask Clare to drink it for me. Luke declines because he is driving, of course. We make a toast to a fabulous Christmas Eve and the wonderful ladies preparing our food, and continue to talk amongst ourselves.

As I place my napkin in my lap, I can feel his eyes boring into me, I turn my head to look up at his face and I melt instantly at the dimply smile and the look in his eyes that tells me, without a doubt, how in love with me he is. I return his smile and reach for his hand to thread my fingers through his.

"So, you know this entire table is under mistletoe, right?"

"Yep. I do."

"So you'll know I've got to kiss you, then. Right now..."

"Yep," I respond with a huge grin, "I do."

He leans down to my face, gazing right into my eyes, smiling, and rubs his nose along mine. "You're so much more than I ever thought I'd have, Til. I think you're awesome," he whispers.

I could collapse from the force of my swoon, I have no words that could even come close to describing what it does to me when he makes me feel like the most important person in his world.

He slowly touches my lips with his and our eyes close immediately. We kiss softly and slowly. Wherever we are, whatever we are doing; this moment, this absolutely perfect moment is what I have needed since the accident that took my dad. It's the feeling that I have someone to support me, to be with me, to guide me and help me and love me unconditionally. I know I have all of that with Luke and he's going to be there, by my side, as my rock for... well, for what I hope is forever.

"Now, come on you two," Pam says quietly, interrupting our kiss, as she slides past Luke to put a huge bowl of mashed potatoes on the table, "you don't want to make everyone jealous." I look up at her and smile, and she winks at me. I wonder if she has anyone, she always seems to be at the house...

"Please, help yourselves," she says to the whole table, as she and Daniel's housekeeper place the last few bits on the table. I look at the feast ahead of me and my stomach rumbles; a huge selection of sliced meat and fish, mashed potato, sweet potato, green beans and vegetables... it all looks mouthwateringly good.

And it was. About half an hour later, I am slumped back in my chair, desperately bloated, unable to look at the leftovers. I have eaten way too much, but it was all so delicious, I just couldn't stop. I take a swig of my sparkling water and exhale. Luke looks at me, grinning, "Has someone eaten a little too much, Princess?" he asks and to my horror, rests his hand on my belly. I know I'm telling him tonight and everything, but he can't find out like this, here. I sit up in a shot and push his hand off.

He frowns immediately, shocked by my reaction. "Whoa, what's the matter?"

"Oh, nothing... nothing..." *Oh fuck it! What the hell do I say?*

"Hey, Til, tell me what's up?"

"Nothing, I just... I am so full. A bit bloated really..."

He chuckles. "A little bloated belly isn't enough to put me off, sweet cheeks." *Phew, I wasn't going for that but since he thought I was, I'll run with it. For now.*

~~~~~~~

After Bea, Clare and I help take the dishes out to the kitchen, we sit back down at the table for a little rest before dessert. Candles are burning around the room, and the lighting has been dimmed slightly, to create a more romantic, evening setting.

Daniel pours thirteen glasses of champagne, leisurely, and walks around the huge table, setting them down in front of each of us, before calling in Pam and his housekeeper and returning to his place next to Bea. I watch them interact for a while, smiling at each other and speaking quietly together. They gaze into each others eyes, lovingly, and it's only then that I realise... I have what they have. Wow.

Daniel kisses Bea and stands with his glass, "Everybody, I'd like to say a few words before dessert, please." The room calms for Daniel to continue. "As you all know, this is our first Christmas together, and I'd like to thank you all so much for being here. I know how badly Bea wanted her friends and family to join us, as did I, and as usual I have my family and best friend here, to celebrate the festivities, too. We are both very excited to be able to spend the festive period with such a fantastic group of people."

"Here, here," Edwards calls, eliciting a hum of agreement around the room.

"So, I would like to first make a toast to Pam and Marsha for the delicious feast that they have prepared for us this evening. Thank you so much, it has been outstanding." We all agree, and raise our glasses to Pam and Marsha. I don't take a drink, of course.

"I would also like to make a toast to you all. We will of course be doing this again tomorrow for our main celebration at Alexia's house, but, since we're in our home now, I think it only right that we thank you all for coming. To our guests."

Bea stands to join Daniel, "To our guests, welcome and thank you."

Bea sits after the toast as Daniel continues, "And lastly, I couldn't possibly make toasts, without making one to my beautiful Beatrice."

Clare sighs, drawing my attention, and I smile as she gazes as Daniel, watching as he looks at Bea, admiringly; she looks like she'll cry any second. Oh Clare, you really need some romance in your life, you poor girl.

"Bea, you are my world, and I'm not afraid to say it in front of all of these people. I love you more than life itself, as you well know, I tell you at least fifty times a day." Everyone in the room chuckles, warmly. "I don't know how I ever lived without you, and I never want to find out again. Merry Christmas Eve, baby."

Bea raises her free hand and holds his. "Merry Christmas Eve, darling," she says with a huge grin.

"I feel like the luckiest guy in the world right now, I've never been happier than when I'm with you, so I think this would be the perfect moment to ask you something." Bea looks up at him, her face straight. Clare gasps and the tears are already streaming down her face. I look at Emily, who is looking at Edward in question, he simply shrugs with a huge grin on his face. I can't believe we're about to witness this! I grab hold of Luke's hand and stare at the beautiful couple in front of us.

"You know what I'm going to ask you, right?" he asks, grinning.

"Uh... I, er..." Bea stutters, and Daniel chuckles.

"Well, you should, baby, because there'd be no doubt that I would need to ask you this, I couldn't ever live without you."

"Fuck, dude..." Luke whispers beside me and holds my hand tighter as he leans forward on the table, grinning.

"Please, please..." he says, as he sinks to one knee beside her and pulls a sparkling diamond from his pocket, "would you give up being my beautiful girlfriend, to become my beautiful wife?"

Daniel's mum shrieks loudly and stands, her hands covering her mouth. Bea laughs as the tears pour down her cheeks by the bucket load, she looks at the ring and back at Daniel, before grabbing hold of his face and kissing him over and over. "Oh my god!" she cries, "I... oh my god!"

Daniel laughs and wipes her cheeks with his free hand.

"I love you so much," she says, weeping and wrapping her arms around his shoulders, pressing her face into his neck.

"So, that's a yes, then?" he asks, holding her tightly.

Bea giggles and nods, "Uh huh, absolutely, definitely, yes."

It takes a moment to realise that I, too, am crying my eyes out. Not only was that the most amazing thing to watch, my wonderful best friend is getting married! I am so thrilled for her. I release Luke's hand to wipe my face with my fingers and instantly feel his arm around my shoulders. He looks down at me and I up at him.

"Amazing."

I nod, smiling, through a small sob, and he tightens his hold, pulling me into his side. The whole room is laughing and crying, it's such a wonderful moment. I will remember this forever and it wasn't even me getting proposed to!

"Let's go congratulate them, hmm?" he asks, squeezing me against him and I nod.

As we make our way around the table, we hold hands, smiling, excited to get to the happy pair. I wait as Bea finishes her hug with Daniel's mum, hers in floods of tears, cuddling her dad, and soon I am in front of her.

"Bea..." I say with a teary smile.

She bursts into tears again and hugs me tightly. "You're crying!" she says through a giggle.

"Yes, alright, I'm getting emotional in my old age. God, Bea, I knew this would happen but I never thought I'd get to see it! This is wonderful, I am so happy for you. Congratulations, darling. I love you so much."

"I love you, too," she says, sobbing. I take her hand and look at the beautiful ring. It's breathtaking. It has a very large, rectangular diamond in the centre, surrounded by hundreds of tiny diamonds that continue around the band. It looks antique.

"Bea! Darling, this is stunning! You lucky girl! It's so you."

"I know, I need to sit down and just stare at it for a while. I'm still so utterly shocked!"

I give her another long, hard hug and slip out of the way to let Clare in for another emotional embrace.

I watch as Daniel and Luke have their moment, and it's not your average, slap on the back 'dude-like' man hug; it's a big, arms-wrapped-around-each-other hug. Luke's hand is on Daniel's head and Daniel fists at Luke's shirt. This is full on, best-mate emotion and it's almost impossible to watch without getting teary eyed again. Daniel's mum is also watching, crying her eyes out. They exchange some whispered words and grin at each other, before embracing again. Gosh, what an experience - to witness all of this.

I am suddenly ridiculously overcome by emotion, and to save myself too much embarrassment, I make a mad dash to one of the downstairs bathrooms.

I can't hold it in as I approach and sob loudly before attempting to open the door. It's locked. *Oh shit.* The door suddenly opens and to my relief, it's Clare, also sobbing.

"I thought I heard you crying, come in..." she says, with a tissue held to her nose.

I enter, put the toilet seat down, and sit with my head in my hands, crying like a baby. *What the fuck is wrong with me? I don't even know why I'm crying!*

"Come on... stand up," she says, holding her arms open and I throw myself at her, as we cry together.

"Clare, I don't know why I'm crying! It just keeps coming out and won't stop!"

She chuckles slightly, "It's your hormones, darling, and you have so much going on, you're about to break some big-old news to your man, you're scared... as soon as something emotional like this happens, you're bound to have a little episode."

I nod in agreement. It's probably true. "Are you okay? I know you're a cryer and everything, but you seem sad?"

Clare shakes her head. "I'm okay. I suppose I'm just happy for you both, I found out two giant bits of news within a couple of days about my two best people in the world. I'm happy, excited, scared for you. And to be honest, a teeny bit jealous. But I'm okay... Listen, Tilly, I'm not going to go crazy again, but please accept that there is nothing going on with me and Oliver. There really isn't. I would love to have a boyfriend right about now, but I don't. And that makes me a bit sad. Okay?"

Oh my darling, Clare. I'm so sorry. "Okay, I'm sorry. I won't say anything again, it just looked that way, that's all. I'm sorry. We'll find you someone, I mean come on, there's no way Luke and Daniel don't have an ideal man tucked away somewhere for you."

"Good. Can we find him now please?"

"Yep, I'll get right on it."

She giggles and grabs another tissue to clean up her face. I do the same and we both hug, calming ourselves before we make our way back to the dining room.

"Love you," she says, and I respond with the same. How anyone can function without friendship like this, I just don't know. I feel like I have had them all of my life, I don't know how I'd cope if I lost my best friends.

Luke meets us in the hall on the way back to the room. "Oh, hey, I wondered where you went, I was looking for you," he says as he wraps his arms around me. Clare smiles and continues back to the other room.

"I just went to the loo with Clare."

"Great news in there, I can't believe he didn't tell me first!"

"I'm surprised he didn't actually."

"He said he felt that if Bea was going to get married, other than her dad, she should probably know about it first."

Wow. That hits closer to home than I'd have thought. "Well, yes, I'd agree with that. So he picked the ring on his own? That's amazing."

"Yeah, but he does seem to know what she likes."

"He does, you're right."

"So you'll marry me one day, right?" he asks and I burst out laughing.

"What an amazing proposal, thanks!"

He laughs with me. "I'm not proposing, baby, but I wanna know that you'll always be mine."

I smile and stare into his eyes, "Yes, one day, I'll marry you."

"Good. Let's get back to the party. How's your stomach?" he asks, and reaches to touch it again. I scoot away and he immediately holds out his hands and frowns again, "What the heck is it? What's wrong with your stomach? Why can't I touch it?"

Fuck, fuck, fuck. "Nothing, I told you. I'm bloated, it's uncomfortable."

"Shit, since when does it hurt to stroke a bloated belly? Are you like..." *Oh god, oh god, oh god...* "getting your period or something?" *Oh thank fuck.*

"No." I could say 'yes', but that would be lying even more than I already have and we're going to be having the 'talk' later anyway. "Let's just get back. We can talk later, okay?" I ask, rubbing his arm, affectionately.

"Are you sick, or something? Are you okay, baby?" *Oh no, not his concerned face...*

"I'm fine, Luke. Don't worry. Come on."

I take his hand and pull, encouraging him to drop the subject and get back to the table.

~~~~~~~

The rest of the evening was such fabulous fun. Daniel chose the dessert, apparently; we had a delicious choice of warm doughnuts and chocolate sauce (I assume Daniel doesn't know that I know what this represents), and key lime pie. I remember them eating that in Los Angeles, too, I wonder if they did anything dirty with that one...

We retired to the sitting room for after dinner drinks around the fire. Bea and Daniel sat on the floor in front of the fire together, with Bea in between his legs, resting against him, whilst the rest of us sat on the sofas. I curled up with my man, thoroughly tempted to fall asleep in his arms, right there.

When it was time to leave, we all offered another round of congratulations to the happy couple, and headed out to the car to return to Alexia's house. After we park up outside,

Luke helps me out of the car and slowly walks up the steps, holding my hand.

"I know it's late, Princess, but I really want to share something with you."

"What's that?"

"Well, you haven't been up to the hot tub yet, it's incredible at night and I think it'll finish off the evening perfectly. Will you take a hot tub with me? Please?"

I smile, he's so cute, and I think a hot tub sounds amazing, right about now. Just as I'm about to agree, I suddenly remember that I am pregnant! Apart from the fact that I don't want to expose myself, I'm also not supposed to use hot tubs or jacuzzi baths, according to my pregnancy manual... not sure why not. *Oh bugger, now I have to think of another excuse and see that disappointed face again.*

Oliver opens the door and we follow him inside. "I really don't feel like it, darling, but you go ahead. I'm just so tired."

He nods, quietly before responding, and I feel awful. "Okay. No, I'll come to bed with you."

"Are you sure?"

"Yes. I want to hold you. We can do it another night, maybe have a Christmas soak."

My stomach churns as we go up to his bedroom, the nerves of what I'm about to do, the amount of dinner I have eaten not sitting right in my belly, Wriggler having a wild old time in there. It's enough to make me feel really rather sick.

As we step through the door, Luke walks to the balcony again and opens the door wide, sending a freezing breeze through the room, and I stand still by the bed. As he turns back, he looks at me and frowns, "Are you okay? You look... pale, you look sick, Princess." He reaches for me and I run, fast, bashing the en-suite door into the wall on my way in and bend to vomit violently into the toilet. *Omg, couldn't I have done this a little less dramatically?*

It keeps coming and all I want is to close the door and shut the fuck up. There is nothing more revolting than hearing someone being sick. And to my absolute horror, he appears next to me. "No..." I mumble and he ignores me completely, holding my hair back and putting his hand on my forehead, under my fringe.

"It's okay, baby," he says, gently, "just let it out."

As more of the poison leaves my body, I start to cry, I hate being sick, I hate that he is hearing and watching me, and I love him so much for not caring.

"Don't cry. It's okay, you'll feel better in a minute. Just let your body do what it has got to do."

I whimper and then sob. "But..." I wail, "you're here, you can hear it..."

"I know, it's okay. I have seen and heard it plenty times before. It's not going to stop me loving you, sweetheart."

I sob again. "But... it smells of sick... I smell," I cry, mortified.

"It really doesn't. Calm down, stop worrying."

I flush the toilet when my stomach seems to have let go of everything it needs to. And I stand, hunched over, and make my way to the sink to clean my teeth. There's no way I can look at him and talk with sick breath.

He holds my hips. "Is that a little better?"

I nod as I start to brush. I look in the mirror and my face is flushed, mascara running down my cheeks and my eyes red. Wow, I guess this is what Luke's going to have as the memory of being told he's going to be a dad.

When I finish, he leads me out to the bed and starts to undress me. "No, I can do it."

"No, let me. I want to." He reaches for my waistband and I jolt back, away from him. I look up at him, knowing what's coming and a tear falls slowly down my cheek. This is really going to happen.

"Okay. You won't let me see you naked, don't think I haven't noticed, and you won't let me touch you now. You're going to tell me what the hell is going on, and you're going to tell me now." His voice is strong, stern, masterful. *Shit, I really shouldn't be turned on right now.*

I put my face in my hands and nod, preparing myself. I take a long, deep breath in, and exhale slowly. "Okay."

"So what is it, Til?"

My voice wobbles as I ask, "Will you close your eyes? Please?"

"What? Why?" he asks, bewildered.

"Please?" I plead, my voice becoming more of a whimper.

"Okay, okay. Calm down." He closes his eyes and I begin to undress.

"Please stay that way, I will tell you, I promise."

"Okay, my eyes are staying firmly shut, until you tell me I can open them."

"Thank you."

I continue to remove my clothes until I am fully naked, and I tentatively step over to where he is standing, at the side of the bed. Tears fall down my face, my heart races and my skin prickles from the goose bumps as the breeze flows through the room. "Keep them closed," I ask and he nods as I take his hands and slowly move them to rest on my ribs. I sniff, and blink the tears from my eyes as I direct him. "Move your hands down, they're on my ribs. Touch my tummy." I wipe the tears from my cheeks and fresh ones replace them in seconds.

"Tilly, I don't understand, sweetheart."

"Please?" I ask, crying, "Please just slide them down."

He slowly glides his hands down my body and I sob as he reaches my little bump. He slides over it and stops. He goes back up and repeats the process and as he reaches the bump again, he pauses and opens his eyes. He looks directly into mine and all I can do through the tears is frown and silently beg for his acceptance. His face is serious, not an emotion on display. He blinks and his eyes shoot straight down to his hands. And Wriggler.

One hand immediately leaves me to cover his mouth and his eyebrows shoot up. "You're... you..."

I cry and hold his hand to my tummy, desperately needing the contact.

"Shit, Tilly, I... I'm so confused. You're pregnant?"

I nod, petrified of what comes next.

"And this is my baby, right? I mean, you're not gonna let me fuck you with some other guys baby in there?"

"Yes, it's your baby, Luke."

He sits on the bed and looks blankly at the door to the en-suite. "So... so, you knew? You've known? All this time?"

"Oh god, Luke, I'm sorry. I wanted to tell you when I first saw you, I really did but then it got all sexy and then we got all 'together' and everything and I was scared that I'd lose you. Please don't be angry with me." I weep, begging for his forgiveness. I crawl onto the bed next to him and clutch his arm. "Please?"

He looks at me with a frown. "Baby, calm down. Come here." He pulls me onto his lap and I break down again, holding him tightly so he can't let go. "Shh, calm down. I'm sorry, Tilly, but this is all a big shock to me, I don't really know how to react right now. I... I'm, I am a little angry, actually. You should have told me."

"I know. But I was so scared. Are you going to leave?"

"No, we need to talk, I'm not leaving."

"No, I mean, are you going to leave me?"

"No... I... Jesus, Tilly, you're pregnant?" he asks again in disbelief.

I nod, silently.

"How? I mean, when? Oh..." I see it registering, "the pool?"

I nod again. Wiping my cheeks, shaking.

"Til, you're freezing, get into bed please," he says, dominantly.

"Please don't go," I beg.

"I'm not going. I'm going to undress and get in to bed so we can talk about this."

I climb off him and into the bed. Covering myself, I sit up against the headboard and watch as he undresses. He removes his top and starts to unbuckle his belt. He pauses. "So... there's a child inside your body..."

"Uh huh."

He continues to remove his trousers. "And you haven't told me because you were scared? Of what? My reaction or that I'd leave?"

"Both. Scared that you wouldn't want it, scared to never see you again. Lots of things."

He turns off the light and walks over to climb into bed next to me. The light from the en-suite illuminating us both.

He pulls back the cover and looks at my belly. "How pregnant are you? Like, three months or what?"

"No, I'm actually sixteen weeks tomorrow."

"And what's that line going up to your belly button?"

"It's called a linea nigra, apparently it's totally normal. I had to look it up."

"How can I *not* have seen your stomach? We've had sex, like, every ten minutes."

"I was just being... careful."

"Careful not to tell me that I'm going to be a father?"

I pull the covers back over myself and slink down in the bed, to lie down. I turn to face him. "Yes. I'm sorry."

"You keep saying that, Til. I know you're sorry, but I still have questions, okay? I just found out that my girlfriend of one day is four months pregnant. How does that even work out?" He starts to count the weeks back on his fingers.

"You have to add a couple of weeks on to the pregnancy date, it's all worked out from my last period, not the actually conception date."

"Oh, okay. So, what? Have you had one of those ultrasound things?"

"Yes."

"Jesus Christ, Tilly." He runs his hands through his hair and shakes his head. "You have done all this stuff knowing I'm the father of your child and you didn't fucking tell me? I should have been there!"

"I didn't know if you'd have even wanted that, Luke. I didn't think you'd want to change your life to settle down. We weren't an item then, remember?"

"I know, but fuck! I'd have liked the choice."

"Would you have been there? Do you want a baby?" I ask, quietly.

"Shit, Til." He shakes his head. "I am just so out of left field here, I mean, Christ. I don't know what to think."

He stays silent for a minute, just looking at me, and suddenly he jumps. "Oh, fuck, I know you said you hadn't, but please god, tell me no one has touched you or my baby."

I frown, "What do you m... oh... No! I haven't slept with anybody, Luke. Just you."

"Okay. But we've been rough, Til, I've been throwing you about all over the place... shit, that can't be good?"

"It's fine, Luke. We can have sex the way we do without it harming the baby."

"The baby..." he repeats.

I nod. "The baby."

"There is a baby inside your body, that is made of you and me..."

I nod and the tears flow again, just the way he describes it is beautiful to me. The man I love and me made this thing. It might be freaking him out, but I love that fact. "Yes. And no matter how you feel right now," I say with a squeaky voice, thoroughly laced with emotion, "I am so in love with it, because of that. Whether you want to stick around or not, my little Wriggler is part of you, and that makes me love it so much more. And if possible, it makes me more in love with you." I sob as he just stares at me. He doesn't know what to do or say, and I understand that, but I will damn well tell him how much it means to me.

"Til, I..." he shakes his head and I throw the covers back and get out of bed. "Where are you going? Tilly? Are you sick again?"

"I'm just getting tissues. I'm coming back. I'm fine."

When I return to the bed, blowing my nose, I plonk myself down and sit cross legged.

"Get under the covers, Princess, it's freezing."

"No. I'm fine. I need to sit for a minute."

"Okay." He gets out of bed and walks over to the balcony to close it.

"You didn't have to do that, Luke."

"Yes, I did." He sits on the bed behind me and positions himself so that I'm sitting between his thighs, my back against his front. "Now rest back." He holds my hands and places them gently on my belly. I lean against him and turn my head so my face presses against the front of his shoulder. "We've got a baby in here. Wriggler, you say?"

I grin, "That's what I call her."

"Oh, her?"

"I don't know, it's too early for all that, but I say him or her, depending on my mood."

"Okay. And what about your throwing up in there, what was that about? Is everything okay? Could that harm the baby?"

"No. It's okay. I ate too much and I worked myself into a state, worrying about telling you."

"Oh, baby, that's bad. You shouldn't have felt like that. If you'd have just told me earlier, it wouldn't have got that way."

"I know."

"Does anyone else know?"

"Well, please don't go mad. I didn't tell anybody, because I thought you should be the first person to know, but Clare told me today that she knows. She guessed."

"And let me guess, she told Bea. And if she told Bea... then, fuck, Danny knows! Danny knew about my own fucking child before I did? And he didn't tell me?"

"No!" I shout, "Calm down! Bea does not know, and neither does Daniel. Clare knows it's not her place to tell anyone and she hasn't."

"And your sister?"

"No! I told you, I didn't tell anyone."

We sit in silence for a moment before Luke suggests I get into bed. He goes down for a glass of water and I sit waiting for him to come back. It seems like forever before he opens the door again, but as he enters, I see why. He has made us a tray of tea and biscuits. He walks to the bed and puts it down on his side table.

"I thought you could use some tea."

"I really could. Thank you. Are you still mad?"

"I'm not mad Til, I'm just completely overwhelmed, can you understand that or am I being unfair?"

"No, not at all Luke, I totally understand."

"I mean, I got a girlfriend yesterday. I realised I want to get married some day, today, and now I am going to be a dad... I mean, it's not your average Christmas Eve, you know?"

I smile. "I do."

"I just, I can't stop thinking that you've been doing this all on your own... you had no one to talk to about it, no one to go to appointments with. I can't bear that. You should have told me."

"Honestly, Luke, I didn't think you'd be into it and the thought of wanting you so much and then having you tell me you didn't want to play an active part in the baby's life would have killed me. I was so depressed back in England. I knew I had to tell you, but I wanted to do it face to face. And then... well you know how that panned out."

"I fucked you on the kitchen counter. Man, that was good."

I smile. "It was."

"So when you told me that you couldn't get pregnant... it's because you already are. You could have told me then. When we were joking about wanting each other's babies, you were holding this secret. Every time we've had sex, you've been trying to avoid me seeing you... god, this must have been hard for you."

"Oh don't, Luke, it's not about that. It about me being stupid and not telling you sooner."

He pauses and looks at me, holding my hand. "It's about you and me having a baby, Princess."

We continue to talk, I answer all of his questions about the pregnancy so far and all of the situations where I have avoided having to tell anyone about it. He is strangely excited that I am not actually afraid to ski. He is, however, very sad that I can't share a hot tub with him.

"Yes, but don't forget, Lukey, now that you know, we can shower together."

"Let's do it now!" he says, impatiently. "No, wait, that can't be good for the baby, no shower sex. No."

"What? Yes, shower sex, yes!"

"I'm not doing anything that might harm you or Wriggler." *Uh... just sharing that name for the baby makes my heart swell.*

"How is that going to harm either of us?"

"Well you know, funny positions, might not be good... and you might fall..."

"Luke, listen to me. Sex will not harm the baby. Whatever the position. And I am highly unlikely to fall with a giant man like you in there with me. I think you'd catch me if I slipped."

"Okay. Maybe."

"Okay, yes."

"And the ultrasound? Did everything look normal?"

"Yes. It all looks perfect."

"Does he move in there?"

I nod and he raises he eyebrows in delight, "Really? Could I feel it?"

"You couldn't, but I can. It's like little flutters."

We drink our tea and talk about everything he can think of, before we drop off into a wonderful, needed, deep sleep. He holds me tightly from behind, resting a hand on Wriggler, and kissing my neck every time he stirs. It was an extremely emotional experience, but I have to say, it was a lot better than I had expected. Just like Queenie said it would be. I thought he'd get a lot angrier. He seems, if anything, a little excited. I appreciate he's got an awful lot to get his head around, but I think it'll be okay. He still loves me, clearly, and I can only be one hundred percent grateful to him, for making this experience, one that I'll remember for good reasons. He isn't leaving. We can do this. We can be the happy family I so wanted him to help me create.

CHAPTER 12
TUESDAY 25TH DECEMBER - CHRISTMAS DAY

When I wake, Luke isn't in the bed with me. I sit up and again, notice that the balcony door is open so I assume he's out there. I climb out of bed and go to the loo, planning on joining him afterwards. As I return from the bathroom, I find him sitting on the bed, waiting for me.

He smiles, sweetly. "Merry Christmas, Princess." *It's Christmas!*

"Oh! I forgot it was Christmas Day! Merry Christmas, Lukey." I say as I climb back onto the bed and crawl over to give him a kiss.

"Merry Christmas, Wriggler," he says quietly, touching my belly.

"Merry Christmas, Daddy." I whisper, tentatively, assessing his response. He raises his eyebrows and inhales, sharply. Maybe that was too much, too soon.

"Wow. Daddy..."

I nod and hold his hand. "That is what this makes you... but we can take it slowly. Get you used to the idea, okay?"

He nods and smiles at me. "Sure. So, we need to get ready for breakfast, Til, but I wanted to give you a couple small gifts in private, first." *Ooh! Presents!* "Don't expect too much, these aren't big gifts," he says as he leans down the side of the bed and pulls out a small, gift wrapped box.

"Oh, how exciting! Thank you!" I say as he hands me the box.

"Now, this might not be very... appropriate... now, but I bought it back in California, and it's for you. So I'll give it to you anyway."

I peel off the ribbon and open the box, pushing tissue aside to find the gift. I pull out an incredibly sexy, black, corset style underwear set that I seem to recognise.

"I don't know if you remember, sweet-cheeks, but this is what you were teasing me with back in Nordstrom, that day we met. Just before our first kiss. I couldn't get it out of my head. I bought it after you left, in the hope that I'd be able to give it to you, one day."

I smile, remembering it well. "Yes, I remember it. I love it. And yes, it is appropriate, just because I'm prego, doesn't mean I can't be sexy."

"Well you're right there, you're sexier than ever right now."

"Thank you, I love it, and I *love* that you remembered it."

"Good. Here's another little thing..." he says, handing me another box.

"Oh, thank you..."

I begin to open this box, smiling, loving that we are sharing our first Christmas Day moment, alone. I pull out two plush bunnies, the cutest things I have ever seen, really fluffy with huge, floppy ears and a little red heart embroidered on each of their bellies. One is the palest pastel pink and white and the other is beige and white. "Oh, these are so cute!" I hold them to my chest and hug them both.

"Well, you know we're a couple of love-bunnies..."

I giggle, these cute, fluffy little things represent us and our crazy bedroom antics.

"This one is me..." he says, taking the beige one, "and this one is you. See?" he says, pressing their noses together so they kiss. I could cry all over again, this is just so cute! I giggle and wrap my hand around the back of his neck, kissing him.

"I love them, thank you. And I take it it's just a huge coincidence that they have little hearts on their tummies?"

He chuckles. "It is. I thought that when you're in England, and we're not together, you'd have something to cuddle. But as it turns out, you will take a little bit of me everywhere you go anyway."

"I will. Forever." He raises his eyebrows and blows, still finding the whole situation a little daunting.

"Anyway. I have something for you, too. I really don't want you to freak out. I'll be back in a sec."

"Freak out? Oh god. Okay."

I climb out of bed and throw on one of his t-shirts to head straight out to my room to collect the couple of things that I have, that I can only give him in private. Once retrieved, I join him back on his bed.

"Now, this one," I say, as I crawl over to him, "I bought yesterday and it's not intended to scare you or make you get all deep or anything; like your gift, it is for you to take home with you, to remind you."

"Okay..." he says, as he tears off the ribbons and wrapping paper, and holds the small black bear in his hands. He smiles and whispers, "Papa Bear," - the words on the bear's t-shirt.

I hold the tears back, I'm not sure why this is emotional, but it is. "Yes, well, you did say we might have woken the black bears out of hibernation the other day..." I giggle, "but it's just a little something to take with you. To remind you of... you know."

"I do. Thank you." He sits the bear on his table and smiles at it.

"And the next thing is from England," I say with a long exhale, steadying my nerves, as I hand him the box.

"Should I be worried?" he asks with a grin, but as soon as he takes the lid from the box, his face drops. He gazes at it, his mouth slightly ajar. "I... it's..."

I nod. "It's Wriggler's first photo."

He lifts the frame from the box and continues to stare. "I can see... I mean, I can work it out and everything... there's her head..." He continues to stare in astonishment at the perfect scan picture. "This is... this is in there..." he says, looking at my belly as I sit on the bed.

"Yep." I whisper, lifting the t-shirt, exposing the bump.

He shakes his head in disbelief. "I'm sorry, Til. It's still a lot to take in, you know?"

I crawl over to sit in front of him and I take the frame from his hands, before holding them in mine. "Luke, listen to me. I'm not expecting you to suddenly be acting like this is how it's always been. I know it needs to sink in and it'll take a while. It took me a long time to get used to the idea. It's okay to be freaked out."

He looks into my eyes and smiles slightly, before looking down at our hands. "It is a little... daunting. I mean, it's really cool and everything, but I am totally freaked out that someone is going to call me 'Daddy'. I'm worried about you, too. I mean, you're up to date with your appointments and all?"

"Yes, don't worry about me, I'm fine. I had morning sickness for a while, that's gone now, thank fuck."

"But, you had no one to take care of you then! Jesus, that really gets my goat. You should have had support. You should have had someone looking out for you."

"I'm alright, Luke. Stop stressing about me, and concentrate on trying to process the baby news."

"Well, you're a huge part of that, Til."

I nod and sit silently, not really knowing what else to say. Maybe if I'm quiet, he can start getting things right in his head. A few moments pass before he speaks. "I've got one more gift here."

I look up at his beautiful face and see his smile as he passes a box to me. "Thank you," I say, taking it. Inside, I find a small clipping of mistletoe and I grin widely as I pull it out.

"Mistletoe."

"Yeah, I wanted us to have our own mistletoe moment. Just the two... three, of us," he says awkwardly.

I lift it up above my head. "Come on then, bad-boy, kiss me crazy."

He smiles and holds my face in his hands, leaning close to kiss me. He's soft and gentle and slow. His tongue lightly licks at my lips before his hand moves to the back of my head and threads through my hair, as he moves faster. I can't get enough of him, I love him so much, I need everything he offers me. I fist my hands in his hair and sigh loudly, inching further towards him. He pushes me gently to the bed, until I am lying beneath him, loving every inch of his body on mine.

He breaks away to sit up on his knees and pulls his polo-shirt over his head, revealing his outrageously good torso. I still swoon like I've never seen it before. He pushes my t-shirt up my body with his strong hands, until it's bunched at my chest, taking a long, hungry look up and down my naked form. He firmly runs his hands down my sides and lowers back down again, resting on top of my body, returning his lips to mine.

I moan loudly as his tongue twists with mine, my legs bending either side of his body and wrapping around him. I slide my feet into the waistband of his track suit bottoms and push them down his thighs and he chuckles into my mouth. "Well done, I'm impressed," he says, deserting my mouth to lavish my face with tiny kisses.

"I need you..." I whisper, my eyes closed, my body tightly wrapped around his.

He kicks off his trousers and moves to kiss my neck. "I don't want to fuck you hard, Princess, not today," he mumbles against my skin.

"What do you want? I need you, Luke, please?"

He continues to kiss at my neck as he holds one of my boobs in his hand and caresses, divinely. I moan and writhe beneath him. "This is why they're bigger? Because of the baby?"

"Uh huh," I moan, praying he doesn't stop, "yes, but it's so good, don't stop, please don't stop."

He squeezes a little harder, making me cry out in pleasure, all while still kissing and nibbling at my neck. "We can make love, baby, but not hard. Okay?"

I'm assuming this is because of the baby, but I'm not going to question anymore. "Okay, please..."

He kisses my collar bone, slowly moving up my neck to my face before devouring my mouth as he positions himself between my legs. "Is it okay lying on you like this? I'm not squashing him am I?"

"No, no... just don't stop... it's fine..." I respond, holding his head in my hands.

He rubs my nipple between my fingers and I cry out, "Suck it... suck it..." he moves down and takes it in his mouth, licking and sucking indulgently before moving to the other. I moan and throw my head back deeper into the pillow, my mouth open, my eyes clenched shut.

"This is good, baby?" he mumbles against me.

"Oh god, yes!" I cry, and he continues to flick with his tongue and caress with his hands as I reach down between us and take him in my hand, pressing him against me to find his way in. He groans loudly and abandons my nipples to kiss my mouth as he thrusts slowly, sinking deep inside me.

I wrap my legs tightly around his waist, his kiss muffling my cries, his rough moans turning me on immensely. He kisses my jaw as he rotates his hips, pushing into me again and I tilt my pelvis upwards to better accommodate him, to feel every inch as deep as it can go. And it's so deep, almost painfully deep - but so, so good.

He continues to kiss me all over as he makes love to me, his gentleness so unlike him. He's loving me, taking care of me, protecting me... and our baby. I whimper as he glides slowly in and out of my body and I wrap my arms around him, holding him tightly. "I love you," I whisper as a tear falls from the corner of my clenched eyes, down the side of my face. It's approaching and I know I'm going to explode any moment, my skin prickles and heat rushes to all parts of my body in contact with his.

"Oh god..." he says, pained, "fuck, Tilly." He thrusts a little faster and I immediately burst, digging my nails into his back as I come long and hard.

"Yeah!" I cry, moaning and writhing as he thrusts one last time before collapsing against me, his head tucked into my neck. He pants against me and kisses my neck. "I love you, Merry Christmas."

I giggle, "Merry Christmas to you, too. Was that a Christmas shag?"

He laughs with me, "Yup."

"The first of many today, I hope."

"We'll see, it'll be a busy day with people here."

What the fuck? I move my head to the side to force him to move his and look at me. "Since when does that bother you? We fucked in Daniel's *library* yesterday, with a houseful of people..."

"I know, and we probably will, it's just going to be a busy day, is all."

What is that all about? Didn't he enjoy it? Why is he being so vague? "Is everything okay?"

He grins and rolls over, taking me with him so he's hugging me to his chest, on top of him. "Yes, of course everything is okay. I love that we're spending our first Christmas together in one of my favourite places."

"I love it here, too."

"Let's get ready, we're supposed to be downstairs for breakfast soon."

"Okay."

"Just one thing, Tilly..."

"Uh huh?"

"How did I not know? I mean, you've hidden your front from me, your boobs are bigger, you're not skiing, you're not drinking... I mean am I damned stupid or what?"

"Oh god, darling, no. Of course you're not. No one else noticed either... apart from Clare and she only just realised."

"But I've been sleeping with you!"

"I've been devious, okay? I made excuses, I lied, I hid. I'm clearly better at it than I thought. It's not you being stupid, Luke. Please don't think like that, it was all me being cowardly and selfish and I'm so sorry about all of it."

"Okay. Let's not talk about it now. Let's go enjoy Christmas." He grabs my arm as I lift away from him. "But Til, can we just keep it to ourselves for now, until I get used to the idea."

"Absolutely. Whenever you're ready. Clare won't say anything, either."

I have a shower in my room... totally uninterrupted which surprises me, I was expecting Luke to sneak in and ravish me, now that he knows he can. I even left the door open, but he didn't come. I suppose he's still in a bit of a daze, he needs time to get used to it, to let it sink in.

I'm so surprised by how he took it, I mean - I thought he was going to shout and get really angry, maybe even storm out, but he was the height of perfection. He showed his natural feelings, but remained calm for me, he made it all 'okay', and I will be forever grateful to him for that. Telling him about the baby was probably one of the most nerve wracking moments of my life.

I dry off and get dressed in my black, loose-fitting, knee-length, silk dress and heels. I make sure I wear the gorgeous lingerie set that Luke bought me and I feel sexy. A bit fat, maybe, but definitely sexy. I grab my hair dryer and make-up bag, and make my way to Luke's room so I can finish getting ready with him, in case he wants to talk anymore before we have company.

When I step through his doorway, he's nowhere in sight, and I can hear the shower running. *He's* still *in the shower?* I kick off my heels and walk into the en-suite to find him standing there in the cubicle, facing away from me, one arm out-stretched - his hand pressed against the far wall, his other hand pinching the bridge of his nose as he frowns, pained. His head is bowed, the water simply thundering down onto his neck and back as his stands, motionless. *Oh shit.* This is not the stance of someone have a leisurely shower. He's stressing out.

I stand and gaze at him for a moment, worried. He's jovial, he's bubbly, he's not... *this*. He should be singing or whistling, maybe even having a little dance in there... not standing there, fretting. Silently, I unzip my dress and let it float to the floor before I open the door and step in behind him. I don't care that I still have my underwear on, I just want to comfort him, I need to touch him, soothe him. I gently run my hand against the hot, wet skin of his back and step around to his front. "Hi," I whisper when he looks at me, surprised. I wrap both arms around his middle and press the side of my face against his chest.

It takes a moment, but he soon embraces me, holding me tightly, bending to rest his face on my head. "Hey."

"Are you stressing out?" I ask, running my hands up and down his brawny back.

He exhales loudly and smoothes my hair down my back. "Little bit. Little bit."

I squeeze him tightly. "That's okay. You can freak out, it's okay. You don't have to be strong around me."

"I know I don't, Princess. This is just... happening."

"It will. It's okay. Do you want to ask me anything?"

"No, I'm good. But... can I..."

I look up at his face. "What?"

"Can I... touch her again?"

I smile and my heart beats rapidly, I think I just fell in love with him all over again. "Of course you can, don't even ask me that, just do it." I step back a little and pull the lingerie top up and over my belly, and he places his huge, gentle hand on my little stomach. The water runs down our bodies, soaking us both.

"Wow. I have a child in here," he says, somewhat astonished. I remain silent. This is his moment to get acquainted with Wriggler. "You're not big at all, but you do look pregnant, now that I can see you like this. No offence."

"No offence taken, darling, I am pregnant."

He exhales again, and slowly crouches down until his face is level with my tummy. He inspects it, silently, like it's a rare piece of art, both hands resting on either side. He leans forward and gently kisses it, bringing tears to my eyes again.

He stands and holds my face. "Thank you for taking such good care of him. Or her," he says as he leans forward and kisses me gently. *What an odd thing to say...*

"Of course I would..."

"I know, but... you know... thank you anyway."

I smile at him, wondering what he means, and kiss him back. "We'd better go down for breakfast, we'll be really late if we don't get out now."

"You're right. By the way, this looks hot on you. Especially wet. It even looks good with our little bump, here."

I grin, here's a bit of the Luke I know. *And he said 'our bump'!*

Half an hour later, we're dressed and ready and we make our way down to the dining room for breakfast with Clare and Oliver.

"Good morning, you two, we thought you'd never get here. Merry Christmas," Oliver says as he stands from his chair to shake Luke's hand and kiss my cheek. I give him a big hug.

"Merry Christmas, Olly. Sorry we're late."

"Yeah, yeah, I don't want to know..."

I giggle as I move over to Clare, we hug tightly. "Merry Christmas, doll," she says, "all sorted?"

"Merry Christmas," I respond, before continuing in a whisper as the boys chat about something or other, "Yes, sorted. It's okay. He knows you know, but we're not saying anything to anyone else yet. He needs to get used to it..."

She pulls away and simply nods and smiles, as the room goes a little quiet. I move to sit down and Clare hugs Luke. I observe as she squeezes him tightly and kisses his cheek, looking purposefully into his eyes. Oliver frowns slightly, confused, so I quickly divert his attention.

"So, where's my tea Olly? Haven't you poured it yet?"

"Oh! Apologies madam!" He says with a sarcastic tone and a roll of his eyes, and I giggle, cheekily, as he begins to pour the tea from the pot. Luke sits next to me and Clare next to Oliver, opposite us. He rests his hand on my knee and I clutch it. It's all going to be okay.

Our breakfast is delicious, eggs Benedict, at our request, tea and orange juice. The champagne is being put on ice until the rest of the party gets here. Pam is cooking for us yet again, and Marsha - from Daniel's house, is also here preparing the Christmas dinner with her. Either they don't have anywhere to be today, or the Berkeley's are paying them a ridiculous sum to be here.

We retire to the sitting room where we get comfortable on the sofas to wait for everyone to arrive. I wonder how Bea is coping with that ring weighing her down, I bet she hasn't stopped staring at it, it's the most stunning ring I've ever seen and it practically takes up her whole hand. I have no idea how much diamonds cost, I've never checked it out, but I'm willing to bet that this cost more than my annual fucking salary, and then some.

The room is so warm and festive, the tree lights twinkling as always, the smell of incredible cooking floating in from the kitchen, fun Christmas songs playing in the background - kicking back with my best friends and super-sexy boyfriend. I love it.

I look over at Clare as she stands to throw a log onto the fire. She looks effortlessly gorgeous today, her hair is flicky and glowing so perfectly golden, her make-up - spot-on, and her fitted, cream, lambs wool, short dress showing her curves and lengthy legs to perfection. I have to say I'm a little jealous, I feel like a frump in this baggy dress. I look her up and down as she moves around the room, her tiny waist and flat stomach and those big boobies.

Luke nudges me and puts his arm around my shoulders. He lowers his face to kiss my cheek and whispers in my ear, "You look totally, freaking hot, sweet-cheeks. I want to do you all over this room. Stop feeling insecure."

I look up at his face, how the hell did he know what I was thinking? "Uh... thank you. How..."

"I'm watching you watching Clare... I know what you're thinking."

"Well you're right. But have I told you how delicious you look today?" I ask, leaning away from him to fully appreciate the sight. Even the way he sits turns me on. His black trousers fit his thighs perfectly, and the pale grey shirt he wears skims every curve of his brawny torso. His collar open a fraction, I can smell that neck from here. His incredible, Luke smell that sends me into orgasmic overload every time I come within two feet of him. My god. His hair is styled, but tousled, messy but perfect, matching his rough stubble. Crikey, he's so unbearably edible.

"No, but please, go ahead..." he says with a cheeky smile on his face.

I giggle and lean forward to kiss him. "You look fucking amazing, I fancy the pants off you." I mumble against his mouth.

"I love it, but you'll have to fancy them off later, Princess, because I hear the rest of the gang coming."

I pout and he kisses me as the front door opens and everybody tumbles in, covered in snow. "Merry Christmas!" They all cry and we stand to join them and share hugs and greetings all round. I watch as Luke greets Alexia, and for the first time since I met her, I don't feel an ounce of jealousy.

They hug tightly and kiss each other on the cheek, Luke ruffles her hair and she slaps him on the arm. It makes me laugh. Thank god I can see their relationship for what it is now, that jealousy thing was horrific. They're no different to Olly and I.

Daniel and Henry go straight to the kitchen to wish Pam and Marsha a Happy Christmas, and when they return, they bring a couple of ice buckets with champagne and orange juice. Pam follows with a couple of trays of delicious looking canapés. We settle around the fire and Henry begins to pour the bubbly. Clare stands with him and suggests she make the mimosas.

"I fancy one, you do too, don't you Til? Hmm? Mimosa?" she stares at me and I'm clearly a bit behind because I've no idea what she's on about... of course I don't want a mimosa!

"Uh... okay?"

I watch as she prepares a couple and then casually pours a glass full of juice, and hands it to me. Nobody is watching and finally it clicks. "Great, thanks Clare." I say with a grateful smile, and she winks at me in return. Me not drinking on Christmas Day would be like Bea's mum serving up a pizza, so I'm thankful for her quick thinking.

We toast to the perfect day and chat amongst ourselves about how fabulously festive Aspen is and how much we're enjoying our holiday. Apparently, the Berkeley's usually go skiing on Christmas morning, but they decided that with such a large group, they would skip it this year, and asked if we'd like to go for a walk instead. I think it sounds like a lovely idea and I'm quite excited about getting out and about in the crisp, snowy air.

When we finish our drinks and canapés, about an hour or so later, I put on some tights, swap my heels for snow boots, and find my luxurious new coat. Everyone else gets wrapped up warm again and we head out. Daniel's mum, Rose, said there's something going on in town that we might enjoy so we slowly walk together in that direction.

Luke walks with Henry, talking about... something, so I join Oliver and Clare. I slip in between the two of them and link arms. "Hiya, what's new? You're looking particularly handsome today, Olly..." I say, meaning every word; he looks hot. He is a very handsome man anyway, he and Bea have the same colouring, light brown hair, bright green eyes and they both have incredible, long eyelashes - which I always think looks gorgeous on a man. He's probably just over six foot and really fit, he's always had a good body. Not quite as delicious as Luke's, in my opinion, but it's great, none-the-less. The girls have always gone after him. I don't think he's ever been short of a date.

"Thanks, darling, you look pretty stunning yourself. You all do," he says, leaning forward, past me, to look Clare up and down . *Oh yeah? Someone's got passion in their pants...*

"She is looking pretty hot today, isn't she?" I say with a huge, knowing smile as Clare looks straight ahead and blushes.

"He wasn't just talking about me, Til," she says, almost a whisper.

"Of course. I'm just saying, you do. I love that dress on you, your boobs look amazing."

Now it's Olly's turn to blush. Inside, I'm giggling like crazy, they're so easy to play.

"Okay, okay. Thanks Tilly, we all know you like my boobs."

I giggle, it's true. Ever since we met I have have had a bit of a fixation on them. I've always had average sized boobs, quite relative to my size, and Bea is the same, but Clare's are larger and so... perfect. They're big and pert and make her waist look tiny. Most girls pay a lot of money to have a chest like Clare's. She looks incredible in a bikini. And this cream dress.

"So, met anyone new, Olly?"

"You mean am I seeing anyone? No, not really."

"Not really?"

"Not really. Someone's interested back at home, but I'm not sure."

"You've always got someone interested, Ol. Who is she, do I know her? Why aren't you sure?"

"You don't know her, she's a friend of the girlfriend of a bloke I do a couple of jobs with. And I'm just not sure on her yet... she's pretty and everything, I just... don't know."

I roll my eyes and shake my head. There could not be a better matched couple than the two people either side of me, but they won't seem to do anything about it! Although I suspect, as I have already mentioned, that they have had a shag. *Something* has definitely happened. "Well if she's not right, she's not right. I'm sure, one day, you'll see that the perfect girl has been right under your nose all along."

Oliver rolls his eyes and chuckles. "Oh right, and who might that be, darling? You?" He starts to tickle me as we walk along, sliding his hand inside my coat to poke my ribs. I cry out, laughing and trying to push his hand away, I'm too ticklish for my own good. "S..stop, Olly!" I cry through the giggles, and suddenly, I trip on his foot and lose my balance on the icey paving below. "Sh-shit!" I cry as everything transforms into slow motion. I pull my arm from Clare's and grab hold of Oliver and he wraps his other arm around my waist as I fall fast, the only thing racing through my mind is Wriggler. *Please, don't let me hurt my baby...*

Managing to crouch quickly, Oliver's thigh breaks my fall and he grabs me before I hit the ground.

"Fuck!" I hear Luke cry out, loudly and before I know it, he's right there. "What the fuck do you think you're doing? You asshole!" he shouts furiously, glaring at Oliver as he grabs hold of me and lifts me to my feet. "Asshole!"

"Hey! Luke! Stop it, it was an accident!" I cry, my heart pounding. Thank god.

"Jesus, what the hell were you doing?" he asks again, angrily.

"Luke!" I shout, patting his chest with my hand, everyone around us has stopped walking, watching what's going on. "He didn't do anything, I was teasing him and he tickled me, I slipped, that's all, it's not his fault, calm down!"

He rubs his forehead with his gloved fingers, his other hand holding me tightly against him. "Tilly, are you okay? You've got to be careful!"

I glare at him, everyone is going to wonder what the hell is wrong with him. "Luke, I'm fine! He caught me," I take a deep breath, my nerves a little shot. "You're overreacting," I add in a whisper.

"Hey, Til, I'm sorry..." Oliver starts and I interrupt.

"No, Olly, it wasn't your fault, I slipped. Everyone just carry on. No big deal, I just slipped! Luke... I'm fine."

"Sure," he says, closing his eyes and dropping his head before taking a deep breath and looking at Oliver, "sorry, Oliver. I was out of line."

"Don't worry about it, mate. Shall we make a move..." he says to the group, clearly picking up on our need for a quiet moment.

Everyone continues to walk and we step to the side, waiting for them all to pass. I slip my arms around his waist and hug him, needing a little comfort. He cuddles me back and rocks slightly. "I'm sorry, Princess. I didn't mean to shout," he whispers.

"It's okay, Luke, but really, I'm fine. It wasn't Olly's fault."

"I just saw him messing about and then you falling... I got mad."

"I know you did! But we mess about, it's what we do, just like you do with Alexia. He doesn't know that I'm pregnant, Luke. He'd never do anything to hurt me, and chances are, even if I had fallen, I wouldn't have hurt the baby."

He nods. "I'm sorry."

We release each other and hold hands to continue walking, "I suppose you'll just have to walk with me instead of Henry, and look after me," I say with a smile.

"Sure thing, do you want to ride on my back again?"

"I want to ride on something again," I reply, winking, "but yes, I'd love to go on my boyfriend's big, strong back again."

He grins and crouches down to let me climb aboard. It's lovely to hug him so close to me like this, Wriggler wedged between us, my face pressing against his.

As we arrive, I can smell something sweet and delicious. "Where is this?"

"This is Wagner Park Clock Tower, and if I'm not mistaken, we're here to make S'mores."

"Oh my god, I've heard people talk about them on tv... tell me more!" I say, excitedly.

"Well, come, let's follow everyone and go make some."

CHAPTER 13
TUESDAY 25TH DECEMBER/CHRISTMAS DAY (CONT.)

Wow. Had I known the disgustingly gooey amazingness of s'mores, I would have demanded the ingredients be brought to me sooner. Toasted marshmallows and melted chocolate wedged between sweet crackers is the most delicious thing I have ever eaten and I could keep going until I am twice the size I was this morning.

Luke looks at me and laughs as I lick every last bit from my fingers. "I think you like s'mores."

"I love s'mores... maybe even more than I love you, Luke. We might have a problem. You need to make me them, every day for the rest of my life, in order for you to stay in my good books. Okay?"

He chuckles again. "You could never love anything more than you love me, baby, and you know it. I'll make one exception, and that'll be all."

"Just one? So, you don't want to have more than one child?" I ask, more interested than worried. I hadn't thought that far ahead.

"Whoa... wanna give me some time to get used to the idea of one first? Geez..." he says, totally seriously.

"Oh, okay! Sorry, I was only wondering, I wasn't... um..." I feel a little awkward, that wasn't the response I was expecting.

"Hey, Danny, have you made s'mores for Bea before?" he calls out, totally disregarding the conversation we are having, pissing me off a little bit, actually. I mean I wasn't expecting him to say he wants five kids and a country cottage, but he could at least have made me feel a bit better after his panic attack response before entering a conversation about how many fucking s'mores Daniel has made for Bea. *Okay, calm down, Til. He's still getting used to it... give him time.*

Rose and Emily walk over for a chat, apparently this is one of the activities in Aspen's twelve days of Christmas event. I am trying to get into the conversation, but I can't stop worrying about Luke, who has now walked off somewhere with Alexia. *Maybe she's had enough of licking her fingers and wants to lick a bit more of Luke's arse again, instead.* Oh god. Here we go again, I thought I was over this stupid jealousy business.

I nod and smile, not really listening to a word these two lovely ladies are saying. *Where has my man gone?* We mill around for a while as the Berkeley's mingle and introduce their new in-laws to some families they know here. There are a lot of children, I think as I sit back on a bench and observe the happy little faces munching on s'mores.

There's a little toddler girl here being chased by her dad and big sister; she can't be much more than eighteen months, toddling along in her snowsuit - complete with bear ears, holding the gooey treat in her chubby little fingers. I smile as she giggles loudly, her dad giving chase while she wobbles on her feet. She's the cutest little thing with big brown curls exploding from the front of her hood. She waddles over to her mum and throws herself into her arms, covering her mum's ski jacket in chocolate and marshmallow. It makes me laugh out loud, I'm going to have to get used to the idea of my clothes getting filthy... and my house, wherever I live.

I stare at the family, imagining my life in LA with my baby and my Luke - and I get butterflies. I can't believe I've got my man and I'm getting a baby, I didn't even want any of that just a few months ago, but I can't even express how much I want it now.

If I'd never have met Luke, I'd never know this feeling, because I can pretty much guarantee that no one else could make me feel like this. If we hadn't got drunk and persuaded Bea to come to LA with me, I'd never have met him. If we hadn't forgotten a condom that night in the pool, Wriggler would never even be here. These things were so unplanned, but so incredibly necessary to make my life complete.

An arm slips around me and for a moment I think it's my man, but the ever-so-familiar scent of Chloe perfume wafts to my nostrils.

"Hi darling, wotcha doing?" Bea asks, happily.

I rest my head on her shoulder, affectionately. I love how happy she is. "Hello my lovely, I'm just looking around, enjoying the festivities, remembering to thank you."

"Thank me? For what?"

"Well, apart from inviting me along on this amazing holiday; for letting us persuade you to come to LA, for having a fling with Daniel. If it wasn't for you..."

She squeezes me tightly. "Tils, if I hadn't come with you, you would still have met Luke one way or another. If it's meant to be, it's meant to be. And you two... are definitely meant to be! And anyway, I should be thanking you. I'd never have met my Daniel if it wasn't for you."

I grin. "Come on then, show me that gem again, make me jealous."

She giggles and pulls her leather glove off, I'm surprised it fits over that bloody great rock. "I never thought I'd hear you say that, darling; jealous of an engagement ring? Well I never! It won't be long before you have one of these, the way you two love-birds are going."

I hold her hand and admire the intricate details of the ring, the beautiful setting and elegant stone. "I very much doubt I'll ever have one like this Bea, he's definitely not short of a few bob, but he's only a personal trainer, not exactly a Berkeley!"

"Hmm... really? Okay then..." she says with a confused expression.

"What?" I ask, "Is he secretly Daniel's cousin or something?"

"No!" she laughs, "It's nothing... just... maybe ask him about that, okay?"

"Why? Is he a multi-gazillionaire as well?"

She laughs again, "just ask about the trainer thing. Okay?"

"Okay. Oh, he did tell me he could give that up if he wanted to, has he told you he's going to?"

"Yeah... yeah, that's it. Just confirm it with him."

"Okay..." I ask, perplexed.

"Oh, and what was that all about earlier? I though he was going to deck Olly!"

"Oh, I don't know. He thought it was his fault that I slipped. I put him straight, it's okay. Obviously a bit on the over-protective side."

"Yeah but he throws you all over the place, I've seen it with my own eyes..."

"I don't know. Maybe it's okay when it's him or something. Anyway, I'm sure he'll apologise again later."

"Yeah, probably. I know Alexia was telling him off before they saw their friends."

"Oh is that where they are?" *What the fuck is she telling him off for? Doesn't like him being protective over me, eh? Jealous bitch.*

"Yes, they met some friends. Don't be jealous, it's so unlike you."

"I'm not!" I cry, protesting a little too forcefully.

"Okay, okay. But please believe me when I say Alexia is a lovely person. She's not after your man."

"I know, he's already told me that." *And she's obviously able to pull the wool over Bea's eyes, as well."*

She puts her glove back on and pulls me up. She links arms with me and walks over to Daniel whose face lights up when he sees her. He kisses her as we reach him and he leans down to kiss my cheek. "Hey Til, how were your s'mores?"

"Daniel, I am thoroughly displeased that you have not introduced Bea to these tasty treats already. She could have been making them all this time!"

"It's all my fault, I apologise," he says, bowing slightly with a gorgeous smile. "Baby, I demand that you invite Tilly over for s'mores when we get back to the UK, we'll take home some of the traditional ingredients."

"Perfect!" I cry, loving this idea, "They can be dessert after Chinese and 'Mad Men'!"

"Oh, I've missed you on our 'Mad Men' nights. Please come back."

"I will, can't wait."

"So what's going to happen with you and Luke now? Are you going to do long distance or what?" Daniel asks the obvious question.

"Well, we discussed me moving to LA briefly, but I'll have lots to organise before then, so I'm assuming we will have to do long distance at first."

"We'll talk about that, Princess," Luke says, surprising me as he approaches from behind and wraps his arms around my tummy. I almost flinch, before remembering he can do that now; he knows what's hiding in there. It's soothing actually, I've got a bit of a stomach ache and his hands slowly rubbing me feels good. I could probably do with a poo, to be quite frank about it.

Pretty soon, the whole gang joins us and we decide it's time to go home, so we slowly walk back to the house; the couples, hand in hand. Oliver threads his arm through both Clare and Alexia's. *Charmer*.

"Sorry about that, I had to talk with some people and couldn't get away. Why didn't you come find me?"

I shrug. "I don't know, I thought you were busy."

"I would have introduced you. I was worrying about you."

"Worrying? Why?"

"I just was."

"Oh god, seriously Luke, you need to get used to this. You can't be with me twenty four seven. I am a grown up and quite steady on my feet most of the time."

"Til, don't. Okay? I don't know how to deal with this, I'm just doing what comes naturally."

"Okay. Sorry." *This could get annoying, is he going to check up on me every five minutes?* I decide to change the subject. "When we get back, I want to show you something, just you and me."

"Okay... I don't think we'll have time for fucky-fun..."

I giggle but wonder why he's starting to say no to sex... he never says 'no'. "No, it's not fucky-fun, although that's not such a bad idea..." I say, testing the water to see how he responds.

"We'll see. Why are you rubbing your belly like that?"

"Hmm? Oh, I've just got a bit of a tummy ache, that's all. Don't start worrying, there's nothing wrong with me or the baby."

"Okay, if you're sure," he says, squeezing me tightly, pulling me into his side.

~~~~~~~

As we walk through the door, the wonderful aromas and warm heat of the roaring fire welcome us, there's nothing more homely than a log fire and dinner in the oven. We all remove our boots, coats and accessories before Alexia and Henry arrange some more drinks.

I excuse myself to go and get these uncomfortable tights off and visit the loo, hopefully that'll make my belly feel better. It's probably something to do with the tights digging in to my belly, too. I'll have to remember to buy bigger ones. Maybe stockings, tights are so hideously unattractive.

As I sit in the bathroom, waiting for something to happen, I hear a knock on the door. "Yes?" I ask, who on earth would need to bother me while I'm on the toilet?

"Are you okay? Is your stomach better?" Luke asks.

"Yes, Luke. I'll be down in a bit, okay?"

"I'll wait. You wanted to show me something..."

Oh for gods sake. Can't a girl poo in peace? "Yep. Be out in a sec," I say, deciding to give up, nothing worse than someone - a boy in particular - knowing you're having a number two.

I wash up and open the door, finding him perfectly sprawled on my bed, staring at his scan picture which he must have brought it in with him. God, I love this man so much, I'll forgive him disturbing my bathroom moment purely because he's so gorgeous.

"So, sweet cheeks, what is it that you wanted to show me?"

"Well..." I say as I bend to retrieve my iPad from my bag, "come and see this." I sit on the bed and he moves next to me, wrapping a leg around my side and sliding me into him. I can only imagine how hard the muscles in his thighs are flexing right now... *mmm...*

I open my Bounty Pregnancy App and slide the gauge to sixteen weeks, before placing my iPad in front of him. "Here you go. I look at this every week to see what Wriggler is up to. I thought you could read it first this week, so you know something about the baby before I do. Then, maybe you can tell me about it. Role reversal, what do you think?"

He looks at the screen expressionless before looking back at me. He unexpectedly kisses me, hard, holding my face in his hand. He looks down at my belly region and then back into my eyes. "I think it's awesome. Thank you."

I shrug and smile, brushing his broken cheek with my fingertips.

"So this is what the baby looks like in there?" he asks, pointing to the picture on the screen, "Little arms and legs and fingers..."

"Yep. Cute isn't it?'

"Incredible," he says before continuing to read the page. "Okay, it says you need to think about your birthing plan... do you have one of those? What is it? It asks if you want a birthing pool. When do we need to buy that?"

I giggle, but control it, I don't want him to feel silly. "A birthing plan is deciding how I want to give birth. I haven't done that yet. A birthing pool is a pool you can give birth in, we don't have to buy one unless I want to have the baby at home. I can use a birthing pool at the hospital, depending on which hospital I give birth in."

He rubs his forehead again, a sign of stress I have learnt. "Okay, shouldn't you have done the birthing plan?"

"No, we can do that another time. There's plenty of time, besides, I think that decision should be made with you."

"Thank you," he says as he continues to read for a few moments. "It says you'll need new clothes. So we need to go shopping."

"Luke, we don't need to go shopping. Most things still fit me, I've only been having issues because I'm trying to hide it. I might need to get some of those bellyband things so I can leave my trousers undone, but that's it."

"Yes! Bellybands! It talks about those here! Okay. We better find some of those."

I hold his forearm... wow, my hand hardly goes around it, he's so muscular... *Tilly! Focus!* "Luke, honestly, there's no rush for any of this stuff. Okay?"

"Okay. So, do you use Saunas?" *Oh god, he's on a roll!*

"No. Or hot tubs, as we discussed."

"Okay, so we don't need to worry about that..." he says, mentally ticking off each topic on the page.

He pauses for a minute, reading the next part. "Oh man! It's like... this big!" he says excitedly, making a space between his forefingers. "Five inches! And it can suck its thumb! Holy crap, that's amazing!"

I smile, loving that he's doing this and enjoying it.

"So, you can feel it moving, right?"

I nod.

"That means your placenta lies closer to the back than the front. Did you know that? Is that bad?"

"I didn't know that, so thank you for telling me," I say, stroking his arm again. "And I'm pretty sure it's fine."

"Maybe we should check it out?"

"Luke, stop worrying. It's fine."

He continues to read. "Whoa, your breasts could get even larger and more tender... do they hurt?"

"Um, yeah, they do, but I like it when you touch them. Don't stop doing that."

"Okay..." he says, shrugging, and he lifts his hand to cup one of my boobs as he continues to read, making me laugh out loud. I know he's being funny, but it feels oh-so-good.

"Mmm, don't let go," I say, closing my eyes and resting my head back on my shoulders.

"It really feels that good? I'm only touching it?"

"I know, but they ache and you holding them is like an incredible massage... and it *really* turns me on."

"So if you get hungry in the night - drink milk, the end!" he says before tossing the iPad to the side and pouncing on me. I laugh loudly as I fall back into the bed and he kisses my neck, growling. He slips his hand under my dress and glides it all the way up to my chest, sliding my bra out of the way and holding my boob in his big, strong hand. He fondles gently and I moan loudly.

"You really like that, huh?" he mumbles against my neck, grazing my skin with his teeth and tweaking my nipple between finger and thumb.

"Oh god, yes..." I whisper, arching backwards, forcing myself further into his hand.

"I want to kiss it and lick it. I want to suck on your nipple..." he says as he kisses his way from my neck to my jaw.

"Oh god, I'd come, I know it."

"Are you wet, Princess? Do you want me?" he whispers, seductively.

"Yes... yes..."

He slips his hand away from my chest and I whimper loudly, before I feel his fingers slide into the lace of my knickers. He moves slowly down, past my clit making me flinch, until his finger slowly circles the outside of my entrance.

"You are, baby, you're so wet for me. There's a house full of people waiting on us, and you want me to make you come?" he whispers into my ear, his voice gravelly and sexy.

"Yes, yes... yes..." I moan, my head writhing against the pillow. He kisses the corner of my mouth and brushes my lip with his hot tongue as he pushes his fingers deep inside me slowly. "Fuck yes!" I cry in a whisper, as he pulls his fingers straight out again and glides them up to my clitoris, to circle it firmly.

"You want more?"

"Yes, fuck me, Luke, fuck me..."

He kisses my mouth over and over, hot, open mouthed kisses. "No. No sex. I'm going to make you come right now." He growls as he flicks my clit and swiftly slides back inside me, pushing hard and deep. I cry out loud as he slowly pulls back and pushes in again, twisting his wrist, his fingers moving inside. It's outstanding and he's absolutely right, he is *definitely* going to make me come right now.

I clutch hold of the sheets below me and curl my toes as the waves slowly come forth, his fingers turning, pushing, twisting inside me, brushing against that sweet spot. "Come hard, Til..." he growls through gritted teeth and I moan slowly; one long, continuous cry as it crashes through me, everything tingling, my muscles tensing at this outstanding, forceful orgasm. My teeth clenched, he kisses my face and I can't possibly move to kiss him back... I'm stuck, locked to the spot, riding this fucking amazing orgasm to its very, very end.

His fingers gently twist, moving slowly, easing my body from this rigidity, as I come down and relax my muscles. He kisses my lips again and I grab his neck with my hand, holding him against me as I kiss him back, passionately, sliding my tongue in his mouth, needing him to understand how incredible that was.

We snog for short while before we come-to, realising we need to get downstairs. We've been missing for quite a while now. He washes his hands and I change my undies and brush my hair, before making our way downstairs, holding hands. My stomach still aches a little bit, but I'm sure once I eat, I'll be fine. "So do you have any questions about the baby stage?" I ask on the way.

"I'm pretty sure I will. I'll let you know."

"Okay."

Downstairs, everyone is rosy cheeked and merry, laughing, chatting; it's a perfect Christmas afternoon. The meal will be served shortly, so we're gradually starting to make our way into the stylish dining room. The table is set beautifully with gold decorations and crystal glassware, the centrepiece a huge round vase filled with gold baubles and crystals. The white table cloth is scattered with more tiny crystals, each one glimmering in the light, making the table sparkle spectacularly.

"Wow, this looks fabulous." I say to no one in particular as I stroll around the long table, looking for my place card.

"They did a fantastic job, didn't they?" Alexia responds with a smile from across the table. *Wow! She's talking to me.*

"I think I want a Pam." I say, jovially, feeling a bit awkward given the unkind thoughts I've had about the woman I'm talking to.

"I wish I could take her home with me, she's amazing. They all are," she says, softly.

Luke appears at my side and puts a hand on my bottom. "Are we here, gorgeous?"

I nod and put my hand on his back, stroking his delicious muscles. As we sit, he whispers to me. "What are the foods you can't eat? There are some, right?"

I respond quietly, "Yes, I can't eat soft cheeses, shell fish, or undercooked meat - like a steak that's not well done. But this food will be fine."

"Okay. Good. What will happen if you eat those things?"

Blimey, he really is protective. "Probably nothing, but there's a higher risk of food poisoning with the fish and meat and I read up about soft cheese because I really wanted some brie, apparently it can contain listeria bacteria which can cause listeriosis. The risk is higher in pregnant people because of hormone changes or something so it can cause miscarriage and stuff like that."

"Oh god. Don't eat any cheese."

I smile, "It's only soft cheese that's mould ripened. Other cheeses like cheddar are okay. Don't worry, I won't eat any cheese with mould."

"Maybe you shouldn't eat cheese at all, just in case."

"Luke, I can eat hard cheese. Stop worrying."

He puts his elbow on the table and rubs his forehead again as he nods, silently. I wish I could stop him stressing. I stroke his back and lean in to kiss his cheek, whispering in his ear, "Don't worry. We'll be fine."

His eyes close and he puts an arm around me, holding me against him. I see Alexia watching our affectionate embrace from the corner of my eye, she's smiling broadly. Why was I jealous of her again?

The magnificent meal is set in front of us all on the table, the turkey is huge and incredibly delicious looking; golden, juicy and... and... god I'm fucking starving, can we eat now?

Alexia stands this time, to toast everyone. She says that although she isn't staying here, this is still her house and she'd like to welcome everyone, and hopes that Clare, Oliver, Luke and I are all enjoying our stay here. Which we are, immensely. Again, like Daniel last night, she toasts to Pam and Marsha for the fabulous meal and their wonderful decorations. Apparently they are always invited to spend the Christmas meal with the Berkeleys, but they religiously decline, and remain in the kitchen to continue cleaning and preparing desserts.

She toasts the happy couple again, congratulating them on their one day anniversary of engagement, and follows by toasting Luke and I, saying how wonderful it is that we have found each other. I thought that was very sweet, and considering she's shy in social situations - very gracious. I'm such a bitch for wanting to steamroll her.

As we all dig in and load up our plates, I remind myself to be careful and not overload like I did last night. I don't want to have to vomit in front of this perfect man again. How mortifying. Still, he didn't seem to mind. My belly still aches a bit on one side, but maybe after I eat, things will move along. Might even be from retching last night, maybe I pulled something.

Oliver is on my other side, talking with Clare and Luke is deep in conversation with Bea as we begin to eat, when I get a short, sharp pain in my side. *Ow!* I grimace and rub it hard, easing it a little, trying not to make it too obvious in front of Luke, he'll only have a panic attack and take me to A&E for a check up or something. So I continue to eat, forgetting about it, thoroughly enjoying this mouthwatering feast.

I put my knife and fork down for a moment, to reach for my water and as I lift the glass, I get another, sudden, agonisingly sharp pain, in exactly the same place - much, much worse than the last one. I cry out, dropping my glass on my plate, and I double over, screeching my chair loudly on the wooden floor. The room silences as I hold my belly and grimace again, not even thinking about where I am, or who's watching me.

Luke stands in a shot, throwing his napkin on the table. "Holy fuck!" he cries, "Til, what's happening?"

I shake my head, I don't know what's happening and I'm scared, but right now, I can't talk, it hurts so much.

He rests his hand on my back and crouches next to me. "Put your arm around my neck, Princess, come on, we've got to get out of here." I manage to do as he says and he lifts me, effortlessly out of the chair, and carries me over to the door. I catch a glimpse of Clare on my way out, she has her fingertips covering her mouth, her eyes watering, she looks so worried. I want to tell her I'm okay, but I don't even know if I am. Oliver looks confused, and I don't get a chance to see what everyone else is doing, I'm out in the lounge before I know it.

"Baby, what the hell is it? Let me get your coat, we're going to the emergency room."

"No... no..." I manage, holding the side of my tummy and closing my eyes. "Luke, no. Let me just lie down for a little bit."

"No fucking chance, Tilly. There is something seriously wrong right now."

"Luke. Please stop. I think I need to lie down, maybe go to the bathroom, maybe even have a nice warm bath. I think it could be...uh, well...I really don't want to talk about it with you."

"What the fuck? Tilly, you fucking tell me right now, this isn't funny."

Jesus Christ, what the hell?! I press my hand against his chest. "Luke, stop panicking. It's easing a little now. I think it might just be that I'm..."

"That you're what? Would you just friggin' tell me?'

"Constipated! Okay? Consti-fucking-pated! Happy now?"

"No way. You don't do what you just did in there because you're fucking constipated," he shouts.

"Luke, be quiet! Please? Just take me upstairs. We can give it a minute, see if I'm right. If you're still worried, or I am, you can take me to the hospital. Okay?"

His face is as white as a sheet. He gawks at me for a moment, he looks totally lost. "Til, I don't know... I mean, I just don't know. What should I do? Make you go? Do what you want? What am I supposed to do right now?"

I clasp both hands around the back of his neck and look him in the eye. "Listen to me. Calm down. What I really need you to do is take me upstairs. Please? Please? I just want to lie down."

He simply nods and takes me straight up the stairs, opening the door to his room and placing me gently onto the bed. He slips my shoes off and swiftly pulls a t-shirt from the drawers. "Let me undress you and get you into something more comfortable."

I slide my dress up my thighs and under my bum and he takes it from there, slipping it over my head. He removes my bra gently and helps me into his t-shirt. "Do you want socks?" he asks, still as pale as anything.

"No, thank you. I'll just get into bed and lie down for a bit."

"Til, is this because of the fall earlier?"

"No, absolutely not, that was nothing."

"And have you eaten anything bad? Cheese? Meat? Oh god, it's not the meat we ate the other night, is it?"

"No, Luke. I'm not... you know... that's not happening. I'm fine, Wriggler is fine."

He helps me under the covers and then disappears into the en-suite. I hear the bath running as I close my eyes and pray that everything is okay. Please let this be a pulled muscle or constipation... okay, so neither has ever hurt quite like this before, but I know there's a hold up in there because... well... no, I don't need to go into details about dates and shit. Quite literally.

He returns to the room and turns the light off, crawling onto the bed next to me and putting an arm around my chest. "Is this okay? Am I hurting you?"

"No. Not at all. I need a cuddle, Luke." I say feeling a little bit teary, and he opens his arms, allowing me to turn and scoot inside, snuggling up to his chest. As soon as he wraps those big arms around me, I let go and begin to cry a little. I didn't realise quite how scared I was downstairs, until now.

"Shh." He rubs my back, soothingly. "How is it now? A little better?"

I nod. "A little bit, it's not sharp now, just a dull ache."

He says nothing, I wish I could see his face, but I don't want to move from the warm embrace I'm locked in. I can feel his heart thudding through his chest against my face.

We lay silently for a moment, alone in our thoughts, together - physically. A knock at the door makes me jump. "Til... Til? Can I come in?" It's Bea.

Luke moves back so he can look at my face, "You want me to send her away?"

I shake me head. "No."

"But you aren't going to..."

"No, Luke. I won't say anything."

He calls out, telling her to come in. She walks straight over to me and sits on the bed next to me. "Til, are you okay? What's wrong? What happened?"

"I don't know, my stomach feels really bad."

"What is it? Have you eaten anything? Do I need a mask?" she asks humorously.

I smile, weakly, I'm just not quite with it. "No, I've been a bit bunged up and it's just gone on a bit too long, that's all. Don't tell everyone that, please?" I ask, managing to pull a mock-horrified face.

Bea grins. "Of course not. Go and have yourself a nice warm bath and a good old shit. You'll feel better in no time." She says, making me giggle out loud, which actually hurts my belly. I still, closing my eyes and and holding my yummy.

"Are you okay?" Luke asks, panicked again.

"Yes, yes." I say, reaching for his hand and holding it tightly. "Bea, just tell them that I have a funny tummy."

"Will do, doll. Feel better, I'm sad you're missing Christmas but I want you happy and healthy. Look after my BFF, Lukey boy."

"I will," he says, not even a trace of humour for Bea.

She stands and walks to the door to leave. "Oh, Bea?"

"Uh huh?"

"Can you tell Clare that I said 'don't worry'?"

"Yes, I will. She's a right old worry wart that one. Feel better, love you."

"Love you."

She leaves the room and I snuggle back into Luke, feeling so sleepy all of a sudden.

"Til, can I move to turn the faucet off, real quick?"

I smile, my eyes closed. "Of course."

I wake up as he climbs back into the bed and suddenly remember what's happening. I feel like I've been asleep for a couple of hours, not a matter of minutes. Panic spreads through me, and I immediately want to go and sit on the loo and prove myself right.

"Luke, I'm going to go to the bathroom."

"Okay, shall I come with you?"

"Uh... no."

"I think I should."

"No. For what I'm going in there for, I really don't need company."

"But you might..."

"Really, no. You may not join me."

He sighs loudly. "Okay, but leave the door open."

"Are you being serious?"

"Absolutely, leave the door open." He has his dominant face on.

"Oh my god." I shake my head as I walk, hunched over, into the bathroom. I push the door to, but leave it slightly ajar, to satisfy the stress-head.

I'm really not sure I need to tell you about what happened in the bathroom, but it was semi-successful. That's all you should want to know. I climbed into the bath immediately afterwards and lay back in the warm bubbles. It was fabulously soothing, and the ache practically diminished after about fifteen minutes.

Luke made me promise that I'd tell him when I want to get out, so that he could help me, so I called out after a while and he loyally arrived by my side with a big, fluffy towel and assisted me out of the bath like I'm some sort of frail old lady. But I love it really, he's so caring.

We get back into bed, this time Luke takes his clothes off, and we snuggle up ready to sleep. I think we both had a shock today and we're quiet, tired and in need of a big cuddle. Well, I am, anyway.

As I curl up in his arms, he kisses my head and whispers to me, gently running the tips of his fingers up and down my back. "So you're feeling a lot better, sweet-cheeks?"

I nod against his chest. "Yes, much better, thank you."

"I'd still be happier if you'd let me take you to the emergency room."

"No, I'll be fine. The ache is very slight now, I'm sure it'll be gone soon."

"What, you mean it's still there? The ache?"

Oh gawd... "Yes, but it's not a lot at all. Stop worrying, Wriggler and I are fine."

He doesn't say anything else, he just lies there holding me while I drift off into a deep sleep.

~~~~~~~

"Til... Til..." Luke's voice stirs me easily.

"Hmm?"

"What's wrong?"

"Nothing?" I say, puzzled and still half asleep.

"You're moaning and moving around a lot, is your belly hurting again?"

I still for a moment and realise that it is, the ache is back and it's quite intense. It's not the deep pain from earlier on, but it definitely hurts. "Mmm, yes. It is."

"Right, come on. Where are your boots?" He turns the bedside light on and I attempt to sit up, barely able to open my eyes in the brightness.

"What? Why?"

"We're going to the emergency room and I'm not taking no for an answer."

"But Luke," I begin.

"No, Tilly, no. There's no room for discussion, we are going." Bossy boots is back!

"Can't I just..."

"No! Where are your boots?"

"Um..." I rub my forehead, trying to think. "Downstairs by the door, I think."

"Okay, good. Stay there."

He leaves the room quietly and I check the time, it's two in the morning. I could try to contest further, but I don't think it'll work, and he'll only get angry with me. And honestly, I believe I know what the source of the pain is, but I'm no doctor and I have no idea if my diagnosis is correct. I'm a little... okay - a lot worried, too.

I slowly slip my legs out of the bed and prepare my sleepy body to get up when Luke re-enters with my fur coat hanging over his arm, my scarf, gloves and head band in one hand and a bottle of water in the other. He drops everything on the bed to put my coat on.

"Can't I put some trousers on first?"

"No need, my t-shirt is more than sufficient."
"I need trousers."
"No, the coat is long enough."
"Luke. Stop. Please go and get me some trousers, I will not go anywhere without some on." He stops and looks at me briefly, before realising I'm quite right and nodding. He makes his way to my room and I get wrapped up.

A few moments later, we're quietly making our way down stairs, careful not to wake anyone. He helps me put my boots on and slowly walks me down the steps to the car. I start to feel nervous, what if something *is* wrong? He lifts me into my seat and dashes around the car to get in himself. "It won't take too long, baby," he says and I nod with a half smile. He clutches my hand as he reverses out of the drive.

~~~~~~~

The journey home from the hospital was silent. You could have heard a pin drop in the car, between the occasional snivel. It was a highly emotional, very moving couple of hours and I think it will be etched into my mind for as long as I live.

Walking in to the house at about five, everyone is still asleep so all is noiseless and still. I take my boots off, and make my way up to the bedroom alone, as he goes to the kitchen. It doesn't take long for me to undress and slip into bed, the poignant early hours of the day tumbling down on my composure; tears trundle down my cheeks as I break down, alone.

The anxiety increased ten fold on the journey, and by the time we reached the hospital, we were both nervous wrecks. They were particularly thorough, they listened for the heartbeat, they performed an ultrasound scan, they checked me from top to bottom.

I think watching Luke through the whole process was what affected me the most. He was petrified. He comforted me one minute, and then had to leave the room the next. I couldn't understand his behaviour, and I still don't. Wriggler is happy as Larry in there, and I am fine. It took a simple dose of medicine to get everything moving and for the worry to be gone.

I still can't forget the relief I felt when I heard those first few thumps of Wriggler's heart. And Luke's face... he looked like he could cry. Although he didn't, of course. He stood up though, and walked around the room with his hands clasped at the back of his head.

Then when they did the scan - after much pressing by Luke - he was absolutely awestruck. I was hoping he might have held my hand or even kissed me, but once he had stared at the screen for a few minutes, captivated, checking everything is where is should be, he left the room. Just... left. I've no idea where he went, or what he did, and when he finally returned, he offered no explanation whatsoever.

It was so... lonely. I needed him, I wanted to smile with him and celebrate that everything was okay... but he left me. Alone in a strange room with a sonographer who was wondering what was going on with the parents of this child, I was happy but embarrassed, excited but alone - again, just like I have been all along.

I tried to make conversation when we left the hospital, but he was short; not unkind, but not loquacious in the slightest. It's making me feel really rather uneasy, and when all I want to do is sigh with relief and share it with Wriggler's dad... his distance is disconcerting and frankly, very upsetting.

I try to stop crying, but I can't. Although I did think it was a very painful bout of constipation all along, I started to worry very much that something was wrong. I have never experienced pain like that before, just from a simple bowel issue. So I was very worked up before we finally found out everything was okay, and it's all hitting me now.

Luke has been downstairs for quite some time, I must have been in bed a good ten or fifteen minutes and there is still no sign of him. What's wrong with him? I soak up my tears with a tissue and slowly sink down into the bed, giving up on waiting, and drift off to sleep quickly and easily.

CHAPTER 14
WEDNESDAY 26TH DECEMBER

I feel like I've slept for a lifetime when I stir, and am relieved to find myself tightly wrapped in Luke; my face on his chest, both of his arms holding me tightly against him, one leg hooked over mine. I'm almost a little squashed, and very warm. I kiss his chest as my heart swells. He loves me. Maybe he'll be able to explain last night to me, later; he seems to have returned to his normal self, if this overly affectionate sleeping position is anything to go by.

He squeezes me even tighter and I close my eyes, revelling in it. I have had so many years of meaningless, fun sex with good looking, entertaining men and not once did I feel I was missing out on something. But right now, in the arms of the *most* good looking, *most* entertaining man in my world, I can't possibly imagine living without the affection and love that I absorb from him. I need it now, and giving it back comes so unequivocally naturally to me.

My eyes feel swollen and I still have a tissue balled in my fist from last night. I could do with a long, hot bath. I wriggle slightly, getting comfortable, and Luke groans, releasing me a little.

"Are you okay?" he asks, his voice deep and croaky.

"Yes, I'm fine. How about you?" I ask, touching his cheek with my hand. I always seem to be drawn to his broken side, for some reason. Maybe it's a protective thing... I don't know.

"I'm good," he says as he stretches. "It must be late."

"I don't know, I don't really care, I don't need to be anywhere." I snuggle into him again, getting cosy, needing some of that affection back.

"But I might," he says, bluntly, and I feel a little taken aback. He's awfully moody all of a sudden. He turns to check the time on his phone on his side table.

"Oh, sorry, I didn't really think that you'd be going anywhere today."

"A bunch of us usually go out on the slopes the day after Christmas and I was thinking of going, I have been staying in too much and haven't done enough boarding."

Oh. He never mentioned this before, and he has said every single day that he doesn't want to snowboard, he wants to spend the holiday with me. Now I feel a bit embarrassed about being presumptuous, but on the other hand, a bit annoyed. "Um, actually, Luke, you were the one who said you didn't want to go out, and you've just made me feel a little bad about it, I'm not sure that I appreciate that very much. I have told you loads of times that I want you to go out and that I'd be fine here on my own."

"I know. I'm not trying to make you feel bad. I'm just saying, I want to go out today. Is that a problem?"

"No, no. That's fine by me." I shake my head, attempting to start over. "Go and enjoy yourself, you could probably use it after yesterday," I add, trying to get a little friendliness back into the conversation.

"Yeah," he says, nonchalantly.

"Luke... have I done something to piss you off?"

"Not at all."

I move and look up into his face. "So why are you acting so... coldly?"

"I'm not. Do you want a bath?" he asks, disregarding my question completely. He releases me and begins to sit up to get out of bed.

"Will you have one with me?" I ask flirtatiously, giving him an open opportunity to right whatever this is.

"No, I'm going to have a shower and get out of here, see if I can catch up with the others."

"Oh. Okay. Um, yes please, if you're going in there."

He says nothing and walks purposefully to the bathroom and I watch as he goes. He doesn't look at me once. My heart aches, what have I done? I hate that he's being so... mean. It's not like Luke at all. That I know of... I suppose I haven't known him that long, maybe this is another, uglier Luke that I have been lucky enough not to come across yet. My eyes water a little. After everything that happened yesterday, I just want a day in bed with my boyfriend, loving me.

He emerges, not looking at me once, and walks towards the door.

"Luke," I call, stopping him.

"Luke, what have I done?" I ask, sitting on the side of the bed, my hands clutched together.

"Nothing!" he replies, impatiently.

"Clearly I have. Is this about yesterday? We can talk about it, I went through it, too."

"Why the hell have you only just told me, Til?" he shouts and I jump a little, not expecting it. "What if you hadn't told me before yesterday? What if all that had happened and I didn't know you were pregnant? You'd never have gone to the hospital to make sure *our* baby was okay. I had to make you go!"

Holy shit. He's really mad. "Oh... I, I would have gone. I was worried, too, Luke. But the point is, I did tell you before yesterday, and the baby is fine. I told you before how sorry I am that it has taken so long for me to tell you..." I feel highly emotional and my eyes sting as the tears start to fill them. "Is this why you're going out today?"

"Can't I want to go out with my friends now?" he asks, angrily, and emotional correctness goes out the window, the tears roll down my cheeks and my chin quivers as my body prepares itself for a great, big sob.

"Of course you can..." I whine as I begin to cry, my voice an embarrassingly high pitched squeak. I put my face in my hands, not wanting him to see me, although it's perfectly obvious that I am sobbing my heart out.

He stands still for a moment, before I hear him moving towards the door and leaving, closing it quietly behind him. I wipe my cheeks and stand to go to the bathroom to check on my bath. I hate this, I don't understand it. Why is he being so... hateful?

I turn off the taps and can't help but smile through my tears at the amount of bubble bath he has put in here, it's a frothy, white mountain. He has also folded a small towel and placed it at the head of the bath, for me to rest back onto. How can he be so mad at me, but still make these perfect little gestures?

I pull off his t-shirt and climb in, sinking down slowly into the warm, soothing liquid. I take a deep, stuttered breath and exhale through pursed lips, trying to calm myself. He's just a bit freaked out. I shouldn't take it too personally, he just needs to get used to everything. I suppose this is more like the reaction I thought I'd get when I told him. But after last night, I just want a little comfort, why doesn't he? Another bout of sobbing commences. *I'm getting a bit pissed off with all of this shit, stop fucking crying!*

Luke enters, unexpectedly and looks at me briefly as he walks to the shower to turn it on, and then he walks back out again, I presume to undress. I sniff, trying to compose myself before he comes back in. I feel the silent treatment coming on.

I close my eyes and sink back, I decide to think about Wriggler. Those thoughts make me happy. My hands automatically find the melon and stroke it, lovingly, feeling for anything new. There is nothing, but just knowing what's in there is enough. I think of his lovely little nose, or her cute little mouth and I smile. *My beautiful baby; I can't wait to see you.*

I hear Luke entering again, and I keep my eyes closed. I don't need to see him glancing at me, only to say or do nothing. I hear him enter the shower and I try to stay focused on thoughts of my dinky baby. Luke said it can suck it's thumb now. That is pretty impressive, and ridiculously cute. I wonder if it will have hair...

An image suddenly pops into my head of our tiny baby in Luke's enormous strong arms, his hand cradling that teeny little head, his gorgeous lips kissing it's miniature nose - and my lips twitch again, I just can't stop. I need to let it out, I need to have a big, fat cry and a cuddle and get it over with.

I wipe under my eyes and open them wide, blinking, trying to suppress the emotional instability, at least until he's gone. I look over at the shower and am surprised to see him standing still, staring at me, frowning. Our eyes lock, neither of us moving, smiling... anything, we just stare at each other.

He slowly steps forward and places both hands on the glass, steam dancing around his wet, naked body. He tilts his head ever-so-slightly to one side and offers me the smallest smile. I wipe another tear from my cheek and stand slowly, stepping out of the bath, not taking my eyes off his for a second. I pick up a towel and open it to wrap around me, and he subtly shakes his head, beckoning me towards him with his finger. So I drop the towel in front of me and walk across it so as not to slip. He opens the door and holds my hand to help me in, closing it behind me.

Immediately I am wrapped tightly in his arms and I break down, sobbing against his chest. He puts a hand on my head and gently rocks me, soothingly. It's such a relief to have him back. He lifts me gently and I wrap my legs around his waist as he holds me close and walks to the glass wall, pressing my back against it.

He doesn't say a word, just simply looks into my eyes, frowning. He leans forward and brushes his lips against mine before kissing me softly. His tongue gently stroking mine, we kiss so perfectly; smooth, slow, loving - exactly what we both need. I wrap one arm around his neck and with the other, I find his hand, and guide it to rest on my tummy, trying to ease his worry; Wriggler is here and she's fine.

His fingers sprawl across it, holding the baby as best he can, all the while still showing me that he cares, his lips grazing mine, alleviating my distress, reassuring me, consoling. I hope he's feeling that too, because it's exactly what I'm offering back, a sense of calm; everything is okay.

He doesn't make love to me in the shower. I know he's turned on, his boner is practically holding me up, and I am, too, but this isn't about sex. This is about comfort and security. Helping each other through an emotional time. He's apologising for upsetting me, without so many words, and I'm telling him it's okay to be scared. It's a totally unfamiliar, alien situation for both of us.

Eventually we stop with the kissing and holding, Luke turns off the water, and we get out together. He wraps me in a fresh towel before we return to the bedroom and I sit on the bed as he gets some underwear.

"We missed all of the gifts yesterday, that's a shame. I have a couple of things for you under the tree." I say softly, the first words spoken between us since before the bathroom.

He smiles and sits next to me, stroking my cheek with his fingers. "I have something for you, too. Why don't we do that a little later?"

I nod. "What time are you going out?"

"Pretty soon. Do you mind?"

I shake my head. "No. Go and have some fun, I want you to enjoy yourself."

"I enjoy myself with you, too, Tilly, a lot. I just wanted to have a catch up on the slopes and forget about yesterday. Is that bad? Do you want to come?"

"No, thank you, darling, you go and enjoy yourself on your own. And no, it's not bad, not at all. I want to forget about it, too. When you get home, can we have some time, just us? Maybe we can watch a film in the cinema room again?"

"Sounds good. We'll try to actually watch the movie this time, and not fall asleep." He smiles. "I'm going to get ready and go, Princess, do you want anything before I go?"

"Just to know that you still love me and that we're okay."

He looks at me with a slight frown. "I won't ever stop loving you, baby."

I close my eyes and lean against his side. He kisses my head and holds me tightly. "I love you so much, Tilly. My heart hurts when I think of anything happening to you. Please be careful. Look after both of you."

I frown, "I'm not going to be without you for too long, Luke. Just long enough to sort out moving to the States. You sound like we'll never see each other again."

"I just worry. That's all."

"We're fine. Don't worry. What time will you be back?"

"It's hard to say. I'll be arriving late so I might stay a while longer."

"Okay, well I'll pick us a nice movie while you're gone."

He smiles and nods before getting up and continuing to dress. I lay on the bed and watch him, feeling very sleepy again. Maybe I will catch up on some sleep while he's out.

~~~~~~

I had a couple of hours sleep and woke refreshed and chirpy. I threw on some comfies before I went downstairs to eat some very late lunch and choose a film for later. I'm really looking forward to him coming back. I realised I hadn't eaten for nearly twenty four hours, no wonder I polished off a huge plate of Christmas Day food in about four minutes flat.

When I have flicked through the huge catalogue of films and chosen one of my favourites of all time; 'The Blind Side', I throw on my ski gear and take myself out into the trees for a stroll. It's lovely to get out in the fresh, daytime air, having been in bed for what seems like a week.

The snow creaks under my boots again and I smile as it tumbles down around me, huge, great clusters floating to the ground. I walk for a while before I find 'our place' and I sit. Clare and Oliver are out skiing with Bea and Daniel, hopefully they left before the shouting started, I'd hate for them to have heard all of that.

I check my phone to see if I have had anything from Luke, but he's probably too busy charging down those slopes, enjoying himself, because there's nothing. I hope he is having lots of fun. I decide to text him, instead, to let him know that I'm thinking of him.

-

26 Dec 16:06
Hiya, love-bunny :-). Hope you're enjoying yourself, I'm sitting in our spot in the trees with the snow falling, thinking of you. Can't wait until you get back, you sexy mutha fucker. Mwah xx

-

I smile and rest back onto my elbows, imagining him receiving that text. I bet he's smiling right now. I wonder if he is with Matt and Queenie, they're so much fun, he'll definitely enjoy his day with them. Although maybe they'll be with their little boy - Logan, I can't see them taking time away from him over Christmas. Maybe they've taken him out skiing today, just the three of them. I think about their gorgeous little family, I've never met Logan but I can imagine him to be the cutest, coolest little boy ever, with super-fun, loving parents like his.

I will definitely enjoy spending time with them as we grow as a family, I will take all of the advice Queenie can give me, she seems to know what it takes to make it work perfectly.

I'd love for Wriggler to be able to ski from an early age, hopefully Luke feels that way, too, we could all come here and take him or her out on the baby slopes. I wouldn't mind spending all of my time with our child while Luke goes off to snowboard, I could ski with it, take it out to play in the snow... maybe we could all stay at Bea and Daniel's place and then the baby and I could use their pool, too.

I lay back in the soft snow, my warm ski clothes protecting me from the cold underneath me, and close my eyes to let the flakes fall onto my face. I'm so peaceful here, so calm and relaxed, such a change from this morning when I was sobbing all over the place. But it's okay now, we're over it; time to move on and help Luke get used to the idea of being a dad, and then break the news to everyone.

~~~~~~~

"Tilly..." his deep, sexy voice calls to me from somewhere. *Hmm?* "Til, wake up, what are you doing out here? You'll freeze!"

I stir, realising I've fallen asleep out in the snow. As I open my eyes, he's crouching over me, taking his jacket off and I smile at him, reaching one hand up to his chest. It has started getting a little darker, the sky a deep, electric blue and it feels much chillier than it was earlier. I can only have been asleep for half an hour or so, though.

"What are you doing?"

"Hello, darling, I was sitting out here, thinking, and must have drifted off. I haven't been here long," I say as I stretch, shivering, noticing just how freezing it is. "Did you have a great time?"

"It was fine, but forget that... here," he gestures for me to sit up and as I do, he brushes the snow from my hat and wraps his jacket around me, rubbing me to warm me up. "We need to get you indoors, this was really dumb, Til, you can't fall asleep out here on your own for Christ's sake."

Oh wow, bossy boots is back! "Luke, I haven't been out here for long, don't get like that. I'm fine." I say as he helps me stand and I lean against him for a hug.

"It's not just you, though, is it? I mean come on, do you ever even think about this baby?"

Whoa! I am not fucking having that! I shove him away suddenly and step back. "How dare you!" I shout, the cold suddenly vanishing, I am red hot with anger. "I think about my baby twenty four seven and you should fucking well know that! He or she is what I live for now, I'd do anything to protect my baby. I could have gone skiing, I could have been having the odd drink to help hide the secret, I could be eating whatever the hell I like and having hot tubs and saunas, but I haven't, because our baby is too important for any of that shit so don't you dare ask me if I ever think about this baby. You bastard! I fell asleep outside for half an hour, I am wearing skiing clothes for fucks sake, feel it, feel it!" I shout as I lift my clothes to reveal my naked belly.

He stands, gawping, saying nothing. I grab his hand and pull his glove off, throwing it in the snow, and I place it on my belly. *Oh bejesus, his hand is freezing...* "See? Can you feel that? He's fine! My stomach is warmer than anywhere else because I wrapped up appropriately. I am and will be a good mother, Luke, and I don't appreciate your bull-shit, making me feel otherwise." *What an arse-hole.* I hope I'm not getting a glimpse into life with Luke, I couldn't be with someone who tries to make me feel like a bad mother.

He stands still for a moment, staring at me, his hand pressed against my stomach. My face must be scarlet, I am so massively furious. He rubs his forehead with his other hand and then looks down before pulling me against him, slipping my top down again. He wraps his big arms around me and kisses my head. "I'm so sorry, Princess. I'm sorry," he whispers. "I didn't mean that, it was unfair. I know you take care of our little Wriggler. I know. I'm sorry."

I close my eyes and sigh, relaxing into his body. "You do know, which is why that comment makes me so fucking mad. Don't do that shit, Luke. I can't listen to stuff like that."

"I know, I know. I was being a total ass, I don't know why I said that. I just worry..."

"But why? Don't you trust me to look after myself? I've done a good enough job so far."

"Yes, you have. Come on, let's get you inside and forget it." He picks me up and carries me to the house. I rest my head on his shoulder and snuggle against him. I hope he gets over this quickly, or we're going to have some pretty bad teething problems.

We curl up in front of the fire once we have changed into our comfies, Clare and Oliver are on one of the sofas talking, while we sit on the floor together, soaking up the heat from the smooth, amber flames. I lean back against his chest and close my eyes, Wriggler is having a dance and I automatically put my hand on her. It's a good thing I'm not facing the other two.

"What is it?" Luke asks, and I subtly take his hand and rest it against the spot where I felt it move.

"Nothing, it just moved that's all. I wish you could feel it too." I whisper.

"That's so cool," he says and I look up at his face. He is smiling beautifully, those dimples make me want to squeeze him like crazy.

"It is cool. Can we... um, can we like, get back to normal now? Try and get along? Because these few fall-outs of ours have killed me. I hate not being 'us'. I know we have a lot to think about, but we're in this together. Please try not to get cross with me and I will try to remember that you need time to get this clear in your head. What do you say?"

He tightens his hold on me and kisses the side of my face. "Sure. Of course, I'm sorry about everything, I love you so much, you know that don't you? You are everything."

My heart aches with love for him. He is my everything, and more. "Yes. I do, and I hope you know how desperately I'm in love with you, Luke. I missed you so much today."

"I missed you, too. I came home straight after you texted me."

"Oh yes, I forgot about that. Did you come back because you missed me, or because you wanted to make sure I hadn't gone bungee jumping?"

He chuckles. "Bit of both... maybe... I panicked a little when I couldn't find you and then remembered your text so I went out there looking for you."

"And I was rudely awoken. You could have given me a big pash or something..."

"And I should have. What a wasted opportunity. Kiss me now," he says, leaning down to reach my face with his. He moves his hand from my belly to my face and strokes it gently as we begin to kiss. He is so slow and caring, making the most of each second. He pulls away after a few moments and looks into my eyes. "Now suck my big dick, hot stuff."

Of course, as always I laugh out loud. He's so funny. "I am so up for that, you know I can't resist your man-sausage, let's do it."

"Where do you want to go? Bed? Balcony? Kitchen?"

I giggle again, "Garden, boot of the car, Daniel's library..."

He grins, "Tub?"

I get a rush of excitement immediately. "Definitely. Let's go."

We stand to excuse ourselves and just before we speak, Pam enters to tell us our dinner is served. *Fuck it.* Luke hangs his head and grins. "I forgot about eating. Later, Princess. Alright?"

I sigh loudly, "Okay. I suppose we do need to eat."

~~~~~~~

Dinner was delicious. A big, hearty, turkey and ham casserole with dumplings, it definitely warmed my cockles after my chilly sleep earlier. Luke was constantly asking if I needed anything else, or if I'd had enough, it was very sweet but I'm still quite concerned that he is so worried all the time. *Is this normal?* I don't think it is but then again, I have nothing to compare this to, it's not like I've ever done this before. I wish I could call and ask Gem. He's being very affectionate, but he's just a bit... odd.

Clare and Oliver decided to join us in the media room to watch the film, so no hanky panky went down in there. Well... okay, so there might have been a little bit of hanky panky under the blanket. He's a naughty boy like that... and I love it. But we didn't have sex or BJs or anything too fun, just a few snogs and a little 'touchy feely' - nothing obvious.

When we finally go upstairs after the film finishes, Luke turns the bath on and I sit on the bed, excited, looking forward to getting down to it. He comes back in and immediately goes to the door. "Be right back, Princess," he says with a wink and disappears. *What's he up to?*

He arrives back shortly after, with his arms full of Christmas gifts. "I don't know how many you got me, Til, but I picked up the ones with my name on, and of course my gifts for you."

"Ooh! Yay! I totally forgot about the presents!" I respond, bouncing on the bed with enthusiasm, "how exciting!"

He sits opposite me and places the gifts between us. "You first," he says, looking at the gifts and choosing one for me to open.

"Thank you!" I say with a huge smile as I open the large, festive box. Inside, I find a tan cowboy hat, quite plain with a simple twisted plait around the base. I grin, broadly as I pull it out and put it on. "Wow, you *did* get me one in my size, I love it! I can't believe you remembered that you said that. What do you think, cowboy?"

He leans forward to brush my fringe out of my eyes and reposition the hat, smiling deliciously. "I think you look smokin' hot. It really suits you."

"Thank you, it's so cool." I rise onto my knees and lean forward, wrapping my hands around his neck. He puts both hands on my bottom and squeezes, making me giggle into our kiss. I look directly into his eyes and smile at him. "I mean it - thank you. I really love it."

"You're welcome, babe. You always turn me on, but I seriously want to do you in that hat right now."

I laugh and immediately follow with a moan of anticipation. "Let's do these gifts quickly because I need you."

"Okay. You want another one?" he asks.

"No, you have one first - although I only have a couple for you. You pick."

He chooses the larger, flatter gift and slowly begins to tear open the wrapping. He pulls out the white, rectangular jigsaw with a picture of two hearts meeting at their points. One heart is the Union Jack, the other - Stars and Stripes, representing the two of us. In the middle, where they meet, it says 'I love you'. I watch as he looks at it with an odd expression on his face; he looks almost... sad.

It takes a while for him to look up and speak. "Til... I..." he begins, and I start to freak out a little, what's happening? What is he about to say? He looks up at my face and drops the gift on the bed, leaning towards me to pull me close and he kisses me hard. He's passionate, fervent and desperate, kissing me like he hasn't seen me for months. I get totally carried away by this unexpected gratitude for my little jigsaw, and thread my hands into his hair, moaning as I kiss him back, forgetting my worries instantly.

He takes my hat and throws it onto the floor as he grunts, sexily. I immediately want to tear my knickers off, he doesn't even have to say words - just hearing his delicious noise turns me on. I pull him further against me with his head, fisting my hands and tugging his sexy hair hard, trying to take control. We kick the gifts out of the way as we slink down in the bed together, legs sliding against each other, bodies writhing. He holds me down, his tongue expertly working mine; he's taking me, he's in control and no amount of hair pulling is going to change that, so I lay back and let him, enjoying every single second of submission, my skin tingling in anticipation.

"I love you, too," he utters beneath his breath as he pulls back slightly to begin kissing and licking my jaw. Suddenly, he looks up, abruptly. "Holy fuck!" he cries, leaping off me, making me jump.

"What the... what?"

He rushes to the en-suite, shouting as he goes, "The tub!"

Oh, whoops. Fucking bath, ruining our moment. I lay back and catch my breath, I was getting seriously worked up there.

He emerges with a smirk on his face and leans against the door frame, looking at me. "Well that was close."

"Tell me about it..." I look him up and down slowly, taking in his gorgeous physique through his casual clothes. His hard cock presses through his tracksuit bottoms and I become utterly preoccupied - focusing on that and not a lot else. It is so inviting, so big and ready... I could just pull those trousers down and let it spring free in front of me...

He clears his throat, obviously. "You, uh... you want something in particular?"

I grin as I tear my eyes from that favourite place and look at his face. "Yes. Yes I do. Are you going to give it to me?"

"Maybe," he says cooly.

"Maybe? Oh, I see. Well maybe I'll just take what I want?"

"Oh you will? Hmm, okay. Let's see how that works for you."

"You know I can get what I want from you with very little effort. You love it."

He pauses and grins from ear to ear. "Really? Like the other night in the club? You got something - but did you get what you really wanted?"

"No. But you were being mean."

"Oh right, and what makes you think I won't be mean now, Princess?"

"Because you love me too much. Because you can't help but give me what I want because I have your cute, little baby inside me."

"What?!" he cries, "You can't use that!"

"Why not? Because I'm right?"

He pouts and narrows his eyes, crossing his arms. "Maybe."

"See... I'm going to get what I want."

He raises an eyebrow, challenging me so I slide off the bed and sink to my knees on the floor. I crawl over to him and look up at his face; he is grinning perfectly. I smooth my hands up his thighs slowly until I reach the waistband of his trousers and slowly hook my fingers around it. I smile at him and gently tug them down, slowly, staring into his eyes as I do. It's incredibly difficult not to break this eye contact to gaze at my favourite appendage, but looking at him like this, while I slowly strip his bottom half, is so overwhelmingly erotic. I'm ready for him, but more than anything, I want to taste him.

My eyes locked to his, I take him in my hand and firmly run my fist back and forth, feeling him swell further with each stroke. His mouth opens and he blows out, looking alternately between my eyes and my hand caressing him. Keeping eye contact, I lean forward slowly and reach his tip with my tongue, and I lick it indulgently. He groans out loud and grimaces as he rocks his head back to rest against the wall.

I know he's loving it and it makes me need him all the more. I look at him in my hand and get that tingle down in my lady bits, it's just so perfect. I don't waste a second before I plunge him into my mouth as far as I can take him.

"Oh sweet Jesus, carrots, and peas..." he cries and the laughter rumbles in my throat, but I refuse to remove him from my mouth. "Fuck, baby... so good..."

"Mmm," I moan, sucking, lapping, plunging deep. I love that I can feel him like this, so intimate, so close. Kissing him in the most erotic way, tasting that part of him that I adore, the part that gave me my purpose in life. It gave me Wriggler.

It's an erotic, sexual experience, of course, but I truly love this part of him and the deeper I take him - the harder I suck, the more I feel I am expressing exactly how much I love him. All of him.

He raises his arms and thrusts his hands into his hair as he groans loudly again. I caress his balls with my other hand, gently, moving the precious flesh with my fingers as I move faster with my other hand and mouth around his cock. "Oh god..." he moans, preparing me for what's coming, and I get a buzz of excitement. I love it when I make him come, however I do it, just knowing that I can do that to this big strong man - take him to that place of complete ecstasy - makes me revel in excitement.

"Til... oh shit, holy fuck... Tilly!" he moans loudly as he comes hard, grunting and growling. One hand slips down to rest on my shoulder - not holding me against him or using me for leverage, just gently resting against my skin, affectionately, as his orgasm weakens and finally diminishes.

He stands still, panting for a moment as I slowly lick him lightly and ease him from my mouth.

He grunts quietly through pants and I reach up, running my hands under his t-shirt to rest on his taut abs. I adore this body, I would adore his body even if he wasn't so immaculately built, it belongs to him and that's what I love. But it is a super-fantastic bonus that he's an adonis and I get to stare at him forever and know that other women want him. He's mine bitches.

I slowly stand against him and wrap my arms around him, resting my cheek on his chest. His arms snake round me and hold me tight. "Fuck, Princess - you're definitely an expert at making me blast off..."

I giggle. "That's because I love it when you 'blast off'."

"I love how you say that, *'blahst'.*" he says, chuckling, "Your accent is hot."

"Thanks. So, shall we have a bath now?"

"Yeah. Can we stand here for a minute first? I don't think my legs are gonna work."

I laugh again, "Of course."

We bathe together, our wet bodies sliding against each other, it's just as well I'm so small, he barely fits in the bath himself. It's comforting, warm and wonderful lying here with my big bad-boy, having him hold me and wash my body. We don't say much, he seems a little quiet but that's okay, he's probably still coming down from his forceful climax a few moments ago.

I think that we are finally getting back to the way we were, he's still getting used to it, but he's coming around. We're getting there. I lay back against him, close my eyes and smile. This is us, our family here together, in love. I have got exactly what I never knew wanted and I feel so lucky. I can't wait to tell everyone now.

We finish unwrapping our gifts in bed; Luke opens the 'long distance' pillow cases that I bought him, one with a drawing of a girl skiing, her tracks leading all the way over to the next case, with a boy tumbling down the mountain behind her in a heart shaped ball of snow. When I saw it in the shop I thought it was so sweet, and relevant to us. He seemed to like them a lot.

I open my last two gifts from Luke, the first - a bunch of rabbit themed socks, 'tube socks' as Luke calls them. They make me laugh, they are very cute, and I know they will turn

Luke on as soon as I put a pair on. Who'd have thought that socks of all things would be considered 'hot'.

Of course I slip a pair on straight away, teaming them with Luke's t-shirt, before opening my final gift. A beautiful pair of tear-drop, diamond stud earrings. They are amazing, you could see the sparkle a mile off and I absolutely adore them. I am so surprised to have received diamonds from Luke, and I instantly throw myself at him, tightening my arms around his neck.

"Lukey, thank you so much. They're beautiful. Thank you. You didn't have to spend so much on me."

"Til, enough of that. I'm glad you like them."

"Oh, I do, I do! I love them," I say as I kiss his lips.

"Let's sleep," he says, somewhat nonchalantly, taking me by surprise.

"Oh, okay." I respond, confused. "Everything okay?" I start to clear the bed, moving the gifts and wrapping paper to the floor.

"Sure. Careful, Til..." he says loudly, grabbing my hip as I lean over the edge of the bed to drop some more paper.

"I'm perfectly fine, Luke."

"You could hurt yourself, come on."

"Oh god. Seriously, you have to let me live, you can't wrap me in cotton wool, I am only leaning over the edge of the bed, I won't fall off, I won't pull anything, I won't harm either of us."

He rubs his forehead with his fingers again and I can see I'm trying to hold back. He wants to say something.

"What, Luke? Spit it out."

"Nothing," he says, lowering down into the bed, "forget it, let's just get some sleep."

Maybe he's realised he's worrying too much. I don't know, but I think it best to just lie down with him and forget it.

I snuggle into my pillow, watching him get comfortable, and decide to change the subject. "So do you want to take me, bad-boy?" I ask with a wink and he smiles at me, running his fingertips up my arm.

"Not tonight. I'm kinda tired. That okay?"

What? No to sex, again? "Um, yeah. Is everything okay? Ever since I told you, you don't seem to want to have sex as much."

"No. Everything is fine. I'm just tired after snowboarding today."

That excuse isn't washing with me, but we can broach the subject tomorrow, I don't think I'll get anywhere tonight. Maybe I'll sit down with him and discuss my concerns about his worrying and about the sex thing. It's so unlike him.

"Okay." I turn and face away, wriggling back against him.

He holds me close and kisses behind my ear. "I'm sorry, Princess," he whispers , and I wonder just what it is he is apologising for.

CHAPTER 15
THURSDAY 27TH DECEMBER

I stir very early, it must be about three, and Luke is kissing my shoulder and neck over and over again, his hand firmly holding my tummy as he whispers about how much he loves me. It's too early to wake fully and I feel myself falling back into the deep sleep of a moment ago with a contented smile on my face as he continues to kiss. His sniff is the last thing I hear as my dream takes me down a dark corridor of the school I went to as a child.

I stir again a couple of hours later, his hands leave me and the mattress moves as he climbs out of bed. "Mmm... come straight back..." I mumble, hearing his feet pad around to the en-suite. I fall back asleep again, looking forward to being wrapped up safely in his warm body.

I roll over to reach for him when I wake again, feeling cold and lonely. I open my eyes, realising he's not back, and I turn to check the door to the en-suite - that feels like hours ago, he can't still be in there... and he isn't, the door is wide open. I sit up and look at the balcony, the curtains are closed and still so the door must be closed; he's not out there. He must be downstairs, I think, as I yawn and rest back against the headboard, rubbing my eyes. Maybe he's getting us breakfast in bed. I hope so, how fun!

I turn to my bedside table to check the time on my phone and my heart thuds hard in my chest when I see what's on there. The jigsaw I bought him, split in half, just the Stars and Stripes left; his heart. Immediately, I check his bedside table to see if 'my' heart is over there. It isn't, and neither is his 'Papa Bear', or his phone. I sit bolt upright, beginning to panic. *What the hell is going on? Why has his stuff moved?*

I kick the covers back and run over to the drawers, closing my eyes as I grab one of the handles, praying that I am being irrational in thinking he's done a runner. I open it slowly and my heart falls deep into the pit of my stomach; his clothes are gone. *No... no, no, no! He can't have, he wouldn't have!*

I walk back to the bed, searching for clues about where he might be and why he would need to take his clothes.

I look at the jigsaw again and press the button on my phone next to it, to see if I have any messages. I do; one, from him. *Please, please, please - let this be something totally normal, let me be forgetting about something...*

> **LA Luke 27 Dec**
> **I will love you forever, Princess. You have my heart, no one will ever take that from you. I'm sorry. x**

I drop to my knees on the floor, my chest constricting tightly around my pulverised heart. I drop my phone and clench my hands at my sternum, needing some relief from the pain. I bow down, hovering over my bent legs, wondering what the hell happened. We were okay... we were cuddling and kissing... he says he loves me. *Why has he gone?* Is he coming back? Does he ever want to see Wriggler? *Oh god... Wriggler...*

I moan loudly, letting this pain get out anyway it can. Rocking forwards and backwards I cry, loudly. "No, no, no..." I say over and over. He can't do this to me, Luke would never do this to me.

My door bursts open and I don't even bother to look up when I hear Bea calling out to me. I continue to rock, crying loudly, clutching my chest.

"Til? Tilly, darling, what's happened?" she says as she runs to me and sits on the floor, holding me.

I lean into her and sob. I don't bother to talk, I need comfort, I need to cry this pain away, I need... him.

"Darling, it's okay, just tell me what happened..." she says in a soft voice as she rocks with me. My heart feels like it's in my throat, thumping hard, making me nauseous. This can't be happening.

Daniel appears at our sides and rubs my back, too. Where did they come from? How did they know I was upset?

I bury my face in my hands and try to compose myself, maybe Daniel knows something. I take a deep breath and look up at the two of them. "Why... why are you here?"

"We knew something was wrong, Luke sent a text message to Daniel early this morning asking us to get round here quickly to make sure you're okay."

"He did?'" I ask, hopeful. "What did he say? Where is he?"

Daniel moves forward and takes my hands in his. "He didn't say, but I knew he wasn't with you. Til, he said that you need to tell us something and asked me to tell you it's 'okay'. What is it? Are you alright?" He softly rubs my back, comfortingly and I remember again why we all love this man so much. Bea is so lucky. I thought I was. Even last night when we'd had a few 'words' with each other, I still felt so lucky to have Luke, but now I feel like I don't - I've lost him. *Have I really lost him? Has he gone for good? Does he just need a break?*

"Daniel, where is he?" I ask in desperation, pleading with him.

"Sweetheart, I just don't know."

"Did you ask? Can you call him? Text him?"

"I have, I've been calling him and texting him ever since I saw his message, all the way over here. It's switched off, I can't get hold of him. I'm sorry."

I nod. "He's left me," I say, quietly. "Has he? Has he left me?" I ask Daniel, hoping that he will miraculously have all of the answers, knowing full well that he will not.

"I don't know, Tilly. I have to speak with him. I don't understand what's happening though. Has his stuff gone?"

I nod. "Yes. I don't know why, we were so happy - he was kissing me and cuddling me in the night... why would he do this? What happened between those sweet kisses earlier and... whenever he left? When did he leave?"

"I don't know. I'm so sorry, Til. I need to fucking speak with him, this is wrong," he says, shaking his head and running a hand around the back of his neck.

"Til, what was it you need to tell us? I am so confused. First we get a text from Luke to get around here - he's gone, you're crying because you had no idea he was going - so what can you tell us? I don't understand."

"Oh..." I moan, fresh tears streaming down my cheeks, "Oh god, Bea, I feel so sick. Why is this happening?"

"I don't know, darling..." she says looking at Daniel and shaking her head, helplessly. "I just don't know what to do or say. Could he have changed his mind about the girlfriend thing? Did you fight or anything?"

"He wouldn't do that, baby, he loves her too much. He wouldn't just take off because of a fight," Daniel answers.

"We have been arguing a little bit, but... I just thought he needed to... he needed to get used to the idea."

"Of having a girlfriend?" she asks, nodding.

I shake my head and put my face in my hands again. "No."

She frowns. "Til, I just don't understand. I'm sorry."

I take a deep breath and slowly get to my feet, sitting on the edge of the bed. They two of them stand in front of me and I take a hand from both of them. "I love you. I need to tell you something."

"Oh god," Bea says, putting her spare hand to her mouth. "Oh god, what? What is it?" she asks panicking and Daniel immediately puts an arm around her back, comforting her.

"Bea, I'm fine, nothing like that."

"You're pregnant." Daniel says, surprisingly, his face knowing, and I see things all clicking into place for him.

"What? No, she's not..." Bea begins and looks at me as she speaks, coming to an abrupt halt when she sees my face. "You're... you're having a baby?"

I nod and look down, hating that they don't already know this. Bea's mouth drops open and she stands in silence, taking it in.

"Oh, sweetheart. This makes a lot more sense to me now," Daniel says as he sits down next to me on the bed and puts his arm around me, holding me tightly against him. I slip my arms around his stomach and let myself soak in the comfort. It feels so good just to have someone hold me.

"Darling... I... who? When?" Bea asks, dropping to her knees in front of me and reaching for one of my hands.

"It's Luke's baby, of course. It happened while we were in LA."

"What?" she cries, "How long have you both known?"

And this is the bit I really don't want to have to go through again. "I told Luke on Christmas Eve. I have know for a long time, and I'm sorry I didn't tell you Bea, I really am, please don't be upset. But I wanted Luke to know first. You know?"

"Oh, Til, of course I do, I'm not upset... I am absolutely gob-smacked though. I mean - this must have been so hard for you?"

I nod, nonchalantly, I did what I had to. "Darling, Clare knows, but not because I told her, she guessed the other day and I asked her not to say anything until I told Luke. And then Luke didn't want to mention anything until he got used to the idea... which... I guess he won't now. But since he told Daniel I could tell you - now you know."

She stands again and bends to hug me hard. "Oh gosh, doll, you poor, poor thing. And that fucking son of a bitch!" she shouts, pulling back and looking at Daniel. "You better bloody well get hold of him and tell him what the fuck I think of him right now," she shouts to Daniel, quickly followed by, "sorry, darling. I didn't mean to shout at you," and a quick peck on the lips. *God, 'in love' is not what I need to witness right now.*

"I know, and don't worry. I'll track him down. I know what's going on now."

"Do you? He better fucking know what's coming to him from me," Bea says, firmly.

"No, Bea," I respond, defending him, "it's not his fault. He's not the dad type, I'm surprised he was even the boyfriend type. I suppose I thought this would happen, I just fell too far... in love... with him..." I say slowly through sniffles as I melt again.

"What can I do? Let me get tea," Bea says, warmly.

I nod, wiping the tears from my face. "Okay, thank you. Daniel please can you try and get hold of him, tell him I need to talk to him. Tell him I won't be mad - I just need to tell him that I love him and that it's okay."

"It's not fucking okay!" Bea shouts and Daniel frowns. "Okay, okay. I'm sorry, Til."

I smile, even in a 'situation' these two are so cute.

"I will keep trying, sweetheart," Daniel says as he kisses my cheek and stands to leave the room, I presume to start trying to make contact with him. "Do you know what time he left?"

"No. I know we woke up really early and he was kissing me and... and holding my tummy, "I whisper, the pain ripping through me as I recall, "and then I woke a couple of hours later when he was getting out of the bed to use the toilet. Or so I thought... I don't remember him coming back to bed after that... oh god..." I say as my stomach churns painfully and I rock forwards again.

"Okay, I'll be downstairs if you need me. I'll let you know if I get a hold of him."

I nod and watch as he and Bea leave the room.

I enter the en-suite and lean against the vanity, looking in the mirror at my ugly, morning, cry-baby face. *Ugh.* I run the sink taps and splash myself, washing off the sleep and salty tears, praying it will refresh me just a little bit.

When I return, Oliver is sitting back on my bed looking his usual, cool self, resting against the head board, his ankles crossed, waiting for me. "So, we're going to have another little person in the group, eh? That'll be fun!" he says with a huge smile as he opens his arms to offer me a cuddle. I immediately well up again and throw myself at him, laying on the bed, holding him tightly.

"Alright, darling. Everything will be okay. He's just scared and being a bit of an arse-hole, we all have our moments, men are useless. He'll come around," he says, making me smile.

I nod against him, saying nothing. I'm fed up of talking, I just want to lie here, enjoying one of my best friends; my hand-picked brother.

"And you know, he is a really good bloke. He seemed a bit strange on a couple of occasions, but that's all understandable now, given the circumstances, but he's decent. He will come back, don't you worry."

I nod again, sniffing. "Do you think so?"

"I know so, and even if I happen to be wrong, which - let's face it - I never am, that baby will be so unbelievably loved. You *know* I'm going to be the best uncle ever, and my mum and dad will seriously adopt that child as their grandchild - don't doubt that." I grin and squeeze him tighter, grateful for his love. "I'll help you, Bea and Daniel will and you know Clare will be more than enthusiastic about being a hands-on auntie. But that won't even be necessary, because Luke will be back when he's reorganised his head a little bit, and you'll be back to being the best looking family, ever. Okay? So you stop worrying your little self, stress won't help anyone right now."

I smile, loving his wonderfully caring nature, but it just isn't washing with me. It's very easy to say all of this, but when you're the one who has just been left, pregnant and alone, it's not such an easy pill to swallow. *Bastard!* How can he do this to me? Oh... stop, Til. It's not his fault, he has never seen himself as a dad and he didn't ask for this either. He must have been so overwhelmed to go as far as to leave me.

"Shall we just lie here, darling? Bea is going to bring up some tea and food - you need to eat - and I'm sure Clare will be joining her. You just know they're downstairs doing all that girly shit, worrying about you and getting all excited about buying baby-grows. Now I realise why there was a search on Clare's iPad for 'cot sheets with the highest thread count'."

I giggle out loud and swat his belly. "There was not."

He laughs with me. "Okay, there wasn't, I didn't hear about any of this until Bea and Daniel just came down and told us. You know he's trying to get hold of Luke now, don't you?"

"Yes."

"Good. We all love you, Tils, and you won't have to do any of this alone. We're here and we'll stay here with you as long as you want us, until Luke sorts his head out and gets back. I'll be your baby-daddy for as long as you need me. Just don't try anything gross..."

I giggle and squeeze him again, gorgeous man. "Don't worry - I'm *so* not into you. No offence."

"Bloody charming. Thanks for the vote of confidence!" he says, amused.

"Be quiet, you know the whole world and it's sister wants you. And if you know what's good for you... you'll pick the right one." Just because I'm broken right now, doesn't mean I can't give him a point in the right direction - as if he doesn't know it.

"Yeah, yeah."

We lie together in silence for a few more minutes and my mind races, I still don't think I'm quite believing what's happening. But maybe I just need to give him the day, maybe he just needs to get his head straight... but what about? I mean, he's known for a couple of days - and yes - he's been overprotective, but he was fine - we were still kissing and affectionate, he was even holding my tummy and stuff.

He hasn't shown any signs that he would just up and leave... has something happened? Does he have someone else? As easy as it would be to believe that - given the type of man he is - I just don't. He loves me and I know it. I am so confused; broken and thoroughly confused.

As I wipe some fresh tears from my cheek, I hear the door creak open, and Bea and Clare stroll in with trays of tea and snacks. I smile as Clare walks over to me and plonks the tray down on the bed. "We'll get him back. Don't you worry," she says softly and kisses my forehead. "In the meantime, I'm very excited to be able to talk about our exciting news. This trip to Aspen has been quite a celebration, first Bea and Daniel and now you and this little wriggly-bum," she says, touching my belly.

"Congratulations darling," Bea adds, "I'm sorry I didn't say it before, I was away with the fairies."

"Thank you, and don't worry. It wasn't really a 'congratulations' type of moment anyway."

Bea walks around to the side of the bed with my tea, and I shuffle to a seated position, still leaning against Oliver. He's my current rock and he will have to stay there for as long as I need him. If he needs the toilet... tough luck. I take the tea and thank her, before she sits on the edge of the bed next to me. "So..."

"So, can you see it and touch it and talk to it?" I say with a smile, knowing what's coming.

"Exactly!" her eyes sparkle with excitement at my words. I lift Luke's t-shirt, revealing my bump and teeny tiny knickers to my best friends. Oliver rolls his eyes at the sight of my underwear but it doesn't phase him at all. I notice Clare frown a little at my almost-exposed nether regions being displayed in front of Oliver, but I really couldn't care less. We don't see each other that way - and I'm sure he has seen his fair share of female crotches in his lifetime.

Bea gasps and places a warm hand on the little bump. "I can't believe you have a bump and I never even noticed."

"Like I said to Clare and Luke, I have been working pretty hard to try and conceal it."

'Wow...'' Oliver says, "So... does it move and everything?"

I nod, loving that he's taking an interest, too. I watch as Clare smiles at him.

We spend a while like that, drinking tea - looking at the bump and talking softly. I put a pair of trousers on, in case Daniel walks in and gets an eyeful of my lace covered pubic region, and I enjoy the distraction of my friends for a while. Every time I remember the situation, I get a huge twang in my belly that makes me feel ill, but I manage not to vomit like the last time. The last time... when I told Luke... *ouch*. Remembering hurts.

Everyone tries to make me eat one of the fabulous goodies that they brought up from Pam in the kitchen, but I just can't stomach anything. I tried to take a bite of an apple but it was flavourless and sat in my mouth like I was chewing on cloth. I am constantly wondering whether or not Daniel has got hold of him and itching for him to come in the room and give me an update.

When he finally does come to the bedroom, we all look up expectantly. He walks over to the bed and looks down. *Oh god - bad news*. "What? Daniel? Have you spoken to him?" He nods, slowly, saying nothing. "And? What? Where is he? Is he coming back?" I ask desperately.

"Come on, let's leave them to talk," Bea says, standing and making her way to the door. Oliver kisses my head and releases me to follow the others out.

"What's happening, Daniel? Please tell me something." I ask softly, holding back the tears. He sits on the bed next to me and holds my hand.

"Sweetheart, he's just landed back in LA," he says, tenderly. I frown and drop my chin to my chest immediately as my tears flow. I'm so thoroughly hurt, so heartbroken - how could he possibly do this to me? What is so bad that he couldn't stand to stay with me until the end of the holiday? He actually left me in bed to go to the airport, book a flight and board a plane to get away... When did he book the flight? Had he known he was going?

"He is so worried about you, Til. His head is messed up, he doesn't know what to think or do, all he knew was that he had to go. This is what he said to me."

"He can't be that worried," I say, my voice weak and wobbly, "he knew I'd be a mess if he left. Why has he gone? Did he say? I need to know, maybe I can make things better? Does he need time?"

Daniel takes a deep breath and exhales slowly before squeezing my hand and responding. "Tilly, he said that you should go on with your life and forget about him. He said he just can't do this."

"No!" I cry, my heart tearing in two again, "he can, he can! I'll help him... Daniel, why can't he see, it'll be okay?"

"Sweetheart, there's more to it than just leaving you. I can't tell you any more than that, I'm so sorry. He loves you, you need to know that he loves you."

"No, if he loved me - he'd be here, keeping me from this agony. How is there more to it? What is it?"

"I.. I just can't say. I'm so sorry, Tilly."

"Will he talk to me? Can I call him?"

Daniel shakes his head. "I don't think so. But listen, Til, I am going to call him non-stop. I am worried about both of you, you both mean a lot to Bea and I and I will do everything I can. I will try so hard to make him see sense and come back, but Tilly, he seems pretty firm on this. He's so confused, but he seems confident that this is the only way forward. I will try my hardest to make him see otherwise."

"Is there someone else in LA?"

"No, no. Nothing like that. He's totally, one hundred percent in love with you, and I can't see that ever changing, but he has issues that he needs to deal with, and he doesn't feel that'll ever be possible. I, however, do, and I will do anything I can. Okay?" I break down again as I nod in defeat. "Come here, sweetheart," he says as he moves forward to embrace me tightly. "We'll be here for you, always. You know that."

I nod again, whimpering and weeping; nearly ten years worth of tears have appeared in the last few months and I feel like I now have an endless supply. I clutch my tummy with both hands, trying to comfort her. I can't help but feel like she's hurting too, like she knows he's left us and it's because of her - I think... I don't even know what or who is the reason. Despite filling up with this beautiful little being, I feel hopelessly hollow. Just so... hollow.

Sitting here, being rocked, soothingly by Daniel, I think about that word... hollow, and one of my favourite songs comes to mind, 'Goodbye my Lover', by James Blunt, and it's all I can think about, the lyrics going round and around in my head. It's painful, terribly painful and I can't sit still anymore; I need to move, to be different, change my position - anything to ease this discomfort; the torturous ache.

I break away from Daniel's embrace to climb off the bed and stand, but I immediately need to put my hands on the bed and bend over, nauseated. I take some deep breaths but feel the churn again at the slightest thought of him. I'm going to be sick.

I stumble to the toilet and bow down as I heave, over and over. I haven't eaten anything since yesterday so it hurts as I wretch, fruitlessly.

"Shit," Daniel shouts as he dashes in to be with me, "Baby!" he shouts loudly, calling for Bea. She appears within a few seconds as Daniel strokes my back and holds back my hair.

"It's okay, doll. It's okay."

Daniel leaves swiftly, thank god, how many men do I have to throw up in front of this Christmas? Bea simply stands with me, holding me, letting me get this over with.

~~~~~~~

Laying in bed with a bottle of water at my side and a slice of toast forced down, I curl up in a tight ball, holding Wriggler. Everyone has left me, except Oliver. He says he's going to stay with me today, and if I don't want to talk, he'll have a kip next to me. He reckons he needs it... wonder why that is.

"Wanna spoon?" he says, making me giggle.

"You won't try and hump me or anything, will you?" I ask, grinning.

"You should be so lucky. Come on, give us a hug."

He makes me want to cry all over again. But I don't, I don't think my body could cope with anymore, my head feels like it's about to explode, my eyes are like pea holes in snow and I have a great, shiny tomato for a nose. *Attractive.*

I wriggle back against him and he hugs me tight, "Now go to sleep, you look like shit," he says, making me laugh.

"You bitch."

"You could never look like shit, Til, but you do need a bit of a kip. You'll feel a lot better and will be thinking clearer after a sleep."

I nod. "I know. Night night, Olly."

"Night, darling. Sleep tight."

~~~~~~~

Being wrapped up so warm and tight is lovely, as I wriggle and stir. I stretch and turn, and my gut drops as reality returns, Oliver still fast asleep beside me, holding on tightly. For a split second as I woke, I thought it was Luke, I had forgotten what has happened and was blissfully immersed in my dream of his beautiful body enveloping me. And I feel horrible for being so disappointed to see Olly, but I thought for a minute that I was still happy. Olly only reminds me of the ache that doesn't seem to be easing.

His eyes flicker and he stretches, looking at me. "Hiya, you alright?" he asks, sleepily.

"Mmm hmm..." My eyes well up and I bury my face in his chest. He holds me, rocking ever so slightly but remaining silent. Such a true, true friend, I love him dearly.

We stay that way for a good twenty minutes or so, total silence except for my whimpers and sniffles. Eventually, he hands me a tissue box that Bea left on his table. "I think you could use one of these, tears are one thing but do you have to snot on my t-shirt?"

I giggle and take one to blot my eyes and nose. "Cheeky shit."

"Ah, you love me really."

"I do. Thank you, Olly."

"Don't be silly, none of that please, just get on with feeling better."

"I'm not sure I can, I can't think of anything else, he's all I want, I need him. We need him," I say, holding my tummy.

"I know, I know. We'll get him back. So, tell me some more about this baby then, I want to know stuff."

I grin and blow my nose to a hilarious, disgusted look from Oliver, and I begin to tell him everything I know about Wriggler. It's a soothing distraction, because I am always excited to talk about the baby - now that I can, but I still want him here to share the experience with me.

A little later, everyone surprises me by coming up to the room with a late lunch, and eating it in the bedroom with me. It was lovely. I wouldn't have gone downstairs, I don't want to leave my 'Luke' pillow, but I was fully expecting to eat up here on my own, maybe with Oliver if he didn't want a change of scenery; so having everyone eat in here is wonderful and unexpected. I manage to stomach the soup that the girls asked Pam for, it's much easier to eat than a sandwich or something bulky, and I feel a little stronger, having filled my belly.

The rest of the day is spent in bed with Oliver. He does a little work on my iPad, makes a couple of calls and sorts out some business issues back at home, and I doze. I had a bath and changed pyjamas, washing my hair and face to refresh my body. I stood on the balcony for a short while which I thought I would enjoy, but it proved too painful, and I had to return to bed as the tears and memories came speeding back.

I adore Bea and Clare more than anything, they are the most caring friends a girl could ever ask for, but there's something about being with a man that comforts me right now. I can hug him, fully platonically of course, and feel that masculine warmth that no-one but a man can offer. I can spoon him without feeling weird or sexual, and just have that feeling of protection that I get from these boys. They are all similar in that way, go to the ends of the earth to protect the people that they love, and luckily, all of these men love me. It's just a shame one of them can't be near me anymore, for some reason.

CHAPTER 16
FRIDAY 28TH DECEMBER

"Til, darling, I brought you tea..." Clare's soft voice echoes as I wake, my eyes swollen and heavy to open. And thud. It hits me again. I close my eyes and take a deep breath, attempting to compose myself before I go into meltdown when I haven't even said a word to anyone yet.

I nod and smile, I just know if I open my mouth to speak, a sob with fall right out onto the pillow. Luke's pillow. I had to swap them so I could smell him, and so Olly didn't change the smell with his own fragrance, it's all I have left of him, apart from the jigsaw heart and my fluffy bunnies that I can't bear to look at.

I sit up and take a sip of the tea, the hot liquid gliding down my cold, tense system. Olly is already awake, drinking his coffee next to me. "Morning," he says, "I think I enjoy this 'playing husband' shit, suits me I reckon. How does it feel waking up next to a stunner like me? Bet you feel like you've hit the jackpot, don't you?"

Instantly the giggles tumble from my body, exactly what I needed. "You'd make a wonderful husband one day Olly, but sadly, not mine. And anyway - how are you playing husband? You have woken up next to many a girl in your time, and you didn't even have sex with this one!"

"I don't spoon, and I definitely don't wake up with my hand on someones pregnant belly. I mean, what the fuck? I freaked myself out."

I laugh, "Did you? You were touching my belly?"
"Yes! Keep it away from me."

I have to put my cup down, my body jolting with laughter. "You don't mean that, you're just getting close to your little buddy, you are going to be the best uncle ever, Ols."

"I won't argue," he says, polishing his nails on his t-shirt. "Oh, and next time you want to steal one of my t-shirts, can you nick an old one? I only wore than once and have been looking for it for years, I thought I'd lost the plot!"

Damn it! I've gone forever without him seeing this! "Oh... yeah..." I offer him a cheeky grin and he rolls his eyes.

"Til, I know you want to stay in bed, but we thought we'd all go to Bea and Daniel's today, chill out around there in a different environment. It'll be good for you." Clare says. "And, we could all have a swim or something?"

On the one hand, it sounds great; a change of environment as she says, another exploration of their fabulous house, and a swim in the luxurious pool, but I think I just want to be on my own today - so I can cry it all out without any witnesses and do whatever it is that I need to do. "Actually, I think I might just stay here on my own. But you all go, please, I think I'll have a day to myself."

"Til, no. You have to come with us. We've spent so much of the holiday apart, and we have all missed you a lot. Now we're going to spend the day together, taking care of our Tilly and our baby, okay?"

I smile slightly and nod. "Okay." I really need to force myself to do this, as much as I really don't want to move. Wriggler needs fresh air and so do I.

After they leave me to get ready, the first time I've been properly alone since he left, I try to keep busy. Clothes on, clean the teeth, tidy the mess away, make the bed... sit... smell the pillow... collapse on the bed and hug the pillow... *Oh dear, not what I had planned.*

I inhale so deeply, trying to almost ingest this little bit of Luke that remains on the pillow. I don't know how I will cope for the rest of my life with his child, knowing he's Daniel's best friend; knowing that Bea will be seeing him regularly and that she'll know his son or daughter, yet he won't.

If he ever comes to London, I'll have to miss out on any social gatherings, for fear of seeing him and knowing that he doesn't want me or my beautiful baby. I will always love him, and seeing his face will be like getting zapped by a taser, *'here's what you can't have, Til, the man you want more than anyone else'.* And I'll have to watch him with other women... what if he likes the idea of having a girlfriend, now that he's had one, briefly? What if he brings one to England and she meets all of my friends? *Oh dear god, I feel sick again.*

I take one last deep breath with my face pressed into his pillow, and place it back on the bed, tearing myself away from it to grab my iPad, handbag and phone and make my way down stairs. *It's a fucking pillow, Til. You're not leaving a real life Luke in the bedroom. He's already fucking done that to you.*

Arriving at Bea's, we're welcomed at the door with big mugs of spicy chai latte, such a welcome treat after the cold trip from the car to the house. It's freezing today and the snow is coming down in sheets. We curl up in front of the fire and relax with our drinks, canapés already centring the coffee table.

Everyone chats but I find it very hard to concentrate, continuously running through our last few moments together. Why didn't I wake up before he left? Why didn't I hear him packing and stop him? Why didn't I talk to him the previous night about my concerns, instead of leaving it to the morning, when it would be too late? I might have been able to stop him. But what was so bad? I mean he cuddled me, he kissed me over and over, he was holding our unborn baby in his hands... how could he leave that? How could he leave us to do all of this on our own? How could he leave me to feel like this? That *bastard!* How could he!

I can't sit here anymore, I want to scream or break something, at the very least growl with anger and throw cushions. How dare he leave me like this after telling me he loved me and letting me believe we could do this? I need to excuse myself, and I know where to go.

"Bea, I'm sorry to interrupt, can I please go and sit in the library for a minute? I just need some time on my own, away from noise and talking and everything. I'm sorry, I just need to have a little melt down and I just want to do it alone."

"Oh darling of course, help yourself, spend as long as you like up there. All day if you have to."

I exhale deeply and smile, appreciatively. "Thank you for understanding."

"Of course, go and do what you need to do."

Everyone resumes conversation, refraining from making a fuss, as I stand and make my way out of the room with my bag. I practically sprint up to the library and as soon as I get there I double over, putting my hands on my knees and moaning out loud. I don't know how to keep this pain in, I need to cry and scream and let it out! Noise is the only thing I can think of to do that.

I stand straight and immediately walk straight over to the ladder that we had sex on, and shove it hard. It hurts my hand more than anything but I don't care. "Uh... bastard!" I shout, knowing no one will here me and glad for the freedom. "Fucking bastard! Arse-hole! Selfish fucking prick! Uh!" I cry, throwing the nearest book I can find at the wall.

Oh shit... that's not mine. I move to go and pick up the book, feeling bad to have damaged one of the books in the beautiful room. *Whoops.* After careful inspection, I note that the book isn't damaged at all, and I place it on the small table as I drop down in the love seat. *Fucking love seat, more like 'stupid-motherfucker-for-falling-in-love'-seat'.*

I take my phone out of my bag and go straight to Luke's number, ringing it. I haven't tried so far because Daniel told me what he'd said, but I'm so angry right now. He can't just leave and not give me any answers! What a wimp! It rings and rings, but he doesn't answer, angering me even more, so I stay on the line to leave a voicemail.

"You're a fucking bastard! How dare you! Don't you give two shits about us? No, obviously you don't or you wouldn't have just upped and left in the middle of the night without so much as an explanation! You're a pussy; a stupid, bastard, arse-hole pussy and I fucking hate you for this!" I scream down the phone, the tears of anger running down my cheeks. "I trusted that you loved me, I trusted that you would change for me, I let myself believe we could be a family, a happy fucking family! My poor baby, god knows what he's experiencing in there, I hate that I'm like this with a baby inside me, my baby... your baby... our... baby..." I say, slowing to a halt as I begin to weep down the phone. "I love you so much. I love you... and I hate you. So much, Luke. Why did you go?" I cry, sobbing down the phone as I hang up. It's going to do no good, but I need him to hear it, to know what he's done to me.

I drop my phone on the table and rest my head in my hands, letting go, releasing the overwhelming emotion that has been building up since I left my pillow. *This* is why I don't have relationships, *this* is why I didn't want to get involved with Luke again; I knew I'd fall so deep that I couldn't climb out, and that he'd leave me down in that ditch. If he'd have done this the moment I told him, it might have been a little easier, I would have understood that he didn't want this, I thought all along that he would probably leave when I told him.

But he was nice - shocked, but nice; lovely in fact. He touched my tummy, he tried to bond a little, talked to the baby, reassured me and made me believe we'll be happy raising Wriggler together. Why did he do all that if he was just going to leave anyway? It makes this so much more painful. The unexpected hurts so much more than my original fear of losing him immediately. *Bastard!*

I curl up in the chair and cover myself with the big furry blanket draped over the back, trying to calm myself enough to start thinking of my plan for the future. I need to focus on something to get me through, I'm going to have to find somewhere to live. That in itself is a sharp stabbing pain to my system; for the last few days, I've been mentally picturing myself in LA with Luke and have gotten so excited about where we'll live, being close to Gemma and spending weekends together with her and our families. Thinking of having to move out of my maisonette to find somewhere else, on my own, in England is a huge blow.

I could still move to LA to be closer to Gemma, but then I would have more of a chance of bumping into Luke, and knowing he lives so close but hasn't met his own child will hurt like nothing else. If I haven't got him, I need my friends. I need Gemma, too, but I can't live so close, yet feel so terribly far from Luke.

Minutes, probably even a couple of hours pass as I sit in the same position gazing out of that huge round window to my right. Bea opened the door at the bottom of the stairs to my left, a short while ago and brought me up a hot drink and a little bit of lunch. I smiled as she got to the top of the stairs. "Hello, doll," I said, my voice quiet and weak.

She just shook her head and said, "Shh," leaving the food, kissing my forehead and smiling at me before disappearing back down the stairs and closing the door at the bottom. She knows how to deal with me in all sorts of situations, they all do, and considering I never get emotional like this, they are getting it spot-on. I really didn't want to talk - she knew it, and respected it, like the perfect friend that she is.

I haven't heard anything from Luke since my crazed voicemail and it frustrates me. I so want to hear his happy, sexy voice, feel the tingles that spread across my skin when he laughs, the joy that blooms within when he says something funny or romantic.

I take my phone, deciding to text him.

-

28 Dec 14:03
I'm sorry for my voicemail. I am just so frustrated, hurt and so horribly sad, Luke. Please talk to me? Please tell me why you left? I won't get cross - I just want to speak to you. I miss you so much, I can't explain how much I hurt, wanting you. Please explain it all to me? I LOVE you. T. xxx

-

I leave the phone on the table and snuggle back into the blanket, pulling it up to my face and watching the heavy snowstorm belting down outside. It's very cosy and if I was here in the arms of my boyfriend... ex-boyfriend... whatever he is now, I would be in my element.

I fall asleep again, the crying too much for my exhausted body to take while it's trying to grow a baby. I am cosy, warm and comfortable and I sleep deeply for a good couple of hours. The vibration of my phone on the table wakes me with a jolt and my hand grabs it faster than lighting, expectantly. My eyes sleepy and blurry, I have to blink a few times to be able to focus clearly on why my phone was vibrating in the first place. Text Message. From... Luke!

I sit up straight and immediately click into the message.

-

LA Luke 28 Dec 17:11
I can't. I love you, Tilly, more than anything, and I'm so sorry for what I have done. I am all of

> the things that you called me, and more. I miss you, too, but please try to move on, it will be easier for you. I will never love anyone like I love you. Goodbye my Princess. xxxx

I immediately hit reply.

> 28 Dec 17:13
> Luke! Please don't stop - talk to me, will you call me? Please? It's okay, we'll be okay, I promise. We can take things slower and get you used to it all. It won't be hard, darling, we can do whatever it takes to make you feel comfortable about all of this. Just talk to me. Please? Don't say goodbye. xxx

> LA Luke 28 Dec 17:15
> Stop it, Tilly. I can't do this, you're too good for this shit, stop trying to 'help' me. I'm an asshole. It's not going to change. I'm sorry. I can't text anymore. We can't speak. Take care of both of you, promise me that. xx

The frustration builds again as do my tears. I'm angry.

> 28 Dec 17:16
> I'm not promising you anything, you **FUCKER. YOU BASTARD.**

I throw my phone on the table and snarl, so disappointed. I had him - he was communicating... and I lost him again. What could I have said differently to have made him talk? How could I have kept him there to remind him of what he's missing? *Nothing. Because he's a wanker. A wimpy, wankerish fucking wanker.*

~~~~~~~

   I spent the rest of the afternoon/early evening up there, collecting my stuff and heading downstairs only for dinner before we left. I didn't contribute to the conversations, I just sat there like a miserable bitch, needing 'me time'.
   We left pretty much straight after dinner and as soon as we get home, I run up to Luke's bedroom - where I intend on continuing to stay - and I turn on the shower and start to strip. *Don't sit, don't stop. Keep moving and then get straight into bed.* I need to totally preoccupy myself with routine until I can go to sleep and forget again.
   Oliver offers to sleep with me again tonight, but I decline - I need to be on my own to work through this now. I needed them so much yesterday, but today I am needing alone time, I can't be crowded.
   My plan works, and before I know it, I am asleep, heading into tomorrow with - hopefully - less swollen eyes and some emotional stability.

CHAPTER 17
SATURDAY 29TH DECEMBER

Nothing about waking up this morning was eventful or worthy of remembrance. In fact, everything in my world has gone dull and colourless again. So I will resume functioning much like a zombie, as of a couple of weeks ago.

During breakfast, Clare tells me that the boys are going skiing with all of the folks, and that Alexia and Bea had wanted to have a girls day out in town. It sounds like the last thing I could ever wish to do today, but Clare is so sweet - turning her down would be too hard.

"Please would you come, Til? I thought..." she says as she covers my hand with hers, "well, I thought maybe we could go and buy something little for the baby." Her voice is so gentle and soothing, she could sell a cage to a wild lion - this one.

I roll my eyes and grin, "Okay, okay, you don't need to give me the puppy-dog eyes. I'll come, but please don't expect me to be all lively and shit, okay?"

"Oh goody!" she says, bouncing up and down in her chair.

We meet Bea and Alexia in town after a car picks the two of us up. Strolling around in the cold air is refreshing, but the beautiful fur keeping me warm is a constant reminder of him, and making conversation is tough. Alexia is very smiley and loquacious today, and talks to me a lot more than usual, asking how I am and questions about the baby. She's quite nice really.

Clare leads us to a beautiful baby boutique, smiling and excited. "I wish we knew if it was a boy or a girl, I would love to buy something pink or blue," she says sweetly.

"I know, me too. I haven't bought anything but a pair of socks. When I was feeling really rough, and no one knew, I had to buy something tiny to make myself feel a bit better."

"I can understand that," Bea says, holding the door open for me. The shops smells lovely and the huge array of beautiful baby items is wonderful.

"Oh my god! Oh my god, so *cute*!" Clare cries, holding up the tiniest, most gorgeous pink, flannelette baby-grow with soft ruffles on the bottom. It is ridiculously cute, if I knew I was having a girl, I would buy it in a heart beat. "I wonder if they sell it in white..." she says, rummaging around the racks.

"Clare, it is gorgeous, and I do really want it if I am having a girl, but if it's a boy - bottom ruffles really aren't the look I'll be going for."

"Oh yes... didn't really think about that. Does that mean I can't buy a white dress?" she says with a pout.

"He won't be wearing a dress either - if it is a boy, white or not."

"Damn. Can you have a girl then because girls' stuff is so much more cute."

"No! I disagree!" Bea says, "look at this!" She holds up a white vest with a pale blue baby elephant embroidered on the front. It's also very gorgeous.

"Oh my god," Clare says, walking straight over to Bea and snatching it, "can't it just be twins and then you can have one of each! Or... ooh," she looks at Bea with a mischievous look.

"Don't look at me! I'm not having a baby yet, no thank you!" she suddenly looks at me, worried. "Oh god - sorry, I didn't mean... oh, it's not bad that you're pregnant... I meant..."

"Bea, it's fine, I know what you meant. You two are enjoying each other, you will have a baby to make it perfect one day - but for now, you are just loving the time to focus on you. It's lovely, and had Luke and I had the chance - we might still..." I look down, pausing, "well, you know."

Bea rubs my back and I take a deep breath before changing the subject. "I would love to buy something in here, so let's look for something neutral."

I really enjoyed shopping in that little boutique, it reminded me that even though I have lost him, I still have my beautiful baby, and I have so much to look forward to with him or her, even without Luke. It'll be horrible knowing he's missing out on one of the best things to happen to us, but I will be the lucky one, he can fuck right off if he thinks his life is better without our baby.

I bought a gorgeous, white, baby blanket made of the softest most luxurious fabric you could imagine. I adore it. Clare found a little crocheted elephant that she couldn't put down - so she had to buy it for Wriggler, and Bea bought a vest with a little bumble bee on the front. They didn't have to buy anything at all, but they said they couldn't help themselves, and I know they are trying to cheer me up.

We stroll around leisurely, window shopping and people watching. I am surprised that I feel a little stronger, I mean - I still feel sick every time I think of him or see something that reminds me of him, but I feel okay walking around like this, occasionally contributing to the conversation. Maybe concentrating on the baby for a while is helping. I just wish I could get back home and show him the goodies we bought, share the excitement with him.

Alexia wants to show us a fabulous shop selling all sorts of exquisite accessories. It is warm and cosy in this small, glamorous boutique. The blues music in the background is sexy and fun, a great noise to shop to. There are no other customers in here with us, and the attentive member of staff immediately offers to help Bea as she tries on a beautiful hat. I feel a little exhausted and stand resting against a counter, watching as my friends try things on. I'm not really interested in buying anything, I've just come along for the ride.

The song changes and my mind wanders to Luke, wondering what he's doing, whether or not he's thinking about me, hoping he's boarded another flight to come back to me. *Oh, who are you kidding, Til? He's not coming back.* Oh dear, that chest pain is back again and my eyes well up as I rest on my elbows and bend to try and ease the pain. I close my eyes and try to gain composure, just listening to the music.

Bad idea. 'I'd rather go blind' by Etta James is probably the worst song to try to compose myself to. I love this song so much, I adore the stunning sound of her voice, but those words, those utterly too-true words are agonisingly real to me. Okay, so she's singing about another woman, but those words take me right back to how I felt when I saw him with

Alexia. Funny how things become clear later; there's nothing going on with them at all.

But her first words make me want to scream, 'but *nothing* told *me* it was over', I had no clue that he was about to leave me. I wish I had, I might have been able to better prepare myself. I feel every ounce of passion in this song, every ache in the words, it's exactly how I feel and without even knowing it was coming, I sob loudly, and crouch down to the floor.

Luckily, everyone is further towards the back of the small shop, and the music hides my noise. Or so I thought. An arm wraps around me and holds me tightly, and as I look up, Alexia shakes her head. "Shh, just let it out. Cry your heart out," she says, sweetly.

I simply look into her eyes and continue, I can't stop it. She's being so sweet, the song is so painful, and I just can't stop needing Luke. She remains still, kneeling on the ground next to me, hiding behind a rail full of belts. She hugs me hard and comforts me with whispered words.

"I don't know his reasons for leaving, Tilly, but he truly loves you more than anything. I have never seen him so infatuated by a woman, and he told me some wonderful things about you. His face lit up every time we spoke about you, and when you came into a room - wow. You do something to him that I've never seen before. His reasons must be valid, he wouldn't do this to you, easily. I have tried to call him and text him, but we won't take my calls or reply. If I can help in anyway, please tell me. I just want you both together and happy. You belong together."

I attempt to smile but my facial muscles just drag my mouth back down. I attempt to speak and nothing but stutters come out.

"Shh, it's okay, don't speak. Just take some good, long, deep breaths. Here..." she hands me a tissue from her bag. "Wipe your eyes, think happy thoughts. You are so strong, if I were you, I'd be a mess."

"I am!" I manage, pointing to myself with a very slight giggle.

"You're really not. I've had guys screw me over before, and trust me - I couldn't move out of bed for at least three weeks."

I giggle again. She is really sweet, I can see what Bea is talking about now, I'll be sure to keep the steamrollers away from her.

I have calmed down somewhat by the time the other two get back to us with their purchases. "You okay, darling?" Bea asks.

I nod, "Yes, but I think I need to go home now, if you don't mind. You all stay out and have lunch, I'll be fine on my own."

"No, we'll come back, are you all done?" Clare asks, and the other girls nod, so we all head back home together.

When we arrive, I excuse myself and go straight up to Luke's room and sit on the bed, cuddling up to the pillow. I wonder if Alexia will mind if I take it home with me...

I have another little cry and a long think about the situation. It's time for me to realise that he's gone and he's not coming back. I just wish I could talk to him to say goodbye properly, to have a pleasant conversation where I'm not screaming at him - just to end things a little better. I pick up my phone to try to call him, but as I had expected, he doesn't answer and it wrenches my heart just a little.

I decide play some music on my phone and for some torturous reason, I play that song that I love so much, the one that was going around in my head the other day when he left; 'Goodbye my lover' by James Blunt. It's so beautiful and it hurts so much, but I can't stop listening. It's everything I'm feeling right now, but I want him to hear it, to know how I feel.

I grab my iPad and open up a new email. I have to send him something, if he won't talk to me.

-

To: Luke Summers
From: Me
Subject: Please let me say goodbye.
Attachment: 1

-

Luke,

I love you, I miss you, but I always knew this might be too much. I'm sorry I kept it from you for so long, I was afraid to lose you, and obviously, I was right to be afraid. But if I could re-do everything, I would do it exactly the same way, just so that I could get that time with you again.

I don't know your reasons, I wish I did, all I know is that you have them and I will respect that. Neither of us asked for this, but I'll be honest with you and say that I feel more than blessed to have your child growing inside my body. If he's anything like you, he'll be a wonderful human being, and I'm lucky to be his mother.

Of course, I will never forget you; every time I look at my baby, I will think of you, want you and miss you. I don't think I will ever be able to stop loving you, not only because you're the only man I have ever needed, other than my dad, but because you have given me this precious gift. I will forever be grateful to you, for that.

I need to say goodbye to you now, and it's so difficult, my beautiful, big bad-boy.

I love you, I miss you, I don't know how I will live without you. I know I will never be alone, but I'll always be hollow without you.

Tillifer xxxxxxxxxxxx

P.S. I have attached the link to a song I would like you to listen to. Listen to the words, from me, to you. X

-

Sent from my iPad

-

I hit send and curl up against the headboard, wondering what he'll do when he reads it. If he reads it.

Bea knocks on the door and pops her head around, "You okay, doll?"

"I'm... okay. Actually, no, not really. I feel like shit."

She comes into the room and sits on the bed with me. "We're all supposed to be going to this wine and cheese thing later, do you fancy it?"

"What wine and cheese thing?"

"You know - that event in the Aspen 'Twelve days of Christmas' thing... at the Sky Hotel, a wine and cheese tasting."

"Oh... what time?" I say, unenthusiastically.

"Four until Six-thirty."

"Honestly, I really don't feel like it. Do you mind if I don't come?"

"Not at all, darling, but we will miss you. Would you like me to stay here with you? I totally don't mind - it might be fun!"

"No, please go - I love you and thank you, but I just want to sleep and be quiet on my own."

"I understand. No worries," she says, rubbing my arm, "Just text me whenever you need me, okay? Daniel has been calling Luke non-stop, you know. We'll get this sorted."

"Thank you. But things aren't going to change, this is it now and I have to accept it, I can't force him to want to be with us, and if he doesn't want it more than anything else in the world, then I really don't need him as much as I thought. Me and Wriggler need more than that."

"Don't give up."

"I'm not fighting for someone who wouldn't fight for me, Bea."

She smiles and nods in understanding. "Okay. I love you, try to relax and enjoy the afternoon."

"I will."

CHAPTER 18
TUESDAY 1ST JANUARY

Happy New Year. Or miserable new year, if you're me. What a sorry few days these last few have been. After Bea left me to my own devices on Saturday, I spent the day wallowing in the bedroom. I ventured out onto the balcony in the freezing cold, with the duvet and a cup of tea, and I curled up in the chair and slept again. I'm doing a lot of sleeping, but I have needed it, and this crying is really wearing me out.

I woke up in the evening, freezing cold, so I had a hot bath and went straight back to sleep again. At least I enjoyed my first half of the holiday; right now, I am just sitting by, waiting for the time I can go back home and indulge in my self pity in the comfort of my own room. I also need to get planning, looking for a new home and thinking about how I can look after the baby on my own, whilst still earning money to live.

Yesterday, New Years Eve, I went for a walk outside again, but that was yet another painful reminder. I should have known something was wrong the last time when I fell asleep out here. He went crazy at me. Maybe I shouldn't have done that - maybe I should have been more careful so he didn't worry so much. Oh, I don't know, there are so many 'maybes' it's ridiculous, I'm not to know what I could have done differently.

There was a huge New Years Eve party here at Alexia's house last night and I couldn't even face going downstairs. There were people overflowing from room to room, and I just wanted the solace of my own space. My wonderful friends came upstairs with a champagne glass of sparkling Apple juice for me, to toast in the New Year, and that incredibly thoughtful, newly engaged couple didn't even have a midnight pash, to save my feelings. Of course I physically pushed them out onto the balcony and told them to snog, or else. Everyone who can, should snog at midnight.

It marked the beginning of a new era for Wriggler and I; our first New Year together, the year in which he or she will be born; the best of my life. It doesn't feel like it will be, but the day I get to hold my newborn, will be the most special I have ever had.

I called Gemma earlier in the day, told her everything and let her know that I would be out to see her just as soon as I could get more leave from work. She cried her eyes out, first at the good news, and then because I am in such a state. She worries about me so much and I know she wants to be with me.

It was so wonderful to talk to her, tell her everything, and she had some fantastic pregnancy advice. It was so good to finally talk and share the experiences that we have experienced during our pregnancies. I am a little under half way there, so she told me so much about the lovely things I should expect in the near future.

Wriggler has been extremely active over the last few days, it's so obvious now and I can feel so much more. It's bittersweet, really. I love it, it's the most wonderful feeling but I want to share it with someone. Yes - I can share it with my friends, but they aren't its dad. It's not the same, they aren't my lover; someone I can lie naked and hold my tummy with.

I'm seventeen weeks today. It's been a week since Luke told me all about Wrigglers developments and got horny about my boobs. Thinking about it makes me clench inside, *god,* I could do with a big, hard fuck to knock me out of this 'funk' - as my favourite American people would call it.

Today, on the Bounty pregnancy chart, I am told that the progesterone may slow down my bowel movements and cause constipation. *You don't say?* Maybe I should read the week ahead of me this time - just in case! Apparently, Wriggler is practising breathing movements and is in a crucial stage of lung development. She has little taste buds, too. How cute. I wish I could tell Luke. Maybe I should... no, he wants to make a clean break. Will he never want to know anything about his child? I just can't imagine him not caring or needing to know that he's doing well at school, or that she's top of her ballet class... or when he or she first starts to walk as a toddler.

I don't know what everyone else is up to today, but as we're going home tomorrow, I intend to pack up my stuff and get ready for reality. God, the thought of having to go back to work after this roller coaster of a ride is fucking hideous.

As I pack up the last of my clothes from my room, I drag the case through to Luke's, to get the rest of my things. Pam meets me on the landing with a large pile of towels.

"Hello, Pam."

"Hi, Tilly, how are you?" she asks following me into my room.

"I'm okay, thank you."

"You're missing Luke though? I know I am, that boy is something special, I always miss him and Daniel when they go back. Never a dull moment with one of those two around."

I smile. "Yes, I miss him a lot."

"He'll see sense, sweetheart. He's a good boy."

"Everyone says that, it's just a little hard to believe sometimes. Do you have a family? You seem to be here all the time."

"No, I couldn't have babies back when I was married so I never got one of my own. I used to take care of other people's children, as a nanny, and that was perfect for me. When I divorced, I was looking for a new job and a friend of mine, Marsha - you met her, told me about a family she had met whilst working in a restaurant, who were looking for house staff. That's how this all started."

I sit on the bed as she potters around the room, folding blankets and lightly tidying. "So, where do you live?"

"I live here, didn't you know that?"

"No..."

"Well, in the laundry room, there is a secret staircase leading to my private dungeon," she says in a story-telling voice, making me smile. "I live in the downstairs part of this house and I work in whichever of the three houses I'm needed in."

"Oh that's great. Well, hopefully one day, I'll be able to come back here and meet you again, when the baby is here."

"I know you will, I can't wait to meet that little bundle. Hopefully I'll see you next Christmas."

"Well, we'll see, if Luke's going to be here... I probably won't..." I begin, and she interrupts.

"Less of that talk, you'll be back at Christmas as a family - if you choose to spend it in Aspen, and I am looking forward to it already."

I won't argue. She's too nice. So I just smile and nod, silently.

She leaves a couple of fresh towels, as she has every other day, and takes away my old ones. She gives me a warm smile before slipping out of the door and back out to the rest of the house to carry on working. What a lovely woman, I bet she was a wonderful, warm nanny.

Lunch time comes and goes, and during the afternoon, I take another long walk out in the garden. It snows heavily on me, and I get really cold, but I endure it, just to savour these last moments of Aspen. I had wanted to go back up to *'Sundeck'* on Ajax Mountain, take another trip in that gondola and gaze at the view, but only with him. I would have liked to have gone back to *'Peaches Corner Cafe'* for one of those delicious roasted vegetable sandwiches... but remembering all of the flirting that we did in there, reminds me exactly why I just couldn't stand to be there again, without him.

We all eat dinner together at Bea and Daniel's house again, to say goodbye to Alexia, Rose and Henry, and to toast to the wonderful holiday that we have enjoyed. Well... in my case, *half*-enjoyed. It was a lovely evening, considering my crappy mood, and by the time we get home, I am absolutely exhausted and ready for my bed. I send Luke a quick text message, because I just can't seem to fully let go. I can't accept it.

-

1 Jan 23:47
Happy New Year, Lukey. I can't stop thinking about you. One minute I hate you, the next... I am so in love with you. Either way, it still hurts so much. Come back to me? I want to move to LA to live with you, hold your hand every day, be your 'Princess' again. I want us to go house hunting and buy Wriggler a cot. I want that life. I want you. Love you, Til and Wriggler. xx

CHAPTER 19
WEDNESDAY 2ND JANUARY

As usual, I slept with my phone under my pillow, just in case anything came through from Luke in the night. I don't want to miss it in case it's my last opportunity to communicate with him, although I fear I may have already had that moment. There is nothing on my phone when I wake, which isn't a surprise to me, but it still hurts.

I continue with the morning as usual, trying my utmost not to cry every five minutes. We enjoyed breakfast together, Olly and Clare a little sad to be going home, they have so enjoyed this holiday.

We sit and chat around the fire for a couple of hours after we have all gotten ready to leave, our cases waiting by the door. We're leaving after lunch, at about two, so we can relax and chill out around here for a while before the busy journey home. I wish we could just get on a direct flight and be done with it so I could at least try to sleep through it, ignoring the memories I'm leaving behind in Aspen.

When we have finished Pam's deliciously filling roast chicken salad, we have about half an hour left. I'm not sure what Clare and Oliver do with their time, but I use it wisely... saying goodbye to the bedroom, my favourite view from the balcony and that pillow that I have become to attached to. I sit on the balcony, hugging it close to my chest, burying my face into the soft fabric. It still smells of him, faintly.

I stay there until I hear a car horn beeping from the front of house, indicating the arrival of the car. I feel terribly weepy, and I squeeze the pillow tightly before taking it back to the bed and slowly retreating towards the door. Pam surprises me there, *has she been watching me?* "Oh! Pam, you gave me a fright."

"You car is here, Tilly, would you like any help bringing anything down?"

"No thank you, I left it all by the door downstairs."

"Okay, I'll have a quick once over in the rooms while you load into the car," she says, shooing me down the stairs. I'm pretty sure she won't find anything, but it's always good to have someone else check it over for you.

Once everything is packed up, Pam joins us at the bottom of the stairs to say goodbye. "Only a couple of things, Oliver - you left this..." she says, handing him a brand new wallet, if I'm not mistaken - the same wallet Clare was looking at in Ralph Lauren before I confirmed to her that I was pregnant. *Did she go back and buy it for him?* Interesting...

"You need to be more careful with your wallets, Olly, especially expensive new ones like that..." I say, suspiciously and Clare looks away.

"Yeah - I can't believe I almost did it again," he says, giving nothing away.

"And sweetie, you left this..." she says, handing me a full carrier bag. I look at her questioningly. "Off you go, it was so lovely to meet you, I can't wait for everyone to come back next year."

I take a look in the bag, and inside, folded in half and wedged in tightly, is the pillow. She hugs Clare and Oliver, and then me. "You should take it, everyone needs a little comfort, that's where you find yours right now. We have plenty more where that one came from, sweetheart."

I hold her tightly and nod, so grateful to her for understanding. "Thank you, Pam."

"You're welcome, I'll be seeing you next year, as a happy family."

I smile weakly and let go, entering the car behind Clare and Olly. I gaze out of the window at Pam as she waves the car out of the drive. I think I love her.

Again the journey to the airport is quick and painless and before we know it we're inside, greeting Bea, Daniel, Emily and Edward. Before we move over to the check in desks, Daniel stands next to me and puts an arm around my shoulder. "Hey, Til, can we talk for a minute?"

"Yes, of course, what is it? Is Luke okay?"

"He's okay. Come sit with me," he says, walking me over to a couple of seats near the door. "He won't talk to me anymore. I can't get a hold of him any way I try. I spoke to his housekeeper, she says he's at his place but acting strangely, so at least we know he's there."

"Oh good! That worried me," I say, my hand on my heart. "Why has he stopped talking to you?"

"Last time we spoke, he got mad, told me to butt out of his business and to concentrate on worrying about you."

"Oh."

"Yeah. You have got to get him to talk to you, Til. You guys really need to talk about what's going on here, and I know he's not going to come to you, because he's got it in his thick skull that you're better off without him. I think he's gone crazy if he believes that. He has something he needs to tell you. He didn't want you to know about this, and I'm not going to get any deeper into it - it's not my place, but you have got to talk to him."

"Daniel, I text, I emailed him, I try calling... he won't answer... what is it?"

"I know," he says, slipping an envelope into my handbag. "Decide what you want to do. Whatever you choose, I'll back you all the way." He kisses my cheek and stands, making his way back to the group. *What?*

"But... what? What do you..." I don't continue, he's too far away to hear me and is already embracing his fiancee.

I look down at my bag and pull out the white envelope, *what the hell is going on?* I tear it open quickly, and inside I find a paper with all of the booking details for a first class flight from Aspen to LAX... in a few hours. *Holy shit...* I hadn't even thought of going to him... now.

Crap, how am I supposed to make this kind of a decision this quickly? Everyone is waiting for me to check in... this LA flight leaves about an hour and a half after my flight to London. Oh shit, what do I do? I need to go home... go back to work and start living the life I need to get used to again. But... what if? What if I just jumped on this direct flight to LA? Would we be able to sort it out? Would he tell me this big mystery? Would he be happy or go crazy? I'd lose my job, for sure. Oh shit... I don't know what to do - I want him so badly... and this is my chance, but he doesn't want me... he just fucking left me on my own to bring up a baby!

Yes... yes he did do that shitty, arse-holey thing. He left his pregnant girlfriend without even saying goodbye. What kind of shit-head does that? One that probably shouldn't get a second chance Til... Stop forgetting that you want him more than he wants us... that's a bad relationship, it'll never work.

No. I'm so grateful to Daniel for giving me the option, but I can't do this. I would have my heart trampled on again and then I'd have to make the long journey back to England anyway. I stand and join the rest of the group, and we immediately head to the check-in for the flight.

We stand in line, awaiting our turn at the desk, everyone chatting quietly, discussing home. Bea and Daniel hold each other tightly, it must be so nice for them to be at the airport together now, after that heart wrenching moment when they had to separate at LAX with no hope for their future - now they get to fly everywhere, knowing that they'll always be together. And this time they return engaged.

I smile at them with envy, they knew what they wanted and they've got it. The difference between them and Luke and I, is that Luke and I aren't on the same wavelength. I want something that he doesn't. I sigh as we step forward, next in the queue to check in, and my handbag vibrates. I know I live in hope, but I get that tingle in my belly that it could be Luke. Every time my phone makes a noise I get excited - just in case. It's silly, but I can't help it - it never is him but I can hope.

I pull my phone out and check the screen... Oh my god, it *is* him. *Please, please, please don't let him tell me to stop texting him...*

-

LA Luke 2 Jan 14:45
Happy New Year to you, too, Princess. I miss you so badly. I hate what I have done to you.
xxx

-

I stare at my phone for a minute, my heart hurting. He misses me, too... so why can't he be with me? I need answers - he's clearly got something going on that has to be bad, if he really does miss me that much but still can't be with me. Does he hate kids or something? No... he was great with Jack in LA, and Queenie says Logan adores him, he must be good with kids. Oh for fucks sake, I'm just so confused.

"Earth to Tilly..." Clare sings with a giggle.

I look up, in question. "Hmm? Yes?"

"We need your passport."

"Oh, yes - sorry..." I rummage around in my bag, retrieving my passport - that white envelope distracting me. I slowly pull the passport from my bag and hand it over to Clare, my eyes locked on that white paper.

"Thank you," she says, handing it to the lady at the check-in desk.

"No..." I say suddenly, "no - I need that back," I look over to Daniel and back to Clare. "I'm not coming - don't check me in," I say to the check-in staff, "I'm not getting on that flight."

"What?" Oliver says, "What are you talking about?"

"I'm... um... I'm going to LA..." I say, only just realising that I've made my mind up. I nod, determined. "Yes, I'm going to LA, I'm going to find out what the hell is going on."

"Good for you," Daniel says, putting an arm around me and kissing my cheek.

"Darling, that's great. Go and tell him off and then find out what the problem is. You'll sort it out," Bea says, still quite angry with him for what he's done.

I hug everyone good-bye and go and sit for a moment to collect my thoughts. What the hell am I doing? I'm at a strange airport, all by myself, about to fly to LAX to confront the man who can - and has - broken my heart into a thousand pieces. This is fucking crazy! I would never, *ever* have done this for any other man before. *Never!* So this is what people mean when they say: 'the things you do for love'. Lose the plot.

I get myself together and check in for the flight after a while of shaking my head and talking to myself about how stupid this is. People must think I have some serious issues. I do. I spend the rest of my time waiting, contemplating taking up nail biting and pacing, neither of which has ever taken my fancy before.

When I finally board the tiny aircraft, I'm shaking with anxiety, even though I'm so excited to see him, however he reacts. Just to see his beautiful face, touch his skin, smell him... it'll totally be worth the rejection that could be so, very real.

I sit down in my navy, leather seat, one of the six, first class places on the aeroplane. The plane is so tiny... not what I'm used to at all, but that's okay, I'm not concerned about my surroundings for the next couple of hours - what I'm concerned about is what's going to happen when I get there. *Oh crap... what am I doing to myself?*

I sit back and close my eyes, hands on the bump as the plane fills up and we begin to taxi. This is it... I'm on my way to LA again. I think about what'll happen when I arrive - shall I go straight to his? Shall I go to Gemma's first to dump my bags and give her a big cuddle? She has no idea that I'm on my way.

If I go to hers, it'll just delay it - I don't think I can handle the nerves for any longer than is absolutely necessary. Daniel told me just before they went through to the departure lounge, that a car will be waiting for me, to take me wherever I go and that I could use it however and whenever I need to, which is fantastic. It means I can just do whatever I need, without relying on Gemma to change her plans to accommodate me.

Daniel is an amazing person... he'd never leave Bea in this mess, but then again - he doesn't have the issue that Luke has, whatever it is. Does he? I mean who knows, it's all a great mystery. Hopefully in a few hours, I'll get some answers, if he doesn't send me packing the minute he sees me.

My stomach is in knots, Wriggler is moving around like mad in there and I'm starving but I just couldn't eat a thing. I have a bottle of water to sip and that's about all I can manage right now. The closer we get to LA, the tighter the knots get, the more I writhe in my seat with worry.

God, I hope he won't be annoyed with me, I hope I don't come across as some needy, stalker-like psycho. I just need answers... and to say a real goodbye. Maybe he'll need me to force my way in and do what has to be done, Daniel clearly thinks so or he wouldn't have bought me this ticket. *So sweet*, I'll have to pay him back for this somehow... *oh crap*, I didn't think about that.

A couple of hours later, we're landing. The journey was definitely a little more lumpy-bumpy on this little plane, I would not recommend Bea do this trip - she'd be climbing the walls. I'm at a place now, where I just want to get off this plane and straight to Luke's house to snog his face off... or get turned away... you know - whichever. Preferably not the latter.

I'm not used to getting into this airport from a domestic flight, but I manage to get to my bag as quickly as I can, through passport control and straight out to meet the driver who swiftly gets me packed up in the car. Wow... I'm actually on my way to see him. My stomach rumbles noisily and I wriggle around in the seat, desperately trying to ease the anxiety. It's not working. *Oh god.* I'm so nervous I could definitely use a toilet before we get there, I'm absolutely crapping myself.

I know the name of Luke's apartment complex by heart, and of course, the driver knows where it is anyway - he's one of Daniel's drivers. It's about twenty five minutes of sheer terror. What the hell is going to happen? I mean, I need to see him, I can't get there quick enough, but I'm so scared of what he'll do or say when he sees me. *Oh fuck...*

We pull up outside part of the complex, and I ask the driver to hold on to my luggage. I'm not dragging a suitcase all over the place. I jump out of the car and walk quickly towards his apartment. I hope he's there, I hope he answers... *holy shit, I hope he's alone.* I stop dead in my tracks. Fuck, what is he's with someone? Ouch... that hurts. I take a deep breath. *If he's with someone, Til, he's with someone, and you need to know about it and get the fuck over him. Come on, you can do this...*

I nod to myself as confirmation; I'm doing it. I continue to walk at a fast pace, my heart pounding and my lungs working overtime. As soon as I see his door, I start to run, I can't get there soon enough, I need him. I near and pause as I approach, noticing that it's ajar with cleaning products holding it open.

I take a deep breath and push it, stepping over the products and into the hallway. The vacuum cleaner is growling from the lounge and I see his maid, turned away from me. I look in the kitchen to my left, no - not in there, and I step forwards a few steps to put my head around the doorway of the den... not in there either.

Two more deep breaths, and I'm making my way up the stairs, tentatively. I reach the top and tip-toe to his bedroom, hoping to god that I find him alone. When I reach his room, I find his door wide open, and I step inside and walk through to the main area.

There he is, beautiful, semi naked, sitting on the end of his bed, his legs apart, elbows on his knees and his head resting in his hands. His phone is on the bed at his side. He looks gorgeous. Tears immediately run down my cheeks, my heart hurts with how much I love him.

He looks sad, helpless, confused. I so want to help him. I sniff, without thinking, and he shakes his head. "Honestly, I'm fine, you can go - you don't need to stay any longer, the place is spotless..." he says softly, without looking up.

I remain silent, just staring at him, resting my weight against the wall at my side. I can't move, I can't talk, I can only gaze and weep at the sight of my big, strong man looking so weak and tired. I haven't even seen his face, but his body just sitting there like that, looks so... defeated. *What is it?*

"Please... I'll be fine..." he says and turns to look at me. He stills and his mouth drops open as his eyes run from my feet to my eyes and back again. I frown as the tears turn into sobs, and he stands and clenches his fists. "I... what..." he says, before he storms towards me and I have absolutely no idea what is coming next. Is he happy or sad? Angry?

He surprises me by wrapping me tightly in his arms and squeezing me so hard, I can barely breathe. I hold on tight, pressing my face into his bare chest to soak in all the Luke I can get. He releases me suddenly and drops to his knees, pulling my top up and yanking my tracksuit bottoms down below my belly. He hugs me, pressing his face against Wriggler, kissing over and over again, repeating the whispered words, "I'm sorry, I love you."

I thread my fingers in his hair as I cry. Watching this grown man down on his knees, talking to my belly, desperate and needy. His arms wrapped tightly around my hips, he doesn't let go. He just kneels there, holding me, whispering to Wriggler.

I reach around and pull his hands from my bottom, and crouch down to join him on the floor. I hold his face, tears filling his eyes, and I kiss him softly. "I missed you too much, Luke. I need to know."

He looks down and immediately back into my eyes as he nods. "I know... I just... I can't."

Anger rises, unexpectedly. "You can't what for fucks sake? You need to tell me! How could you do this? Have you any idea what you did to me? You bastard!" I cry, smacking him on the arm. He doesn't flinch, but it felt good. "Bastard! You.... you bastard!" I cry, over and over, smacking him harder. I growl loudly in frustration and slap him in the face. He doesn't even move, he just sits there and takes it... what the hell is wrong with him?

I break down against his chest, as his arms wrap around me, comforting me. I sob my heart out, squeezing him tightly, praying that I don't have to let go of him again.

"I'm so sorry," he whispers, "I hate that you're like this, and I know it's my fault. I'm sorry. Is the baby okay? Are you... are you okay?" he asks.

I nod. "Yes... we're okay. Considering."

"I know. I... I can't believe you're here... I was just thinking about you on your journey back to London and thinking about booking a flight out tonight... I can't cope without you, I'm just such a mess, I don't know what to do, Til."

I sit up and wipe my cheeks with my fingers. "I know exactly what you can do, sweet-cheeks," I say, adding a little bit of humour into the situation because we sure as hell need it. "We're going to go over there and get into bed and you're going to hold me really tight and tell me what all of this is about. I know and you know that we're going to be happier together. Nothing you say can be that bad."

He nods. "Okay. It's hard for me, I don't like to talk about it."

"Okay, I understand that, darling, but this is me. You can tell me anything and I will still love you. I need to know what this is so we can work through it, I need to know your issue with having a baby. Or a girlfriend, but I don't think the girlfriend is the problem."

"No, it's not," he says quietly.

We both stand and I strip down to my underwear, Luke watching me the entire time, his gaze frequently returning to my belly. I climb into bed and he follows, scooping me up into his arms. He inhales deeply and snuggles into me.

"I have missed you so much. The minute I got on the plane I knew I had made a mistake, but every time I think about the baby, and the way I was acting with you - I get a panic attack and feel like this will be best for you."

"Okay, is it because you're scared to be a dad?" I ask, softly, I really do want to understand this so we can work through it, together.

"No. I'm not afraid to be a father, not at all. I like that idea."

I smile, that's a relief. But... then what is it? "Well that's good... so what is the problem? I'm so confused Luke."

"I know, and it's just... you might not even think it's a lot - but it's issues I have, that I need to overcome. It's a big deal to me."

"Okay, it's fine. I want to understand..."

He squeezes me tightly and nuzzles his nose into my neck. It's so soothing, his hands touching my body, his face against my skin... it's hard to concentrate.

"I know I made a mistake. I realised today that I would have to come after you and to work through my issues." He takes another deep breath before he continues. "Do you remember the girl I told you about? The one who I kept it in my pants for?"

"Oh yes... the mysterious one..." *This is to do with her?*

He nods. "Yes, the mysterious one. She wasn't mysterious, I just don't like to talk about it, we were young and I got... affected by stuff."

"What happened? Oh my god..." It dawns on me. "She got pregnant?"

He holds me close and kisses my neck. "Yeah. This is really hard for me."

"I know. Take your time."
"I love you."
"I love you, too."

"Okay," he pauses briefly, "we were nineteen. It was an accident, we didn't plan it, and didn't tell anybody when we found out. But... I loved her, or so I thought, and we decided that we'd forget college, move in together and be a family."

"At nineteen?" I ask, shocked.

"Yeah. I felt adult enough to take care of her and a child, so we just... agreed to do it."

"Wow. So... you have a child?" I ask, absolutely flabbergasted, this is something he seriously should have told me.

He pauses again and shakes his head. "No."

"Oh god," I say, holding his hands that are pressed firmly against my belly.

"We moved in together, it wasn't right, we argued all the time, she wanted to keep going out to parties, I wanted her to stay at home. I got mad and she hated me for it. Then one day, we were having another fight, she started getting mad and then doubled over in pain."

"Oh god..." I am so upset by what he's telling me, what he must have gone through, and then I am reminded of my own doubling over moment on Christmas Day, and I wonder what on earth must have been going through his head.

"She lay down for a while and the pain got a little better, so we thought maybe this was normal. Then, later on in the evening, it happened again, only this time she was bleeding real bad. It turns out she'd been having pains for a while, but she thought it might be normal. We hadn't had an ultrasound because it was still early days."

"Oh Luke..." I say, turning in his arms and holding him tightly against me, pained by what he had to go through.

"We lost the baby. We hadn't even told our parents yet, she was still in the first trimester."

"Darling... I don't know what to say."

"Nothing, baby, it is what it is. We moved back home with our families afterwards, and broke up pretty much straight away. At first, she told me I had caused it, by fighting with her all the time, that people shouldn't get stressed when they're pregnant, and although I know now that it wasn't that - she did call me a few years later to apologise for saying those things - I just never got it out of my head that I had something to do with it."

"So this whole time, you've been worrying that something is going to happen to our baby, and that it'll be your fault?"

"Maybe... I don't know, Princess. I just couldn't handle making you so upset all the time, we kept fighting."

"But we weren't fighting that badly, Luke, that wouldn't have an impact on the baby."

"Then there was the whole constipation issue..."

Wow, thinking back to the hospital... now I understand why he was so weird... it was all too real for him... he'd been there before. "Oh Luke..." I begin to cry again, my poor man, he must have been so horribly tormented by all of this.

"It was only today that it really struck me, I had probably done more damage by leaving, than anything else. I just couldn't stand to be there, making you mad because I was so paranoid, knowing I might lose you in the end. Both of you. It felt easier for me to leave you and know that I'm not going to drive you away, or have to go through all of that again, believing I am to blame."

"Darling," I say, sniffling, "you didn't cause that miscarriage, and if anything like that happened to me, it couldn't possibly be your fault. These things just happen. Me getting mad and shouting at you won't harm Wriggler, and your paranoia could never drive me away. It only shows me how much you care for us. I need you, you need to look after us, be with us all the time. Your baby was still very, very young when that happened, you were only in the first twelve weeks..."

"Nine."

It breaks my heart that he remember this all so clearly. "Exactly, nine weeks is so little. You have seen Wriggler, you have seen the scans and heard the heartbeat. Doesn't that make you feel better?"

"Honestly? Not really. It makes me think how much more I have to lose. I love you so much it hurts, and Wriggler, too. I think I would die if anything happened to you. I know how it felt to lose that first baby and I don't think I can do that again."

"I can't guarantee you anything, Luke, but Wriggler is doing fine in there, he's break-dancing right about now. I can't do this on my own, I need you. We'll be stronger together, whatever the future has in store for us. But right now, we have a lovely little baby on the way, and we need to celebrate that - not worry about something that will probably never happen."

He nods with a smile and lifts the covers to look down at my tummy, "I know you're right. I'm so sorry about everything. I should have told you, but it's so hard for me to talk about - especially to you... I don't want to worry you. I thought you might panic that it'll happen to you, too, knowing it's happened to me before."

"Luke, we have to let nature do it's thing, however it goes. Maybe that's easier for me because I get to feel this life growing and moving around."

"Maybe. Thank you for understanding. Thank you for coming to me. Thank you for being you and for looking after our baby the way you do. I'm sorry I ever made you feel like you weren't being the most perfect mommy-to-be."

"I understand now, I only wish you'd have felt you could have told me this earlier. It explains so much, and now that I know, we can work through it, together. It wasn't that bad after all, was it?"

"Actually, no. It was a lot easier to talk about than I thought it would be. You're the best baby-momma ever."

I giggle as he kisses me crazily all over my face and neck, breaking the sombre mood. "Thank you, hot baby-daddy. By the way - she's moving a lot more over the last few days and I can feel it so much."

He smiles excitedly and wriggles his way down the bed to hold my little bump in his big hands. He makes me laugh as he starts talking to it.

"Hey, baby, it's me, daddio, what's cookin'? So someone told me you've got tastebuds now... how cool is that? You're growing up fast in there..."

Hang on... I didn't tell him that... "Have you read the development stage page?"

"Sure have, I downloaded it on my iPad as soon as I got home, same one as you got. I wanted to know what's going on in there."

I smile so broadly. Thank god I came here. Although it sounds like he'd have been coming to see me if I hadn't. "Luke, you can be as paranoid as you like, okay? We can work through this together, I'll tell you everything I feel, you can come to all of the appointments, we'll do whatever it takes to make you comfortable about the pregnancy. Just promise me you'll tell me everything that worries you."

"I will," he says, crawling back up my body and straddling me on his strong arms and knees. He kisses me softly.

"And never, ever leave me again."

"I won't..." he says, kissing me again, moving his soft lips all over my face and neck.

"And promise me... promise me..." I moan, closing my eyes and arching into his body as he kisses and licks my neck indulgently.

"Mmm hmm?"

"Promise me you'll make love to me every day, properly, no holding back... fuck me and fuck me good. It won't hurt the baby at all."

He growls, grinding his pelvis into me, his erection digging into my leg, "I'm gonna fuck you so good, baby, all night long, and again in the morning, and then again at lunch time..." he says as I wrap my legs around his waist and he positions himself.

"Yeah..." I moan, desperately anticipating the ecstasy ahead.

"Yeah." he responds as he pushes slowly inside me, making me cry out.

The door suddenly closes and we both jump, looking at each other, *what the...*

"Whoops, I guess the maid didn't see you arrive..." he says, and we both laugh out loud. It's so typical that we have spent a whole week in Aspen, fucking every which way possible, but only when we're having sex in a bed in Luke's bedroom, do we get caught.

CHAPTER 20
THURSDAY 3RD JANUARY

Waking up this morning is perfect. I am, of course, tightly wrapped in my man's huge arms, erection digging into my bum cheek and gorgeous, soft lips caressing my face and neck.

"Mmm... good morning, bad-boy..."

"Good morning my Princess," he mumbles, his voice so low and gravelly... *sexy beast!*

"I like this..."

"I like it, too," he says, holding my hip and rolling me onto my back. He crawls down the bed again and kisses my tummy, chatting away to it under the covers, making me laugh.

"So, mommy is moving to California to be with Papa Bear, how cool is that?" he says.

I lift up the covers and look at him, smiling. "She has quite a lot to do first, darling."

He comes back up to lay next to me. "Sure. I thought we'd fly back next week, after you've let me bone you for a few days," I giggle as he continues, "and then we can sort out you leaving your job, getting all of your stuff over here and the logistics of a Brit living in the States. There'll be a lot of paperwork. I also want you to show me around, and take me to go meet your dad."

"My dad?" I ask, confused.

"Sure, I want you to introduce us, he needs to meet his grandbaby's daddy. You can take me to where he is and we can sit there all day and talk about him. Okay?"

I well up and swallow that huge lump in my throat, hard. I nod and smile at him, stroking his handsome face with my fingers, he's perfect.

"Great. So let's get some flights booked in a little while, okay?"

I sniff and compose myself. "Yeah, sounds good, but it's going to cost a pretty penny, all of these flights, I need to sort out my finances first."

"I was thinking about that, too, sugar-lips, do you want to be a stay-at-home mom, or are you going to want to work?"

"I don't know yet. If we need the money, maybe I can find something that fits in with being a mum, as best it can?"

"You won't *need* to work, Til, but if you want to, you could work with me."

"What?" I cry, "I'm no fitness trainer darling, and you should know that.

"Oh - that's right, we didn't discuss this part. So, I'm not just a personal trainer, that's what I have done for 'fun'. I told you I'd stop doing that now, right?"

"Right... so what else do you do?"

"I own fitness centres and sports clubs around the US. I don't tell people about it, it's something I own, but I have a lot of people working for me, making it easier for me to live a different life. I do get involved, I just keep that part of my life separate, I never saw myself as a serious business type and I didn't want anyone else to either, but deep down, I love it.

"What?" I cry, "You have what? And you didn't tell me this?"

"I don't talk about it much, because I'm a fitness trainer to most people. It really doesn't come up that much."

"You are so ridiculously blasé about this... you have a chain of fitness centres?"

"Yeah. My dad gave me a big chunk of money when I was twenty one, to invest in the business plan I had. I bought a gym and he funded most of it. I gave it a huge make-over, did some great shit, and it took off in a big way. The business just grew from there, with the financial help of my folks here and there. Now it's a major success. I can't wait to get into it with you. I'm going to be a dad and husband now, so I think it's time for me to take a more 'public' role."

"A husband?" I ask, amused.

"Hell yeah! Don't think you're getting away from me, pumpkin, we're getting married for sure. Preferably before the baby is born."

"What the fuck?" I cry, this morning is full of revelations.

"Why not?" he asks with a grin.

"I... you... we..."

"You wanna be my wife, Princess, or what?"

"Er... ask me properly and then maybe I'll think about it."

"Can I sink inside you while I do?"

I laugh loudly and swat his arm, "No, you may not."

He smiles beautifully, those dimples popping, "Tilly, please, and when I say please, I mean *please*... will you marry me? I want a hot piece of ass for a wife."

I giggle and grab hold of him, cuddling his beautiful body. "Absolutely. I'll so *totally* marry you."

"Good, I've never wanted anyone the way I want you. Now... sit on my cock and sex me, baby."

FIVE MONTHS LATER
FRIDAY 14TH JUNE

CLARE

"Oh my god, oh my god... you're doing so well, Til, I'm so proud of you..."

"Clare..." Tilly groans, "shut the fuck up..."

Luke rubs my back sympathetically as I put my palms on my cheeks, *why can't I just do as she asks and shut the fuck up?* "I'm sorry... I just can't,"

"Clare, darling," Bea whispers from behind me, "don't worry about apologising, best just keep quiet before she rips someone's head off," she says with a roll of her eyes and a smile.

It's just so incredible, I have never witnessed a baby being born, apart from on the TV - and when it's on the TV, it's not one of your BFFs! I nod at Bea and sit back down in the chair at the side of the bed.

Luke is holding her hand, his face down on the pillow with hers as he bends over to comfort her. They gaze at each other with such undeniable love - it's wonderful. She lifts her hand to stroke his cheek, and I see her face start to screw up again.

"Oh holy fuck, I'm having another one..." she cries, letting out a long, deep wail. Jesus, this looks like bloody agony! She squeezes Luke's hand and he wraps his other hand around the back of her head, she seems to like this, she wedges her face into his neck and he holds her there until the contraction ends. There's not a lot she does like right now, so I think Luke is doing anything that seems to comfort her. She's so uncomfortable, bless her.

This does - strangely, make me want a baby. Is that abnormal? I mean, I'm in this hospital room watching one of my best friends howling in agony as her body prepares to birth her baby, and all I can think is... *I want to do that*. I am so weird.

"I need to move, move me quickly, please help me," she cries to Luke.

"Sure, Princess what do you want?"

"On my knees, I need to be on my knees, now, before another one comes... please!" she shouts desperately, and he supports her upper body so she can move onto her knees. "Hold me, hug me, let me stay like this, oh god... oh no..." she says, wrapping her arms around his neck tightly and burying her face in his neck again. She's kneeling at the edge of the bed, her man holding her upright as he stands in front of her. She begins a low moan, her hips swaying from side to side slowly, and as the moan gets longer and louder, her movement stops and she bears down, the moan progressing to a grunt.

"Holy fuck, she's pushing! Bea - Clare! Go get the woman! Tell her! Press the button! Fuck, someone get help!" he cries in a panic, and Bea darts out of the room and shouts down the corridor for help. I stand, helplessly behind her, watching the two of them. "It's okay, baby, it's okay, she's going to be here any minute now, the midwife is coming. I wish I could take this pain, I wish I could do this for you. You're amazing, you're just... so amazing."

"I love you," she says as she bursts into tears, scared, and I quickly follow suit. This is unbearably emotional. "Luke... I want to push, I need to push, and oh god... oh no..."

At that moment, the midwife bursts through the door, pulling on her latex gloves and coming around to my side of the bed, behind Tilly.

"She wants to push and she's having another contraction," Luke says, informatively.

"Wow, you sure move fast, don't you little baby," the midwife says as she prods and pokes about down there.

"Oh holy shit-bags, don't touch me... don't touch me... ugh..." she starts and continues with a long, deep, guttural moan, burying her face into Luke's shoulder again and doing that bearing down thing.

"You can push sweetheart, go ahead, you're ready," the midwife says doing lots of things around Tilly's nether regions. Another lady runs in as Tilly shrieks. She stands to the side of the other midwife, and I move slightly to see what's happening.

Oh holy mother of... OUCH! That looks horrible! But... oh, oh my god... that's her little head right there... it's almost out... I raise my hands to my mouth, this is the most incredible thing I've ever seen in my life.

Tilly calms once more, panting and stroking Luke's neck and hair with her hands. "Shh, you're doing so well, she's almost here, baby!"

She nods and makes a light, high pitched sigh.

"Tilly, I know I should shut the fuck up,' I say tentatively, "but... but she's got hair, lots of dark hair... her little head..." I say and my chin starts to wobble and I burst into tears like an idiot. "I can see her..."

"Did you hear that, Luke?" she says with an emotional giggle, "Clare can see hair!" she says excitedly before being brought back to this painful reality. "Oh... oh god, oh..."

"Okay, Tilly," midwife number one says, "you push nice and smooth, let's get her head out with this one..."

"Oh god..." she shouts, squeezing Luke's shoulders. He puts his hands on her lower back as she begins another of her deep wails. It goes on for forever, and I watch as she pushes, her grunt long and hard, and the baby's head moves down... oh my... it's, it's coming out... I see her face! Oh god... are they supposed to look like that? She looks... oh dear, she looks a funny colour.

Midwife two, who appears only to be watching, looks at me and with a slight smile, she says, "Yes, dear. That's what they should look like. Perfect." *Phew!*

I look to my left as Tilly has her breather, and see Bea watching, just as enraptured as I am. She looks at me in utter amazement, how can our little friend be doing all of this? She must be some sort of Superwoman.

"Okay, Tilly - a real big push with the next one, lets get this little baby out now."

Tilly moans and mumbles into Luke's skin, "I can feel her head, I can feel it... it's like I shat a warm, wet coconut out of my mini..."

Luke can't help but smile a big, broad, handsome smile, but has managed to control it, so as not to giggle. She'd probably murder him if he laughed right now. She sounds exhausted too.

I look at Bea and she has her hand over her mouth, desperately trying not to let her laugh be heard. Tilly is just too funny, even in labour!

She begins the next contraction very quickly, and I see her preparing, holding him tighter and positioning her legs a tiny bit wider. She groans and pushes, the low grunt from the depths of her lungs and as the baby slides a little further, Tilly suddenly yelps, loud and high pitched, and the baby dislodges and slips all the way out, the midwife holding her between Tilly's legs doing all sorts of weird suction things to her nose.

Oh my god, she's so tiny, so weeny! And I got to witness this - to see her before even her parents have. I burst into tears at the miracle of it all, and can hear Bea whimpering in the other corner, along with me.

"Here, sweetie," midwife one says, "get your baby, reach between your legs, I've got her..."

Luke holds Tilly up as she leans back and pulls her baby up from between her legs, and sits back on her haunches. The midwife quickly wraps a blanket around her, in Tilly's arms. "She needs your skin contact and warmth, Mama, so wrap her up tight."

She holds the baby close to her chest, and I lose my view, but just watching the back of Tilly as she looks down at her baby, hearing her cry, hearing the baby make those funny squeaky noises... watching Luke melt as he watches and holds his beloved wife and their beautiful little girl... it's the most emotional thing I have ever seen, and I would like to go somewhere for five minutes and break down.

"Hey baby Emily, you're so pretty..." Luke says as his eyes sparkle with love for his new little daughter.

We step out of the way of the midwives as they check things with the baby, jot notes and generally move around the room like the professionals that they are. We slip out together, to leave the happy family together for a few moments... to get acquainted with each other.

We hug each other tightly, we have just shared the most precious moment of our lives. After a few minutes, we move down the corridor a little way, until we get to Daniel and Oliver. Daniel scoops Bea up in his arms and she cries, telling him everything, quietly.

Oliver steps close to me... it's a bit awkward. "You okay?" he asks, reaching to touch my arm, but pulling away at the last minute.

I nod, but burst into tears on the spot, covering my face with my hands.

"Oh, darling, come here," he says, wrapping his arms tightly around me and pulling me into his body as I sob.

"Oliver, that was... she's just so... she's beautiful. Tilly is amazing... Luke... they are all so special. That was the most amazing thing I have ever seen."

"I can't begin to imagine. Was does she look like?"

"We didn't see much of her, but she's such a tiny little thing! With a full head of thick black hair!"

"Black hair? Where'd she get that from?" Oliver asks, amused, and I giggle, regaining my composure, and realising I should probably get out of his embrace about now. If *she* was here, she'd probably have ripped my hair out by now.

"I'm going to have to get back soon," he says. I see, she's cracking the whip even when they're on holiday and one of his best friends has just given birth... bitch.

"No, Olly, you can't!" Bea scolds, "You have to stay and meet little Emily! Screw your bloody curfew."

"Don't start Bea. I don't have a curfew. Okay, I'll hang around. I am excited to see her. So they did go for mum's name after all? She'll be over the moon when we tell her."

"I know. Emily Summers, it's so cute, isn't it?" Bea says with a huge smile. "Speaking of parents, Luke's should be here soon, who knew she'd have such a quick labour!

We all sit and wait for a while, I know something else has to happen with Tilly - she has to birth the placenta and stuff. God I hope she doesn't have to have stitches... ouch, stitches in your pop tart? No thank you! Bea and Daniel hold each other tightly and whisper to each other, whilst Olly and I sit in silence, a few seats down. I hate this. We used to be so close, and now she's come along, ruling the roost, telling him who he can and can't be friends with... it has got so awkward.

I was really looking forward to this holiday. We've got plenty of staff in to cover Bear's and I have been so desperate to come to LA and see all the amazingness that the girls rave about. I couldn't wait to see Bea and Daniels place at the 'W' and Tilly and Luke's impressive new pad in the Hills... it's a dream holiday. Not to mention the road trip to Vegas we're all taking in a few days to leave Til and Luke to bond with Emily, it could be a trip of a lifetime, but Oliver's new girlfriend had to tag along, and she's making my life hell.

She hates me. She won't let Oliver and I be alone in the same room together anymore, she thinks I'm in love with him and that I'll pounce on him the minute her back is turned. Stupid wench could be further from the truth. I love him, yes, as a best friend. He's not interested in me, he never has been... well apart from those few occasions when we both got carried away... but that happens sometimes with two, single best friends... doesn't it?

Anyway, I've got my eye open for my own perfect man, and I have a nice possibility who looks like quite the catch... I'm just trying to decide if he's my type or not. I don't know what Olly's new bitch's problem is, but I'm not it. He doesn't want me and I'm not after him anymore. Those days are long gone. I just hope she doesn't make Vegas a great downer for me, I've wanted to do this trip for far too long to let someone I don't even know spoil it for me.

I stand to go to the loo, I'm fed up of sitting here like a loser, waiting for him to say something to me. Our friendship was something wonderful before, and now we don't even talk without feeling awkward.

I splash my face, I didn't bother to apply my make-up when we got the shout to leave for the hospital at one thirty am, so I needn't worry about smudged mascara. I blow my nose and make myself feel better, that experience was so incredible, but it broke my heart a little bit... I'm not sure why... maybe it's their love for each other... their beautiful new family... I want one of those. I'm nearing thirty and I want a husband and a baby, god damn it.

I growl and flush my tissues down the toilet, taking a deep breath before I head back out to Mr Misery and the love birds. I can't wait to go and see little Emily Summers. I just love that they found out the sex at the twenty week scan, before the big move to the States, it meant I could buy a whole range of gorgeous pink dresses for my little sort-of-niece.

I open the bathroom door and am shocked as I get pushed backwards by a huge, powerful force... a masculine one... a gorgeous one. It takes a couple of seconds to realise that I'm locked in a bathroom with my ex-best friend, Oliver. I look at him, questioningly... what's happening? Why are we locked in here?

"Clare... you okay?"

"Er... yeah, just emotional... what's happening?"

"I don't get any time to talk to you anymore... I want to check you're okay."

"Yes, I'm fine. Let's get back to the baby."

"Can we just... I'm sorry, okay? I'm sorry about Stacy, I know she's a bit jealous..."

"Oh Oliver, let's not. It's fine."

"No, I'm going to talk with her, she'll understand. I don't want to lose you, we have a great friendship and I hate that things are getting weird between us."

"Okay... it's fine. You talk to her. I don't like it either, but sometimes you have to give up things for the people you're falling for... you know?" I say, fishing for information... is he? Does he love her yet?

He stands still, silent for a moment. "Can I... can I have a hug?" he asks sweetly and I smile. God, why does he have to be so bloody cute? I step forwards into his embrace, and inhale his scent. I think he's smelled the same ever since I first met him and totally fell head over heels for him. Oh, those hideous days when I felt alone and empty, watching him with that amazing, skinny girl on his arm every weekend. Gosh, I was so jealous of her.

He holds me tightly for quite some time, before pulling back slowly and looking down at my face. I look at him, expecting him to say something... but he doesn't. He just locks those sexy, bottle green eyes with mine and stares. It's a little torturous, actually, I haven't had any kind of... 'interaction' with a man since... well... since Aspen. And these eyes, that soft, sexy mouth so close to me, is a hugely unfair temptation. He's dangling a whopping great carrot in front of me and I... *whoa!!! Wanna pash mate?* Crikey, I am taken totally unawares as he kisses me, amazingly... passionately, it's so hot!

He pushes me against the wall and groans as his tongue feels for mine, his hands rubbing my body until he finds one of my breasts and holds it firmly. *Oh holy mother, what are we doing?* His mouth so fervently kissing mine, I am taken away somewhere that it's okay to have a great passionate snog in a hospital toilet while your BFF has her 'hoohaa' stitched up.

He grunts loudly and slows the kiss... clearly remembering that he has a girlfriend. He closes his eyes and shakes his head, before stepping back. "Shit, Clare... I'm sorry. I'm so sorry - I shouldn't have done that... I got a bit... you've been upset... I just..."

"Oliver, it's okay. We won't mention it. It was a mistake," *for you.* "I haven't... you know... for a while so, I suppose I just got carried away myself..."

He stares at me and runs his hand through his ruffled brown hair. "You're... um... you haven't, since..."

I shake my head and he closes his eyes and frowns.

"Let's get back, Oliver, hmm?" I say, moving towards the door and he grabs my wrist, pushing me back against the wall again, his face determined, raw, hot... *Oh please, Olly... don't do this to me again?* I silently beg, knowing how I feel after he does. Sated, amazing...empty.

###

About the author

Sexy Summers is Dani Lovell's second novel, book two of the Sexy series.

Although British, Lovell has quite an obsession with all things 'Stateside' and often dreams about the fabulous trips she'll one day take across the pond.

Lovell lives in Hertfordshire, UK, with Daniel, Luke, Oliver and the rest of the sexy gang (all in her head, of course), and her real-life family.

If she's not working on her latest Sexy story, you'll find her taking care of her children, planning her latest fantasy vaycay or eating her weight in goats cheese.

You can contact Dani here:
Facebook: **https://www.facebook.com/pages/Author-Dani-Lovell/345108372283119?ref=ts&fref=ts**
Twitter: @AuthorDaniL
Email: **authordanilovell@gmail.com**

Coming next:

Book three of the Sexy Series; Sexy Hart - The story of Clare and Oliver.
Estimated: March 2014

Printed in Great Britain
by Amazon.co.uk, Ltd.,
Marston Gate.